The Drum King

The Drum King

by

Richelle Kosar

TURNSTONE PRESS

Turnstone Press
607 – 100 Arthur Street
Artspace Building
Winnipeg, Manitoba
R3B 1H3 Canada
www.TurnstonePress.com

The quotation from *Crackhouse* by Terry Williams (Addison Wesley Publishing, Don Mills: 1992) is used with permission.

The quotation on page 238 is from *Middlemarch* by George Eliot.

The quotation on page 387 is from *Emma* by Jane Austen.

Turnstone Press gratefully acknowledges the assistance of the Canada Council for the Arts, the Manitoba Arts Council and the Government of Canada through the Book Publishing Industry Development Program for our publishing activities.

Le Conseil des Arts du Canada DEPUIS 1957 | The Canada Council for the Arts SINCE 1957

Cover artwork: Brigitte Dion
Author photograph: Ted Johnston
Design: Manuela Dias

This book was printed and bound in Canada by Kromar Printing for Turnstone Press.

Canadian Cataloguing in Publication Data
Kosar, Richelle, 1950—
The drum king
ISBN 0-88801-220-9
I. Title.
PS8571.079 D78 1998   C813'.54   C98-920066-3
PR9199.3.K65 D78 1998

To the boy with the drum, Providencia, 1990

Contents

Acknowledgements

I would like to thank Jean Kosar, Jacqueline Borowick, and John Sakeris for reading the original manuscript and offering much-needed support and encouragement. I am grateful to Carlos Torchia for his advice and suggestions on Spanish phrasing—any errors are mine, not his. Thanks also to Brian Henry, Manuela Dias, Marilyn Morton and David Arnason.

And finally, I would like to give special thanks to my parents, Anthony and Margaret Kosar, for teaching me about what matters.

Prologue

Now i dream of buenos aires almost every night, extraordinarily lush and vivid dreams. The moment I close my eyes my mind begins to fill up with southern colours and smells. I feel easy and slow; I seem to be walking through a warm, aromatic wind, my clothes rippling softly on my body. Against the burnished sky the bronze tips of the palm trees droop in the November heat. Lacy jacaranda trees veil the air with a delicate mauve scent, slender orange trees display their opulent amber fruit, even in the poorest and shabbiest streets. I keep walking and walking on the endless glittering pavement, half-dazed by the dreamy beauty of the late afternoon sunlight, it flows over the city like clear honey and changes the languorous, muddy Rio de la Plata to a river of dark gold. Then shadows lengthen on the boulevards, electric lights begin to blaze from the long windows of restaurants, and waiters stand in the doorways, wearing coats so intensely white that it hurts my eyes. Elegant *porteños* stroll past arm in arm, tracing fiery circles in the air with their cigarettes. The Teatro Colón has opened into the gassy, star-filled night like a giant golden flower. In La Recoleta steamy moonlight softens the silent contours of Evita's last palace. An old poet walks ahead of me and turns into a shadowy laneway, scraping his cane on the cobblestones, dreaming of mysteries and famous *conquistadores*. Rich women are sitting with their *amigas* in bright cafés; they seem to hover above the ground, to float in a cloud of scent made up of perfume, rich coffee, and cream-filled pastry. They lean together in a burst of laughter, and carelessly toss coins to the dirty little beggar-boys on the sidewalk, gaily oblivious to their hungry, watchful eyes.

I see all this, it passes before me like a drug-induced hallucination, and I'm filled with such a longing, I have such an ache in my throat, as though I am missing something I used to have and then lost somehow, a long time ago.

And—why neglect any cliché?—out of a gloomy alley, littered with garbage, tango music echoes along the damp concrete, cheap and brassy and haunting; a couple dances with dramatic gestures, both slim and dressed in black with touches of scarlet, their pale faces luminous in the dark. Since it's a dream I glide dreamily into the woman's place, why not, I hold a rose in my lipsticked mouth, I feel the feverish urgency of my partner as he presses his body against mine, his lips are hot, his hand caresses my naked back, he raises a knife and lightly pricks my throat until the pearl-white skin is marked by a dark red drop of blood.

God, my dreams were never so baroque before.

Chapter One

THEY SAY IT'S IMPOSSIBLE FOR TWO PEOPLE to tell the same story. I think I remember every detail of that day and night last April, but no doubt he saw it all very differently. I can imagine him spinning it out for some rapt or sceptical listener. Likely his version would be much wilder and more flamboyant than mine; he would cram it with more of everything: music and violence, fireworks and guns. All I can say with certainty is that this is how it happened to me, this is how it unfolds in my memory, over and over again.

I remember that the city streets were bright with the first bit of pleasant weather after a long, cold, wet winter. The trees remained absolutely bare, you couldn't discern even the most subtle, elusive beginning of green, and puddles of melted snow still lay here and there in the grass, reflecting the ragged, milky sky. But it felt like spring just the same. The sun was shining and a mild, fresh breeze drifted over the windowsill, smelling piercingly of earth and rain.

I was teaching an undergraduate class on The Novel in the Nineteenth Century. It was my last class of the year. The students were young and callow and their main concern seemed to be finding out what questions would appear on the final exam. I couldn't help feeling a little restless, a little irritable and distracted. My eyes kept wandering toward the window. I saw a fat man crossing the courtyard. He was wearing shorts and carrying one bright red balloon on a long string, like someone in a Fellini movie.

A girl in the front row asked a question about *Emma*. I blinked and tried to focus my attention but before I could formulate an answer, a boy at the back, a tall, thin boy with gingery hair and a very pale face, a boy who had missed many classes and had barely spoken on those rare occasions when he did make an appearance, suddenly piped up with "Who cares?" Everybody turned to look at him.

"I think Jane Austen is totally petty and stuffy and boring," he said. "Why should we have any interest in all these rich twits and whether they get married or not?"

Needless to say, it wasn't the first time I had heard this view expressed. But I pretended to be incredulous. "Well," I said, "you shouldn't be quite so ready to dismiss Austen's characters as 'rich twits.' If you had—"

He was too excited to wait for me to finish. "But what's so great about her? Look at Dickens. He wrote about high and low and rich and poor and every kind of life. When you're reading Dickens at least you can breathe. He doesn't stick you in a parlour with a bunch of fat cats fussing about etiquette and having little intrigues and making polite conversation. Big deal. It strikes me as a total waste of time."

I asked myself why I was letting this obnoxious twerp walk in on the last day and take over my class in such an aggressive way. I should have flattened him at once but my energy didn't seem equal to the task; what I felt like doing was sitting down and closing my eyes. Instead I lifted one eyebrow and smiled. "Perhaps Austen would be more to your liking if she'd inserted a car chase or a shoot-out here and there.

Would that add a bit of manly significance to the text?"

His face went beet red. "That's not what I mean at all!" he declared angrily. "I'm saying is this stuff relevant to most people today?"

A girl in the front turned her head sharply. "Look," she said, "you're taking a really simplistic attitude to complex material, and if you—"

"Complex? Hah!" He leaned back tensely in his chair, rocking it on two legs. "What's so complex about it? It's irrelevant, that's all. It doesn't mean anything to anybody living an ordinary life and working and struggling in the modern world!"

He was an ugly young man with a protruding Adam's apple, the kind of man who was probably very awkward with women, who had lots of trouble getting a date. I could picture him sitting in a cluttered, messy room in a dorm somewhere, smoking one cigarette after another, flakes of dandruff on his shoulders, poring resentfully over his books, searching for things he didn't like.

"All right, let's look at Dickens since he seems to have escaped your contempt, Allan—or is it Albert?" I said. "I'm sorry, we've hardly seen you all semester, so I'm not sure of your name."

He sat stiffly upright, staring at me with undisguised spite. I stared back, right into his eyes, smiling questioningly.

"Alvin," he mumbled.

"All right, Alvin. Why do you think we still read Dickens today? Is it because of his social relevance or his practical applications? No, we read him because he creates an imaginary world that captivates us and makes us believe in it. He engages our emotions and enlarges our vision of life. Those are the only things literature is obligated to do. That's what we read Dickens for. And that's why we read Jane Austen too. And Shakespeare. And Tolstoy, and any other writers we love."

For a moment he seemed to be struck dumb. I thought I had actually managed to silence him, and I began to stack my books. "Well, it's getting late, so—"

But he had only been gathering his wits for another assault. "In Russia ninety per cent of the people weren't even

Richelle Kosar

literate!" he cried defiantly. "What about all those millions of poor slobs who couldn't even read Tolstoy's stuff? All those poor slobs slaving in coal mines and chopping down trees and farming on the land. Why should they have cared what Count Tolstoy had to say? Maybe they had their own stories to tell! But when did they get the chance? What happened to all their stories? Those are the ones I'd like to study! Where are the books with those stories?"

"Literature isn't found only in books, Albert," I said. "Sorry . . . Alvin. Most cultures have a rich oral tradition. That includes folk tales, songs, rhymes, street theatre . . . they're all primitive forms of literature. There's even a school of thought which holds that *The Iliad* and *The Odyssey*, two of the seminal works of Western civilization, weren't written by a single poet named Homer but were a compilation of stories and myths that came down to the Greeks from antiquity through generations of oral story-telling. If you're interested, Professor Bartoli has a course that examines the origins of narrative in the context of social history."

He gave a loud, high-pitched laugh. "Yeah, right!" he said with bitter sarcasm. "The common people get to make social history, and Count Tolstoy gets to write the books!"

It was clear that he was ready to go on picking at the same bone forever. The room seemed unbearably stuffy. It had been a very long year, and I wanted it to end. I took a cursory glance at my watch and said, "Look, we're already overtime. If you had such a burning desire to discuss these issues you should have come to class more often during the term, Alvin. But right now the rest of us want to get out of here."

This produced an emphatic clapping of hands. Alvin What's-his-name flushed resentfully and slumped down in his desk.

"I want to wish you all good luck on your exam," I said. "You've been a good group and I've enjoyed our time together." I said essentially the same thing to all my classes at the end of the term and I thought it came out sounding rather tired and facile, but they didn't appear to notice and gave me a round of applause. I kept my head down as they talked and packed up to leave, but

I could sense the shape of Alvin What's-his-name sitting motionless, staring at me with rancour and need, wanting more attention, more arguments, more of something. However, I was through with him and I refused to encourage him by looking up. Instead I rearranged the papers in my briefcase and waited for him to go. At last I heard his chair scrape as he pulled his lanky body awkwardly erect. I was aware of his lingering shadow in the doorway of the lecture hall, his head turned toward me for one last angry, demanding glance. But I didn't lift my eyes until I was sure the room was empty. Then suddenly the breeze from the courtyard came into my nostrils, cool and fresh and sweet.

USUALLY I RODE THE QUEEN STREETCAR all the way to Neville Park Boulevard and then walked down one block to my house. But that day I got off in front of Kew Gardens. Maybe it was because the lake was showing a brilliant summery blue down at the ends of all the sidestreets, and you could see thousands of swaying, sparkling diamond lights and white sails skimming above the water like birds. And the air was heavy with evocative odours: damp ground, plants coming to life, succulent foods cooking in the backs of restaurants. I wanted to walk, I wanted to fill up my lungs with oxygen, I wanted to eat a large meal. I went past the Beaches Library and the William D. Young memorial drinking fountain, then down through the trees, through the delicate, shifting patterns of light and shade.

A band was playing in the bandshell. They were Kinsmen, I think, or Rotarians, a group like that, and they were playing not well, not badly, old-fashioned band music like "Le Carnaval de Venise" and "The Debutante." You could close your eyes and imagine that it was 1910 and ladies in long dresses might come strolling by, carrying pastel parasols. But even in 1910 they weren't always so refined; they had sensual pleasures and hidden longings; perhaps while the cornet played its strong, slow melody and the percussionist burst in with an electric clash of cymbals, those ladies walked beside their lovers, stirred by the voluptuous sound, going further into the trees, into the shadows, gloved hands trembling as they lifted their skirts....

I had two exams left to set. I had many things I should have been doing. But for some reason I kept sitting there in the park, uneasy and half-dreaming, feeling the warmth of the sunlit wooden bench under my legs.

I think all along I had a sense of someone standing nearby, off to one side. I didn't look, but I knew someone was there, someone was standing and listening to the music, occasionally lifting one hand to take a drag on a cigarette. I think as much as half an hour went by, and I was aware of him all the time, but I looked straight ahead at the bandshell, at the portly Kinsmen with their straw hats and shiny instruments. Then a child called out, far across the lawn, something about ice cream, about dropping her ice cream. It gave me a reason to turn my head and finally I looked straight at him. He was younger than I had thought he would be, maybe in his early thirties, several years younger than I. He was wearing a white shirt open at the neck and slim brown pants. He had glossy brown skin and his hair was dark and wavy and long on his neck. One leg was crossed casually over the other, one hand rested against his hip, one arm hung loosely at his side, and a cigarette burned between his fingers, giving off a trail of bluish smoke and an ashy aroma. He was motionless, as if for a moment he had been caught in a timeless suspension. I thought of a title for his portrait: *Gypsy Man in Kew Gardens, 1992.* Or perhaps something more modern and abstract: *Cityscape 529,* and he would be broken up into shards and rectangles of colour and light: black and brown and yellow and white with flashes of red. There was something striking, dark and vaguely exotic about him. And something else. I'm not sure why I thought this: it wasn't his clothes, it wasn't his face or his posture, it was nothing that I could have specified, but I had a clear impression of something disreputable, something slightly off, something sleazy. That was what interested me, that was what I liked the most. I felt my heart thudding inside my chest, slow and hard. I didn't know what I should do, whether I should go ahead. I hadn't done anything risky for two or three years and I had told myself I was getting too old to take chances like that anymore. But then I decided. Oh, yes, why not, yes, go on, do it, go ahead.

"Not the most exciting music in the world, is it?" I said.

He turned his head at once, and his eyes passed rapidly over me, down to my toes and up to the top of my head, one swift glance that seemed to absorb and assess everything about me, my looks, my age, the style of my clothes and how much they cost, who I was, what I might want. I didn't find it insulting. Instead it seemed to demonstrate something alert and intense in his personality, as though he wanted to be aware of every possibility, to miss nothing. He appraised me, he made up his mind, and then he smiled, all within two seconds. His smile was a radiant flash of white in his smooth, brown face, and it seemed to recognize me, approve of me, and express delight in my existence.

"No, not exciting," he said. "But pleasant."

His voice carried only the trace of an accent, barely detectable and impossible to place. Spanish, I thought. Maybe Turkish. I had no idea.

"Do you like it?" I asked.

"Yes, today. It seems just right for today." He didn't come closer, but he had turned his whole body toward me. He was wide awake, he was ready for anything.

The stout cornetist spoke brightly into the microphone. "Here's a special old favourite," he told his audience of approximately ten (including a dog and a squirrel).

"Oh, no, not 'Believe me if all those endearing young charms!' " I laughed. "They certainly have a complete repertoire of old chestnuts."

The Spanish/Turkish man smiled and nodded, but I had the distinct impression that he'd never heard of "Believe me if all those endearing young charms" and possibly was mystified by the phrase "old chestnuts" as well. However, he didn't let it slow him down. "Look at him, though," he said. "He loves to play it. I think clearly it's his best one."

The Kinsman was trying hard. His face was flushed and

damp from his exertions, but he was tapping his foot energetically. "Yes, I think you're right," I said. "Do you ever go to the jazz festival? It happens right here in Kew Gardens every year at the end of July. It's marvellous. You can bring a blanket and on a warm summer evening you just lie here listening to cool jazz and hot jazz until it puts you in a trance."

"Well, now I can hardly wait till July," he said.

"I think you'd like it," I said. "Because you seem like the jazzy type."

He caught the signal instantly and acted on it. "I do?" he said, with a soft laugh. And he walked swiftly across the grass and sat beside me on the bench. His arm touched mine, the cloth of his shirt was warm from the sunlight. "But now the important question is, do you like the jazzy type?" he asked playfully.

"Oh, yes," I said. "I think it's my favourite type of all."

We looked at each other, laughing a little breathlessly. His eyes were the colour of clear tea. I had a slight sensation of vertigo, as though the earth had begun to turn very fast and he was the only solid thing on it. Yes, it all came back to me as quickly and easily as that, all the things I hadn't felt for a long time: dizziness, a tightness in my chest which made it deliciously difficult to take a deep breath, an ache through my body so painful, so pleasurable, so profound I could have moaned out loud. He was close enough that I could smell his skin, his musky cologne, his freshly laundered shirt, the shampoo he had used to wash his hair, his smoky breath. I thought that in a minute the bench we were sitting on might rise from the grass and whirl out above the trees, over the lake, and spin in the bright air like a kite. I thought that I wasn't old at all; I was still young and crazy and I was going to go on living for a long time. I had never been with a Spaniard or a Turk before.

WHEN WE LEFT THE PARK THE SUN WAS GOING DOWN. All the roofs on Queen Street East gave off flashes of honey-coloured light, all the alleys began to fill up with deep blue shadows.

"I'm in no hurry," he said. "I didn't have any special plans."

"Neither did I," I said.

The twilight had started to deepen, spreading into the city like a wash of ink, and lights sprang up and floated across the murky sky and lake like sparks. We walked aimlessly, and occasionally his arm brushed against mine with a little electric shock. He indicated my briefcase with a casual gesture of his cigarette. "You work in an office?"

"Sort of," I said. "Yes."

A tall, thin-faced man, lounging in the shadowy doorway of a corner store, lifted his hand in languid greeting. "Hi, Eddy."

My friend turned his head and grinned. "Hi, Steve. Hey, can't you take a break? Get somebody else to hold up that wall for a while."

"Ha ha," Steve replied in a very soft voice. "You're a real comedian, man." His eyes flickered toward me curiously, but he didn't acknowledge my presence. "Catch you later."

We went on. "You know people around here," I said.

"Well, I've been around the neighbourhood a couple of years now. I've met a few people."

"I've lived here most of my life and I don't know anybody," I said. "I guess I'm not very friendly."

He grinned at me. "No?" And suddenly he reached out and took my hand. For some reason that made me feel a bit uncomfortable and I had to repress an urge to jerk away. There were certain things I wanted and certain things I was prepared for, but that childish gesture struck me as somehow too intimate. For a moment it put me outside myself and I saw how ridiculous I might look, walking down a street in the Beach carrying my briefcase and holding hands with a sleek and flashy-looking foreign man who was obviously younger than I. But his fingers were warm and dry, and he stroked my palm with his thumb, a light tactile caress that I felt all the way up my arm and down my body to my groin. Then I wanted to stop somewhere in the shadows, close my eyes, forget everything but that one sensation.

"You don't look like an Eddy," I said.

"No? Well, it's Eduardo. Eddy's my nickname."

Eduardo. Spanish. Possibly Latin American. My mind clicked along and then stopped. "I'm Grace," I said.

"Grace. That's nice. I like that for a name."

"Do you know what I want?" I said.

His eyes flashed at me; he smiled and squeezed my fingers.

"What?" he said meaningfully.

"I want to drink a glass or two of red wine," I said. "Eat a plate of pasta."

"Oh," he said, surprised.

"How about Luigi's Trattoria?" I said. "Have you ever eaten there?"

"Luigi's. Sure. Lots of times. Are you so hungry?"

"I'm starving."

"Well," he said. "Let's eat, then."

"Luigi's is only a couple of blocks from where I live," I said in a moment. "Afterwards we can go there. It's right on the beach. I'll show you the view."

"Oh. Yes, that's good," he said, with a soft laugh. For a moment he leaned against me, his upper arm against my shoulder, a very slight pressure that seemed to leave a brief, fiery imprint on my flesh.

Luigi's Trattoria is small and dimly lit, with checkered tablecloths, candles in Chianti bottles, and various other atmospheric touches, including a rotund man who comes out and plays a concertina. In the summer you can sit on a patio beside a vine-covered trellis, but it was too early in the year to do that. We sat inside, by the window. The candlelight was soft and rosy and tiny flamelike reflections danced in the dark glass. He leaned back, resting his arm casually on the back of his chair. His shirt looked very white against the olive-brown colour of his skin.

"Hi, Eddy," the waiter said. "How's it going?"

"Hi, Brian," he responded. "Not bad. A typical Friday night, huh?"

"Man, it's been murder," Brian said. "What can I bring you?"

"Well . . ." He looked at me.

"Oh, a bottle of Pinot Noir would be nice," I said.

Eddy nodded. "Sounds good to me."

"You really do know everybody," I remarked after Brian had bustled away. "I come in here fairly regularly, but I don't know any of the waiters by name."

He smiled and shrugged. His posture was relaxed and easy, but there was a certain tension about him. I had the same thought as when I first laid eyes on him, that he was keenly aware of everything around him, that he was ready for anything to happen, anything at all.

"Can I tell you this?" he said suddenly. "You have beautiful hair. I've never seen hair that colour before."

I imagined that this was probably the kind of thing he always said to women. "It's just red," I said dryly. "My father had red hair too. I guess that's where I got it."

"Is it very long?"

"I guess it's about halfway down my back. Sometimes I pin it up like this to keep it off my neck. Look, you don't have to pay me compliments."

"Will you show it to me later?" he said softly.

For a moment I found it absurdly difficult to draw a deep breath. Yet at the same time there was a twinge of uneasiness and embarrassment, exactly the same feeling I'd had when he took my hand on the street, a feeling that maybe he and I were operating on different levels. Maybe he had the wrong idea about me, maybe he thought I had to be flattered and admired and fussed over, maybe he thought that was what all women liked.

"I might," I said, rather sharply, feeling ridiculous. It annoyed me that I couldn't seem to look him in the eyes. Even when Brian returned with the wine, I was still looking down at the tablecloth.

"I was going to mention, Matt was in here earlier this afternoon, and he asked if I'd seen you," Brian told Eddy.

Eddy's voice was cool. "Oh, yeah?"

"I said I hadn't seen you for a couple of days."

"He knows where to find me," Eddy said. "Here, Grace, is it okay?" He nudged his glass across the table so that I could taste the wine.

I took a sip. "Yes, it's fine."

"Thanks, Brian. We'll order in a couple of minutes." He leaned over to pour me a full glass. I drank some quickly, hoping to recover my composure. Instead the alcohol seemed to enter my bloodstream in an instant and it intoxicated me, left me somewhat dazed. Why am I doing this? I wondered. I said I was through with this sort of thing. I promised myself.

There was a tiny beeping sound. I hardly registered it at first, but all of a sudden Eddy was patting the pocket of his jacket. "I've got to make a phone call," he said, getting up. "I'll be right back."

"What was that?" I asked incredulously, half-laughing. "You've got a pager? Don't tell me you're a doctor."

"No," he said with an easy, casual grin. "It's my office. Sometimes they need to get hold of me."

That pager unnerved me a little. Was he going to turn out to be some kind of young entrepreneur, a real estate agent perhaps, well-known throughout the Beach, always in contact with his office, eager to be a success, entertaining political ambitions? I had to take another swallow of wine to calm myself. He moved smoothly between the tables, slim, good-looking, carrying that indefinable aura of something that was not quite right, not quite real. Doctors and real estate agents weren't the only ones who used beepers; bookies used them too, so did drug dealers. That was all right; that might be interesting. I had never been with a bookie or a drug dealer before. I watched his white shirt, the dark thick hair curling on his long, graceful neck. Someone else knew him, a woman this time, a young blonde who looked up at him big-eyed and flirtatious, putting her hand on his arm as he bent down to speak to her. He smiled right into her eyes, his face close to hers. I took another drink of wine. I thought, Of course I could get up and leave right now, while he's on the phone. He'll come back and I'll be gone. He disappeared into the darkness at the back of the restaurant. Now, I said to myself. I could just stand up and leave. Walk casually down the street, turn the corner.

I didn't move. I took another drink of wine and listened to the concertina. I was in Italy. I was on holiday and when

14

you're on holiday it doesn't matter what you do. The wine tasted good; it was dry and clear and sunny. Soon we would have to order another bottle.

Eddy came back to the table. "I'm sorry," he said. "That was just—"

"It's all right," I said. "You don't have to tell me."

Smoke from the candles drifted up, burned my eyes. There seemed to be gold in the room, gold light and red light, coloured bottles glittering behind the bar, blue lights on the beer taps, all floating in a soft smoky haze. We ordered food and it was brought. The steam rose from my plate and warmed my face.

"It's good," I said. "It's delicious." But I hardly tasted it.

"Have you ever been to Italy?" I asked him.

"No," he said.

"Well, you should go sometime," I said. "You'd like it."

"What's the best part?"

"Florence. No—Venice."

"Maybe we'll go together someday," he said.

"You really are awfully charming," I said. "Don't work too hard at it."

"All right," he said, with a laugh.

There were people all around us, and a steady murmur of soft conversation. Luigi's isn't a large place; the people at the next table were only a couple of feet away. But the more wine I drank, the more I felt as if he and I were set apart from the rest, the only bright clear images on a dim backdrop.

"I met a man once in Italy," I told him. "It was in a train station. He had dark curly hair and green eyes. He was the best-looking man I'd ever seen. He was a young soldier who was in Rome on leave. You remind me of him."

"Oh, yes?"

"We got into a train compartment together. I had a first-class ticket but I got into economy class with him. He turned the light off. He kept calling me 'angel' and 'Madonna'—I think those were the only words he knew in English. He was just a boy, really. He was only twenty. I was young too, I was only twenty-one. I remember the window was open at the top and a wonderful smell was blowing through the train, like fields of clover at night. . . . He took off his shirt and he was wearing a white undershirt and he looked so beautiful, it took my breath away. He pulled my blouse open and all the buttons popped off and hit the sides of the compartment like little bullets. There were four other people in that compartment, two other soldiers and an older man and a woman. None of them said a word, none of them moved. They were barely breathing. I think they were either shocked speechless or else they were afraid we'd stop. But I don't think we'd have cared if there'd been a hundred people watching. He took the waistband of my underpants in his teeth and pulled them right down over my knees."

Eddy was staring at me incredulously. "Jesus," he said. "What are you doing to me? Have mercy. Did this really happen?"

"Of course," I said. "He got off the train at two a.m. in a town whose name I've never been able to remember. He and the other soldiers. They all got off. I leaned out the window as the train was pulling out of the station, and he was standing on the platform, and I threw him my underpants. As a souvenir. I still remember it, I watched him getting smaller and smaller, running on the platform and waving my underpants in the air like a flag. It was great. I didn't wear underpants for two weeks after that, in his honour."

I always enjoyed telling stories like that to strange men. I liked to watch them become startled, agitated, excited. It amused me.

"I'm not interested just in the sex," I said. "It's the quality of the entire experience."

After a moment he laid down his fork, pushed his plate to one side, and began to talk in a soft, melodious voice. "One summer I was home from school," he said. "I went home to our *estancia*—our ranch—outside Buenos Aires. There was going to be a wedding, a friend of my father's was going to marry his third wife, and he wanted to have the ceremony at our *estancia* because it was such a beautiful setting. My father's friend was in his fifties but his fiancée was much younger, half his age. There were two hundred guests and after the ceremony we had a barbecue on the lawn and whiskey and champagne, and an orchestra playing. My father had had a stage built for dancing. It was beautiful after sunset, everybody in their suits and evening dresses, dancing in the twilight on the lighted stage. I danced with the bride and her breath smelled of champagne, she was holding a glass of it and taking sips while she danced and drops of champagne splashed on my neck. She pressed against me and pressed her face into my throat. I was young and not very experienced, so of course I started to get hard, which was really embarrassing, but when I tried to move back she just held me closer and rubbed against me till I thought I was going to die. No one saw what was happening, too many people were dancing, all whirling around and bumping into each other, and everybody was a little drunk, and the bride's new husband was sitting at a table smoking a cigar and arguing about politics. When the dance ended she took hold of my arm and said, 'Come with me.' And we walked away from the stage and across the lawn in the dark. We went down into the orchard, until we were surrounded by trees. It was very quiet in there, the laughing of the wedding guests seemed to come from a great distance. I remember the smell of oranges and lemons, so strong and sharp it made you dizzy. She stood with her back against a tree and lifted up the skirt of her wedding gown, right up above her waist, great bunches of white lace, and she wasn't wearing anything underneath, I saw her long legs and her . . . *cosita*, I don't know the word in English, and she took my hand and held it there. I could hardly talk, but somehow I got the words out, I said, 'M-my G-g-od, are you crazy? Your new husband is so close and all the wedding guests!' And she said, 'They're all pigs and I don't care!' and she hopped up and wrapped her legs right around my waist. She was light as a feather. Her skin felt like satin. She opened up like a beautiful flower, petal by petal, soft as velvet, and I felt as if I exploded inside her, like a fountain, like fireworks, like confetti. And far away the orchestra was still playing, first happy then sad, happy then sad. But her husband wasn't as interested in politics as we thought. He must have seen us leave the dance floor and followed. All of a sudden—bang! A bullet flew right past my head! I saw drops of bright red blood splash across the white sleeve of her bridal dress. They had to knock the pistol out of the husband's hand, they had to hold him back to keep him from killing me. The next day I was sent back to school in disgrace. The young bride was never seen in Buenos Aires after that. They said the husband kept her locked up in his house in the country and only let her out for an hour every morning so he could feed her oranges on the patio."

He leaned back in his chair and smiled. We looked at each other across the table. Never in my life had a man talked to me that way. Never before had a man come back with a better story than mine. I was astounded, enthralled, I felt a weakness in my knees.

"You just made that up, didn't you?" I said.

"I still have the scar from the bullet," he said. He leaned across the table and lifted up the hair on his temple to show me a white crescent-shaped mark above one ear. It could have been caused by any number of things. It could have been a birthmark.

"Yes, I see," I said.

He smiled and tilted his head back to drain the last drop of wine from his glass. "Shall we go?"

"Yes," I said. "Let's go."

The street was completely dark by then, the streetlights were on, and the air no longer felt summerlike. But I was hot from wine and food and erotic talk, and I had a giddy desire to laugh out loud, although nothing was particularly funny. He put his arm around me. My skin was so alive that I thought I could feel the texture of his fingers through the fabric of my thin jacket.

"I must be drunk," I said. "I'm afraid I'm going to say something really stupid in another minute."

"Go ahead," he told me. He leaned down and put his mouth against my ear. "Say something really stupid." His breath was hot and silky. His collar brushed against my cheek and made me shiver. The wind had come up strongly over the lake, sending black waves to break into foam on the glistening sand. The CN Tower and the golden skyscrapers of the city wavered above the restless water like a mirage. Our feet crunched on the damp boardwalk, moving swiftly. My thigh rubbed against his. The night was carnal, everything in it, the wind, the littered beach, the distant spires, the white and blue hut where the lifeguards changed their clothes on hot afternoons in the summer, the shadows of leaves flickering on his white shirt. I wanted that wild walk to go on for a long time, and yet I wanted to hurry, hurry.

"It's right over there," I said as we stepped off the end of the boardwalk into the soft sand. He stood beside me in the electric darkness as I unlocked the garden gate, fumbling with the key. He was so close that I could feel his breath in my hair.

My house seemed still and hushed after the noise of waves and wind and blowing branches. The streetlamp at the end of the boardwalk sent a diffuse white light through the tall windows onto my living-room floor.

"I'm not going to turn on the lights," I said breathlessly. "I like it this way." I had walked straight through the hall, not waiting to see if he was following me. I saw a magazine on the coffee table, open at an article I had been reading that morning before school. It looked strange to me, as though it must have been put there by someone else.

He was standing behind me, a foot or two away. I thought he might grab me roughly, but he didn't. He was just out of the light. I could see the liquid glitter of his dark eyes.

"Show me your hair now," he said.

"Oh, you know, it's ... really ... it's not that special," I heard myself stammer, like a teenage girl.

"Please," he said.

My fingers shook as I reached up to remove the bobby pins. There seemed to be so many of them and I didn't know what to do with them so I dropped them on the floor one by one. Long loose pieces of hair swung down over my shoulders.

"There," I said hoarsely. "See, it's no big deal."

He moved closer and stood next to me. His voice came softly out of a shadow. "It's like a waterfall," he said. "So many little ripples. Did you have that done, or ... ?"

I felt as though I were bending over a bonfire. I couldn't think straight. Surely I was making a fool of myself, standing there in the dark listening to him talk about my hair. "No," I said. "It's just got a bit of a wave in it, that's all. It's no big deal." He took some of it in his hand and held it against his face, across his mouth and nose, with a long intake of breath, as though he were inhaling perfume. "God," he said. "I love it." It moved me that he would do and say things that could so easily have made him ridiculous. It moved me that he didn't seem to care if he was ridiculous. He sighed and his breath tickled the roots of my hair, made them tingle. I turned blindly and pressed him against me with shaking arms. It felt as if I had waited a long time to do that, it was like relief from pain to feel the whole length of his body against mine. Then we were kneeling on the carpet, he was kneeling beside me and pulling his shirt out from his belt with a swift, graceful, impetuous gesture. While I struggled with the zipper on my skirt, he bent forward and kissed my neck and whispered, "Yes, hurry, I can't wait to see how beautiful you are." I felt myself go rigid for a moment. It made me wince to hear such absurd flattery. I squeezed my eyes shut and said sharply, "Please don't be so corny or it's going to turn me right off." He drew back for a moment, startled, but then gave a soft laugh and shook his head. I felt the flutter of his eyelashes against my skin. He lay on his back like a boy to pull his pants off, and like a boy he rolled back up into a sitting position, slender and naked in the white light from the tall windows, and began to feel in the pockets of his clothes, searching for something. I heard a crackle of plastic and saw what he was holding.

"Oh, no," I said. "Let's not use those."

His eyes flashed up in surprise. "No?" he said. "But why? It's dangerous otherwise, isn't it?"

"Are you afraid?" I said. "Because that's exactly what I want. I want it to be wild and scary and dangerous as hell."

He sat looking at me for a moment, smiling faintly. Then he tossed the plastic disc over his shoulder.

Chapter Two

I AWOKE FROM CONFUSED DREAMS, swirling darkness, rock music beating dully inside my head. I was lying in my own bed, covered neatly with my blanket and linen sheet. My body felt like a heavy weight against the mattress. The skin on my face and shoulders was tender, as though it had been rubbed raw. Between the slats of the closed blinds I could see glimmers of pale fresh light. There was no sound in the house.

In the past when I was having little adventures more regularly, I usually chose to go to a neutral place like a hotel. But not always. Every once in a while there would be an occasion when I felt particularly reckless or daring, or maybe I'd had a bit too much to drink, and then I didn't care and brought the man home with me. Of course it wasn't the smartest thing to do. The next morning that always became crystal clear. It was best when they got up before dawn and left in a hurry, eager to escape before I woke up. I usually helped out by pretending to be so fast asleep that I was unaware of all the noises they made as they crept around searching for their clothes and bumping into unfamiliar furniture. Then the downstairs hall door would shut with a discreet click and I could let out my breath in a long sigh of relief. But that April morning seemed different, for some reason. When I saw that my exotic Spanish lover was gone, what I felt was not relief but a curious sensation almost like hurt, almost like regret. Then I thought of my purse. Once I woke up at the Waverley Hotel after a man's silent departure and found that he had stolen my wallet. Not only that, but he had told the desk clerk that I would be the one paying for the room. I had to let the hotel manager keep my watch for security while I walked to my bank to get some money. The manager was a seedy man with a fringe of greasy hair above his ears, and he treated me like a twenty-dollar whore, which I found kind of amusing. Apparently he didn't realize that the watch he was holding could easily have paid for a year of nights at the Waverley Hotel.

I sat up at once. I couldn't remember what I had done with my purse the night before. I had been too distracted by the things he was doing and saying, and his hands on my body. Well, it was worth it, I thought, even if my wallet is gone. I lay back down and stretched my arms voluptuously above my head. A single shaft of light fingered the objects on the mantelpiece and filled the dim mirror above it with a milky morning radiance. I'll just lie here for another fifteen minutes, I told myself. But it was no good, I couldn't help thinking about my wallet and how much trouble it would be to replace all my credit cards.

The bedroom was chilly and smelled stuffy. I put on my housecoat and went downstairs to the living room. My purse was lying in a patch of sunlight beside the coffee table. The wallet was inside. I took it out and opened it to check that everything was still there. Then I heard a sound from the terrace. When I turned my head I saw him at once through the opened glass doors. He was standing outside in the brilliant morning sunlight, leaning on the stone wall and looking down at the beach, raising his face to the sun's warmth, naked and shameless as a primitive boy who had never heard of the custom of wearing clothes.

"What are you doing?" I said sharply, walking out onto the flagstones. "Somebody's going to see you."

"There's no one out here at all," he said. "It's great." He reached over and pulled playfully at the belt of my robe. "Take yours off too. The sun feels great."

"No, stop it! Are you crazy? You'll have the police here in a minute!"

That sort of thing had happened before too, of course. The man was still there after I opened my eyes, and I had to cope with him somehow. But no one else had ever walked out onto my terrace and displayed his naked body to the whole world.

"Fantastic garden," he said, waving his arm. "I didn't get a good look at it last night. Did you plant it?"

"I had it planted. Look—"

"And that gate at the bottom. That's great. You open it, you're right on the beach."

"Come inside, for God's sake," I said, pulling at his wrist. He followed willingly but stopped just inside the doors, his back against the glass, and put his arms around me and kissed me. His skin was covered with goose flesh and smelled of the fresh cold morning air.

"Mmmmmm," he murmured, rubbing his cool lips against my temple. "You're still warm from bed."

Slowly I relaxed against him. It was too much; no one could be expected to resist very strenuously.

He ran his hand down my arm. He felt the wallet I was holding.

"What were you doing?" he said, leaning back to look down at my face.

"What? Well, I . . . I was just checking to . . . uh . . ."

"You thought maybe something might be missing?"

"Oh, no," I said quickly. "No, of course not. I just wanted to—I forgot how much I'd withdrawn yesterday and I just wanted to check."

"Do I look like a thief?" He didn't seem particularly angry; he asked the question in an offhand way, with a slight smile on his face.

"No! Don't be ridiculous," I said. "I told you, I just wanted to see how much cash I had. I forgot, that's all."

"You don't need to worry," he said, still smiling. "I don't want your money. I've got lots of my own."

"Well, of course. I'm sure you do."

After a moment he slipped his cool hands inside my robe. I stood without moving. I felt as if I could purr, like a cat being stroked. My eyelids became so heavy that I had to let them fall shut. "What a night, huh?" he whispered.

I opened my eyes again, obscurely disappointed, somewhat irritated. Apparently he was like a lot of other men, eager to be complimented on his performance.

"Yeah," I said.

"I'll never forget it," he said.

Oh, I'll bet, I thought. "Really?" I said in a dry voice.

His breath made a circle of warmth on my shoulder. "You have nights like that all the time?" he asked.

I waited a moment. All at once, for no reason at all, my throat began to ache, as though I wanted to cry. I couldn't decide whether or not to tell the truth. Finally I said, "No."

My robe had slipped back. I looked down and saw his long brown hand resting on my shoulder. He looked too. We both seemed to be struck at the same moment by the contrast between his skin and mine. "You're so white," he said.

"Yes, I know," I said. "I can never get a tan. I just freckle or turn as red as a lobster. So I have to be careful of the sun. That's why I always look so pasty."

"Oh, no," he said. "It's like you're made of pearls."

His face was very close; I could see myself reflected in his tea-coloured eyes. No doubt about it, he's good, I said sarcastically to myself. But the cynicism didn't seem to go very deep; it didn't stop my knees from trembling; it didn't stop the blood from rising in my cheeks.

"Well, what a pretty thing to say," I remarked flatly.

He laughed.

Just beyond the glass a squirrel had paused on a tree branch to peer at us inquisitively. Suddenly I remembered that we were still standing against the window, in full view of anyone who might happen to walk past on the boardwalk. Tension squeezed the muscles in my legs. My need to move back, to be hidden, became absolutely compelling.

"I'm hungry, aren't you?" I said briskly, pulling away from him. "Let's eat something."

I made a big breakfast, something I rarely do. I made scrambled eggs, sausages, toast, hash brown potatoes, coffee, freshly squeezed orange juice. Usually I don't have a big appetite in the morning but I sat across from him at the dining-room table and ate as much as he did, taking second helpings, slathering my toast with gobs of butter and jam, drinking a cup of coffee in two gulps. We both had damp hair from the quick shower we'd taken together as the coffee was brewing. I liked the feel of the damp hair on my bare neck. He lounged back in his chair, bare-chested and bare-footed, crunching his toast, licking his fingers and smiling at me. Sunlight streamed through the tall windows, filling the room with shimmering stillness and warmth. Against the bright glass my geraniums in their clay pots looked like a painting composed of scarlet and ochre, vivid and perfectly designed, evoking Spain or Greece. I could have sat there all day, lazy and luxurious as a courtesan.

"I really like this house," he remarked idly. "Do you rent it, or . . . ?"

"Oh, no, it's mine," I said with a yawn, pouring myself a third cup of coffee. "I bought it in the seventies, before the boom. It's Second Empire style so it has the high ceilings and the arched windows. All the mouldings are original. It's one of the oldest houses in the Beach. It was one of the few lakefront houses that survived when the city was building the boardwalk in the thirties. I was really lucky to get it."

He watched me as I talked and then nodded thoughtfully, looking around. "That painting," he said, gesturing. "I don't know much about art. Is it by somebody big?"

I laughed. "I bought it from a sidewalk artist in Paris. He told me it was 'a tribute to Fragonard.' I liked that."

"The way you have it set up. I've never seen that before."

"Oh, I just got tired of the same old thing, I mean pictures in frames, hanging on the wall. That's a turn-of-the-century French music stand and suddenly I had this idea that the painting would look nice just sitting on it. What do you think?"

He stared at it with a very serious, contemplative expression, almost as though he were memorizing it. "You have good taste," he said, shifting his eyes to my face.

His air of grave judgement made me smile. "Thanks," I said.

"The room upstairs, the one with the pink and blue walls . . ."

"Oh," I said. "Did you go in there?"

"The door was open and I looked in," he said. "Wasn't that all right?"

"Oh, sure." I laughed quickly. "Of course. I don't care. That's the guest room."

"How did you do that? Did you hire somebody?"

"You mean the walls? Well, it's a long story. Provence is one of my favourite places in the world and I often rent a little cottage with a room like the one upstairs, sort of a soft rose colour with blue baseboard and lots of windows and when you wake up in the morning you feel like you're in the middle of a sunny yellow field filled with flowers and the blue Mediterranean is sparkling in the distance. I wanted to have a room just like it here in Toronto. So I could go in and pretend that outside it isn't winter, you know? I have a friend who's a painter and she liked the challenge. It's kind of a *trompe l'oeil* effect. The real windows look out at Toronto and the painted windows look out at the fields of Provence, so when you wake up in that room, sometimes you can't be sure just where you are."

While I was explaining this he stared at me intently, as if he didn't want to miss a single word. It was a bit strange. I wouldn't have thought he was the type to be so interested in interior decorating.

"What are you doing today?" he asked suddenly.

I had a dozen things I thought I should be doing, but I made a quick decision. "I'm taking the day off," I said.

"So am I," he said.

I promised myself that tomorrow I would call it quits, tomorrow I would get back to normal. I just wanted to go on awhile longer, stretching out my wild little escapade, squeezing it for its last drop of juice.

"I'll get my car," he said. "Let's go for a drive along the lakeshore. Then we can go shopping. I'll make you dinner tonight. A special Argentine feast. And after that we'll play music and drink wine and make love in that French room all night long."

"All right," I said carelessly, swallowing a slight breathlessness. "If you go out the front door you're right on Vine Street."

I didn't ask him what he was taking a day off from, where he lived, any of those questions. He didn't ask me anything either. He put on the rest of his clothes and said he would be back in a little while. I heard his beeper making its insistent peeping sound as he opened the front door.

"Do you want to use my phone?"

"No, that's all right," he said. "I'll call them from my place. See you in an hour."

I sat down on the living-room sofa, still wearing my housecoat. All of a sudden I didn't feel quite so carefree or so pleased with myself. I really didn't like that beeper. I pictured him breezing into a trendy office nearby, sitting in a plushy swivel chair and propping his feet on a desk, punching out some numbers on his touch-tone phone and launching into a glib sales pitch full of phrases like "five per cent down" and "rock-bottom rates" and "priceless equity" and "marvellous lakefront acreage." Calm down, I told myself. But he had asked me if I rented or owned. And he had seemed terribly interested in the way the place was decorated. I closed my eyes and prayed fervently. Please God, not a real estate agent, that's all I ask.

I noticed that the magazine that had been lying open on the coffee table the night before was now closed and stacked neatly on top of some other magazines and newspapers. I wondered why he had done that. The room seemed changed in other ways, too, although I couldn't pinpoint anything specific that was different. I wondered how long he had been up while I was asleep, and what he had done during that time, what he had looked at. I imagined him quietly pushing open the guest-room door and going in, staring speculatively at the painted windows and the painted Provençal fields. Had he figured out all sorts of things about me that I didn't want him to know? I tried to remember what I might have left lying around—letters, notes, photographs, a book with writing on the flyleaf? Everything seemed to be in its proper place, yet I felt that something was wrong. I didn't like the idea of his looking into my books, or touching any of my things while I wasn't there.

Of course there was a very strong possibility that he wouldn't come back. I wasn't sure whether I was worried or consoled by that prospect. In the bathroom mirror my face looked pale, with milky grey, lashless eyes. I didn't look attractive at all. He was a flashy guy, he'd been around. I could see him pulling up in front of a loud nightclub, jumping out of a big, ostentatious car that glittered with chrome, opening the door for a tall twenty-year-old blonde whose brief knit dress moulded itself to her big breasts and tight little buttocks. How could I compete with something like that? No, he won't be back, I assured myself. However, I got dressed and waited. There I was, a thin, prim, pasty-faced white woman, not young, sitting on her living-room sofa with her purse beside her, her knees together and her feet side by side on the floor, as the clock ticked away the minutes and hours, waiting patiently for someone who would never come. I was far too old and far too jaded to be so pitiful. I'll catch up on my reading instead, I told myself vigorously, if it's mild enough I'll sit out on the terrace with a drink and I'll read all day, that's what I'll do. And this evening I can start work on those exams. When my doorbell sounded, my body twitched in shock as though someone had shot a gun off over my head.

His car wasn't ostentatious at all. It wasn't large, it wasn't expensive. It was small and white and looked a few years old. I felt half-relieved, half-disappointed. He had changed into jeans, a blue, silky-looking shirt, and a brown leather jacket with the sleeves rolled up on his arms. When I got into the front seat he leaned over and kissed my shoulder. His lips barely touched me but I felt a hot tremor of pleasure ripple through my arms and legs. This is nice and tomorrow it will be a nice memory, I said to myself.

The breeze was bright and chilly that day, but I kept my window open and let it flow through the car as we drove. The lake seemed as brilliant and vast as an ocean, endless waves capped with white foam, stretching to the horizon in a haze of sunshine.

"How far shall I go?" he called above the noise of the wind and the car radio.

"It doesn't matter," I called back through my wind-whipped hair.

"Toronto has nice-looking beaches but they're all polluted," he said. "Do you know what's the best beach in the world?"

"No, what?"

"Montevideo," he said. "It used to be polluted too but they cleaned it up. The highway runs along right beside it for miles. The best time is sunrise. We used to gamble in the casino all night, and then drive home. It was fantastic."

"You gambled?"

"Yeah. I and my friends. Just for fun. One night I lost fifty thousand dollars."

I glanced at him. He was staring straight ahead at the road. The breeze lifted the dark curly hair from his brow.

"What did you do then?" I said.

"I bought drinks for everybody. It's a special occasion when you lose that much. Then we left and drove fast down the highway and watched the seagulls flying over the ocean."

"Did you live in Montevideo?"

"No, but we went there for fun. We were always looking for fun. My friends and I."

"You speak English very well," I said. "You hardly have an accent at all."

"Yes, I went to school in the States for a couple of years. My father wanted me to have an international outlook. It was important for our business."

"Your business."

"Yeah, we have an import-export business."

"What do you export?"

"Oh, many things. Wool, and leather, and lapis lazuli . . . Canada has been a great market for us. That's why I'm here."

He was as entertaining and extravagant as a Hollywood movie. Casinos, rolls of bills, men in tuxedos, the highway along the beach; it was all there. I laid my head back against the car seat and let my hair blow away from my face. The Uruguayan wind was warm and scented with flowers, I was dressed in diamonds and a long black gown, I tossed back a glass of champagne as we drove away from the gaming tables where we had just lost a fortune and then nonchalantly toasted everyone in the place. I laughed out loud.

"What's so funny?" he said.

"Oh, nothing really," I said.

We drove for a long time and the music played. After a while I became aware that I seemed to be talking quite a lot, idle conversation, not important, places I had travelled, summer days long past, old boyfriends, stories about myself that I made up as I went along. If he could make things up, so could I. It was part of the pleasure of the experience—the pretence, the game, being someone different for a while. But he turned the radio down to hear me, and then I heard my own voice, rambling foolishly. He seemed engrossed by every word out of my mouth. His attentiveness made me uneasy.

"I keep expecting your beeper to go off," I said.

"Oh, I didn't bring it," he said. "I didn't want to be bothered."

We strolled around the grounds of the Guild Inn. He had never been there before. He loved the Scarborough Bluffs and found the strange sculptures fascinating. So he said, anyway. Afterwards we sat in the restaurant and had a long, leisurely lunch. It must have been three or four in the afternoon when we drove downtown. He parked in a sidestreet near Hazelton Lanes.

"This is my favourite place for shopping," he told me.

"Really? I think it's terribly pretentious."

He stared at me as though this was something that had never occurred to him before. Then he recovered. "Oh, yes, that's what I like the best," he said, with a laugh.

We went through the glass doors that faced onto Avenue Road, passing under the large, artsy papier-mâché figures of circus performers guarding the entrance. The moment you got inside your nostrils filled with a luxurious odour made up of rich leather, new carpet, fur, polished wood, cappuccino, perfume, candles, pastries. He took a deep breath and lifted his shoulders. "Smell that," he said with satisfaction.

His attitude toward "shopping" was the same as my mother's had been. It wasn't just a simple task, where you quickly chose certain items that you needed, paid for them, and left. It was more like a visit to a museum of fine art, a very serious and intense activity to which a great deal of thought and attention had to be devoted. We had to go into every single store we saw, even one that sold nothing but lamps.

"Do you need a lamp?" I asked.

"Well, we should see what they have, shouldn't we?"

Coming out of Lumière I said, "You know, if you really want to find nice things you have to go to private shops. A lot of the stuff in here is completely tacky and overpriced."

He looked at me solemnly. "You're right," he said.

We spent forty-five minutes in a shoe store, where he tried on ten pairs, looking at his feet in the mirror with great concentration, walking a few steps, standing still, posing in various attitudes, until he finally settled on the two pairs that cost the most. "Don't you want any shoes?" he asked me.

He also bought a beautiful green jacket, dark green, wood-green I believe it's called, made of suede so soft it felt like velvet. He touched the fabric reverently, caressing it exactly the way he had caressed my inner thigh. "Feel it," he said, offering a sleeve to me. "Armani."

I shrugged and touched the material in a cursory way.

"You like him, don't you?" he said. "You were wearing an Armani suit yesterday."

I turned and stared at him in surprise. He was busy examining the stitching on the jacket's collar.

"Was I?" I said carelessly. "It's so old, I'd forgotten. I must have had it for three years at least."

He nodded, opening the jacket and feeling the lining.

"Designers' names don't matter to me," I added after a moment. "But I can only wear certain kinds of materials. Natural fibre. Synthetic fabrics irritate my skin. I break out in a rash."

"Of course," Eddy agreed. "Names are nothing, good quality is what's important." He glanced at the clerk with a nod. "I'll take this."

The clerk, who had a deep tan and long wavy hair and looked like a male model, held up a pair of gloves. "Did you see these? They're a perfect match with the jacket. Driving gloves. Kid leather. They're so soft and supple they almost feel like a second skin."

Eddy gave the gloves a brief, appraising glance. "Okay," he said.

He also bought three ties, two shirts, five pairs of socks, a pair of Calvin Klein jeans, and a bottle of Obsession. He paid for everything in cash. He didn't display the money in any obvious way, but whenever he made a new purchase, there were more bills in his wallet to cover it. He wanted to buy me something too. "Anything," he told me. "Just say."

But before I could answer his attention was distracted.

"Wine," he said. "We've got to have lots of wine with our dinner."

The Vintage Wine Shoppe had a resident wine expert. Eddy asked for him at once. He was a small, fair-haired man of about thirty-five. Eddy stood there holding all his bags, bags with labels like Ralph Lauren and Hermes, bags that tell everybody who sees them that you have lots of money to spend.

"This wine is distilled from white grapes planted late in the season in the south of France," the expert told Eddy, holding up a bottle he had chosen from a rack marked "$80." "It has a distinctive smoky flavour, not too fruity, rich but dry, a very slight tartness that really brings out the taste of seafood or chicken."

Eddy nodded solemnly, studying the label. "And that one?" He pointed at some tall green bottles positioned artfully on top of a barrel and surrounded by ornamental grasses.

"Ah," said the expert. "Now that's a very pleasant South American wine from Mendoza, Argentina."

"I know," Eddy said with a laugh. "I was testing you. I'm Argentinian."

"Really," said the expert. "Then you know all about Mendoza wine."

"Better than French," Eddy said. "But I guess I could be a little bit prejudiced."

"Mendoza produces some of the best wine in this hemisphere," said the expert smoothly. "Some people are predicting that Malbec is going to be *the* wine of the twenty-first century on the world market. As you can see we have an excellent Martins, and a lovely Trapiche which is top-of-the-line. Of course you know that if you're looking for *vino blanco* you have to leave Mendoza and go north to Salta. It's a strange fact that when the Torrontes grape is grown in Spain it's practically unusable, but when it's grown in Salta it produces a marvellous dry white wine with an overwhelming bouquet. Now to make this lovely Alba Blanca, the grapes are picked the moment they're ripe and the wine is aged in special casks underground. These bottles are 1976 vintage. The taste is very clear and crystalline, very pure. A perfect complement to shrimp or chicken breast with vegetables sautéed in a light oil."

Eddy spent two hundred dollars in the Vintage Wine Shoppe. Then we rode the escalator to the main level, our arms full of bags and packages. They were all Eddy's purchases. I hadn't bought a single thing.

He paused inside the glass doors, looking out onto the bright, windy sidewalk where a woman was blowing past, holding on to her big red hat, anchored by a leash to a tiny white dog in a checkered coat. He frowned, deep in thought.

"I think I'll wear the new jacket," he decided. He took off the old jacket and handed it to me, then carefully lifted the green suede from its silver-striped bag. Swiftly and expertly he slipped his arms into the soft sleeves, pulled down the cuffs of his shirt, and straightened his collar with one crisp movement of one hand.

"Okay?" he asked me.

It was hard not to smile. I couldn't quite make him out, but he amused me. I thought that all in all he was really rather a silly man. But his silliness didn't diminish my attraction in the least. As he looked down at me with his dark, thoughtful eyes, waiting for my reaction to the look of the jacket, a *frisson* of excitement passed through me like a crackle of electricity.

Out on the street you had to squint in the sudden brilliance of sunlight and wind. A dirty-looking beggar was sitting outside the Book Cellar with a basket beside him, a basket that held a quarter and a nickel. His smell was so strong that your nostrils flared in protest as you got close; you had to hold your breath as you hurried past. I saw a five-dollar bill flutter down into his basket, almost as if by accident, and then Eddy stuck his bulging wallet back into the pocket of his new jacket, casually, without even turning his head. All afternoon he had behaved like the consummate big spender. I wondered if he thought he was impressing me. Or perhaps he only wanted to show me how unnecessary it had been to check my purse that morning.

"I'm surprised, you don't see panhandlers in Yorkville very often," I said. "You know, it really isn't helping to throw big bills at them. You should donate to the Salvation Army or something instead. If you hand them cash they'll only spend it on cheap booze."

"Oh, let him have a good time," Eddy said with a shrug. "Why not?"

IN THE SIXTIES YORKVILLE was a crowded, crazy street full of hippies and musicians, but years ago it changed into its present incarnation: a chi-chi neighbourhood where people own expensively renovated apartments and out-of-towners flock to shop in stiff little boutiques. The psychics provide one of the few reminders of its old chaotic ambience. I suppose they're attracted there by the crowds of tourists eagerly looking for ways to empty their pockets. They set up their tables at frequent intervals from one corner to the next, with bright tablecloths, crystal balls, and tarot cards. Some of them look like gypsies, others appear to be university students trying to make some extra cash.

Eddy paused, considering. "Let's ask about my future," he said.

"Oh, you're kidding," I said.

"Why not? Just for fun." He stopped in front of a middle-aged woman with unbelievably bright chestnut curls under a black scarf. She had the usual accoutrements, including a hand-lettered sign informing passers-by that she was "Madame Serena—seer and psychic, superior above all others, 99% accurate."

"Good afternoon, sir." She spoke in a slow, guttural voice and seemed haughty and condescending, as though she were doing us a favour, not just hoping to make a few bucks.

"Can you tell me something great about my future?" Eddy asked her with a grin.

Madame Serena didn't grin in response. She looked up at him with cold, blue, heavy-lidded eyes. "I'll tell you what I see," she said. "Good or bad, that's not up to me."

"But if it's bad, I should at least get a discount, right?" Eddy winked at me and I smiled. But Madame Serena was determined not to encourage any levity. Her lips remained firmly straight. "Tarot cards, ten dollars," she said sternly. "Palm, five."

Eddy sat down across from her and held out his hand. Immediately Madame Serena got down to business. She grasped his hand in both of hers and leaned over to stare into it, stroking the lines with her thumbs, frowning, licking the corners of her mouth.

"Lifeline is long," she said at last.

"That's good," Eddy said.

"But there's a break halfway. See that? Line breaks right there, then reappears. You will have a serious illness or accident, but you will recover."

"Okay. . . ."

"You have travelled long distances in your life."

He had forgotten that it was supposed to be a joke. Or perhaps he had only pretended it was a joke for my benefit. He leaned over Madame Serena's rickety table, staring intently into his own hand as if he really believed he could see his prospects there.

"That's true, I've travelled a lot," he said.

"And there will be many more journeys. But one day you will settle down and never leave home again."

"When will that be?"

"When you're fifty years old," she said at once, as though reading from a timetable.

"Fifty," Eddy said. "Huh."

"A woman with yellow hair will cause you much sorrow."

Eddy grinned at me. "Not red?"

"Yellow," Madame Serena stated, unsmiling.

I was getting rather tired of Madame Serena. "You can see all that in the palm of his hand?" I asked.

She didn't even bother to glance my way. Instead she raised her head and stared keenly into Eddy's eyes. He looked back, smiling expectantly. She had such a grim expression on her face that I was sure she was going to come out with something really gloomy and cryptic. It was going to be just like a movie scene: there's a gypsy fortune-teller who suddenly refuses to go on, saying that the crystal ball is clouded, so the client leaves, starts to cross the street and is killed by a speeding car.

She waited so long before speaking that I looked rather pointedly at my watch and gave an audible sigh. Neither she nor Eddy paid any attention to me. They were too absorbed in the contemplation of his mystical future.

Still gripping his hand, but not moving her eyes from his face, she finally said, "You give off very strong psychic currents. Very unusual."

"Yeah," Eddy agreed. "I've been told that before."

"Scorpio, yes?"

"Right," Eddy answered, surprised. "How did you know that?"

"Danger is high in the month of August when Mars is in your fifth house. You should avoid travel from the twentieth to the thirtieth. If all goes well, Venus is rising in late September and will bring love and riches."

Eddy was so pleased with this that he tried to make me sit down so I could have my palm read too.

"No, really, I'd rather not know my future," I said dryly. "I'd sort of like to be surprised."

Madame Serena tucked Eddy's money into her full bosom and looked at me with a cool stare, as if she could have told me plenty of unpleasant things if I hadn't been such a coward. The wind lifted the corners of her scarf and whipped them around her face like small black flags.

"I went to a fortune-teller in Buenos Aires once," Eddy told me as we walked back to the car. "She had a little dark room with only one window, a round window made out of stained glass, so there was all this strange light, dark red, dark blue. She had ten cats and the whole time you were sitting there the only thing you could smell was cats, until you thought you were going to pass out or be sick. She told me I'd have honours and glory. And she said that someone close to me would die soon. Then I went back to school and there was a phone call from my father, telling me my mother had died that day."

"Oh, God."

"Yeah. Strange, huh?"

"How about the honours and glory?"

"Oh, that's still coming, I'm sure," he said with a laugh.

"Of course it's all guesswork and psychology and tricks, though," I said. "You don't believe they really can tell the future, do you?"

"Oh, I don't necessarily believe it," he said carelessly. "But it's possible."

The weather had changed and the interior of his car felt cold and slightly damp. It wasn't pleasant anymore to drive along the lakeshore with the windows open. Long grey and white strands of cloud blurred the horizon, made the lake and the sky indistinguishable. One drop of rain hit the windshield, then another. *It's spitting,* my mother used to say. And my father would smile, wryly amused to hear such an expression. I thought of a short grey afternoon when I came home and sat in the dark, silent parlour without removing my coat, listening to the clock tick on the indistinct mantelpiece.

But that was a long time ago. We were speeding along on a wet, silvery road. We had bags of groceries, bottles of red wine from hot, sunny countries, tapes of loud, happy music; he was sitting beside me, a frivolous, showy, good-looking man, tapping the steering wheel in time to the car stereo. I laid my hand on his thigh and felt the long, hard muscle tapering to his knee. Everything became intensely clear and poignant: the raindrops on the glass, the curve of the dashboard and its tiny red lights, the pale gleam of the wet road, the black branches blown across the dark, opalescent sky, all charged with brilliance and vitality as though the world had been transformed into an enchanted place full of light and spicy fragrances, peopled by gamblers and fortune-tellers. Soon we would be inside my house and someone walking by on the deserted boardwalk would be able to look up and see my steamy yellow windows shining magically through the darkness and rain.

In my front hallway he put down his bags the instant the door was shut. Before I had a chance to turn around he nudged me gently against the wall and I felt his hand under the belt of my slacks, his cool, sleek fingers sliding down over my belly and into my crotch. I gasped. The pleasure was so intense and violent that it was almost unendurable. Stop, stop, I wanted to say, I can't stand it. But no words formed in my mouth, only a soft groan. He pressed against my back; his body folded itself into mine as though we were two parts of the same whole. My cheek rested against the dark, smooth wall; it held us up, we floated upon it like two people on a raft in the middle of the ocean. One of his bags fell over on its side and spilled things out onto the rug around our feet, bottles of cologne, cufflinks, a tie with a thin golden thread twining through it, rich things that sparkled in the dim light and dazzled my eyes.

Chapter Three

"YOU LOOK AS IF YOU HAVE SOMETHING WICKED on your conscience."

I had been sitting at my desk, staring vaguely out my office window, twirling my pen. I gave a little jump and turned around. Jeremy Venable was standing in the doorway smiling, his eyebrows raised.

"Whoops. Sorry!" he said. "God, you were a million miles away."

I was annoyed with myself. "Hi," I said, taking off my glasses and rubbing my eyes. "I've been trying to come up with some new questions for my English Lit. 102 exam, but I don't seem to have any inspiration at all."

"Why bother? The old questions are plenty challenging enough for the undergrads, believe me." He came in and slumped down in a chair. His hair was long and silky and he shook it dramatically back from his brow. That was a gesture I had once found quite charming, before it started to make me sick. By the end of our brief fling he had developed a similar reaction to some of my habits. The night we called it quits he told me he'd had enough of me to last a lifetime. I'm sure I said some equally nasty things, but I can't remember now what they were. Still, we had stayed "friends." He dropped by my office once in a while to needle me.

"I'm off to Italy at the end of July," he said. "Gwen's coming with me. How about you? Are you doing anything exciting this summer?"

"Not really. I might go to the south of France again. I haven't decided."

"What about *Trewithen*?" he asked after a moment, putting a slightly mocking emphasis on the name. "I can't imagine you'd let a whole summer go by without a sojourn at *Trewithen*."

"Oh, sure, I'll probably spend some time there too."

"The fabulous *Trewithen* of song and story," he said.

"You would have been bored to death," I said. "It wasn't your kind of place at all. I can't believe you're still annoyed about that."

He laughed in amazement and shrugged his shoulders. "Who's annoyed? I could care less. It used to amuse me, though. All those stories in *Muskoka Memories* about the big parties in your father's day, the cavalcade of cars driving down from the city, the marquee on the lawn, the jazz band in the gazebo. . . . Then the Great Tremain's daughter seals it off from the world and never invites a living soul."

"People always kind of spoiled it for me," I said.

"Yes, that was an area where you had a bit of a problem, wasn't it? People."

I imagined reaching out my foot and tipping his chair over, what a pleasure it would be to see him sprawled on the floor in his beautifully tailored, pale grey suit.

"Isn't there a drug to help you with that?" he said. "There must be. There's a drug for everything now. A pill you could pop to improve your social skills."

"I think my social skills are just as advanced as yours," I said dryly.

"Maybe all you need is a toke now and then," he suggested. "Just to loosen you up a bit."

"A couple of glasses of French Chardonnay make me as loose as I want to be."

"Oh, come on, Grace, don't be so bourgeois. A toke might help you to . . . 'relate.' I think that's how we put it in my hippie days."

"Actually, pot never did a thing for me. I tried it once or twice, but nothing. The people I was with would start giggling and bumping into each other, but to me it was just like smoking an ordinary cigarette."

"Poor Grace. Always on the outside, looking in."

Again I had an impulse to tip over his chair. "Well, it's certainly safer on the inside," I said. "I guess that's why you find it so appealing."

His face flushed, but after a moment he shook his head and grinned to show me he didn't give a damn what I thought of him. "Exactly," he said.

"Listen, Jeremy," I told him, "I really should get back to this. It's driving me crazy. I've got to finish today."

He unfolded himself and stood up. He wasn't a bad-looking man, quite attractive really, a lot of women thought so. He was clever, he was cultured, he was well-read, he had a sense of humour, he was entertaining company, he was a gentle and considerate lover. It bored me just thinking of all his good qualities.

"I'll leave you to it then," he said. "If I don't see you again, have a good summer."

"You too. Enjoy Italy."

After his light step had faded away down the hall, I stared at the blank page in front of me. I had been holding a fountain pen the whole time I talked to him, and it had leaked and stained my forefinger with dark blue ink. I rubbed my hand absently against my thigh, and then I felt the flesh, soft and warm from the patch of sunlight in my lap. Some time later I looked at my watch and saw that ten minutes had passed, and the page before me was still blank.

I picked up my pen and wrote: "Discuss the social/ political implications of marriage in Jane Austen's *Emma* and compare Austen's attitudes to those of Charles Dickens in *David Copperfield.* (30 marks)." There, I told myself with satisfaction. Alvin What's-his-name can have a field day with that one.

By four-thirty my eyes were burning and my shoulders and arms felt stiff, but I had finished both exams and turned them in to the secretary for typing. Thick sunlight burned the top of my head as I walked abstractedly through the sunny courtyard. It was very quiet and full of light, like a courtyard in a foreign city. The sound of my shoes scraping on the sidewalk startled some sparrows and they flapped up around me, wings beating in celebration. Holiday was coming, freedom was coming. I passed through the cool shadow of the Charles Street arch and strolled down toward Yonge. It was so warm on the street that I took off my suit jacket. The intersection was jammed with cars. A young guy with long greasy hair, standing humbly outside Coles bookstore, caught my glance with hopeful eyes and said, "Spare any change, ma'am?" Usually I would have walked right past with my face averted, but that day for some reason I opened my bag and found a loonie.

"Thank you, ma'am. Hope you have a nice day," he said. When he smiled he revealed a row of startlingly perfect white teeth.

In Coles I searched idly through the travel section for something new about the south of France. I thought maybe I should get some material about Spain too. Spain was a possibility. Then I saw it, a large book with a picture on the cover showing a city beside water, tall towers shimmering in a fine yellow light, the title in elegant, curled letters: *Buenos Aires, Paris of the South.* I had a sudden strange little spasm of excitement, as though I was about to discover something brand-new, something I had never known before. The book was so large that I had to put down my briefcase in order to open it. On the title page was a quotation.

Hard to believe Buenos Aires had a beginning . . .
To me it seems as eternal as water and air.

(Jorge Luis Borges)

There were dozens of illustrations: "Tango Dancers in La
Boca," "Illuminated Fountain on Avenida Nueve de Julio,"
"Lovers in Palermo Park," "Polo Game at Palermo Field,"
"Interior of the Teatro Colón," "Society Ladies after Mass,"
"Aristocratic Barrio of the Dead." If I let the pages slip quickly
through my fingers the pictures flowed together into one
phantasmagorical panorama: a mythical city of green fields
and romantic parks, carnivals and cathedrals, street dancers
and stone figures glimpsed through trees, tombs as large as
mansions and vast night streets filled with speed and blazing
neon.

I thought I wouldn't be seeing Eddy again. I believed an
experience like that was always better and sharper when it was
very brief, with a quick and final end. That morning I had
stood on the curb watching his white car slip away into the
streaming traffic of the Beach, and I was already experiencing
a sort of pleasant nostalgia. He was supposed to become a
pleasant memory, a little dream full of heat and sensuality that
I could bring to mind whenever I needed to lift my mood.

I didn't even know if he was really from Buenos Aires or if
that was just some story he'd invented. Nevertheless I stood
there for a long time holding the book, staring into it in total
absorption, placing him dimly in each scene: he was one of the
crowd sitting in a café across from La Recoleta, he bought a
pack of cigarettes from a *kiosco* and leaned forward into the
chilly blue neon glow to laugh with the vendor, he was standing with a group of passionate men having a political
argument on Calle Florida, he crossed a busy intersection at
sunset, his hair flaming in the last soft rays of orange light.

I ended up buying the book. A souvenir of the weekend, I
thought. A souvenir of my exotic South American lover.

The sun was red over the lake that night and the boardwalk was quiet. A solitary man passed me, walking a little

brown dog on a long leash. *A wiener dog,* my mother used to call them, until finally my father corrected her with a sigh. *Dachshund, Vivian. Wiener dog, for God's sake.*

There was a rippling scarlet pathway over the water; you could almost believe it was possible to step onto it and walk right into the sky. Gulls were circling across the radiant clouds with wild, faraway cries. It struck me how beautiful and graceful they appeared at a distance; you could almost forget how ugly and aggressive they became when they were up close squawking and trying to snatch a piece of your sandwich. If they always remained remote they might be legendary creatures, symbolic of freedom, mystery and romance.

Someone was sitting on the pier near my house. As I got closer I saw who it was. I saw the wood-green jacket. He was smoking, looking toward the horizon where you could make out the glimmer of lights from the Toronto Yacht Club on Centre Island.

I stopped abruptly, paralysed by a confused combination of dismay and excitement. It crossed my mind that maybe I wanted to duck out of sight and that I should act quickly. I even took a rapid glance over my shoulder, looking for a way I might escape.

Then he turned his head and saw me. He got unhurriedly to his feet and began to walk down the pier, his hands in his pockets, his longish hair blowing in the breeze. As he approached me he began to smile, easily and naturally, as though we were old friends, as though we had known each other so long that there was no need for a moment's doubt or uneasiness.

"Hi," he said. His blowing hair made flickering shadows on his face.

Something squeezed me inside, a sensation so strong that it was almost painful. Perhaps I was angry, perhaps I was happy. Ridiculous, I told myself, there is nothing to be happy about, this is not a happy moment.

"Hi," I said. "What are you doing here?"

My voice sounded brusque and cold, but he didn't appear

to notice the tone. He just kept smiling, looking down at me, perfectly at ease, carefree as a boy. "Waiting for you," he said.

"But how did you know I'd come this way?"

"I thought you might."

"But what if I hadn't?"

"Then I'd have seen your lights go on, and I'd have knocked on your door."

"But what if I'd had someone with me?"

He shrugged, unconcerned. "I didn't think you would."

My face felt hot. "Well, you shouldn't assume things like that. You don't even know me. I could very easily have had someone else with me, a man, for example. What about that?"

He wasn't upset at all. His only reaction was to smile more broadly. "So then you'd say, 'Eddy, this is so-and-so. So-and-so, this is Eddy.' And then I'd just punch him in the nose."

An alarming thought occurred to me: perhaps he was going to turn out to be one of those men who become obsessed with some hapless woman, follow her, spy on her, send her love letters or threats, phone her in the middle of the night to whisper weird endearments. . . .

I stared at him. A humorous grin split his dark face. "That isn't the least bit funny," I said sharply.

"Oh, come on," he said. He put both arms around me and pressed my face into the soft, velvety collar of his jacket. I could smell a breath of cologne on his warm skin. "You don't want any other man but me," he said.

Inside myself I felt a flood of mixed-up emotion: resentment and pleasure, consternation and gratitude, a desire to give in, a desire not to give in. I had to keep talking, the need to talk was very strong, my voice went on and on, muffled by green suede. "Well, you have no idea what I want. I hate it when people just show up at my door without calling first. And the thing is, I have lots of work to do. I want to make it very clear. I have lots of responsibilities. I just don't have time for this right now. You and I, really it's impossible, it was only a weekend, let's face it, it was meant to be just a . . . a brief interlude sort of thing, don't you understand that concept?

And now I'm very busy, I've got so many things I have to do tonight. . . ."

I felt his long, warm fingers on the back of my neck. "Okay," he said. "I'll just come in for an hour or so."

After a moment I said, "Well, all right then."

We started to walk. His arm was around my shoulder, my arm was around his waist. I gave my briefcase a furtive shake so that its contents slipped down out of sight. I didn't want him to notice the book on Buenos Aires and get the wrong idea.

Chapter Four

THE DEPARTMENT SECRETARY HAD LEFT a telephone message in my mail slot. "Prof. Tremain—Call Leslie, (519) 254-7676." I hadn't heard from Leslie in months and I had no desire to talk to her that day. The thought of her breathless, enthusiastic voice filled me with ennui. I hadn't had much sleep the night before, I had supervised two examinations, and there were seventy-five papers on my desk waiting to be marked. I had a lot on my mind and I was tired, too tired to cope with Leslie's relentless energy.

I sat at my desk crumpling the message and then unfolding it. Finally I picked up the receiver and started to dial. The best thing was to get it over with as quickly as possible. She answered on the first ring.

"Hi, it's me," I said.

"Gracie! Well, hi, how are you?"

"Oh, fine," I said brightly. "How about you?"

"It seems like an eternity since I talked to you last. I guess

Richelle Kosar

you're in the middle of exams right now, huh? But at least you're not marking yet. I know better than to call you when you're marking! I'll never forget that time I showed up at your door, Perry and I had had a huge fight and he locked me out of the house, and I was crying and blabbering about what a bastard he was, and you said, 'Leslie, I have five thousand papers to mark, and I have to finish by tomorrow, and I don't have time to sit around *chatting* all night.' Well, boy, did I ever feel like a dipstick. 'Oh. Sorry.'"

"You're exaggerating," I said. "I wasn't that bad."

"Gracie, you have no idea how scary you are when you're marking papers. Your whole face changes, you get tufts in your eyebrows like Spencer Tracy in *Dr. Jekyll and Mr. Hyde. . . .*"

I laughed grudgingly. "Oh, very funny. As a matter of fact, I've got seventy-five papers on my desk right now, staring at me, but here I am talking to you and being perfectly gracious."

"What? You *are* marking? Oh my God, every year I get it wrong. Maybe I have a mental block against it, do you think? Maybe I'm jealous because you're doing something professional and important. Do you think that could be it?"

My office seemed to fade around me. I was lying in a dark bedroom, the windows open onto the garden. Leslie slipped across the floor like a little ghost and wanted to get into bed with me because she was afraid, she always told you how she felt, *I'm scared, I'm lonely, I'm hurt*, as if it were just fine to say things like that out loud. So we lay side by side smelling the cold lilacs. *Shhhhhh, did you hear something? No, she's asleep, she took her pill and went to sleep.* A door opens far below in the deep darkness, Grandpa's cane thuds against the carpet, his harsh voice rises up the staircase, angry and coarse, a bit slurred because all night he's been drinking Scotch, ice melting and clinking in his glass. *I guess you think you're pretty smart, don't you, sonny? You're pretty pleased with yourself. Well, take another look in the mirror, you sly little prick! There you are, the biggest arsehole on Bay Street!* My father's voice murmurs

50

in response, calm, slightly weary, but he doesn't get a chance to finish his sentence. *Hah! Don't kid yourself! You paid too much, you damn fool! When are you gonna wise up? You're as soft as a bloody woman! My damn dog could of come up with a better campaign than that! Isn't it obvious we want to target the young ones? The market's been flat for a year and it's actually falling in Toronto and New York! So think, who do we want as customers, sixty-year-old guys who're gonna croak on us in a year, or nineteen-year-old guys who're gonna get hooked and live a long time spending money on our product? Couldn't you figure that out, dummy? Couldn't you? Huh?* The answer drifts up the staircase, so weary, so quiet, almost unintelligible. *Oh, sure, the numbers. Yeah, yeah. The numbers'll show whatever their God damn accountant wants 'em to show! They're all liars and bastards, don't you know that? Don't you? Huh? Every last one! Liars and God damn bastards!* Then a door slams shut with a thunderous boom like a cannon being fired, and the house is left vast and empty except for ice-blue moonlight and shadows.

"I know this is short notice, but Sid's driving up for a Blue Jay game on Thursday," Leslie told me. "He's sitting in Ted Putnam's box, very big deal. Well, you know how I feel about baseball, and I hate Connie Putnam too. She's such a brass-plated phoney. She called me in January to see if we were going to the Brazilian Ball. Did she call you?"

"No. She never calls me."

"Well, she knows how you hate that sort of thing. Anyway, I said, 'Connie, I'm really not in a ball kind of mood this year.' And she said, 'It's for charity, Leslie.' As if I'm a selfish bitch or something. Well, forget it, I didn't let her intimidate me, and I didn't go. My shrink was proud of me. But anyway, I thought I'd drive up with Sid on Thursday, and you and I could meet and have dinner or something."

"Oh. Well, sure, that would be great."

"Don't sound so doubtful."

"I'm not doubtful. It'll be great. Really."

"You can afford to take a few hours off."

"Of course."

"Let's go to that place with the blue walls and the vines. You know the one I mean?"

"The French Quarter?"

"Yeah. On Bloor Street. Where they had the chocolate pecan pie. Is that the French Quarter? I've been dreaming about that chocolate pecan pie ever since the last time. I can't wait!"

After I'd hung up, I sat for a while without moving, looking at the pile of exam papers without really seeing it. For my sister's first wedding, my father had ten thousand white lilacs flown in by chartered plane from a greenhouse in Windsor to festoon the ballroom of the Royal York Hotel. At the reception Leslie drank too much wine and during the opening dance she stepped on the hem of her gown, tripped, staggered, and fell right into a flower-covered arbour. There was a moment of shocked silence while she rolled herself clumsily into a sitting position, and then she just sat there tangled in her white finery, pieces of wood on her shoulders and lilacs drooping drunkenly over her head. *Oh my God!* she sang out. *Do you think this is a bad omen?* My father leaned back and laughed out loud. No matter what she did, he thought it was funny.

That's what came into my mind as I sat there in my office. I don't know why I thought of it.

For five years Leslie had been living in a quaint little town called Clarendon, about an hour away from the city. She always used to say she would rather die than live in a small town, but that was before she met Sid, who wanted to live in a small town. Then she was all for it, and started talking about how peaceful it was in the country, how clean, how low the crime rate was, how insane a person had to be to continue living in the city anymore. She and Sid bought an elaborate old mansion on three and a half acres of property, and proceeded to renovate. For almost a year the grounds were overrun with architects, contractors, builders, bricklayers, and gardeners, and Leslie was always at the centre of the activity, making friends with everybody, praising their efforts, and ensuring that they had coffee and sandwiches every day at one p.m. By the time the initial work had been done, the place had started to resemble le petit Trianon. *Oh, no, Gracie, this is just the beginning. An estate like this is sort of a lifetime project. You're always working to realize its full potential.* The latest addition had been a small hexagonal summerhouse with walls of glass, where Leslie and Sid could sit on Sunday mornings with their croissants and coffee, looking out at their rustic garden and the golden fields beyond. *It's the light, Gracie, we had to take advantage of that marvellous pure country light.* I don't know why I have such a sarcastic attitude about it. That summerhouse is very pleasant.

Clarendon reminds me of L.M. Montgomery, Leslie says. *Like Avonlea or someplace like that.*

She always appreciates places that remind her of other places. That was probably one of the reasons she remembered the French Quarter. You were supposed to think you were in a bistro in New Orleans. There were vine-covered trellises, hanging ferns, terracotta pots, narrow faux balconies made of a material resembling wrought iron, paintings of jazz musicians and moonlit nights on the bayou. It's on the second floor of an old store, and its windows are high, so you don't see enough of Bloor Street to spoil the illusion. On Thursday I arrived on time, and she was late, as always. I ordered a bottle of white wine and sat there. I told myself there was no point in getting upset, no use looking at my watch every minute. To pass the time I imagined her progress. Absorbed in buying cushions or fabrics in some chi-chi store tinkling with gentle wind chimes, she suddenly glanced at her watch and gasped when she realized how late she was. . . . She dashed into the street to flag down a cab and immediately began chattering and laughing gaily with the cab driver, telling him her sister was waiting and how furious this uptight, difficult sister was going to be. . . . The cab driver was moved to tell a story about the time he was late for an important banquet with drastic consequences, while Leslie listened intently and laughed and nodded her head. . . . The cab pulled up in front of the restaurant, screeching its tires, and Leslie jumped out, giving the driver an excessively generous tip—"No, really, Ahmed, it was worth it just for that banquet story." . . . The cab driver smiled modestly and hurried to pocket the money before she could change her mind. . . . She rushed up the stairs and burst into the French Quarter like an actress making an entrance. . . .

I heard her laughing. She was standing just inside the door, speaking animatedly to the maitre d', no doubt telling him about the cab ride and the fact she was late. She had a compulsion to be overly friendly to service people, just to demonstrate how charmingly down-to-earth she was. She spotted me and waved, rolling her eyes as if to say, Yes, I've done it again. She was decked out in a really bizarre outfit, a yellow smock-type garment, patterned with navy blue circles and triangles, over long scarlet tights. Her shoes were navy blue with big red buckles. Her dangling earrings jingled like tiny bells as she walked quickly up to our table, all smiles and apologies, leaving a number of people staring after her. That was the idea, of course, to attract as much attention as possible.

"Oh, God, I'm sorry! I looked at my watch and I couldn't believe it was so late. . . ."

She squeezed herself into a chair, laughing and shaking her head, trying to fit her purse and many bags between the wall and the table, talking all the time. "Pour me a glass of wine, quick! What a day I've had, you won't believe it. And do we have any ice water? I want a great big drink of ice water. I'm so thirsty! It's really hot today, you'd think it was July. I'm trying to get a taxi, and I can feel the sweat breaking out all over my body, and this is silk, and you know what sweat does to silk—although Sid wouldn't mind if it was ruined, I guess. Do you know what he said to me this morning? He said, 'You look like you're going to be walking a tightrope at Le Cirque du Soleil!'" She leaned back with a burst of laughter and her head bumped the arm of a waiter who was passing with a tray. "Oh, my God! I'm sorry! Are you all right?" she said to him. "Listen, could you bring me an extra-large glass of water? Icy cold? Thanks a lot."

As she settled back in her chair, sighing and blowing a loose curl away from her face, she reminded me momentarily of our mother, although she really looks nothing like our mother.

"So I said to him, 'You're a fine one to talk. Someone who thinks cowboy boots are the latest thing in understated elegance.' He does, you know. He won't wear normal shoes anymore. I think he'd wear cowboy boots with a tuxedo."

"Maybe the country living is doing it to him," I said.

"Well, God, Clarendon is hardly the Wild West." She laughed and leaned back in her seat. "So!" she said brightly. "How are you?"

"Oh, not bad."

"I've missed you! I haven't seen you for so long! Once exams are over you should come and stay for a week or so. Don't you think? Are we going to Stratford this year? Perry's back there, he's doing Juliet's father and Falstaff and Big Daddy in *Cat on a Hot Tin Roof*. Not that I'm dying to see Perry give one of his pah-fah-mances. I know all his clever little actor-y tricks by heart."

The waiter returned with two glasses of water. "Oh, thanks a million," Leslie told him fervently. "You saved my life. My throat is just parched. God, I haven't even looked at the menu yet. Sorry, could you come back in a few minutes?"

She snapped open the menu, which was as large as a road map. "Have you decided yet?" she asked me. "Hmmmmmm . . . what shall I have?" Suddenly her bright blue eyes appeared over the edge of the menu. "Can you imagine what Dad would have said about this place? As soon as he saw the prices, he'd have decided it was no good."

"He wouldn't have waited to see the prices," I said. "He would have walked in the door, taken one glance, and then walked out again."

" 'Forget it, Vivian. Let's go.' 'Oh, come on, Laurie, I'm starving. I just want to eat something.' 'I'm sure, but I'd prefer food that actually has a taste.' " Leslie laughed and shook her head. "Poor Dad, he was always trying to raise Mom's consciousness."

"Yeah," I said. "Poor Dad."

The waiter returned, holding a pad and pencil. He thought he and Leslie were friends now. He grinned at her. "Well, have you made up your minds?"

"I'll have the blackened chicken with okra and rice," I said. "And a green salad to start with, no cucumbers, oil and vinegar dressing."

"Oh, my God," said Leslie, struggling with the giant menu. "There are so many choices. I can't make up my mind."

The waiter leaned toward her solicitously. "Shall I give you a few more minutes?"

"No . . . okay, I've got it. The bouillabaisse. No, wait a minute. No, forget that. I'm not in the mood for shrimp."

"You can have it without shrimp," he said. He was a tall, sandy-haired boy with big square teeth.

"I can? But what about this? The Jambalaya. Mmmm mmmm. 'Tender pieces of chicken, ham and sausage sautéed with onion and two strips of bacon, served in a spicy tomato sauce.' Sounds pretty scrumptious."

"That's an excellent choice," the waiter agreed. "I had some of it myself earlier."

"And it was good, huh? Okay, I'm going to trust you," Leslie told him.

"You won't be sorry," he said.

A ray of fading sunshine from the high windows hit the back of Leslie's head and turned her hair into a corona of pale light. For a moment I seemed to see another scene faintly superimposed on the one before me: a blonde woman, my mother, talking flirtatiously with a waiter, and a small red-headed man, my father, sitting beside her, tapping his fingers on the white tablecloth, looking straight ahead, cool and elegant in a cool blue shirt, waiting until the waiter walks away, and saying, *You think he's pretty cute, do you, Vivian?*

And she shakes her big cloud of blonde hair defiantly. *Yeah, he's kind of cute.*

And his voice doesn't change, it remains quiet and pleasant, as though he were commenting on the weather. *But however attractive you think he is, it's really a bit cheap to make such a display in a public restaurant.*

Perhaps a bit of colour comes into her face, but the change is very subtle, almost imperceptible. She doesn't think she was making a display; she doesn't think she was doing anything wrong. But she seldom argues with him, even though it seems he wants her to, his pose is casual but he watches her alertly, waiting for a sign of anger or resentment or passion. Her large blue-grey eyes go opaque, she raises her wine glass and takes a small sip, looking out across the room, suddenly remote and beautiful as a portrait on the wall.

They were present so vividly for a moment. No, not they, exactly, but a vision of them in which their faces and bodies were in shadow, and only their outlines appeared, silhouettes surrounded by fiery light, sitting side by side at a dim table.

"Do you know what I might do?" Leslie said later, after she had finished a large chocolate dessert and we were sitting a bit sleepily over our coffee cups. "I might have a baby. What do you think of that idea?"

I was surprised, but not too surprised. "Really? I always thought you weren't interested in kids."

"Oh, I know, but I'm thirty-four. If I'm going to do it, I have to do it soon. Maybe I'll regret it later if I don't. Everybody says you end up regretting it."

I shrugged. "I imagine a lot of people who do have kids end up regretting it too," I said.

"Do you really think so?"

"Of course. Say the kid turned out to be a serial killer. Or a politician."

Leslie laughed. "Well, I don't know. I'm thinking maybe I should just go ahead. Do you think that would be wrong?"

"Wrong? You mean because of the population explosion?"

She stared at me with wide eyes. "Huh? Is that one of your causes now?"

"No," I said. "I don't have any causes."

"I meant if I got pregnant without telling Sid. Just stop taking the Pill, but not tell him."

"But why should you do that? You mean he doesn't want a baby?"

"Oh, he thinks he doesn't. But I think maybe we need a shake-up. If we had a kid, someone who needed us and so on, maybe things would be better for both of us. It might give our life some purpose."

"You don't think your life has any purpose?"

Leslie looked at me with a one-sided smile. "Not really a lot, no."

It occurred to me that maybe we should stop drinking coffee and order another bottle of wine. In the high windows of the restaurant, the sky had grown dark. The waiters were lighting candles at every table. "Well, I'm surprised to hear that," I said. "I thought you were happy."

Leslie gave a quick laugh and shook her head so that her earrings danced. "Oh, sure we are. It's not that." Then her eyes dropped and she stared down at her coffee cup, running one finger around the rim, chewing on her lower lip as if searching for the words to express something. "Happy, though," she said finally, with a faint quizzical grin. "Is that all there is to it?" At that moment our waiter arrived beside the table to light our candle.

"Shall I shed a little light on the subject?" he suggested playfully. "Everything okay here? Can I bring you a little more coffee?"

"No, thanks, Roger, everything's great," Leslie said brightly. She knew his name by that time. After he had moved on, she said to me, "What about you? Do you feel as if your life has meaning?"

"Not really," I said dryly. "But then I never expected it would."

Leslie shook her head, laughing. "Gracie, you're such a cynic."

"Why?"

"Have you met anybody lately? I mean, any interesting men?"

"No," I said. "Do you think that would fill my life with joy and purpose?"

"Not necessarily, but you might be in a better mood! It's been a while now, hasn't it? Don't you miss having—what did Aunt Lucy always say?—'masculine attention'?"

"Actually, I don't," I said. "It always gets so complicated and boring. There are lots of better things to think about."

"Well, I guess that's right. That's the best way to look at it. What's that Gloria Steinem quote?—a woman needs a man like a fish needs water." Then she put her hand over her mouth and giggled. "Oh, wait—that can't be it."

"Anyway, men don't really find me attractive," I said suddenly. I don't know why I said that.

"Oh, Gracie, what on earth are you talking about?" She leaned across the table in her eagerness to reassure me. "You got Mom's height, and Dad's red hair—when you walk into a room people just have to turn and look. Remember when you were on the cover of *Chatelaine*, after you got your doctorate? The strapless evening gown and the mortarboard? What did it say? 'Grace Tremain: Socialite to Academic.' Something like that—"

It was a memory that made me wince. "Oh, God," I said. "Please. I must have been out of my mind. 'Socialite.' What does that mean? When was I ever a 'socialite'?"

"But the point is, you were so gorgeous they put you on a magazine cover." Leslie was always paying people lavish compliments, telling them they were gorgeous or brilliant. You couldn't take it seriously.

"They put me on a magazine cover because I was Laurence J. Tremain's daughter," I said. "Don't be so naïve."

"They never asked me to be on a magazine cover," Leslie said.

She insisted on leaving Roger an extravagant tip. "Oh, come on, Gracie, he was so nice." We wandered out into the warm, dark street. The humid breeze ruffled our clothes as we stood on the pavement under the glowing pink neon sign that said "French Quarter." Leslie's fair hair looked like cotton candy in the pink light. We strolled to the corner where Bloor and Yonge intersected. There were lots of people walking up and down, some leisurely, some hurried and frantic, some well-dressed, some shabby and loud. You could smell popcorn and perfume and fried onions. A wild-haired man in a greasy coat went past, waving his arms and shouting furious obscenities.

"Yonge Street is so grungy," Leslie said, wrinkling her nose.

"That's what I like best about it," I said.

She laughed and poked my arm the way she always used to do when we were kids. "There are lots more beggars now. Have you noticed that? More than ever before, I think." She gazed down the broad white expanse of Bloor Street West. "And Creed's is gone," she said. "Who would have believed that could ever happen? Fenton's too. Remember how packed Fenton's used to be every afternoon?"

"Yeah, apparently the Roaring Eighties are really dead and gone. Even Winston's is shutting down this month." I didn't try to analyse why it gave me such satisfaction to say that.

"Yeah, I know! It's lucky Dad didn't live to see it. Winston's! What would he have done if he couldn't go there and have dinner at his special table? It's kind of scary, isn't it? If Winston's can go, you feel as if nothing is safe."

We began to walk south. A scrawny boy who looked about fifteen years old leaned from the doorway of an empty store and called to Leslie, "Hey, chickie, I'll give you twenty bucks for a blow job!"

Leslie rolled her eyes toward me. "Charming," she said, with a laugh. "Remember when Dad had the old silver Cadillac? The upholstery was so soft you felt like you were riding on air? Once we were driving down Yonge Street. I was so small I could hardly see out the window and I had to keep craning my neck. I saw a man with no legs sitting in front of the old Woolworth's store. He was trying to sell pencils. When I saw him, I burst out crying. I don't know why, I guess it seemed so sad for a man to have no legs and have to sell pencils sitting on the dirty sidewalk. Well, you know how Dad hated it if we cried. He kept saying, 'Don't look at him. Just don't look at him.' He even tried to put his hand over my eyes.

Then he started pretending that he and I were on a flying carpet and we were flying high above the city. He said, 'Everything looks so small. I see a tiny little castle. What do you see?' He made it seem so real I forgot about everything else. I started imagining that I saw a tiny little train station, and a tiny man on a white horse, and stuff like that. Dad said, 'Close your eyes. We're going to fly right through a cloud now!' You remember that Cadillac, the engine hardly made a sound, we just glided, and I could imagine a big cottony cloud breaking into a thousand cotton balls when we sailed through it. Every time I'm on Yonge Street I remember that."

"*Dad* said to pretend you were on a flying carpet?"

"Yeah."

"He actually said that."

"Yeah," Leslie laughed. "Why?"

After a moment I shrugged. "It doesn't sound like him, that's all."

She strayed too close to me and her soft arm bumped against mine. All the years of our lives we had been walking down streets together, bumping against each other, talking, laughing, and yet there were still things about her that I didn't know and things about our parents that she knew and I didn't. That gave me an odd pang of anxiety.

She launched into a new story involving a neighbour in Clarendon who raised show dogs, but I stopped listening, because I had glanced across the street and seen Eddy. He was standing with a group of men and women in the yellow doorway of a bar called Sirocco, right beneath a big sign that said "LIVE SEX SHOW ON STAGE!" His green jacket was draped over one arm and his other hand was on his hip. He looked casual, graceful, his body seemed to ripple dreamily in the warm, sultry air. He didn't see me because his attention was occupied. One of the other men, a tall broad-shouldered guy whose suit jacket looked too tight, was yelling into his face. Something like, "The top guy! Get it, greaseball? I don't want any fucking middlemen!" And Eddy was smiling, apparently unperturbed, and saying something so quietly that I couldn't distinguish the words. Leslie and I continued to walk. She kept talking happily, completely oblivious to the scene on the other side of the street. I didn't turn my head. I looked straight down the sidewalk to the faraway glossy towers of the Eaton Centre. But I could still hear the angry, threatening voice of that big, red-faced man: "The fuck you are, pal! Don't fuck with me or you'll regret it! I don't need to calm down! I've had it with your bullshit, you slimy bastard! Fuck you!"

My face was burning. I felt my heartbeat, slow and hard and painful inside my chest. I almost expected to hear gunshots.

"So I phoned her up," Leslie was telling me. "I was so mad I didn't care anymore. You know what I told her?"

"What?" I said. My mouth was so dry I could hardly get the word out.

"I told her I was going to call the Humane Society if she didn't shape up. I really did!"

"Good," I said. We had gone a block beyond the Sirocco. I felt that I could risk a quick look over my shoulder. No one was standing in the doorway anymore. I couldn't see any of them on the street either. They had all dispersed with amazing speed. I had a dazed feeling that I had imagined the whole thing.

"Because you know me, if there's one thing that drives me mental, it's seeing animals mistreated. Well, she—" Leslie broke off. "What are you looking at?"

"Nothing," I said. "Do you feel like another drink?"

"Sure," Leslie said. "You know what I'm in the mood for? I don't know why. One of those big, fruity, tropical drinks. Like . . . what are they called? Mai tais? Singapore slings? The ones with the tacky little paper umbrellas. I feel like having one of those."

We kept walking down the hot street, down toward the lake.

Chapter Five

"Eddy...."

"Yeah?"

"This business of yours, is it doing well?"

We were sitting on my upper balcony with glasses of Argentinian wine, which I had developed a taste for. Below us the waves rolled up onto the beach and fell back, leaving the sand as sleek and shiny as glass. It was a mild evening, with a soft mild breeze, and the clouds over the water were beginning to reveal delicate pastel shades. I had finished marking my last exam that day. I was free for three long months. I had a vague plan that I would go to France in July, and that would bring an end to this peculiar episode in my life. I had no idea why I was letting it go on so long.

He blinked, as though his mind had been far away. "My business? Oh, yeah, it's great."

"You don't seem to work very hard at it," I said in a teasing way.

He grinned nonchalantly. "Well, you see, that's how you can tell it's successful, because it sort of runs itself."

"What's the name of the company?"

"October Enterprises. That's the main one."

"The main one?"

"Yeah, we have a couple of subsidiaries. When you diversify it makes things simpler."

"Why 'October'?"

"Well, because that's the month I first came to Canada. October 1986."

"And it's an import-export business."

"Right."

"Leather and wool. . . ."

"Alpaca, vicuna, yes. And lapis lazuli."

"Lapis lazuli?"

"Yes, the semi-precious stone. We bring it in from Chile. Did you know it's only found in two places in the world? Chile and Afghanistan. Imagine that."

"Oh . . . I thought my mother bought some in Rome once. They told her there was a deposit of lapis lazuli in the Tuscan countryside."

Eddy dismissed this with an airy wave of his hand. "The Italian deposits are so small they're insignificant. And not very good quality either."

He was distracting me. I returned to the main topic. "So you own . . . what, stores where you sell all these things?"

He smiled. "No, it's a bigger operation than that. We don't have stores, we import and we sell to stores."

"So you're a middleman."

He shrugged. "Yes, I guess you could say that."

"And what is it that you export?"

"Fur," he said. "Inuit art. That kind of thing."

"And you make money?"

"We're doing pretty well," he said.

For a few moments we sat in silence, listening to the sound of the waves. There were a couple of children down on the beach. They were tossing a stick into the water, and their big, black dog kept retrieving it and then shaking himself violently, sending up cascades of silvery drops.

I took a sip of my wine. "I was on Yonge Street on Wednesday night," I said casually.

Eddy didn't seem impressed. He nodded absently, turning the stem of his wine glass in one hand, gazing out toward the misty horizon.

"My sister and I were walking down toward the Eaton Centre. I thought I saw you."

That seemed to jolt him a little. He shifted in his chair and looked at me. "Your sister? Why didn't you tell me? I would have liked to meet her."

"Weren't you busy on Wednesday night?" I said. "I thought I saw you on Yonge Street with a bunch of people."

"I can't remember. But I would have rearranged things. I wish you'd told me."

It wasn't the reaction I had expected. All of a sudden I felt a little guilty and began to stammer. "Well ... I just ... I didn't think you'd be interested. It was just boring old family stuff. You know."

He stared at me with impenetrable dark eyes. I pulled myself together. "Anyway, that's not the kind of set-up we have, is it? Where we get all cosy and meet each other's relatives?"

He continued to stare at me for a moment. It was hard to tell what he was thinking. Then he said, "Your sister, she's the small one with fair hair, right?"

It was my turn to stare incredulously. "How do you know that?"

"She's in all the photo albums."

My muscles tightened. Carefully I set down my glass. "You looked at the photo albums?" I said.

"One morning when you were still asleep. What's the matter? You've got them sitting right out in plain view in your bookcase. Wasn't I supposed to look at them?"

"It's not that," I said. Don't be such an idiot, I told myself, forcing a smile. Relax. "I don't care. I'm just surprised that you bothered. You looked at all of them?"

"All the ones in the bookcase, I guess." He was watching me curiously. "What's wrong?" he said after a moment. "I'm sorry, but I didn't know they were supposed to be a secret. Don't we have the kind of set-up where I'm supposed to look at your photo albums, either?"

I heard myself laugh, a completely phoney and artificial laugh. "Oh, don't be silly. I don't give a damn if you looked at them. Why should I? Yes, my sister is the small one with fair hair. She's very attractive, isn't she?"

"Sure," he said. "But the blonde woman—your mother? Wow. Gorgeous."

"Yes, my mother was really beautiful. Everyone thought so."

"And the redheaded guy—I guess I don't need to ask if he's your father, that's obvious."

"Yes," I said. "I guess the hair gives it away."

"Oh, it's not just the hair."

"No?" I said.

"Oh, no." He grinned. "It's the shape of your face, your eyes, the way you stand, the way you hold your head."

"Really." I gave another phoney laugh.

He was scrutinizing me unwaveringly. "You've never been told that before?" he asked.

"Oh, yes, I've heard it before," I said. "I could never see any resemblance myself, except for the hair colour. He and I were really completely different. Sometimes people are so stupid. They notice the red hair and right away they start imagining all kinds of other similarities that don't even exist."

The anger in my voice was unmistakable. I heard it myself. Of course he heard it too. One side of his mouth went up in a quizzical, amused smile. I had begun the conversation expecting to put him on the defensive, and instead I was the one spluttering and tying myself up in knots.

"You don't like your father very much, it seems," he said.

"He's dead." There was a momentary silence, but I couldn't leave it at that. "Of course I loved him," I said in a level voice. "But there couldn't have been two people less alike than my father and I."

"Okay," he said.

I shrugged my shoulders, trying to smile. "It's not important."

"No," he agreed.

He seemed to be humouring me. That annoyed me all over again. "You know, I can't help thinking, I've never seen any photo albums of *yours*," I said. "I've never even seen where you live. You just materialize at my door. When are you going to invite me to your place so I can go through *your* things while you're asleep?"

Again his eyes rested on my face, searchingly, thoughtfully, as if he was trying to figure out what was going on inside my head. Finally he said, "My place isn't very nice. It's pretty bare."

"Bare? What do you mean?"

"I don't have any furniture. Things like that."

"You've been living here since 1986 and you don't have any furniture?"

He shrugged and smiled, open-faced as a child. "I never had time," he said. He waited a moment, tilting his wine glass so the clear yellow liquid flowed to one side. Then he said, "I'd like to show you my boat though."

He was always doing that, jumping ahead of me, producing new tricks from his hat. "What? You have a boat?"

"Yes. I haven't taken it out much yet this year. I thought maybe tomorrow. Would that be okay for you?"

"Wait a minute, though. You own a boat. You mean a sailboat?"

"Well," he said, "I guess it's what you'd call a yacht. A small yacht."

"A small yacht," I said blankly.

"In one of your albums your father is standing on a long blue boat with a name in white letters, the *Firebird*?"

"Yes," I said.

"Well, my boat is a little bigger than that."

"A little bigger than that . . ."

"Right. Mine is called *Caminito*, after a street in Buenos Aires. Shall we take it out tomorrow?"

"Okay," I said slowly. "That sounds great."

We sat quietly for a long while, watching the sky darken over the lake. He raised the bottle of wine and refilled our glasses.

"You're not bored with me yet, then," I said.

He took it as a joke. "No," he laughed. "Are you bored with me?"

"Not yet," I said.

HE KEPT HIS BOAT IN THE CUMBERLAND MARINA on the lakeshore just east of the city. Everyone there seemed to know him; it was "Hi, Eddy," "How ya doing, Eddy?,", "Taking her out today, Eddy?" from all sides. He walked along like royalty, raising his arm to wave, smiling, making quips. I got a few curious glances. I wondered how many other women he had brought there, and what they had been like.

"Well," Eddy said, quickening his pace. "There she is."

It was a big boat, all right. Tall, long, glistening white, shining in the water with a brilliance that almost hurt your eyes.

"Twenty-three metres," Eddy said. "How big was your father's?"

"It was a fifty-eight-foot Trumpy motor yacht," I said.

Eddy was already climbing up onto the deck. He reached down to help me but I shook my head and clambered up myself. I didn't need any help; I was quite capable of climbing a ladder.

"This is a Hatteras long-range cruiser. She has a shipboard computer with electronic charting and a satellite TV system," he informed me proudly. "There's a dining salon that seats six and three staterooms. How many staterooms did your father's have?"

"I really don't remember."

"You don't remember how many staterooms it had?"

"I hardly ever saw it and I was hardly ever on it," I said.

He seemed to find that strange. "He didn't take you out on it?"

"Once or twice. It was such a long time ago. I was a little girl when he had it. It was his toy and he liked to play with it all by himself."

"What happened, eventually he sold it?"

"Yeah," I said. "Well, aren't you going to show me around?"

Eddy was happy on that boat. His face was alight; he had dozens of things to demonstrate. "The *Caminito* is one of the biggest boats that docks in this marina," he told me as I followed him down to the main deck. "One day last year, some Yanks stood on the pier for half an hour, just looking at her. They couldn't believe it when I told them she could do twenty-two knots. You see, here's the salon." We walked into a long cool space lined with windows. An L-shaped dark blue sofa filled one corner and six plushy blue chairs surrounded a large round table of teakwood. The narrow slats on the Venetian blinds etched the room with patterns of shade and deep blue light. "All the panelling is teak," Eddy said. There's a wet bar and entertainment centre. Watch this." He pressed a button and there was a decorous hum as a television set high up on a glossy wooden shelf folded itself into the ceiling and disappeared from view. Eddy looked at me to see how impressed I was. "Now it's up on the bridge," he told me. "You can watch it there or here, whichever you want."

"Incredible," I said.

"Here's the master stateroom." He pushed back a sliding door. "See, a queen-sized bed, and it has its own bathroom. All the staterooms have their own baths. With gold fixtures. Let's go back this way. Now, watch your step, here's the galley." He opened a cupboard and took down a finely shaped wine glass that appeared to be made of crystal. "Look at this," he said, laughing with pleasure. "Hold it up to the light."

Engraved on one side, in very delicate and graceful lettering, was the word "Caminito."

"I had it done to all the glasses and cups," he told me. Then suddenly he seemed embarrassed and shrugged his shoulders. "I liked the idea. Do you think it's too much?"

"No, not at all," I said. I was rather touched by his unexpected boyish awkwardness. "It's pretty."

The lake was radiant with sunlight that day. We skimmed over the water as lightly as a paper boat on the surface of a pond. He stood at the helm on the flybridge, the bright wind blowing his hair and revealing highlights of red and gold that I had never noticed before. His white shirt and pants flapped and folded themselves against his body. There were lots of other boats out too, boats with coloured sails, motorboats darting past and leaving jets of white foam to melt in the water, orange paddleboats, canoes whose red sides glittered with moisture, windsurfers dangling from triangles and rectangles of striped canvas, all in motion like a huge, vibrant ballet. I'm not a particularly happy kind of person, but that afternoon, sitting there on the deck in the streaming wind and sun, I thought, This is what happiness is like.

"Did I ever tell you, I was in a hurricane once," Eddy said suddenly.

"What? A hurricane?"

"This was in the Atlantic, off the coast of Florida. I had a boat out, a smaller one, not the *Caminito*, and the sky started to get dark. Not black, it was more like dark green, like you could almost see green particles in the air. It came over the radio, a storm warning, Hurricane Ida. I thought, okay, I'd better get back to the harbour. But then—no, I'd never seen a hurricane before. I wanted to see what it was like. It was funny, I wasn't even afraid. I didn't think I'd die. But I thought, well, I'll just get close to death, you know? See how close I can get to it."

As with all his stories, I wasn't sure how much of this was true, or even if any of it was true. But it didn't seem to matter. The possibility that he was inventing everything actually pleased me in some obscure way.

"Do you think you got close?" I asked.

"Yeah, I think I did," he said. "I kept holding on to the wheel. The waves were so huge they'd lift the boat twenty feet in the air and then throw her down again. The wheel was shaking like a jackhammer. It was more than wind, it was like the whole universe was speeding and roaring and turning into water. Man, what a rush!" He grinned at me. His eyes were shining behind the lenses of his sunglasses. "When it's something that big, you almost think you wouldn't mind so much if it took you," he said. "You think what if I just let go? But then you fight against it anyway."

"Well, obviously you survived," I said after a moment.

"I was soaking wet, I had bruises all over, there was a big gash on my head where a pail blew through the air and hit me . . . blood all down the front of my shirt. I steered the boat into the nearest harbour and all these guys came running down to the dock, they couldn't believe their eyes, that I'm still standing and I can throw them the rope. One old man kept staring at me and shaking his head and saying 'Jesus Christ. Jesus Christ.'"

I smiled, raising my arm to shield my eyes from the sun. "I guess Lake Ontario must seem pretty tame after that," I said. "You must be a wonderful sailor. Does it run in your family?"

He thought about that for a moment. Finally he said, "No. But it was always something I wanted. I used to stand in the Puerto Nuevo and watch all the boats sailing in and out. There were some beautiful boats at the Buenos Aires yacht club. I said to myself that someday I'd have one too."

"And now you do," I said.

"Yes," he agreed. "And someday I'll go back there with the *Caminito*. I can picture it, I'm going to sail right into the bay of the Rio de la Plata, and all my old friends will be there on the dock to see me. I'll be standing right here on the upper deck, dressed in my fanciest clothes, and I'll wave to them and they'll say, 'My God, it's Eduardo coming home! *Parece millonario!*' In English it would be, 'He looks like a million bucks!' And I'll slide right into the yacht club and moor the *Caminito* there." Suddenly he turned his head to smile at me. "You can come with me too," he said.

"All right," I said.

THAT NIGHT AFTER WE'D EATEN DINNER, he told me he had some things he had to do. He stood beside me, lifting my hair off my neck, wrapping it around his hand. "I'll come back later though," he said. "Okay?"

"How much later?" I said. You can't let them take advantage of you, you can't get all soft and understanding and womanly. You always have to be on guard against that. "I'm sort of tired and I might go to bed early."

He bent down and put both his arms around me from behind. His cheek rested against mine and the scent of his cologne entered my nostrils and passed down through my body in ripples of pleasure. I had to stop myself from letting out a sigh. "I'll come back and wake you up," he said softly against my ear.

"Okay," I heard myself answer in a breathy voice that sounded completely unlike me. Sometimes I felt alarmed at the power he seemed to be gaining over me. It was a relief to remember that in July I could go to France and leave him behind. I thought longingly about boarding a plane and soaring away from the earth, how strong and free I would feel then.

"I'm just going to leave this here," he said, holding up a duffel bag that contained his sailing clothes. "I'll put it in your hall closet, okay?"

As soon as he was gone, a heavy silence settled over the house. I stacked the dishes in the dishwasher and every sound I made seemed magnified by the surrounding stillness. I walked down the dim hall to the living room, turned on the stereo and sat on the sofa. My watch said nine o'clock. I wondered what things he had to do at that time of night. I wondered when he'd come back: in two hours, in three hours? I didn't feel like reading or watching television. I couldn't think of anything I felt like doing. However, it was too demeaning to sit there staring at the clock, waiting for his return like some sad, dumb chick. The devoted girlfriend, helpless without her man. Disgusting.

It was obvious that there was something highly suspect about his excessive charm. He was like one of those con men you read about, the ones who move into your life, seduce you, dazzle you with lies, and then disappear with your life savings. But I wasn't stupid, I couldn't be fooled, I had been warned about things like that long ago. *Your biggest attraction is going to be money*, my father always told me. *That's the way it is. A lot of men will act as if they're crazy about you but in reality it's your money they'll be after. So don't get all womanish and lose your brains just because some good-looking phoney pretends to be in love.*

My restless eyes fell on the row of photo albums in the bookcase. In a moment I had them piled up all around me. I hadn't looked at them in a long time and I wanted to see exactly what Eddy had seen. I wanted to know what he might have discovered about me, what he might have found to use against me.

Some of the albums were really old, dating back to when my parents were first married in 1950. There were photos of them in Palm Beach on their honeymoon, old black-and-white pictures with white, serrated edges, showing them sitting on a terrace above a curve of white sand, my father small and urbane in a pale shirt and shorts, turned to my mother with a slight smile, and my mother looking not at him but at the camera, her eyes hidden by dark glasses, her shoulders and round white arms gleaming with a pearly radiance. She was only twenty-two, at the absolute peak of her beauty, dressed in a black bathing suit with a big full skirt and a neckline that was a bit too low for good taste—and I'm sure my father must have commented on that, I'm sure he must have looked at her with a slight lift of one eyebrow and made some dry, sarcastic remark. But her appearance was the one thing she had complete confidence in, and nothing he said about it would have shaken her. So she merely smiled, adjusted her sunglasses and sat motionless in the perfect sunlight, waiting for the camera to capture her youthful splendour.

Lots of people said I looked like Grace Kelly, she told me once. *She was my favourite actress so I named you after her. Oh*, I said, *I thought I was named after Grandma Tremain. Well*, she said, *yeah, her too.*

I tried to imagine what Eddy had thought when he looked at those honeymoon photos. Had he noticed the luxurious buildings in the background, the glittering table settings, the white sleeves of maitre d's and waiters hovering solicitously just out of view? Had his heart started to beat with excitement, had dollar signs popped up in his eyes as though he were a character in a cartoon? Of course he always seemed to have plenty of money, and he apparently owned an elaborate yacht. But con artists often had fronts like that. Once Leslie went out with a guy who claimed to own a five-bedroom penthouse condo at Harbourfront, but he turned out to be renting it by the week and had accumulated debts amounting to $750,000. He wanted Leslie to put up the money for a new real estate venture which he swore would pay big dividends within a year. Even Leslie wasn't dumb enough to fall for that one.

I thought probably Eddy would soon be asking me for a "loan," or offering to sell me a unique piece of lapis lazuli at an inflated price, or suggesting that I invest in his business. He was in for a big disappointment.

There were the usual embarrassing shots of myself as a baby, naked on an elaborately embroidered comforter, waving fat arms and legs and drooling above my mother's awkwardly written notations: "Grace, 5 months," "Grace, 7 months." I had to ask myself what had possessed me to keep those albums and to leave them in my bookcase where anybody could pick them up and look through them. Wasn't there something a bit strange and neurotic about a person who saved baby pictures of herself and kept them right in her living room, ready for presentation at any time? I don't even know why I had the damn things, Leslie should have had them, she was the one with the country house and the snug domestic atmosphere where old family photos belonged.

I turned a page and there we all were, in front of our old house on Neville Park Boulevard, standing on the steps. My grandfather was still alive then, sitting behind us on the verandah, half in shadow, his gold-headed cane planted between his knees, a frown on his face, as usual, holding a glass of Scotch, as usual. My father stood on the top step, his head uncovered, his hair blowing silkily across his forehead, one hand resting on my mother's shoulder, and she was one step below, holding Leslie, a tiny baby wrapped in an expensive crocheted shawl, and I was on the lowest step of all, a solemn-looking six-year-old with bright red hair in tight braids and big shiny glasses. God, that was my most hideous age. And the glasses everybody wore in those days, how could anyone have thought they were attractive, those cat's-eye frames with the designs on them, ugly beyond belief! But my mother looked ravishing, the sun lighting up her cloud of pale hair, and the house rose behind us, large and beautiful with its shadowy verandah where you could discern the vague graceful outlines of white furniture and ferns. You could also see the curve of the driveway off to one side, and the glistening front fenders of the Daimler and the Cadillac.

I hadn't seen that house in years. It was only a five-minute walk from where I lived but I never went there. I never strolled down that street to look at it. I remembered how the dusk would fall over the garden, the magical feel of it, the powerfully sweet scent of lilacs half-hidden by dark, glossy leaves, and we had a fountain too, with a white basin that looked ghostly in the twilight, and on a hot summer night the sound of splashing water was so refreshing, as my mother used to say. They had big parties sometimes, they had long tables set up on the lawn, with tall white candles and bottles of champagne and ten different kinds of dessert. Once it was a party for my father's friend Perry Chandler, the actor, the one who later married Leslie. In honour of Perry's starring roles at Stratford there was a great white swan made of marzipan coated with spun sugar, I remember how that swan gleamed in the dusk and golden candlelight like an enchanted bird in a fairy tale. I watched from my bedroom window, we were too young and parties weren't for children, we were supposed to be asleep, but I looked down at the gay people in their beautiful clothes, holding glasses of golden fizz, and my mother in a narrow red dress that showed off her figure, sitting by herself, because she never knew what to say to Laurie's stuck-up friends. Then suddenly I was on my feet, my fingers against my lips in horror, because my sister Leslie had broken the rules, somehow she had escaped from the supervision of our nanny and there she was, teetering across the lawn in a pair of my mother's high-heeled, silver-spangled shoes, and she'd pinned up her hair and draped a fringed shawl around her shoulders and shakily outlined her baby lips in cherry red lipstick. My mother jumped up in alarm but it wasn't my mother's attention that Leslie wanted. *Dad! Dad! Look at me, Dad!* And he turned, his face tight with anger, all the way up in my room on the third floor of the house I saw the cold flash of his grey-blue eyes, and Leslie saw it too, her voice went on with a desperate vivacity, high-pitched and clear, *But Dad! Wait, Dad! See, Dad, I'm Marilyn Monroe! I'm Marilyn Monroe, Dad!* Some of the guests laughed, and then the moment of fearful tension ended and my father's face relaxed into a grin. He picked Leslie up and swung her around in the air until one of my mother's silver shoes fell from her foot into the grass.

Leslie could always handle him. She could always get away with it. As for me, I never broke his stupid rules. I wouldn't give him the right to castigate me—or worse still, the chance to exercise his royal prerogative and show his indulgence instead.

The nanny, whose name I can't recall, was fired the next day. My mother was supposed to do it, because household matters and child care were a woman's responsibilities and my father was trying to train my mother to be a proper woman. I was sitting on the terrace, reading *Anne of Green Gables*, and I heard their voices through the half-open French windows. *I don't see why it was such a big deal*, my mother said. *Well, Vivian, it was a "big deal," because she had one simple job to do and she couldn't handle it*, he replied. *You don't reward incompetence. Get rid of her.* There was a silence. *Go and do it now*, he said. *I don't want her here when I get home tonight.* Later Leslie and I stood in my room upstairs, watching that nameless nanny, a thin woman of about thirty, walking down the drive, carrying a suitcase. *It's your fault*, I told Leslie. *Now she's going to starve to death. She'll have to walk the streets all day and all night until she can't go on, and then she'll lie down in a dark alley and die, and it's all your fault.* Leslie began to cry hysterically. Then I was satisfied.

Leslie and I stood side by side in front of the cottage, we sat on a beach in St. Tropez, drinking lemonade, we posed at Christmastime, opening presents below a huge, over-decorated tree. We became closer in height, our hairstyles swelled and flattened, lengthened and shortened. I was the serious one, Leslie was the funny one. In every picture she was grinning, rolling her eyes, making gestures, laughing, mug-ging, while I stared into the camera, stiff and unsmiling. Maybe Eddy had shaken his head in amusement at how dull and lifeless I appeared to be. Maybe he had thought, *She's just waiting to be plucked*, like a dry little apple from a tree. I always hated to have my picture taken and when I was very small I used to hide my face or turn my back. *Grace, don't be such a child*, my father would say, bored and irritated. *I have no time for this.* I hated to be the cause of that impatient, exas-perated tone, so I learned to face the lens, but nothing could make me smile. He would hold the photographs between his thumb and forefinger, as if there was something mildly repul-sive about them. *As usual, Grace is as grim as a ghost.*

Beside the gleaming plate-glass window of a café whose name I don't remember, we sit together in a patch of bright sunlight, my mother and Leslie and I. My father must have taken the picture, his shadow can be made out in the fore-ground, a faint shape on the checkered tablecloth. My mother has a cigarette in one hand and a drink in the other and she's looking older; although she's still more attractive than most people her eyes have become a bit tired and bleary. Leslie is fluffing up her hair and vamping like a movie star. My hair is puffy and has been forced into those horrible twists in front of the ears that we used to call "kiss curls." My glasses are shin-ing so that my eyes are invisible, and I'm sitting bolt upright, my hands lying side by side on the tabletop.

It was a café on the island of Rhodes, I remember that. I

remember that someone began a dance and several patrons got up to join it. They formed a line, arms around one another's shoulders, and began to move back and forth in a narrow space in front of the kitchen, dipping their knees and then rising to kick their legs in unison. We sat watching their antics in superior, amused detachment. Then suddenly, without warning, my mother stood up and went to join them. Leslie and I were horrified; we glanced at each other in wild disbelief. *What is she doing!* Even our father, who was seldom surprised by anything, seemed completely dumfounded. He had been about to light a cigarette but he just sat there holding it halfway to his mouth, staring at my mother out on the tiny dance floor with her arm around the waist of a strange, beefy-looking Greek, jumping up and down so that her breasts bounced inside her silk blouse, shaking her hips, actually laughing out loud, actually waving her free arm in the air. She had never done anything remotely like that before; I wouldn't have believed she could ever be so gauche. I sat with frozen limbs, my ears burning with embarrassment, and Leslie bumped against my arm and hissed, *What's come over her?* Finally my father smiled thinly and placed his cigarette between his lips. *I guess your mother must miss all those happy Bohunk dances of her youth*, he said, snapping open his gold lighter with his long, graceful fingers. I had never heard him use a word like "Bohunk" before; he never said things like that. But how descriptive it seemed, how perfectly appropriate for the spectacle she made that day, bouncing around in that bucolic rabble, flushed and untidy and rather crude. I felt ashamed of her; I felt we were very far apart. When she came back to the table her eyes were averted and she didn't offer any explanations or apologies. She just patted her hair and took a sip from her drink, as though nothing unusual had happened at all.

One day Leslie and I were in my mother's bedroom while she sat at her bureau, getting ready to go out somewhere. She looked at herself in the mirror, her long hair, still lush and blonde, the tiredness of her eyes carefully masked by makeup, the softness of her jawline which was becoming more difficult to hide. As she got older she worked harder to maintain her looks, exercising daily, eating very little, spending hours at the beauty parlour, rubbing her face with creams and lotions, remaining at her makeup table until she was satisfied that she had done her best to conceal every minuscule flaw. *You know what, my name isn't even Vivian*, she said suddenly, *I never told you kids that, did I? Your name isn't Vivian? What are you talking about? It's . . . guess what? Don't laugh. Polly! Can you believe it? Do I look like I could ever have been a Polly? Polly Popowich!* Leslie squealed with laughter and fell back on the bed, grabbing a pillow and pressing it over her mouth. *Isn't that awful?* my mother said. *Isn't it the absolute worst? I had to change it. I was tired of getting a laugh every time I introduced myself. So I decided I was going to be Vivian Porter. Vivian Porter sounded so nice and English.* A sudden breeze blew one of the long white curtains across the bureau, sending up a burst of scented powder, and she laughed and coughed, waving her hand. *But, you know what, Polly Popowich was the prettiest girl in Saskatchewan*, she said. *It's true, everybody said so. Everybody said I looked like a movie star. I thought why should I waste it on a bunch of farmers? So what did you do, Mom?* we said, already knowing the answer. *I packed a suitcase, this old cardboard suitcase my mother used when she came from Ukraine. And I walked down the road to the place where the Regina bus stopped. The bus driver says, "And where are you going, beautiful?" And I say, "I haven't decided yet."* *Do you think you'll ever go back there, Mom?* She stared at herself in the mirror. *No. Why would I want to go back there? Does Dad know your name used to be Polly? Well, of course*, she said. *Your dad knows everything, doesn't he?*

Had Eddy thought she looked a bit foolish and trashy with that cigarette and that drink and that full mouth covered with red lipstick? No, *Wow*, he had said. *Gorgeous.* I'm sure different words had come into his mind when he saw me in my school uniform, the short pleated grey skirt, the navy knee-high stockings, the scuffed black shoes, the inevitable shining glasses, my mouth gaping as though I'd just been hit hard on top of my head. What about Leslie, always laughing and carrying on, had he thought, Wow, gorgeous, when he looked at her? Had he yawned cynically over the photos of my various respectable boyfriends, from Kevin Whitman, who took me and his mother to the ballet when I was fourteen, to Jeremy on a street in New York, looking handsome but sulky because I had insisted on going to a revival of *A Streetcar Named Desire* even though he thought Tennessee Williams was affected and overwrought?

None of the interesting men in my life had ever been photographed for the family album.

I found the picture of my father standing on his boat, the *Firebird*. He was probably in his late thirties at that time, short and sturdy, wearing a blue sweater and a white hat. Not a captain's hat, my father never put on anything that could be considered corny or pretentious. It was an ordinary white hat that covered his hair and made an elegant shadow over his eyes. He was leaning on the deck railing and staring off into the distance with a smile on his face. I don't know who photographed him that day. I don't think it was my mother because she always jiggled the camera, and that picture is clear, perfectly focussed. It's like an ad in *Gentleman's Quarterly*: a young, handsome, well-dressed man in a dashing pose, a man who gleams with wealth, a man who always gets what he wants. Something else comes across too; it shows in the line of his body and in the tight, upward curve of his lips: a restlessness, an edge of dissatisfaction which almost amounts to anger, because no matter what he has it's not enough, he knows there has to be something more and he has to get that too.

An hour had gone by and Eddy hadn't returned. I put the albums back in the bookcase. I was upset. I'm not sure why. Because he had been gone so long and evidently expected me to wait for him all night? Because he had poked through all those damn albums and seen all those pictures? I wanted to put the albums away in the closet, but I knew he would notice if I did that and he would think it was strange, or worse than that, funny. No, I decided I would wait until the end of summer, after I got back from France, after I had got rid of Eddy. Then I was going to take the bloody albums to Leslie's and leave them there. I didn't want them around anymore.

I took out the Toronto telephone directory and looked up October Enterprises. It wasn't listed. Then I remembered his duffel bag. I decided to look through it. I didn't really expect to find anything. It was an ordinary, well-used duffel bag; he'd brought it with him in his car and carried it on board the *Caminito* and I'd seen him taking out a pair of jeans, a sweatshirt and sneakers, and stuffing the same items back into the bag before we left the boat to come home.

I just wanted to look through something of his while he wasn't there. It felt like I was paying him back for some obscure wrong he'd done me.

He had tossed the bag carelessly into the closet in my foyer. It was heavier than I had expected. I dragged it into the living room and dumped its contents onto the carpet. The soft lamplight made red glints on the studs in his crumpled jeans and on a couple of quarters and a nickel that had fallen out of his pockets. I picked up his sweatshirt and the scent of his cologne drifted out of its folds. I held it to my face and took a deep breath. No one was watching me so I could do whatever I wanted. But then I tossed the sweatshirt quickly aside, because what if he suddenly returned and caught me smelling it like a lovesick teenager? His sneakers were surprisingly small. I held one up to look at it and an object fell out onto the floor, a thick plastic keychain in the form of a palm tree— big green fronds and a trunk shaped like the body of a naked woman. Charming. It held one key, a key to what? His apartment, his boat, his car? I felt in the pockets of his jeans and found nothing but a packet of matches from a place called the Casa Roca (restaurant, motel, nightclub?) with half the matches torn out. The duffel bag had several pouches and I opened them all. They were all empty except for a small zippered slot which contained a piece of dirty paper with a name written on it in pencil, "N. Roberts," and the beginning of a number, "224—" The rest had been torn away.

I sat on the bed and stared at the meagre collection of articles as though they were pieces of an intricate puzzle that I had to solve somehow. If only I could figure out the connections between them, I would know something about him that he meant to keep secret. A pair of jeans, a sweatshirt, a pair of sneakers, a keychain, a torn piece of paper with writing on it. The electronic clock on the sideboard made a faint whirring noise as the digits turned over and told me it was now eleven p.m.

I was particularly interested in the torn piece of paper. I thought surely the other half was somewhere in the duffel bag. That made sense. Perhaps the number was a phone number or an address, something I could investigate later. I searched through all the pouches and slots again. Nothing. Then I felt carefully in the bottom of the bag. There was a flap of cardboard or stiff canvas fitted there to give the bag shape, and beneath it there seemed to be a bit of space in which I thought I felt an edge of paper. Aha! I thought, struggling to get my fingers around it and pull it out. Then I had a momentary flash of disappointment, because it wasn't plain white paper at all. It was money. A twenty-dollar bill. He must have put it in the bag and it had somehow worked itself under the canvas flap and he'd forgotten about it. But possibly the same thing had happened to the torn piece of paper I was looking for so I kept searching. I pushed my fingers further under the flap and sure enough, I felt more paper there. A lot more paper. I pulled out another bill. Fifty dollars. And another. Then another twenty. Then a hundred-dollar bill. By that time I was kneeling on the rug holding the bag open as far as it would go and prying the flap back. There were dozens of bills, all neatly arranged in rows, twenties, fifties, hundreds. My hands began to tremble and my heart seemed to throb right at the base of my throat so that it was impossible to swallow. I thought I could hear a car door slamming down in the street—he was back! He was going to come in before I had a chance to return everything to its proper place! But maybe he had expected me to look, maybe he had wanted me to find it, maybe he wanted me to know! Maybe he was eccentric, maybe he didn't believe in banks, maybe he kept money in boxes under his bed and carried it around with him night and day, maybe to him that was perfectly normal behaviour! I was so excited and unnerved that I could hardly concentrate, but I tried to count it. I had to start over several times, but the figure I finally arrived at was twenty-five thousand. He had been carrying twenty-five thousand dollars around in a duffel bag all day, tossing it into the back seat of his ramshackle car, leaving it behind in my closet while he went out to roam around the city.

I don't know how long I sat there holding that bag in my lap. It seemed a long time. He didn't appear. Finally I got up and put everything back in its place. The torn piece of paper went into the zippered slot, the keychain was returned to the toe of one sneaker, the loose change was restored to the pockets of his jeans. I threw the bag into the closet. Then I went upstairs, undressed and got into bed. I didn't fall asleep. I lay on my side, watching squares of moonlight shift and stretch along the wall beside the window. I was thinking, thinking, thinking so intensely that it seemed almost like a physical exertion.

Sometime during the night he came back. I didn't look to see what time it was, I didn't move. I heard him downstairs, unlocking the door with the key I'd given him. I heard his light tread on the stairs. In a moment I felt him standing inside the bedroom. He was breathing softly.

"Are you awake?" he whispered.

I didn't answer. I heard him unfasten his jacket. I heard his clothes drop to the floor and the bedsprings squeaked as he got into bed and pressed his nude body against me from behind. I felt hot and he was cool all over, almost cold, and so smooth, so firm and pliant; he put his cold hands over my breasts and his cold face against my neck and it made me shiver from my scalp to the tips of my toes. He smelled of cigarettes and mist and a whiff of gasoline, it was as though he carried the scent of the whole wild urban night in the contours of his body.

Richelle Kosar

"Oh, you feel so warm," he breathed into my ear. "Sorry I was gone such a long time."

"It's all right," I said. "It doesn't matter at all."

Chapter Six

THE NEXT DAY THE STREETCAR CARRIED ME west on Queen
Street, clanging along merrily like a ride at the fair. I sat with
my briefcase on my lap, businesslike, professional, middle-
aged, but inside I felt as though I were a teenage girl with my
hair in a ponytail, and I was swinging my legs, biting my fingernails, making myself dizzy with wild daydreams.

I transferred at Osgoode Hall and took the subway north
to Museum. When I came out onto Avenue Road, a thin warm
rain had begun to fall. I had forgotten my umbrella and in a
moment my hair and shoulders were wet through. The rain
seemed as fine and delicate as the mist from a spray bottle; it
settled over me like a veil, made me aware of the texture of my
blouse and each strand of hair on my head. I had thought I
was going to my office. There were lots of last-minute things
to do before my vacation—course outlines to review, books to
order for next year, materials to upgrade—but I didn't want to
do any of them. Without actually making a decision, I turned

around and walked north. The city seemed brand-new to me, the colours were different, the street corners were unfamiliar. I felt like a stranger just arriving, full of anticipation, eager to see things I had never seen before. I liked the look of the tall girls in bright plastic raincoats jumping into taxicabs, the hot-dog vendor turning over his sizzling wieners under a striped canopy, the fair-haired man waiting at the corner for the light to change and giving me an absent smile in the shadow of his big black umbrella. In the rain-streaked store windows my reflection flickered past, a fleeting image of someone interesting, daring and quick, with striking auburn hair. Someone in the middle of an adventure. A short, intense adventure that would end soon. Perhaps it was going to be my best one, the one I would never forget.

At ten o'clock I went into the Metro Library and rode the little glass elevator to the third level: Business and Social Sciences. The tables were filling rapidly with high school students who whispered, giggled, and passed books back and forth. "No, Shirley, like, forget it!" a chunky girl shrieked before being hushed by her friends. I walked up to one of the computers. "Subject?" it prompted me. I placed my briefcase to one side and stared for a moment at the flashing cursor. Then I typed "Narcotics."

In a moment the screen filled with choices:

Narcotics
    1. Narcotics, addiction
    2. Narcotics, control of
    3. Narcotics, crime and
    4. Narcotics, distribution and

I typed "3." The selection of books on "Narcotics, crime and" was not as long as I had imagined it would be. However, I got out a pen and notepad and copied the list. Some of the titles were direct and businesslike: *Drugs and Crime*; *The Billion-Dollar Connection: the International Drug Trade*. Others had brief and rather jazzy names: *Snowblind*; *Blow*; *Hooked*.

And still others seemed rather inflammatory: *Merchants of Misery*; *Embracing the Devil*.

In a few moments I was sitting at a table below a slanting skylight which sent reflections of raindrops trailing across the pages of each book I opened. My favourite was dramatically titled *Hard Drugs, Short Lives*. I was struck by the frontispiece: a black-and-white photograph of two dark figures huddled in an alley, their heads close together, the streetlight outlining their bodies with an eerie glow and casting elongated shadows along the wall beside them as they carried out their sinister transaction.

I didn't know a lot about drug dealers, except what I had absorbed from the popular culture, where they seemed to be everywhere: you read about them in newspaper stories, magazine articles and books; you saw them on countless TV shows and in every second movie out of Hollywood. It was something I had suspected from the beginning. The only reason for doubt had been that it was such a cliché. A Latin American drug dealer. Of course. In the movies they were always Latin Americans, except when they were blacks. As soon as a movie actor spoke with a Spanish accent, you suspected what role he was going to play. But the thing was, I wasn't at a movie, yawning, safe and quiet in the dark. This was something real happening in my life, happening to me.

Anyone who noticed me would have guessed that I was preparing to write a research paper. I sat with piles of books at my elbows, leafing through one volume after another, reading sections that caught my eye and making notes on things that seemed particularly pertinent to my thesis.

Cocaine first used in Inca religious ceremonies

Spanish conquistadores forbade coca use, then
rescinded their ban when coca's work-prolonging
powers in native labourers was realized

Indians still chew coca leaves to combat fatigue and
lessen effects of strong winds and cold temperatures
at high altitudes in which they work

Latin America supplies all cocaine sold in U.S.
(*narcotraficantes*)

Entry routes mainly by commercial or private planes
and boats, body carriers . . .

Deal in cash, harder to trace . . . one man caught
carrying a suitcase containing $500,000

Use pay phones to make deals, not residence phones
as they can be tapped or traced, many carry *beepers*

"Cocaine is like our World Bank, it is our product.
Without cocaine my family would starve . . . The
reality is the big drug guys, the Escobars and the
Ochoas, are like folk heroes because they take the
money and give it back to the people. Pablo Escobar
has built homes for the poor in Medellin. Other guys
have used cocaine capital to boost the lives of the
poor. This is more than the politicians down there
can say."—Jamaican drug dealer

"Anyone with brains knows that there are no Robin
Hoods among the criminal classes. Whatever drug
kingpins may give to the community, they take back
a hundredfold in the destruction and human misery
they cause."—Florida attorney

In Colombia murder is the primary cause of death
for men 15 to 44 . . . 400 people murdered every
month in Medellin . . . Guns a necessity in the drug
trade . . . use violence to defend own territory, to take
over new turf, to punish informers . . . Osvaldo Silva

shot to death in Sloppy Joe's, investigators found
only the body in the deserted bar . . . Ramon
Gonzalez machine-gunned in the front seat of his
brand-new Cadillac at noon on a busy Miami street,
no witnesses found . . . Tommy Delgado killed in a
back alley shootout behind the Gold Coast Lounge, a
Key West drug hangout. . . .

I sat for hours at the heavy yellow table, hardly moving
except to turn pages and put words into my notebook. When
I had finally closed the last volume, I glanced at my watch
with bleary eyes and realized with amazement that it was three
o'clock. I hadn't had any lunch, I had gone into a sort of
dream. My head was aching, my neck and arms were stiff, and
in front of me were twenty sheets of lined paper covered with
untidy, scribbled writing that hardly looked like mine.

Out on the street, I felt almost as though I had been
dropped from another planet and couldn't do anything but
gape, dazed and uncomprehending, at the long bright shafts of
sunlight pouring through the clouds and shimmering on oily
puddles in the gutters. It was a cool June afternoon, and cars
were streaming down Yonge Street, shoppers were jostling each
other with bags full of merchandise, two cyclists pedalled by
on the slick pavement and turned a corner, the chrome on their
bikes flashing with blue-white light. Everything was in motion,
everything was dangerous and alive. I stood in front of
Britnell's Book Store, pretending to look at the window display,
holding my briefcase with the twenty pages of information
inside. With each breath I took I seemed to feel a little flicker
of something just below my diaphragm, a little spasm of sensation so sharp and potent it was like the prick of a knife blade.

WHEN I CAME DOWNSTAIRS, he was sitting on the sofa watching a soccer game. I wasn't the least bit interested, but I said,
"Who's winning?"

"Argentina," he said, grinning. "Naturally. Did you take a shower?"

"Yeah. I was caught in the rain this morning on the way to my office and I've felt sort of dirty ever since." I sat down in the armchair. I was naked under my terrycloth robe. Its rough fabric rubbed against my skin, producing little currents of heat in my arms and legs. It felt good. He glanced at me with his clear, tea-coloured eyes. His hair was dark and lustrous, his skin was brown, the collar of his shirt looked white as milk against his glossy neck. He seemed exceptionally vital, more than real.

"Have you ever used cocaine?" I asked.

He didn't gasp or turn red or give a guilty start. He just looked at me, with a smile. "Why?"

"Just curious."

After a moment he shrugged. "Sure," he said. "Everybody has."

"I haven't," I said.

"No?"

"Do you think I should?"

He didn't answer. After a moment I said, "What's it like?"

"Oh, it makes you feel good. Lots of energy. Like you could go on forever, like there's nothing in the world you can't do."

"That sounds pretty nice," I said. "Don't you think I should try it?"

His eyes hadn't moved from my face. I let one side of my robe slip down over my shoulder. The exposed skin seemed to tingle with pleasure. "Don't you think I should?" I said again.

"Why would you want to?" he said.

"For the experience."

He waited. Finally he said, "You could. But sometimes it gets people into trouble."

"What kind of trouble?"

"Oh, sometimes people get hooked. Can't get enough. Spend all their money. Besides the main problem."

"Which is?"

He looked at me with his faint smile. "It's against the law."

"But you've tried it and you never got into trouble," I said.

90

"Did you?" I put my feet up on the coffee table and opened my knees. The robe fell apart. I felt as though I were drunk. I wanted to shut my eyes from the unrestrained pleasure of that giddy drunkenness. He was staring at me expressionlessly.

"If I wanted to try it, you could get some for me, couldn't you?" I said.

"Maybe," he said. "What are you doing?"

I moved my knees lazily back and forth. "I'm still wet," I said. "I'm drying myself." My blood was washing slowly through my body, heating me from the inside, heating my skin.

"I've never seen you act like this before," he said.

"Haven't you?" I said. "But really, we hardly know each other. I'll bet there are all sorts of surprises ahead."

He gave a soft laugh. My throat felt so constricted that it was difficult to speak.

"Are you terribly interested in that game?" I said huskily.

"No," he said. "Not terribly."

"Then why don't you come over here. You're sitting so far away."

Without taking his eyes from me he raised the remote control and shut off the television. In the sudden silence I could hear the fast, crazy, trip-hammer beat of my heart.

"Come here," I said. "Come on, Eddy. Hurry."

Chapter Seven

IT WAS THE MIDDLE OF A LONG NIGHT. He often wanted to sleep in the room with Provence on the walls, so that's where we were. I had opened a window and we could hear the waves washing up over the beach, a lulling, sensuous rhythm. We had pulled one thin sheet over our bodies; it rose lightly and drifted down as he breathed in and out. His hand rested on my leg. There was no sound anywhere in the world except for the waves and the soft hiss of our breath. We floated on a vast moon-washed sea, alone, and in the distance the painted fields and painted flowers rose up dimly, like hallucinations.

"How many women have you slept with in your life?" I asked.

He stirred slightly. "Why?"

"Just idle curiosity. Lots, I imagine."

His body vibrated against me as he laughed modestly.

"How many? Too many to remember?"

"What do you want, a number?"

"You can round it off to the nearest hundred, if you like."

"Thanks," he said. There was a brief silence. I waited, but he didn't speak.

"Is it a secret?" I said finally.

"Eight hundred and thirty-three," he said.

I had to sit upright to look at his face. "Come on! Are you serious?"

He was grinning in the darkness. "One," he said after a moment. "You're the only woman I remember."

I was annoyed with myself for feeling pleased by that bit of flattery. "Oh, of course," I said, flopping back down beside him. He moved his hand caressingly up and down on my leg. "I've slept with lots of men," I told him suddenly. Then I caught my breath in surprise at myself.

"Don't brag," he said softly.

"It's true. Not so much in the last few years, since AIDS, I'm more careful now. But before that. I used to go out and pick them up. Sometimes two in one weekend. It was a favourite pastime of mine."

It was the first time I'd ever spoken about it to anyone. I waited for him to react. Of course he was a criminal and had probably seen and heard things far more shocking than anything I could tell him, but you never knew with men, even the roughest ones could have some very puritanical attitudes about sex. I thought he might be scandalized or even disgusted; I thought he might call me a slut. I almost hoped he would. I waited breathlessly. But he didn't speak or move. He continued to stroke my leg. Then I wondered if he was even listening. Possibly I was boring him. Possibly he was drowsy and just wanted to go to sleep.

"I'd go to the most unlikely places I could think of," I said. "Union Station at eleven-thirty at night. The Burger King on Yonge Street. The racetrack. The Green Light Tavern on Queen Street West. I'd sit down, I'd look around, I'd pick someone out. I'd think, Yes, he's the one."

Again I waited for him to say something, to express some

kind of astonishment, excitement or revulsion. He didn't say a word.

"I was never afraid," I said. "Not really. For some reason, I could never believe that anything bad was going to happen to me. I realize that must sound a bit naïve."

He didn't seem to have an opinion on whether it was naïve.

"I met a baseball player in the Green Light Tavern," I said after a moment. "Oh, not a Blue Jay or anything like that. I wouldn't have the slightest interest in a Blue Jay. This guy was one of those minor-league players and he was old for a ball player, thirty-six or thirty-seven, something like that. His hair was starting to get thin on top and he needed a shave. He sent me over a drink."

His hand continued to caress me. His eyes were open; he was looking at the ceiling.

"He looked kind of seedy. I liked that. So I waved at him to come and sit with me. Actually he didn't seem like an athlete. His skin was pale and he had stubble all over his cheeks and his hands trembled a bit when he picked up his glass. He acted like a drinker. But he said he'd been with some minor-league team, oh what was the name of the town? I can't remember. But anyway, they'd released him a couple of months before. He didn't know what he was going to do next. Playing ball was all he'd ever done in his life. That was his story anyway. He had a room at the Garden Hotel—do you know it? A real dive way down on Queen West. An awful little hole of a room with a bathroom down the hall. His window looked out on a fire escape. He kept apologizing for it. 'I don't know Toronto very well, I'm only staying in this dump till I find something better.' He had a bottle of rye whiskey in the bedside cabinet. He brought it out and poured two drinks into two big tumblers with chips out of them. We sat side by side on the bed and drank. You could look out the window and see the red neon sign, GARDEN HOTEL. It was perfect."

"What do you call this?" he said thoughtfully. "There's a word in English . . . slum. Slumming. Is that right?"

For some reason I felt a bit offended, as though he had trivialized me. "No," I said, "it wasn't like that at all."

The quiet was profound. He didn't ask me to go on, but after a moment I did.

"Every time I drive by the Garden Hotel, I remember him. He seemed so wild and desperate. I think that was what I looked for. The ones on the edge. The wild, desperate ones. They were exciting. They always seemed to be more alive than other people."

In the silence I twisted my head around to look up at him, and then he smiled vaguely, as though he was thinking of something else. I was a little deflated, I had expected a much stronger response.

"I was on a train once," he said. "I was coming home to Buenos Aires from Mar del Plata and I'd spent all the money in my pockets and I knew my father was going to go through the roof when he found out. I was nineteen and just back from school in the U.S. and he always said I wasn't responsible enough, I was too loco, too crazy, I was supposed to be learning the value of money. So I wanted to get some more money somehow, so I wouldn't have to hear this big lecture. I'm walking through the train and I see this woman sitting alone in a compartment. You take one look and you can tell, this woman's a rich *porteña*. That's what we call people from Buenos Aires— *porteño, porteña*—of the port, you see? She's got European clothes, she's got rings on her fingers, her luggage is expensive, she's been in Mar del Plata for a little summer holiday and now she's heading back. So I knock on the door of the compartment. I say, 'Is this compartment full?' She looks at me, she decides, no, it isn't full. So I go in and sit down. She's cool at first, she's not talking much, but every so often she raises her eyes and gives me a look. I tell stories, I'm charming, after a little while I casually get out a deck of cards and start playing *solitario*, and it's a long boring ride on the train, so she shows an interest. Soon we're playing gin rummy. I say, 'We could bet a little money, don't you think that would be more fun?' Sure, what does she care, she's got a purse full of bills, she's not worried."

"You were playing gin rummy?"

"Yes. Gin rummy. The Latino version. It was the only game she knew. I didn't care. I'm good at all card games. Soon she's lost all the money in her bag. She shrugs her shoulders, she says, 'I have no money left.' I'm leaning back in the seat and she's looking at me. I say, 'I'll take your dress then.' It's expensive, made in Europe, some famous designer, it's worth a couple of thousand right there. She's a little red in the face. She says, 'Please close the blinds.' So I reach behind me and pull down the blinds so people going by in the corridor won't see what's going on. Then she stands and unzippers her dress and steps out of it and hands it to me. And we play some more, and she loses again. She looks at me, waiting for me to tell her what to do. So I say, 'Take off your stockings.' And she takes them off and hands them to me, one at a time. We go on playing. Pretty soon I've got all her clothes and her jewellery piled up beside me and she's sitting there naked, holding her cards. It's hot and I feel very lazy, I'm lying back and looking at her. It's late afternoon, her back is to the window and just past her shoulder I can see the green hills of Atlantida and some kids on a road, and I can imagine those shabby little kids looking right into the window of our compartment and seeing a naked woman playing cards on the train. She loses again and I'm starting to think she's losing on purpose because nobody could be this bad at gin rummy. She says, 'I have nothing left. What now?' So I say, 'Well, there's only one thing to do. Lie down.' I don't bother to get undressed, I just climb on top of her and unzip my pants and stick it in hard. She gives one gasp and after that she's quiet. Then I climb off again. But I make her wait till we're almost in Buenos Aires and then I make her write me a cheque to buy her clothes back. She says, 'Would you give me enough cash to pay for a cab?' I say, 'Sorry.' The last I see of her she's standing in the middle of the train station with her hair rumpled and a bunch of bags all around her, helpless as a baby. I've got all her jewellery and her money and her cheque in my pockets and I walk away."

During his recital of that story, he continued to touch me

caressingly and I lay against him, my face resting heavily on his hot, smooth shoulder. But I felt cold suddenly, as if I had been cut loose, as if I were adrift in cold water, all by myself.

"What's Mar del Plata like?" I asked finally, just to break the long, strange silence. I already knew what it was like; there were pictures of it in my book on Buenos Aires: golden beaches, blue-green water, brown-skinned, long-legged girls in tiny bathing suits, the sun setting behind the dark hotel, turning the ocean into an expanse of shimmering gold. Eddy still didn't know I had such a book. I'd put it on the top shelf of my closet under some boxes. I looked at it only when he wasn't around.

"It's a vacation place," he said after a moment. "Everybody in Buenos Aires goes there during the summer."

"Everybody?"

"Everybody who can afford it."

"It's expensive?"

"There's one taxi company that only uses Mercedes-Benzes."

"You're kidding."

He seemed to be warming to the subject; his voice took on a sudden vibrancy. "You rent a cabana on the beach. Someone brings you a cool drink. People play cards. You do whatever you please. There are boutiques and galleries that stay open all night. There are beautiful cliffs overlooking the ocean. People have summer places there. My family had a house there."

"Really?"

"A small house," he said quickly. "We'd usually spend the whole month of January there. La Perla del Atlántico. I've got lots of happy memories of it."

The bed rocked gently beneath us like a boat on the sea.

"My family has a summer place too," I said. I was surprised to hear myself say that.

"Yes?"

"A cottage in Muskoka. We went there every year as kids, at the beginning of July. You drive up a steep hill and when you reach the top you suddenly see Azure Lake spread out below, and our cottage on the shore. My father always used to say the same thing, we'd swoop up over that hill and he'd say, 'Ladies and gentlemen, we are now entering the domain of Trewithen.' Trewithen is the name of our cottage. It's from the old Cornish language, it means 'place of trees.' " I couldn't imagine what had possessed me, prattling on in such a foolish, childlike way. I knew he wouldn't be interested. Hastily I returned to a subject I knew they always wanted to talk about.

"That's where I first had sex," I said.

He laughed. "Yes?"

"I was seventeen," I said. "A university friend of my father's had come up from the city for a weekend. Dean was his name. He was having some sort of crisis, his wife had left him for one thing, and he was losing his family's business too. He wanted my father to be a white knight, buy up a lot of stock, something like that. But my father wouldn't. 'It just isn't a good investment for us at this point,' that's all my father said. Then Dean got a terrible look on his face, as though he was going to burst into tears. My father said, 'Get a hold of yourself, for God's sake.' My father thought you were a pretty poor specimen if you couldn't even control your emotions. After that Dean stopped talking about his problems and tried to be sociable, you know, laughing and telling jokes, like a good guest, but he didn't stop drinking all day, straight bourbon, one after another. We had dinner on the verandah, and Dean drank a whole bottle of wine by himself. Then he went to his room and passed out on the bed. My mother was really annoyed. She hated people who drank too much. But my father thought it was sort of amusing. He said, 'Just let him sleep it off.' They were going to a dance at the Azure Lake Country Club and they took my sister Leslie with them but I wouldn't go, I pretended to be sick. I was never a very social person, I always liked to spend time alone. After they'd left I went down to the lake. We had our own private beach and I liked to swim after dark on hot nights. I swam for a while and then I lay down to dry off. I remember the sand was still very warm, even though it had already been dark for an hour. The next thing I knew, I opened my eyes and Dean was there. He was kneeling in the sand right beside me, breathing his liquory breath all over me, and sort of pulling at the top of my bathing suit. At first I was horrified, I almost screamed, but then I saw he wasn't really very threatening. In fact he seemed more scared than I was. He kept pleading with me not to make a noise. 'Sh-sh-sh. Sh-sh-sh.' And he kept whispering, even though there was no one else around for miles. 'Just let me have a look,' he said. 'Please, just one look. Please.' Well, he seemed to want it so badly, and I thought, what harm can it do? So I let him take down the straps of my bathing suit. His hands were shaking and he kept turning to look over his shoulder, he expected to be caught any second. He was whispering and paying me compliments but I could hardly listen to him because I was so nervous myself. I didn't mean to go very far, but he seemed so upset and scared that I almost felt as if I were the older one and I had to help him. Everything he did, he asked for permission first: 'Can I do this? Is it all right if I do this?' So before I knew it my bathing suit was right off and I was lying on my back in that warm, silky sand and the sky seemed to be spinning over my head as if I were the one who'd been drinking, not him. I expected it to hurt, but it didn't. I thought it was marvellous. He wanted it so badly. I wasn't stupid, of course I knew it was partly because he wanted to get back at my father. But it was the way he did it, the way he treated me. He made me feel like a queen who was granting him an enormous favour. Afterwards he helped me put my bathing suit back on. His hands were still shaking and all the time he was still looking over his shoulder. He said, 'Don't tell your dad, okay? Your dad would kill me if he knew.' I promised not to tell. It wasn't hard, because I never told my father anything anyway."

"This guy was another desperate one," he commented. "Right?"

"Well . . . yes, I suppose you could say that. He went back to the city right away the next morning. No, no, he'd changed his mind, he couldn't stay the whole weekend after all. I saw him every once in a while after that. He always had trouble looking me in the face, but nobody except me ever noticed that. I didn't blame him, though. He didn't want my father to be angry. He always said my father was his best friend."

"I don't think much of him."

I smiled. "He's dead now. He died of cancer when he was only fifty-two. It's strange, I actually cried when I first heard."

"Did you think I was desperate when you met me?" he asked suddenly.

I was startled for a moment. I didn't know what to say. But I had to answer him. "No," I said. "That was something different."

In the distance I suddenly heard the sound of a car's tires crackling on pavement, then a little burst of music from a radio, a sad, harsh voice backed by drums and violins. It faded away in the night.

He said, "There's a cemetery in Buenos Aires where all the rich and powerful people are buried. La Recoleta Cemetery. Evita is buried there. One afternoon when I was about fourteen I skipped school just so I could wander around and smoke cigarettes and eat ice cream in the sun. I was walking in the neighbourhood of La Recoleta. The jacaranda trees were all in bloom, it was a beautiful day, and I saw a woman coming out of the gate of the cemetery. She was a young woman, at least I thought so from her figure. I couldn't really see her face because she was wearing a long veil made of black lace. She was all alone. She only walked a few steps and then she sort of stumbled a little and had to reach out and lean against the cemetery wall to keep from falling. Buenos Aires is very busy, people are in a hurry, no one seemed to notice this woman's trouble, only me. So I crossed the street and went over to her and said, 'Do you need some help?' She turned her head and I noticed right away that she was wearing lipstick the colour of cherries and her eyes were full of tears so they looked like violets under water. She said, 'I'm so thirsty.' I was holding an ice cream cone, it was half melted, but it was all I had to offer, so I held it up to her, and she lifted her veil and took a little bit of ice cream into her mouth. She said 'Thank you,' and then she put her arm through mine, as if we were old friends, and we started to walk. She didn't say a word so I didn't talk either. We hadn't gone very far before she said, 'I'm so tired.' I said, 'Do you want to sit down in a café and have some tea?' She said, 'No, come with me.' We walked down Calle Azuenaga, which is a street right beside the cemetery, full of *hoteles transitorios.*"

"Full of what?"

"*Hoteles . . .* transitory hotels? Does that make sense?"

"Flophouses, you mean?"

"Flophouses," he laughed. "That's good. I haven't heard that one before. What does it mean?"

"Oh . . . cheap places where transients can get a room for the night."

"Ah. No, that's not it. Certainly there aren't any flophouses in La Recoleta, it's a very exclusive neighbourhood. No, *hoteles transitorios . . .* places where people can go for a few hours to have a good time, with no one knowing."

"No! Right beside the cemetery?"

"Yeah. I think it's excellent, don't you?"

"And this woman took you there?"

"Yeah. We went into the Hotel Florida. She leaned on my arm and told the man at the desk that I was her brother and we had been through a terrible experience and we needed a place to rest for a while. On the Calle Azuenaga they don't care what you tell them. He gave us a key. It was a room with faded blue walls and long windows opening out on a little iron balcony and you could look right across and see the cemetery. City of the Dead is what they sometimes call it in Buenos Aires because it looks like a city, the tombs are big as houses and they have domes and towers and stand in rows like buildings on a street. Rich people have to have mansions, even when they're dead. The woman told me to lie down on the bed and then she went into the bathroom and shut the door. I was scared and excited. I didn't know what she was going to do. I remember there were long white curtains on the windows and one of them kept blowing across my face. She stayed in the bathroom a long time, but finally the door clicked and she came out and she had taken off everything but her shoes and the veil. I thought I was going to faint. I'd never seen a naked woman before. My mouth was sticky from ice cream and I felt like such a kid. I didn't have any idea of what to do. I just lay there and stared at her. I think I was shaking from head to foot. She climbed onto the bed very slowly, like a cat, and started to unfasten my pants. I didn't move. Her fingernails were long and they were painted the same cherry-red colour as her lipstick. I let her take my pants off. As if I had any choice! She had me in her control and I had to let her do whatever she wanted. Her thighs were as smooth and white as cream. I remember her face up above me, all in shadows behind her veil, with the cherry-red lips and wet dark eyes shining through the black lace. It was like she was pulling everything out of me, not just *esperma*, but the air in my lungs, my blood, my brains, everything was pouring out of me and into her. And it was good, it was great, it was as if I was getting lighter and lighter until I was going to fly up into paradise. Afterwards I fell asleep and when I woke up she was gone and the wind was blowing those white curtains into the empty room. It was already getting dark and without even getting up from the bed I could look out the window and see right into La Recoleta, all the stones so white and strange, and this is funny, but for a long time I was afraid to move because I got this idea that I'd actually died and I was trapped inside my own dead body, and *Dios mío*, it was so lonely."

I lay quietly, looking up at the shadows on the ceiling. Finally he cleared his throat.

"Then, it was about three weeks later, I had sex with the bearded lady from the Circo Espléndido," he said. "Now that was really something."

His words hung in the air for a moment. All of a sudden I was laughing so hard that it seemed to come from somewhere in the very core of my body. Water filled my eyes. He laughed a little too. I had to turn and press my face into his neck.

"So you're always going to come up with something to top every single story I tell," I said.

"Maybe," he agreed, spreading my hair across his throat.

I said, "But mine are true!"

"So are mine," he said.

Chapter Eight

MID-JUNE BROUGHT A SERIES OF HOT, SUNNY, humid days and because the previous summer had been unusually cold, with rain every weekend, people were grateful for the good weather and walked along the boardwalk smiling, faces uplifted to feel the sun. A few bold characters even ventured into the cold, polluted water of Lake Ontario and then ran out again, shivering and yelling and wrapping themselves in towels. I saw them from my upper balcony as I stood drinking my coffee on mornings that were already steamy by nine o'clock. Sometimes Eddy would be sitting beside me in a wicker chair. Sometimes he would still be sleeping, behind me in the bedroom, sprawled across my bed with his face hidden by pillows. Sometimes he had already left because he had "things to do."

It was thirty-two degrees Celsius the day I met David Marr, one of the family lawyers, for a drink. He suggested the Aquarius lounge, which was beautifully cool and fashionably ferny. We sat at a small round table beside a wall of glass,

looking down over the hazy glitter of the city, and a sleek blonde
waitress placed two tall white wine spritzers in front of us.

"Well," David said, taking some papers out of his briefcase. "They're not happy."

"I'm sure they're not." I took a sip of my drink.

"I thought Silverstone was going to break down and weep.
He said, 'The Foundation's always had such a good relation-
ship with the Tremain family.'"

"Well, fine. But they knew how I felt about giving the
Tremain Prize to Walkman Peters and they went ahead anyway. I don't want our name associated with a farce like that
ever again."

"He kept insisting that an independent jury made the
selection."

"I don't care. Walkman Peters is a joke. We haven't got a
fortune to throw around anymore. I'm not going to fund pres-
tigious literary awards for trash that appeals to the lowest
common denominator."

"Silverstone claimed that Peters was called 'an exciting
new talent' by the *New York Times*."

"Well, even the *New York Times* has an occasional lapse. In
my opinion Walkman Peters is crude and empty. And to put it
bluntly—I'm the one signing the cheques."

"They've suggested a compromise."

"Not interested."

"They're very upset. There's a good chance they'll go to the
papers."

"Let them."

"Well, Grace, as usual you know what you want." He put
his papers away again, leaned back in his chair and smiled.
"It's really good to see you. You've been so busy lately.
Whenever I phone you, you're not at home. Or else you're just
not answering. What have you been up to?"

David and I were friends. That is, we liked each other in a
casual sort of way, occasionally he came to my place for dinner or I went to one of his parties, he laughed at all my jokes
and I participated in long discussions about the foibles of his

partner Ben, the house he and Ben were renovating, the book he was writing about the legal aspects of deal-making in the nineties, and whether the theatre was finished as an art form.

"Up to?" I said. "Oh, nothing much."

"Well, thank God it's vacation time. Here's to long, beautiful vacations in foreign climes! When are you leaving for France?"

"Oh, the last week of July, I think."

"Where are you going to stay? Are you taking the same villa as last time?"

"Actually, I haven't decided yet."

He looked at me. "You haven't decided? Don't you have to make the arrangements pretty far in advance? If you're leaving the last week in July—that's only four weeks away."

I shrugged, running my finger around the rim of my glass. I couldn't think of an explanation for my unusual lack of preparation.

"Come on, Grace, confess," David laughed suddenly. "I'm dying to hear all about it."

I stared at him. "Confess what?"

"Something's happening, isn't it? You've met somebody. Come on, spill it."

"Why do you say that?"

"Oh, I don't know . . . you're sort of vague and absent-minded, you haven't arranged your trip yet, the Mistress of Organization, Grace Tremain. . . ."

"Well," I said, "this year I felt like being more spontaneous."

"And there you were at Canada's Wonderland on the weekend . . ."

I took another sip of my drink and held it in my mouth for a moment, tasting the wine and soda water and ice, squinting out at the brilliant white afternoon light.

". . . getting on the Dizzy Dipper with a very cute guy in a green jacket? I was going to wait and say hello to you, but we had Ben's kids with us and they were screaming to go into the Haunted Cave, so I couldn't. You certainly seemed to be having a lot more fun than I was. You were laughing at the top of your voice. I don't think I've ever heard you laugh like that before."

I crunched on some ice for a moment. Then I set down my glass and looked at him with an amused frown. "You must have been hallucinating," I said. "Me, at Canada's Wonderland?"

He kept smiling. "Oh, come on, Grace, don't be coy. Ben and I both saw you. With a tall, very good-looking Latin type in a green jacket, getting on the Dizzy Dipper."

I burst out laughing. "The Dizzy what?"

"The Dizzy Dipper. That capsule where you shoot straight up and then straight down? I couldn't believe that you were actually getting on it, when you're so afraid of heights."

I shook my head, still laughing. "David," I said, "you were dreaming. I've never been to Canada's Wonderland in my life, and I hope to keep it that way."

The smile faded from his face. He stared at me as if I'd gone crazy. "But we saw you. Ben and I, we both did. He said, 'Boy, it looks like Grace got lucky.'"

"Maybe I have a doppelgänger," I said.

His eyes were very round and blank. I could see his mouth moving slightly, trying to form some sort of argument. I smiled at him.

"Sorry, maybe I was getting too personal," he said at last.

"Not at all. But I wasn't there."

"You weren't at Canada's Wonderland on Sunday afternoon, June seventeenth."

"I'm afraid not," I said.

He gazed at me, bewildered. He was beginning to doubt himself. "But it had to be you. That red hair, and you were wearing that yellow blouse I've seen you in a hundred times. . . ."

"Well, I'm not the only person in the world with red hair," I said, "and it's against my religion to wear anything a hundred times. Come on, David, think about it. Can you really picture me at Canada's Wonderland, riding the Dizzy Dripper?"

"The Dizzy Dipper. Well, of course I thought it was a bit

bizarre." He shook his head slowly from side to side. "Am I losing my mind? I could have sworn it was you."

I shrugged lightly. "Sorry," I said. "I think you need a holiday too."

"I guess so." He laughed, but his eyes were still perplexed. "Shall we have another one? Or do you have to leave?"

"Oh, what the hell," I said. "Sure, let's have another." And I signalled the waitress. "So, how are Ben's kids these days?"

"Well, don't get me started. . . ."

WHEN I UNLOCKED MY FRONT DOOR and walked into the foyer, a black shadow flashed across the span of light on the floor and then a hand seized me by the shoulder. I had a moment of terror before I realized who it was, before his hot cheek slipped across mine and he pressed his lips briefly against my ear to whisper, "Jesus, where have you been? I thought you said you were going to be home early." Before I could answer his tongue was in my mouth. He had already pushed my skirt up around my waist and was holding me against him with both hands. He was like that sometimes; he would behave as if he had been shut away in solitary confinement for ten years, and had to have sex within the next five minutes or he was going to explode. Then I would feel the same urgency, such hunger and fury that I would start pulling at his clothes as though they were an intolerable barrier between his skin and mine. Only later would the thought cross my mind that perhaps he had only pretended to be so voracious because he knew it excited me. We staggered into the living room and fell clumsily down on the soft carpet. He opened his jeans; I yanked my underpants and pantyhose down around my knees. When he came into me I screamed out loud. I had never screamed during sex before, never wanted to scream, always had trouble believing that there were people who actually yelled and made a lot of noise. The scream roared up through my body from the tips of my toes, burst out of my throat and bounced off the silent, shadowy walls.

Afterward he collapsed and lay heavily against me. His hot face dampened the fabric of my blouse. "I've been thinking about this all day," he whispered.

"Me too," I said, resting my shaking hand on his moist, curly hair. Suddenly I was aware that I was trembling all over, my neck, my hands, my knees, my lips, even the roots of my hair seemed to be trembling. Water trickled from the corners of my eyes and pooled up in the hair just above my ears.

We lay there for a long time, not speaking. He was lying across one of my arms and it began to go numb, but I didn't want to disturb the trance we were in by moving it. After a while I stopped trembling. Instead I began to feel so light, so weak, that if the curtains had caught fire I doubt whether I could have summoned enough energy to stand up. My legs lay across the rug like dead things. I could feel the soft material of my underclothes, still tangled up around my limp knees.

Finally he rolled away from me, lay facing the ceiling for a moment, and then sat up. I looked at the smooth curve of his back.

He cleared his throat. "Sorry if I was too rough," he said.

"That's all right," I said. "I like it when you're rough."

He turned to look at me. His eyes were dark and glistening in the dim light. "And I like it when you're not rough too," I said throatily.

After a moment he turned away again. "I have to go," he said.

I always tried never to show surprise or dismay, no matter what a man did or said, not even if he made violent love to me and then wanted to leave ten seconds later. "Oh?" I said casually.

He nodded, staring at the wall. "I have to meet some guys. It's a business thing."

"You always seem to conduct business at such strange times," I said, with a bright laugh.

"They're from out of town. You know how it is."

"Oh, sure." I forced myself to yawn. "Well."

"Well." He stood up and began to fasten his jeans.

Suddenly I became aware that I was still lying on the floor with my skirt up around my waist and my underpants twisted around my legs. Not a very dignified position. I struggled to my feet and briskly began to rearrange my clothes. "Are you going to come back later?" I asked. A second after the words were out I wanted to bite my tongue off. I tried never to ask questions like that; it was too demeaning.

"I'm not sure," he said. He still wasn't looking at me. "It depends."

I couldn't understand why he had become so distant all of a sudden. Usually he went out of his way to be charming and tender, especially after sex. But that's what you had to expect from men, they changed from one day to the next, you could never be sure where you stood, you always had to remember that you couldn't be sure of anything at all. I thought perhaps his change of attitude signalled the beginning of the end. And about time, too, I told myself.

"Well, that's all right," I said. "Because actually, I have a lot of work I should do tonight so it'll be good to have some time to myself." I was pleased with the way my voice sounded, quite careless and unconcerned.

He nodded. "Okay," he said. He walked over to the door of the foyer. Then he paused, without turning, his hands on the door frame, as if he was going to say something important. I waited. Finally he said, "Okay. Well, good night." And the doorway was empty.

As soon as I heard the front door click shut behind him, I ran to the kitchen and looked out the window. His car was parked at the bottom of the driveway. I stood behind the half-closed curtain and watched him come out from the shadow of the house. He was walking lightly, his shoulders moved in a relaxed, easy way inside his green jacket. Something about him seemed strange, absolutely remote and unfamiliar; I could hardly believe that I had just had him inside my body, that only moments before his hot flesh had pierced me like a sword. He got into his car and I saw his dark silhouette as he leaned forward to turn on the ignition. He pulled away from the curb, made a tight U-turn and headed north on Vine Street. Then I knew what I was going to do.

My purse was lying on its side in the foyer where I had dropped it when he caught me by surprise. I slung it over my shoulder like a weapon. My keys were on the floor where they had fallen. I grabbed them up in one hand as I rushed to the door. Outside the air had not been cooled by the darkness; it was still warm and sultry, with an ashy smell. My hands trembled so much that it was difficult to insert my key in the lock to turn the deadbolt. I walked briskly to my own car. I hadn't driven it in weeks, but it started instantly. That seemed like a favourable omen. I had thought of following him many times without ever making a move. You see, I said to myself, listening to the hum of my motor. Tonight is meant to be the night.

By the time I turned slowly onto Vine, he had already reached the intersection of Vine and Queen. I could see his little white car, a bit ghostlike in the humid darkness, blinking its green signal, waiting to turn west on Queen Street. I pulled over to the curb and waited until the traffic light changed and the white car entered the intersection. Then I pushed the gas pedal down and shot up the hill with a faint roar. I was excited. I'd never followed anyone before.

It was about nine o'clock at night, so there were lots of vehicles on Queen Street, and lots of strolling pedestrians idly stepping off the sidewalks, which meant that I had to keep stopping with a jolt and then starting up again. But it wasn't hard to keep that white car in view. I followed it all the way through the bright, glittery congestion of the Beach, past the Greenwood racetrack with its parking lot radiating the moonlit chrome of a thousand automobiles. After that the streets grew shabbier and greyer, the curbs became weedy and littered, and there were boards nailed over the windows of abandoned stores. The white car led me on, never pausing, never veering away, floating ahead of me, hypnotizing me, going straight west into the darkness of the city. I slipped the Gipsy Kings into my tape deck and turned up the volume. The rhythmic guitars, the clapping hands and harsh Spanish voices seemed appropriate to the occasion. The air conditioning was beginning to work and I felt the perspiration drying on my face. In my cool, leather-scented capsule I floated past all the young shabby men smoking cigarettes in the dark doorways of cheap cafés, a fat woman fanning herself as she leaned through faded curtains at a second-floor window, a grey-haired drunk holding on to the base of a streetlight and shouting "Fuck you!" to the impersonal air. I fell into a sort of dream. It was an area that I went through almost every day, driving or riding on the streetcar. To me it was nothing more than a vaguely unpleasant blur that you had to pass through to reach your destination. Then all at once Eddy's car floated to the curb and came to a stop. This was so unexpected that I couldn't pull over in time and had to drive right past. He was opening his car door and didn't look around as I shot by. I saw him in my rearview mirror, slamming the door with a flourish, walking around the front of his car, lightly bounding up onto the sidewalk with a careless gesture of greeting to a dark figure sitting on a front stoop, then pushing open the doors of a place called Hot Mamas and disappearing into its black interior.

I had to drive around the block. Hot Mamas was on the corner of Queen and a sidestreet called Wistaria Lane, a misnomer if there ever was one. I parked on Wistaria half a block back from the intersection, out of the glare of Queen Street but with a vantage point where I could see both the white car and the side entrance of Hot Mamas. It was a strip club. I had driven by it a thousand times; its exterior was completely familiar to me—a shabby block of red brick with a blue neon sign in the shape of a voluptuous woman holding up a red neon glass of champagne full of tiny blue bubbles that blinked on and off. Many times I had smiled dryly at that glass of champagne, because I would have been willing to bet a large amount of money that no patron in the entire history of Hot Mamas had ever ordered champagne. GIRLS, GIRLS, GIRLS! promised a hand-painted sign in one of its dark windows, and TABLE DANCING, $2.50, and THIS WEEK: MISS NUDE

CALIFORNIA. It was rather pathetic to think of some woman travelling all the way from California to take off her clothes in the loud, beery, rancid air of Hot Mamas. Once we were driving back from our cottage, my parents, Leslie and I, and on the outskirts of a hamlet called Victory we passed a strip club with the fanciful name Esmeralda, which promised "the most beautiful exotic dancers in the world." I tried to imagine the women who came to that forsaken place, I pictured them walking along the weedy road in their shaky high heels and gaudy nylon, going through the shabby doors, climbing onto a dirty platform and straining to be sexy for a bunch of— what? Farmers, tractor salesmen, gas station jockeys? Leslie said something about how horrible it must be to make your living that way, and she couldn't understand why anyone would want to do it. My father said, *Well, I imagine it's the only thing they're capable of.* My mother had the car window open and was leaning against her arm, letting the wind blow across her face. *Isn't that right, Vivian?* my father said. *That's right,* my mother said immediately, without even turning her head.

Two men were standing outside a convenience store, smoking and staring at me. They had watched me pull up to the curb and park, and since then they hadn't been able to take their eyes off me. A woman alone at night is something few men can ignore. Especially a woman alone in a Porsche. Lights go on in their brains: sex! money! at least let's scare her stiff! I glanced around to make sure all my doors were locked, and slumped down slightly. I felt sure that I could handle them, though. I was ready for anything. Adrenalin was pumping through me like a drug. I thought that if I leaned up to look in the rearview mirror I wouldn't see myself, perhaps I would see a dark, fiery Latin woman with a scarlet mouth, waiting to entrap her unfaithful lover, waiting to stick a knife in his guts.

His white car was still sitting outside the door of Hot Mamas. He had been in there a long time. I could picture him standing at the bar, sipping a drink, smiling while some naked eighteen-year-old girl shook her breasts in his face. She would be pretty, she would have a perfect body, slick with sweat, he would slip a ten-dollar bill into her G-string, letting his hand linger on her damp thigh. He would murmur, "When are you finished here, sweetheart?" That's what you have to expect from men: they stick it into you, and an hour later they're ready to stick it into somebody else.

So I sat there. I thought I would wait until he came out, even if I had to wait all night. There was a sort of pain in my throat. I wanted to see him come out with his arm around that eighteen-year-old blonde. I just wanted to see that, and then I could go home.

The two men at the corner finally worked up the courage, or whatever it takes, to come over to my car. I stared at them coldly through the windshield as they approached. They were grinning and weaving around, making motions with their hips and fingers. As they got closer, I saw that they were only teenage boys, which made me feel even more sure of myself— God knows why, since teenage boys can be far more dangerous than forty-year-old men. The taller one knocked on the car window. When I turned my head, he signalled that I should roll the window down.

"You must be joking," I said, more to myself than to them. I shook my head vehemently.

He put his hands together in a prayerful way. "Oh, come on, please," I heard him say through the glass.

I shook my head again.

"Take us for a ride," he said. "We'll make sure you have a good time." He was grinning. He had long, straggly hair that fell in pieces across his eyes. Furtively he glanced around and then pulled a little plastic packet part-way out of the pocket of his jeans, just to let me see it. It contained a small amount of white powder which I assumed was a drug of some kind, although it could have been icing sugar for all I knew. I kept shaking my head. He held out his hands helplessly, as if to ask what else I could possibly want. Then suddenly he pressed his lower body against the car window next to my face and rubbed himself up and down on the glass with a long-drawn-out moan, while his friend went into a fit of hysterical laughter and began jumping around on the pavement as if he needed to urinate.

I did nothing, I didn't even bother to watch. I looked straight ahead through the windshield and gave an ostentatious yawn. The taller one became annoyed and slapped angrily at the glass as if to warn me that he was through fooling around. But I wasn't afraid, not in the least. I looked up at him through the glass and that glass seemed as secure as a steel wall. He couldn't get to me.

Of course they were incensed by my attitude and had to demonstrate their feelings by shaking the body of the car, kicking the tires, and banging on the hood. I sat and watched them, my arms folded. I thought that if it got really bad I would simply turn on the ignition and drive away. But after a few minutes they got bored and fed up. The taller one leaned down in front of the windshield with a sneer and said "Bitch!" I nodded calmly in acknowledgement, as though he had paid me a compliment.

I suppose there might have been a moment when they thought of crossing the line into real violence—slashing the tires, breaking the windows, dragging me out onto the sidewalk . . . it could have gone through their minds. But something prevented them from trying it. I don't know why it happens sometimes, and other times it doesn't. For some reason I felt quite inaccessible to them, quite certain that they wouldn't be able to harm me. Finally they began walking away, making gestures of disgust and dismissal, muttering insults whose import came to me in stray words: "bitch . . . stuckup . . . straight to hell." I wasn't trembling; I felt completely cool, as though I had been doing nothing but sitting quietly and listening to my happy Mediterranean music on the radio. The white car was still parked in front of Hot Mamas. I looked at my watch. It was ten-thirty p.m. I was surprised that it was so early. It seemed more like two o'clock in the morning.

The side door of the club banged open suddenly and a girl ran out. She was wearing tights and a long, loose blouse; her hair was gathered up into a scraggly ponytail. She was carrying a package of cigarettes in one hand and a lit cigarette in the other. She was very thin and young; her face had the finely drawn, famished look of a high-fashion model. I wondered if she could possibly be a performer. She certainly didn't resemble the photographic display outside the front entrance of Hot Mamas: a series of flamboyant, grinning women with breasts so gigantic they reminded you of a Wonderwoman cartoon. The girl with the cigarettes seemed to be about fourteen. But if she wasn't a performer, then why was she coming out the side door of Hot Mamas? She paused on the sidewalk for a moment, then ran across the street, passing right in front of me without a glance in my direction. Even in the dark, I could see that her lipstick was smudged and her eyes looked blurry, as though she had been crying. She turned the corner and disappeared from view. I tried to imagine her prancing around on a stage, teetering in her stiletto heels, flaunting her scrawny body and tiny breasts, smiling nervously and blinking her big, sad eyes. I didn't understand how anyone could find that erotic. But then I didn't understand how anyone could find the Wonderwoman type erotic either. Eddy was still inside though, so something was obviously holding his attention. Possibly he was sitting at a table with a foamy glass of beer, grinning, cheering lustily as Miss Nude California removed her spangled bra. Or he was standing in a dark, water-stained washroom, furtively dispensing little plastic envelopes and pocketing dozens of bills. I looked at my watch again. It was ten forty-five. The effects of my air conditioning were beginning to wear off and I could feel a trickle of perspiration in the middle of my back. His white car sat there, empty and silent, reflecting glints of blue neon. The bars had to close at one a.m. At the most I had only two hours and fifteen minutes left to wait, I told myself with a wry smile. The Gipsy Kings were loud enough to send a slight vibration through the car's upholstery. It made me aware of the heaviness of my body in the seat, the feel of my clothes against my skin, the thickness of my hair on my moist neck, the thin crust of dried semen between my legs. I didn't know a word of Spanish, but I felt sure the raspy male voices were singing about summer nights, tropical breezes, luscious fruits, red silk dresses swirling around warm brown thighs, heat, desire, sex, juice, rage, passion. A digital sign above the door of a café said that the temperature was twenty-nine degrees Celsius.

Then Eddy came out of Hot Mamas. I sat up straight, almost honking my car horn in the process. Then I slumped down again, remembering that I was supposed to be inconspicuous. He seemed to be alone, and he seemed to be in no hurry. He paused for a few moments on the sidewalk, lighting a cigarette, tossing the match carelessly away. He was waiting for someone, that was it, Miss Nude California was going to join him, any second she would come running out, her mane of blonde hair bouncing on her shoulders, she would have long legs, and lots of white teeth, and a laugh like a tinkling piano, just the kind of chick someone like Eddy would go for, of course he would. I sat absolutely still, hardly breathing, my shoulders hunched, my head down, just in case he looked my way. But he didn't. He stood there drawing smoke deep into his lungs and breathing it slowly out. Then he walked around the front of his car, unlocked the door, and got in. I found myself gripping my steering wheel with such intensity that my knuckles hurt. He was starting his car, he was pulling away from the curb, he was leaving, he was still alone. It was disappointing; it was a relief. Nothing was resolved. It wasn't going to be so easy after all. The air was sweet in my nose and mouth, as if it had its own scent, its own flavour. As I turned onto Queen Street, the Gipsy Kings went into "Ritmo de la Noche," reducing their vocals to inarticulate cries of longing that were barely audible above the rush of guitars and drums. Those faint, high voices thrilled in my ears, made the hairs on the back of my neck stand up. The images of Queen Street were glamourized by the rough, poignant guitar chords; the people moved to a syncopated beat and made sense. In my rearview mirror I saw the waif-like stripper standing a few feet up from the convenience store, talking to the two boys who had tried to get into my car. The tall one was showing her the plastic packet in the pocket of his jeans. The blue neon woman with the red champagne glass drifted away, the streetlights floated across the sky, bodies walked and ran and stood on the steaming pavement, and I followed the white car, weaving in and out, moving slowly, then quickly, stopping on red, starting on green, performing an endless ballet to the sound of gypsy guitars.

EVENTUALLY WE TURNED NORTH on Logan. It was an abrupt transition from lights and cars and crowds to quiet darkness. I had to drop back because there was no other traffic on the street and he might have seen me. He sailed far ahead of me through black leafy shadows that rippled over the soft white of his car, making it appear that he was driving underwater. When he stopped at an intersection, I pulled over to a curb and waited until he was in motion again. I'm getting good at this, I congratulated myself.

As we crossed Gerrard I realized he was heading home. He lived on the top floor of an old white house right across from Withrow Park. I stopped, parked at the end of the block, and watched him pull into his driveway. As he got out of his car he glanced quickly up and down the street, but I slumped down and he didn't seem to see me. He went inside. In a moment two tall rectangular windows on the top floor filled up with yellow light. After a while I started my car and slowly, cautiously moved it forward until it was just across the street from the house two doors down from his. On my other side, a wide, grassy slope stretched away, dotted with park benches, white in the moonlight. Because it was such a hot evening, there were still quite a few people strolling on the pathways or sitting under the trees. I rolled down my window and breathed in the warm, earthy scent of leaves and cut grass.

I had been in his apartment once, for about five minutes. He had to stop to pick up some extra cash (he said) and wanted me to wait in the car while he ran upstairs. I said, *No,*

119

I'll come up with you. He said, *Oh, no, it'll only take me a second, why bother?* I said, *I'd like to see your apartment, that's all, I've never even seen it.* He couldn't very well argue with that, so he had to let me come up. The apartment was large, many spacious rooms with high ceilings, one opening into another through tall, arched doorways: a kitchen, living room, dining room, and three bedrooms—I suppose they were bedrooms, although two were completely unfurnished and the other contained only a mattress on the floor. In the living room he had a big, expensive television set and a small, well-worn sofa. In the kitchen were a table and three chairs—not two, not four, but three. The dining room was empty. *Well,* I said, looking around in amazement, *you weren't kidding, it certainly is Spartan. And you've been living here, how long? I told you,* he said, *I'm hardly ever here.* And then he hurried me out.

The time passed slowly and his windows continued to beam their yellow light into the velvety darkness. I wasn't sure why I kept sitting there. Obviously he wasn't going anywhere else and that was the end of it. I looked at my watch. It was after midnight. A strange sort of lethargy seemed to come over me, as though I was too tired to drive home. I listened to the breeze rustling the tree branches. Down in the park a woman was laughing; I could just make out her dark silhouette as she caught hold of her companion's arm and bent over helplessly, her long hair falling across her face.

Suddenly a car pulled up behind me. It happened so quickly and unexpectedly that I froze, holding on to my steering wheel, staring straight ahead. I could hear car doors slamming but I was afraid to turn my head. The rearview mirror revealed nothing more than a dark, moving shape. I expected—what? Banging on my windows, shouted questions like WHO ARE YOU? WHAT ARE YOU DOING HERE? But nothing happened. I sensed that two people were crossing the street, that both of them were staring at me intently. Without moving, without turning, I saw out of the corners of my eyes that they were walking up the driveway past Eddy's car. Their faces were still turned toward me so I didn't dare look around.

They didn't pause at the doorway to knock or ring a bell; they simply opened the door and went inside. They had been looking at me all the while. The moment they were out of sight I had a wild impulse to turn on the ignition and drive away, fast. I don't know why they unnerved me so; I hadn't even had a good look at them, had no idea whether they were men or women, couldn't even be sure they were going to see Eddy. There were two other apartments on the main floor of the house and they could have been visiting one of those—for all I knew they were tenants themselves, simply coming home.

It didn't matter who they were. I couldn't sit still. I got out of my car and walked quickly into the park, down the grassy slope, panting a little in the thick, humid air. I felt much better the moment I reached some trees and entered their shadow. I could still see the house and the yellow windows and the two cars, mine and theirs. Theirs was big and ominous and silvery-looking in the silvery streetlight. I stood silently in the leafy gloom, leaning against a maple tree, furtively spying, like some idiotic secret agent or an obsessed character out of Alfred Hitchcock.

This is ludicrous, I said to myself sternly. Go back to your car and drive home immediately. Instead I continued to stand there, sweating, staring so hard that my eyeballs hurt. After what seemed like a very long time, I heard voices on the street. The two people were returning to their car. They paused on the sidewalk for a moment, looking around. I couldn't hear what they were saying, but I felt sure they were speculating about me, why I had been sitting there alone in my car, why I had now disappeared. They looked right down into the park, but they couldn't see me. I saw them very clearly, though. A tall man with a long ponytail, wearing a suit and a tie, and a woman in high-heeled boots, a short skirt and a thin, sleeveless blouse. They didn't look particularly interesting or dangerous; they could have been anybody, a couple of teachers, a couple of doctors, a couple of actors or shoe-store clerks, out on the town.

Then I realized that they weren't by themselves. Eddy was

with them. They had been talking to him all along. He was standing on the other side of their car, leaning with his elbow against the hood. I saw his head and his white T-shirt and his lean waist. My shoulders gave a violent twitch and I silently cursed myself for leaving my car sitting there at the curb. Surely he was going to see it and recognize it immediately. Damn it, damn it. But he didn't seem to have noticed it; he never even glanced in its direction. And after all, it wasn't an unusual car, there were lots of others like it in the city. Sweat prickled at my hairline. Suddenly the night seemed hushed. All the people in the park had disappeared; it was empty except for me. I could hear the warm breeze faintly stirring the grass, and their voices up on the street, going on in a slow murmur, unexcited, unemotional. Several minutes passed. I couldn't make out what they were saying. They could have been talking about baseball or the stock market or the weather. It became wearying to stand so rigid and motionless. I yawned and water came into my eyes. As soon as they leave, I'm going home, I thought. This is absolutely ridiculous.

Then Eddy stepped forward, easily, almost casually, put his hand on the back of the man's head, and smashed his face down against the trunk of the car. It happened that quickly. There was a crunch of metal and a juicy, snapping noise as the man's nose broke. I had to blink to clear my vision; I couldn't believe I had actually seen that sudden, incomprehensible act. The woman in tall boots seemed as stunned as I. She didn't make a sound; she just stood there beside the car, her hands raised to her open mouth. The man staggered backwards, clutching his face as if to hold it together, and then fell to his knees. Black fluid oozed between his fingers and dripped onto the pavement. Eddy stood beside him, relaxed as a man waiting to cross the street, one hand on his hip, the gold of his expensive watch flashing on his wrist. He continued to speak quietly. I couldn't hear his words, only a rising inflection which seemed to indicate that he had asked a question. When he got no reply he lifted his foot and prodded the injured man's quivering body with the toe of his shoe, lightly, dangerously. At his touch the man gave a jerky nod, still covering his face with his hands. Then Eddy stepped around him and walked toward the woman. I felt the bark of the maple tree under my palm, coarse and rough and inexplicably cold. I was cold too, my lips were cold, and my fingers, and my arms. Although the woman shrank back against the door of the car with a whimper, there was no escape. Eddy pinched her nipples so hard that she winced, and yanked her forward until his face was half an inch from hers. She gave a muffled gasp of pain and tried feebly to push him away, but he wouldn't let go and when she tried to turn her head he just bent closer and murmured into her ear like a seductive lover. "Yes. *Yes!*" she cried, and then he released his hold so abruptly that she staggered and fell back against the door of the car. Without a backward look he turned and walked away. Shakily she began to rub her breasts, huddled against the car door, crying very quietly, as though she didn't want to attract his attention or give him any reason to come back. He might have heard her, but he didn't care. He kept walking, unhurried, like someone out for a stroll on a pleasant summer night. He went up the driveway, opened the side door and disappeared inside the house. The screen slapped gently shut behind him.

After a moment the woman stumbled over to the place where her companion was still crouching, bleeding onto the concrete with his hands over his face. "Let's get outta here!" she said hysterically. "Come on, come on!" She had to struggle to help him to his feet. He clung to her, trying clumsily to rise, smearing blood onto her pale blouse. "Oh, God," she said. "Oh, God, oh, God. Please. Watch it. No, here." "I'm okay," he said in a muffled voice. "I'm okay. Have you got a Kleenex?" There was blood all over the front of his shirt. "*No.* Let's go," she pleaded. "Oh, Jesus. Quick. Hurry." Somehow she got him into the front seat of the silvery car. He laid his head back and even from a distance I could see the wet black blood trickling across his temple into his ear. The woman got into the driver's seat, still sobbing breathlessly, and the car pulled away with a roar of tires.

After a while I climbed back up the slope. It was difficult to walk because my knees felt so stiff. I was breathing in short, shallow gasps; I couldn't seem to get enough oxygen into my lungs. My car was sitting by the curb, silent and pristine, gleaming peacefully in the moonlight. I felt as though years had passed since I left it there. My shoe slipped in something black and wet on the road and my stomach turned over with a sort of sick, queasy thrill. The scene kept replaying in my mind: the speed of it, the way the man's arms jerked outward when his face hit the hard metal, the way he staggered and fell, like a clown doing a pratfall at the circus. There was something horribly funny about it. I had to choke back a desire to laugh hysterically. Go home, go home, my brain repeated in a mechanical way. I unlocked my car door. Only one of Eddy's windows was still yellow. The other had gone dark, and as my eyes adjusted to that fact, I suddenly realized with a shock that Eddy was standing there, his form dimly visible within the dark window frame. He had taken his shirt off and his body looked pale and luminous behind the glass. He was staring at me, looking right at my face. It seemed useless to avoid his gaze. I stood helplessly beside my open car door, looking up at him, my skin burning with shame and fear. He had no expression at all, neither anger nor surprise nor pleasure. Perhaps he had seen my car after all when he was down on the street, perhaps he had been standing at his window waiting for me to appear. I tried desperately to think of some plausible reason for my presence there. An emergency? There was something wrong with my phone but I couldn't wait, I had to talk to him about—what? My mind wasn't working properly; it refused to come up with anything remotely believable. Could I say that I'd followed him as a joke, just for fun? It wasn't the least bit convincing, but it was the only thing I could think of. My mouth began to twist into a painful, foolish smile, I was going to shrug my shoulders and signal that I was coming up to explain.

Then suddenly he moved away from the window. At first I thought that meant he was going to come down. I left my car door open and sat sideways in the front seat. My smile stayed in place, quivering at the corners, making my mouth ache. Stupidly I tried to rehearse what I was going to say. My heart fluttered crazily in my chest. I thought I might faint, but I couldn't faint, I had to be alert, I had to be ready for him. Did he know I'd seen it all? Was he furious? Was he going to push my face through the windshield, throw me to the ground, punch me, kick me? What a fantastic idea, as if he would dare do such things to me. I sat there dizzy and panting, hot with embarrassment and terror, my stomach churning, waiting for him helplessly. But he didn't come. The street remained silent and empty. Far away in the distance a dog barked. After a while I realized he wasn't coming down.

I sat there for a long time after that. The heat went out of my face and body. I felt cool again, almost cold. The summery breeze drifted soothingly across my skin. There were a number of possibilities. He was so angry with me that he refused to acknowledge me or talk to me. Or he had someone up there with him, someone had been standing behind him in the room and had spoken to him, calling him away, making him forget all about me. Or he couldn't explain what he'd done and was going to pretend he hadn't seen me. Or he really hadn't seen me at all—hadn't noticed my car—had been staring in my direction with complete absence of mind, thinking of something else.

Or he was glad I had followed him, he found it amusing, he was glad I'd seen him smash a man's face. He saw no need to explain.

At about one-thirty his other window went dark. A short time after that, I drove away. It took me about twenty minutes to drive home. When I walked into my living room, numb and faint with exhaustion, the first thing I saw was the red light blinking on my answering machine. My throat went bone dry. I rewound the tape and listened. It was Eddy's voice. Of course. He sounded cheerful and ordinary.

"Hi. I guess you must be asleep. I thought we could have lunch on the *Caminito* tomorrow. We could pick up some food and a few bottles of wine and spend the whole day on the lake. Does that sound okay? Phone me in the morning."

I had no way of knowing when he had made that call. Was it possible that he had broken that man's nose, terrorized that woman, and then climbed his stairs and telephoned to leave me a light-hearted message?

Perhaps he had called before he looked out and saw me standing on the street below his window. Perhaps everything had changed after that. Perhaps he was through with me. Which would be fine. Which was what I really wanted, didn't I? Of course this thing with him, whatever it was, had to end. I had always known that. Surely now it was obvious that I shouldn't go on one moment longer. Reading about violence at the library was kind of titillating, but seeing it before my eyes was something entirely different, wasn't it? Surely I hated it, surely I wanted no part of it. I was leaning heavily on the telephone table. An image of his lightning swiftness filled my mind, I saw the dark, steamy street, his arm moving in a flash of dreamlike grace as he shoved that man's head downward into the silvery metal, the glittery spray of bloody drops flying upward. He hadn't given any warning; one moment he was standing there smiling and easy, and then came that sudden, perfect, lethal movement. He knew what he was doing; he was good at it. I always admired people who were good at things. I could still feel his come between my legs. I wanted him there in the room, standing behind me, pressing against me, his face against my neck, pulling up my skirt, I wanted his breath on me, I wanted to feel his rough, skilful hands. Excited tears dropped on my fingers and a hard, painful gasp came out of my throat. I could hardly believe a sound like that had come from me. I'm very tired, I told myself, I'm very, very tired.

I went up to my bedroom and lay down on the smooth, clean-smelling bedspread. I didn't even think of taking off my clothes. I just closed my eyes and fell into a deep black sleep.

Chapter Nine

Wʜᴇɴ I ᴏᴘᴇɴᴇᴅ ᴍʏ ᴇʏᴇs ᴀɢᴀɪɴ, bright sunlight was streaming into the room, although it seemed as if only a few minutes could have passed. His voice was present in my mind: "I called it the *Caminito*, after a street in Buenos Aires."

In a moment I was up on my feet, I was carrying a stool over to the closet and reaching up to the top shelf where the Buenos Aires book was concealed under a pile of boxes. I don't know why I hadn't thought of looking up Caminito before. Obviously there wasn't much chance that it would even be mentioned; after all, there were thousands of streets in Buenos Aires. But I sat on the edge of my bed and turned to the index. And of course it was there waiting for me—had there ever been any doubt? Caminito, pp. 42–43. I turned to a photograph I had glanced at several times before without really reading its caption: "The most bohemian alley in the city: Caminito in La Boca." A sombre grey sky rested above an unpaved thoroughfare lined with buildings and fences painted in brilliant primary colours, red walls, yellow window frames, blue fire escapes, here and there a splash of orange grillwork or green shingle. The colours were so bright and garish that they almost, but not quite, disguised the poverty: the shabby people standing on the corner bartering with a street vendor, the sooty stains on the painted bricks, the bits of trash on the ground, the faded laundry hanging over the balconies.

I sat there in a hot band of sunlight, sweating in my rumpled clothes from the night before, reading:

> In the 1800s the working-class barrio of La Boca developed into a busy dock area. Some of its oldest extant houses are made from sheet iron and tin originally removed from abandoned ships.... Argentine artist Quinquela tried to express La Boca's soul, adorning the alley called El Caminito with many art works and encouraging the locals to use brilliant colours to paint their own houses.... El Caminito comes to an end above a dilapidated part of the harbour which is sometimes pervaded by a powerful stench from the stagnant water.... Tourists may be disturbed by the presence of shabby neighbourhood urchins asking for pesos....

Suddenly the phone rang, shattering the peaceful silence like a scream. My heart was jolted and began to pound. I lay across the rumpled bed and groped for the receiver with a shaky hand.

"Hi," he said. "Did you have a good sleep?"

His voice sounded friendly and conversational. I strained to hear something else in his tone, some underlying hint of hostility or contempt. "Not really," I said cautiously.

"No?" he said. "It's too hot, I guess. I didn't sleep very well either."

"You didn't?"

"No," he said. "Did you get my message?"

"About going on the boat? Yes."

"I think boating is the only thing anybody should do today. It'll be cool out on the water."

I lay there on my stomach, gripping the phone, staring down at the corner of ivory-coloured carpet. I couldn't figure out what was going on. Had he really not seen me the night before? Or was he waiting for me to say something about it, to make it clear just how long I had been there and what I had seen, so he would know what explanations he had to give? My head was still aching, a dull pain behind my eyes. I was too tired and confused to think properly.

"Doesn't it sound like a good plan?" he said.

"What? . . . Oh, yes, it does."

"Should I pick you up in about an hour then?"

"Well . . . sure. Okay," I said. On impulse I suddenly asked, "Did you take care of your business last night?"

"Yes," he answered. "It's all taken care of. See you in an hour." Click. I held the receiver to my ear for another moment before hanging up. Then I turned over on my back and rested my shaky hand on my chest. The feel of my wrinkled silk blouse gave me a strange, half-frightened sense of unreality. It occurred to me that maybe I hadn't gone out at all last night, maybe I had fallen asleep right after we had sex, maybe everything after that had been a bewildering dream.

I went to take a shower.

THE SEAGULLS' WINGS WERE TIPPED WITH RED as they flew across the sun. They squawked noisily and dived over our heads, eager for the bread in our sandwiches.

"They're smart," Eddy said. "That's why they're big and fat."

He was lying on his back, his hands resting on his stomach. His sunglasses concealed his eyes. The boat rocked gently beneath us. We were a long way from shore; no land was visible in any direction. I saw us from a seagull's point of view: two tiny naked creatures floating on a little piece of wood, adrift in a great cold ocean.

As if he had looked into my mind, Eddy said, "I'll bet they hardly notice us at all. All they see is the food. We're just in the way of it."

Restlessly I turned over onto my stomach. I felt uneasy and irritable; my nerves were jumping. I kept remembering how he had stood at the window the night before, staring down at me unblinking for at least two or three minutes. It was impossible that he hadn't seen me. But he didn't say a word about it, not one word. He lay beside me, long and slender and golden, his chest rising and falling with his gentle breath, his eyes hidden.

Who was he? Who was he? Even his name, Eddy Corona, didn't seem real. I looked over my shoulder at my long, bony body. Surely he didn't find it beautiful, surely it wasn't what kept him interested. When was he going to reveal what he really wanted? He yawned and lazily stroked his chest.

"This reminds me of Greece," I said, although it didn't.

"Yes?"

"Have you ever been to Greece?"

"No, I haven't."

"It's beautiful," I said. "I've been there several times. My sister and I spent a summer there once when she was between marriages."

He laughed without moving or turning his head. "How many has she had?"

"Three, so far," I said. "I guess she'll keep trying till she gets it right. Have you ever been married?"

"Me? No."

"Are you sure? Not even one tiny little marriage that happened so long ago you've almost forgotten about it?"

"No," he said.

"Why not? You're attractive, you've got money, you like women, didn't you ever feel like getting married and having children and all that crap?"

"Didn't you?" he asked cheerfully.

"We're not talking about me," I said. "You're a Catholic, I imagine. Aren't you supposed to get married and reproduce?"

He was silent. I didn't want him to notice my agitation. I picked up my glass of white wine. It had been sitting in the sun for some time and had grown warm; its odour was so strong that it seemed to sear my nostrils. "Well?" I said. "Isn't that the way it's supposed to work?"

"I'm not Catholic," he said finally.

"Oh. I thought everybody in South America was Catholic."

"No." His voice was quiet.

I waited but he didn't say anything more. I took another sip of wine, staring at the delicate engraving on the side of the glass. In the sunny stillness you could hear the sound of waves lapping softly against the sides of the boat.

"What was Caminito like?"

"What?"

"Caminito. You said it was a street in Buenos Aires. Why did you name your boat after it?"

He thought about that for a moment. "Because it was such a pretty street. I guess that's why."

"It was pretty?" I wondered if there could be more than one Caminito in Buenos Aires.

"Yes."

"In what way?"

"In the evening, when the sun was setting, it looked like something out of a storybook. Sometimes no traffic would be allowed, and there were street performers who acted out plays right on the road and the sidewalk. The people who lived on Caminito could just walk out on their balconies and be the audience. After a little while you'd almost forget it was a play, you'd think things were really happening."

"What sort of things?"

He seemed half-asleep. He spoke in a slow, drowsy way. "Oh, I don't know, maybe this gorgeous lady would lean out her window and throw a rose to her secret lover. Or there would be a fight with guns, and the loser would die in a pool of blood on the road. Or a wild canary would land on your shoulder, and it would have a diamond in its beak. Maybe the captain of a ship would come back after many years at sea and the woman he loved would still be waiting for him, looking just the same, but he would find out she was only a ghost."

"Things like that happened on Caminito Street?"

"Sometimes in the evening when a play was on, you thought maybe they could."

I raised myself on my elbows to stare at him. He was like a magician in his power to transform himself. It was enthralling; he seemed to contain so many contradictions that I was filled with something like awe. I stared at the dark lenses over his eyes, watching my own dim reflection.

"You know that street pretty well," I said. "Did you live there?"

"Oh, no. But that part of the city was very colourful and *bohemio*, how do you say it, bohemian. We would go there all the time to eat pizza and listen to the tango singers."

"Tango singers? I thought the tango was a dance."

"Oh, yes, it's a dance, but there are songs with words too. Gardel, you've never heard of him? A great tango singer. He died young and thousands of weeping people met the boat bringing his body home to Buenos Aires harbour. He had a song about Caminito. It's sad. All tango songs are sad, even the happy ones. A man has been rejected by his love and he returns to Caminito, where he remembers how he used to walk happily holding her hand. He tells Caminito if she ever comes back, not to let her know that he cried for her. He's tired of living and he wants to lie down beside Caminito and let time erase him forever."

"I think I'd like to see Caminito someday," I said after a moment.

"I told you, we'll go there," he said. "We'll sail right into the harbour, right to the foot of the street, and we'll jump down onto the dock, and everybody will be there, and they won't believe their eyes."

"Yes," I said. "Let's do that."

IT WAS VERY LATE WHEN WE RETURNED to the marina. Stars filled the night sky and floated in the dark, glassy water. I jumped down onto the pier and caught the rope he tossed to me. Laughter and music echoed faintly across the quiet waves from a lakeside café on Toronto Island. Otherwise there was no sound at all except for our voices and our feet on the boards. I thought we were completely alone until suddenly someone spoke right behind us.

"Hi, Eddy."

We both turned at once, startled, and looked into the blank, pale eyes of a fair-haired man in a suit and tie. For a frightened moment I thought he was the same man I had seen on Eddy's street the night before. But of course he wasn't. He was bigger than that man, heavier, and his hair didn't look so long. And his face was intact.

"What are you doing here?" Eddy said without warmth.

"You weren't at home so I figured you'd be down here. I've been waiting an hour and a half." He gave me a curious, wary look, but Eddy didn't introduce him to me, and he didn't offer his name. He just nodded at me, staring hard as if he was memorizing my face. Then he turned back to Eddy with a businesslike air.

"So, anyway, our friend called me this morning. They want to make a deal."

"Good," Eddy said. He was moving around quickly, securing the lines that held the *Caminito* to the dock.

"It's big. Man, I think this is going to be a real big one."

"Relax," Eddy said.

"A hundred keys, he said!" The fair-haired man's voice squeaked with excitement. "By Friday, they want it. Can you get it by then?"

Eddy shrugged carelessly. "Sure." He climbed back onto the deck and began spreading a tarpaulin over the helm. "Tell them I need to see the money first. I see the money, and two days later they get it."

"Yeah, I told them that, and they weren't too happy. They said why the delay?"

"Tell them if they don't like it, they're free to go some-where else," Eddy said, coolly.

The fair-haired man opened his pale eyes very wide and his lips parted in disbelief. "Seriously?" he said. "You want me to tell them that?"

Eddy picked up his duffel bag and jumped lightly back onto the pier. "Yes, I want you to tell them that," he said.

The fair-haired man continued to stare for a moment, but then he resigned himself with a shrug. "Anyway, you know what he said? They've got this guy in Regent Park—"

"I don't need to know that," Eddy interrupted. "That's their business, it's got nothing to do with me."

The fair-haired man shook his head with a faint chuckle. "You're too much, man. Well, so, anyway . . ."

"Call me tomorrow and let me know what they want to do," Eddy said briskly, taking my arm. "If they want it by Friday, I need the money by Wednesday at the latest. Okay?" We started walking away down the pier, leaving the fair-haired man standing alone beside the *Caminito*, staring after us. The feathery ends of his hair looked white in the glow of light at the end of the dock.

"Who was that?" I asked. I was a little breathless because Eddy was walking so fast that it was hard to keep up with him.

"Oh, nobody," he said. "Just a guy. I do business with him sometimes."

I didn't say anything more until we were in his car, back-ing out of the parking lot. Then I asked, "What's a key?" I already knew the answer; I had learned all about keys in my research at the Metro Library. Key meant kilogram, as in kilo-grams of cocaine.

"A unit of measure," he replied glibly. "For merchandise."

I nodded thoughtfully, looking out at the dark, speeding road. "What merchandise?"

"Silver, in this case," he said.

It was almost insulting, how stupid he thought I was. "Why do they have to wait two days?"

"It's the only sensible way. They'll pay by bank draft or

certified cheque and it's a lot of money. You don't want to let the product go until you've had time to check their credentials and make sure they're okay."

"You sell people silver by the kilogram?"

He gave an easy laugh. "Not blocks of silver. But jewellery and *objets d'art*. In Argentina there are many *plateros*, I mean silver workers, and they make really beautiful things. Bowls and goblets and picture frames and figurines. We've sold a lot of silver in Canada because you don't have a tradition of silver-working here."

His lies always sounded so fluent and plausible that I would find myself smiling inwardly and admiring his agile brain. I could imagine him talking to the police, tossing off phrases like "*objets d'art*" and "tradition of silver-working." After a moment I said, "What do they do with the silver after they buy it from you?"

"They're retailers," he said. "They have their own clients."

"He mentioned Regent Park, though," I said innocently. "I can't imagine there'd be much market for silver in an Ontario Housing project, would there?"

He showed no sign of being disconcerted. "Oh, that was something completely different," he said breezily. "I don't know anything about it. Sandy just loves to talk, that's all."

"Sandy, was that his name? You didn't introduce him."

He glanced at me with a charming grin. "I was doing you a favour, believe me."

We drove in silence for a little while. He had turned north on Coxwell and rolled down his window. His hair lifted in the warm breeze. "I think it's a little cooler tonight," he said.

I looked out at the dark old houses clustered together behind small, cluttered yards. The night before, at the very same time, I had been pursuing him through the hot, dream-like streets. Apparently he was completely unaware of all that. It was beginning to seem more and more unreal to me.

"Were you thinking of coming over to my place tonight?" I asked.

He gave me a quick glance and said, "Don't you want me

to?" It was the first time all day that he had shown any uncertainty about anything.

"Well, I have an idea," I said. "I'd sort of like to go to your place tonight. Just for a change."

He looked at me. I turned and met his eyes. His expression didn't reveal anything at all. I tried to keep mine just as opaque.

"Oh, my place," he said finally. "You know what it's like. So bare. Not very nice."

"I don't mind that."

"There's not even a bed."

"I don't care," I said. "I sort of like the idea of a mattress on the floor. It'll be just like back in my university days."

"Did you sleep on a mattress then?"

"Well, no. But you know what I mean."

He laughed uneasily, but he couldn't keep arguing without beginning to sound as if there was something in his apartment that he wanted to hide. He had to give in. "Okay," he said. "If that's what you want."

"Yes, I feel like something different tonight." I sat back against the car seat and waited a moment, letting the dark breeze blow across my face. Then I said, "I'm in the mood to try something new. What do you think?"

He glanced at me with a one-sided smile. "Yes?"

"I didn't mean sexually. Although, if you have anything in mind, don't hesitate to mention it. But no, I meant something else." I looked straight through the windshield and spoke casually. "Remember once you said you could get some coke?"

He didn't answer. "Cocaine," I added helpfully. "Didn't you say you could get some?"

He was driving with one hand on the steering wheel, resting his other arm on the edge of the open window. He turned to look at me. I turned my head and looked back. His eyes were cool and clear.

"Did I say that?" he asked.

"I thought so. I feel like trying it tonight. I'm in the mood. Can you get some?"

After a moment he said, "I'm not sure."

I was still looking right into his clear, black, liquid eyes. I could have said, Look, I know you don't sell silver and I know exactly what you do sell, so let's drop this charade. But I just didn't want to say that. It would have been too easy, too boring. I didn't want to pin him down; I wanted him to be everybody he pretended to be. I wanted to go on with the game.

So I kept looking at him, waiting. Slowly he shifted his gaze back to the street. "This is important to you?" he said.

"Oh, it's not the end of the world. I'm just curious to see what it's like, that's all."

He nodded, thinking. Finally he made up his mind. "Well, maybe I can get some. I'll have to make a stop."

I settled back against the cool upholstery. "Great," I said.

Casually he switched on the right-turn signal and the flashing green light made a little clicking sound on the dashboard, filling up the silence. He didn't speak until we had driven several blocks north on Aird Street. Then he pulled over to the curb in front of a small, old apartment building made of stone. Through its front door you could see a narrow vestibule and a stairwell, dimly lit. Its name, "St. Regis Apts.," was painted on the glass in faded gold letters.

"Wait here," he said.

I sat with my hands in my lap and my head resting on the back of the car seat. Apparently St. Regis Apts. wasn't the kind of building where you had to buzz someone's number and speak into an intercom before being admitted. Eddy merely opened the glass door and went up the stairs, out of sight. Then the street was quiet except for the soft whish of the breeze through the tree branches. After a moment another car went past, moving so slowly that I gave a sharp sidewise glance. It was a heavy black sedan with two elderly people sitting in the front seat, and they were peering straight ahead, so absorbed in their own progress that they had no interest in either me or the St. Regis Apts.

Eddy came back out. I was disappointed. As he slid into the driver's seat I said, "They weren't home?"

He slipped his key into the ignition. "No, he was there."

"He was? You got it then?"

"Yeah." He pulled out into the street with a crackle of gravel.

I was incredulous. "What? You actually got it? But you were only gone about a minute and a half."

He shrugged and smiled dryly. "It doesn't take long."

I still couldn't believe it. I looked over my shoulder and watched the yellow door of St. Regis Apts. fade away through the still, dark trees. "So there's a drug dealer living in that building and you can show up at his—"

"He's just a guy I happen to know," Eddy said smoothly. "And sometimes he has some around. I wouldn't call him a drug dealer."

I looked at his calm profile. "Oh," I said.

I SAT ON ONE OF THE THREE CHAIRS in Eddy's kitchen. Behind me was the tall window where he had stood the night before, looking down at the street. He put a square of black plastic on the table in front of me. He had hung his green jacket on the back of another chair and he reached into the pocket and removed a little cellophane bag. I watched with vague excitement as he tapped out two small lines of white powder. Against the shiny black plastic each little grain seemed clear and distinct. He opened a kitchen drawer and handed me a straw.

"Here," he said. "You can use this."

"You go first."

"I don't want any."

I was surprised. "You don't? Why not?"

He shrugged. "I don't feel like it."

For some reason I felt a bit let down. But I took the straw. "What do I do?"

"Just put the straw in your nose and inhale."

"Just like in the movies."

"Yeah."

I hesitated. "You must think I'm a real bourgeoise," I said.
"Why?"

"Never to have done this before."

He shrugged again. "You weren't interested before."

Suddenly it seemed supremely silly—to snuffle some white powder up into your nose through a straw. I didn't really want to do it anymore, especially while he stood there and watched me. But I had asked him to get the stuff and he had got it, so I had to go ahead. I put the straw at the bottom of one line of powder and sniffed deeply. There was a tickling in my nostril and then a numbing sensation that seemed to reach up into my sinuses.

"Oh, it tingles," I said.

"Yeah, sometimes they cut it with lidocaine or something like that."

"They do? Why?"

He shrugged. "Who knows?"

"Shall I do it on the other side now?"

"Sure."

I sniffed some more powder into my other nostril with the same results. Then I laid the straw carefully across the black plastic. "Well," I said, "I don't feel any different."

He laughed. "It takes a few minutes."

"What's the difference between this and crack?"

He leaned back against the kitchen cupboard and folded his arms. His face looked yellowish and sharply shadowed in the harsh overhead light. "Crack is a little rock that you smoke. It's cheaper and it works faster."

"Maybe I should try that the next time."

He gave a slight smile. "Maybe." Then he moved away from the cupboard and reached out to take hold of my wrist. "Come on," he said.

"Where are we going?"

"To the bedroom."

"I don't even remember where it is."

"So I'm going to show you."

He led me through the large, shadowy, empty rooms. Our

feet squeaked on the bare floorboards. My nasal passages, my throat, and my lungs all seemed wide open, as though I was able to take in more oxygen than ever before. It was a pleasant feeling, but not earth-shattering or wildly intoxicating. Eddy let go of my wrist and slipped away. Then suddenly the walls were washed with soft pink light. We were standing in a high-ceilinged room that had nothing in it except a rumpled mattress, a tall lamp with a rosy shade, and in the corner a tape player and a pile of tapes.

"See?" he said apologetically, trying to fluff up a couple of crumpled pillows. "It's not very comfortable."

"It's fine," I said. "Simplicity. Sometimes simplicity is best."

He snapped a tape into the tape machine and in a moment soft music began to play, something vaguely Spanish, with guitars. Then he pulled his shirt over his head and dropped it to the floor. He turned to me, smiling, moving his torso lightly and half-teasingly in the easy rhythm. "Why don't you get undressed," he said.

I began to unbutton my blouse. "I really don't feel a thing," I told him. "Surely I should feel something by now, shouldn't I?"

"What do you want to feel?"

"Well, I don't know, I thought I'd get a huge rush of excitement or exhilaration or something. Isn't that supposed to happen?"

"Not necessarily."

"Maybe I didn't take enough."

"You had a good hit."

"Then why don't I feel anything?"

He stepped out of his jeans. His underpants looked startlingly white against his glossy olive skin. "Coke isn't for everybody," he said. "It's not so obvious like heroin."

"But the thing is, drugs never have any effect on me," I said. "They never do. That's why I've never been very interested in them. Maybe there's something wrong with me, I mean physiologically, because it's always like that. Drugs don't even touch me. I could be sitting with a bunch of other people all high on pot and laughing and having a great time and I wouldn't feel a thing. It's annoying in a way. I'll bet even heroin wouldn't affect me. I'll bet I could shoot a whole syringe into my arm and afterwards I'd feel the same as usual. Why do you think that is? Could there be a physiological reason why some people aren't susceptible to drugs? Maybe I should do some research on that. It would make quite an interesting paper. Although of course I'm not in a medical field, but you should never limit yourself. That's what my father always used to say. 'Don't limit yourself. There are no limits.'" I stopped for breath and suddenly became aware of my own voice, still echoing high up in the ceiling. "Am I talking a lot?" I said.

Eddy laughed. "It's all right," he said. He leaned over and kissed the side of my head. His lips brushed against my ear as lightly as the wings of a moth. "Do you want to try smoking some pot now?" he said.

"What? Are you kidding? Do you have pot too?"

"This friend of mine left a couple of reefers here the other night. Reefers, that's the right word, isn't it?"

"Yes, Eddy," I said in what I thought was an ironical tone. "That's the right word."

He didn't seem to notice any irony. "So?" he said. "Want to try it?"

"But I told you, it never has any effect on me."

He was smiling. "I think this will have an effect."

"Oh? Why?"

But he had slipped away again, he had disintegrated in the moonlit hallway. I sat down on the edge of the mattress. I felt alert, my senses were so acute that I could hear him opening and closing a drawer all the way at the other end of the apartment. When he returned he was carrying a little twisted cigarette and a lighter.

"I don't want to sound naïve, but is it safe to do this?" I asked. "Should you do two drugs at once?"

"People do it all the time," he said, sitting on the mattress beside me. "It's nothing." He lit the end of the cigarette and

sucked the smoke in sharply. Then he put his arm around my
neck and pressed his lips against mine and breathed the sweet,
pungent smoke into my mouth. "Isn't that nice?" he whispered.
My lungs were still so clear that the smoke seemed to fill them
completely in a second. His arms were around me and he kept
kissing me lightly on my face and body; his lips grazed my
skin like soft, soft wings.

After a while the room seemed to glow with candlelight,
even though we had no candles. I knew there weren't any, yet
I saw them and smelled them. Their bittersweet, sharp, ashy
aroma went up my nose and made me dizzy. He put a new tape
in the tape player and then crossed the shadowy floor toward
me. He seemed to move in slow motion, lithe as a cat. He
leaned over me with a gesture so round, fluid and complete
that it was like a film in slow motion, he cupped my head in
his hand, turning my face up to his. I gazed at him with dazzled eyes.

"Do you want some ice cream?" he asked softly.

"What?"

"Ice cream. Chocolate fudge ripple," he said.

"You have chocolate fudge ripple ice cream in your
freezer?" This struck me as irresistibly funny. There seemed to
be a pool of laughter bubbling around inside me and some of
it overflowed from my mouth.

"Yes, I do," he said. He was laughing too. "What's so funny
about that?"

"Nothing," I said. I tried hard to be serious, but it was
impossible. Another little laugh bubbled out. "Oh, yes. Please
bring me some right away," I said. "I'm starving."

As soon as he had drifted out of the room, I picked up one
of the pillows and buried my face in it to muffle my irrepress-
ible gasp of hilarity. I must be serious when he comes back, I
told myself sternly. I mustn't be smiling, there's nothing to be
smiling about. In a moment's time he was standing in front of
me, I felt his presence, I lowered the pillow cautiously to look
and my eyes popped when I saw that he was holding two cereal
bowls piled high with mountains of chocolate ice cream.

"Oh, my God!" I cried, unable to hold back a fresh burst of wild laughter. "What is it—a pint each? It's enough chocolate rippling futch...fudge, I mean, fudge, to feed a—a—what is it?—an army, that's it, to feed an army!"

He handed me what looked like a tablespoon. "You said you were starving, didn't you?" he reminded me.

I took a huge glob of ice cream and opened my mouth wide to receive it. It was so cold that it hurt my teeth, but every taste bud on my tongue seemed to swell with pleasure at the thick chocolatey flavour. "Mmmmmmmmmmmm," I said. "God, it's delicious."

He sat beside me on the mattress, eating from his bowl with his own big spoon, his legs crossed, his bare knee touching mine. The tape player continued to fill the softly glowing room with gentle guitars. I felt like a child, sitting with my special playmate, and it was a long time ago, and I was so young that I didn't even know how many things were wrong with the world. Nothing was wrong with it at all. We were sitting there together, he and I, spinning on a beautiful little shining planet, and perfect happiness was possible, all sorrows could be healed and all fears stilled. I reached out and put my hand on his shoulder. His skin felt as fine as silk. "I adore you," I said. He wouldn't remember it the next day and if he did I could always deny saying it. Then I looked down at my bowl and saw that all my ice cream was gone. It amazed me that I had eaten such a huge mound of ice cream so fast.

Gently he pushed me down onto the mattress. I looked past his shoulder. The roof seemed to be gone and I was able to see the night sky, it was very warm and close to me, it was a deep purple colour, broken here and there with little white stars that gave off a fragrance like incense as they burned. His body hovered above mine and then he put his ice-cold mouth over my nipple. A delicate, fiery, icy chill went down into my groin and made the tips of my fingers tingle. "Oh, my God," I said. "This is heaven, it must be heaven." He slid into me as easily as a key into a lock, he opened me to all the sweet warm night, and nothing was difficult, nothing was an effort, our bodies fit together like pieces of a jigsaw puzzle, he stayed inside me, we were joined so completely that we would never have to separate, I would never leave him, and he would never leave me.

Chapter Ten

I WAS HAVING A DREAM IN WHICH AN ALARM clock kept ringing and wouldn't stop, even when I threw it onto the floor and smashed it. Then I became fuzzily aware of Eddy's lean brown back, gleaming in the white light from the uncurtained window. He was on the telephone and his voice was crisp and authoritative.

"Look, how many times do I have to tell you, don't use this number. Call me on the beeper, and I'll call you back. Yeah, so, if I don't, then wait a half-hour and call the beeper again. I don't want you to use this fucking number and this is the last time I'm telling you. Emergency, what emergency? These guys aren't Jesus Christ and the Virgin Mary, they're a couple of *cabrones* with some money in their pockets. Bums, bums! Yeah, that's what I said. Shut up, I don't want to know that. I'm not gonna talk anymore on this line. I'll call you in half an hour. You'd better learn to stay cool or you're not going to last very long at this level."

He ended the conversation abruptly, slamming down the receiver. Then he turned to look at me. Instantly I closed my eyes, gave a muffled moan, and turned over on my side as if I were only half-conscious. The truth was, I felt only half-conscious. After a moment he leaned down and put his face close to mine. His hair smelled of marijuana. "Sorry, did I wake you up?" he whispered.

"Huh?" I raised a languid hand and rubbed my face with a feeble show of drowsiness. "What? What time is it?"

"It's about eleven o'clock."

"Eleven? You're kidding. I can't believe it's that late."

"Are you hungry?"

"I'm not sure. I don't think I've digested all that ice cream yet," I said with a weak laugh. His face was still close to mine and the pale light from the window glistened around his head like a halo. It hurt my eyes to look at him.

"I have to go out for a while," he said.

"Do you?"

"Yeah, why don't you get dressed and come with me? We can go have breakfast at Fat Joey's."

"I feel kind of tired," I said. "I think I just want to lie here awhile longer."

"Don't you want breakfast?"

"Why don't you go and do whatever it is you have to do and then come back and pick me up? Maybe I'll feel hungrier by then."

He looked at me, leaning on his arm. His eyes were very clear and blank. I thought he was going to argue with me. Then he merely shrugged and stood up. "Okay."

He went into the bathroom and in a moment I heard the sound of the shower. I lay on my back and looked at the window. I could see a patch of sky, dull and pale, with dirty grey smudges of cloud across it. In my mind I rose to the ceiling and looked down on myself; I saw a naked woman who was getting old, lying on a rumpled mattress in an empty room.

I watched him get dressed. He became so absorbed in the process that he seemed to forget my presence. For several

moments he stood inside his walk-in closet, studying its contents intently. I could see his reflection in the mirror on the back
of the door. He took down a hanger with a pale green shirt, then
put it back again. He fingered a pair of grey pants, then pushed
them aside. Finally, after a lot of careful deliberation, he chose a
loose, dark blue shirt with full, silky sleeves and a pair of soft
brown trousers that fit sleekly over his hips. Once he had
smoothed the shirt-tails into the belt and zipped up the fly, he
studied the effect in the mirror. He didn't ask me what I thought.
He simply faced himself head-on, frowning thoughtfully as he
evaluated the effect he made. Apparently the ensemble passed
inspection because he turned around and walked briskly out of
the closet, snapping his fingers, impatient to be on his way.

"I'll be back in about an hour," he said. "What are you
going to do, go back to sleep?"

"Yeah, for a little while, maybe," I said.

He was standing in the bedroom doorway. "Sometimes
people feel a little down after the coke wears off," he told me.
"It'll pass."

"I'm fine," I said.

His quick footsteps faded on the stairs. When I heard the
sound of his car starting, I threw back the thin sheet we had
slept under and crawled over to the window just in time to see
him pull out of the driveway and move off down the grey,
deserted street. Then the silence dropped down around me
and I felt the resounding emptiness of all those bare, high-
ceilinged rooms.

The closet door was standing ajar. I walked over and
looked inside. It was big enough to be used as a small bedroom, and its interior looked like something you'd see only in
a men's shop: rows and rows of expensive jackets and slacks,
hanging side by side in perfect precision, shelves piled with
neatly folded shirts of various colours, dozens of pairs of
gleaming shoes arrayed in order from dark to light. I had
never seen him wear a hat, but there were several hats sitting
together on a top shelf—a wide-brimmed fedora with a rich,
dark band, a dashing white panama, a velvety brown slouch

hat, even a big floppy straw hat with an emerald green ribbon around it. The smells of leather and cologne and costly fabrics filled my nose and made my head spin with amazement. At that point I had known him for about three months and although he always dressed well, I would never have guessed that he had the consuming interest in clothes which that closet seemed to indicate. In my company he tended to wear jeans, loose shirts, sweaters, loafers. Where did he go in those three-hundred-dollar Italian shoes and silken Armani jackets? I remembered our shopping spree on the first day we had spent together. Apparently he did that sort of thing frequently: bought armloads of merchandise just for the satisfaction of bringing it home and storing it in his closet.

There was a small bureau at the back. It contained a drawer of underwear, all neatly folded and arranged, a drawer of socks, and a drawer of linen handkerchiefs, each one hand-embroidered with a graceful letter *E*. On the top of the bureau was a chest which opened to reveal numerous velvet compartments holding jewellery: gold cufflinks, tie clips, rings, medallions, and expensive watches. Even my father might have been impressed by such opulence. But it existed in an apartment almost completely devoid of furniture, whose occupant slept on a mattress on the floor.

I stepped back and caught a glimpse of myself in the long mirror on the closet door. I looked awful. My hair was standing up at the back, my eyes were smudged with mascara, my lips were pale and dry, and there was a big greenish-purple bruise on my flabby white thigh. It was impossible to believe I belonged in the same space as that closet with its elegant contents. He had looked at my white face and chapped lips and black-ringed eyes and he had smiled and acted charming, as always. What did he really want from me, what was he after? Right at that moment he had to be driving down the street, looking regretfully at all the long-legged girls in shorts and halter tops, thinking of what he was missing while he spent all his time romancing me. Well, I decided suddenly, this is it. You don't have to miss anything any longer, pal.

I went into the bathroom and had a shower. As the soft, fresh water rained down over my sticky face, I made some plans. I resolved to take a taxi home, change my clothes, and call my travel agent to book my trip to France. After that I was going to drive to Azure Lake and stay for a few days. The thought of Azure Lake calmed me at once and made me happy. How wonderful it will be, I thought, how wonderful to be at Trewithen again, all by myself. I seemed to have tears in my eyes, or maybe it was only water from the shower.

As I got dressed, I heard children screaming and laughing in the street below, their feet slapping against the pavement as they ran past. I began to feel better. I thought I would leave him a note. Thanks for everything. It was great fun but we both knew it would have to end sooner or later. I'm leaving to spend the summer in France so I think it would make sense to say good-bye now. That's what I was going to write. I started searching around for a pencil and paper.

His kitchen cupboards were immaculately neat and rather bare. He had a set of plain white dishes with four place settings. He had some wine glasses, some coffee mugs, salt and pepper shakers, nothing unusual or suggestive. He had a silverware drawer. Another drawer was empty except for several spoons of various sizes. His fridge contained a wine bottle, half full, a small carton of milk, a shrivelled lemon, a jar of dill pickles, and an almost-empty carton of chocolate fudge ripple ice cream. Above the fridge was a little cupboard which I had to stretch up to reach. It held a couple of large boxes of baking soda and several more boxes of something called Fioresca Laxante. I took one down and opened the top. It was half full of a thick white floury substance. For a moment I thought it was a drug of some kind, perhaps a different type of cocaine. But it had a sort of chalky scent and tasted sweet. Then suddenly it hit me: *laxante*—surely the Italian or Spanish word for laxative. So he had some boxes of an exotic Italian laxative in the cupboard above his fridge.

The sun had begun to shine. The kitchen window was open and a soft summery breeze drifted into the room, filled with the sounds of chirping birds and fluttering leaves and the far-off whir of a lawn mower. I stood in the same place he had stood, looking across to the curb where my car had been sitting two nights before. There was no way on earth that he could have missed seeing me. He had seen me, and then turned away and shut off the light.

Behind me the whole apartment was steeped in airy, tranquil silence. No clocks ticked, no music played, nothing stirred. He had no pictures—no family photographs, no paintings, no postcards, no cartoons. He had no books or magazines or old newspapers. There were no letters, no grocery lists, no notes of any kind. There was something almost eerie about the lack of personality in those vacant, sunny rooms.

I walked across the polished floorboards, my feet clomping noisily in the stillness. There was another closet in the living room. I opened it. It gaped dimly, revealing his green jacket, another jacket of soft black suede, a long fleecy winter coat covered with plastic, and a pair of tall boots made of rich, reddish leather. Period. That was it. I had gone through the entire apartment and found nothing interesting, nothing significant except a surfeit of expensive wearing apparel. "Damn you!" I said out loud.

Beneath my own voice came a sound close behind me, like someone's shoe scraping on wood. I almost jumped out of my skin. I thought for a moment that he had come back, but when I swung around I caught just a flicker of something at the hall doorway, so brief, so fleeting it was hard to be sure I had really seen anything at all. But surely I hadn't imagined it, surely the door to the stairwell had been open a crack, and someone had been standing there, looking in. I stood frozen for a moment, listening with all my energy, trying to hear through my pounding heartbeat. Again I wasn't sure, but I thought I could make out the faint, faraway sound of a squeaking stair as someone tried to go down very slowly and very quietly.

I walked over to the door and threw it open. I don't know what possessed me. For all I knew someone could have been waiting with a knife or a gun. But I didn't stop to think about any melodramatic possibilities like that. I just had to see if someone was there. The stairwell was very dim, but a thin light filtered in from the door at the bottom. Someone was standing halfway down, leaning back against the wall.

"Did you want something?" I cried shrilly.

The person didn't move or speak. Suddenly a big black newspaper headline flashed through my mind: "SLAYING ON WITHROW AVENUE. Police speculate that a drug deal gone wrong led to the grisly murder of Grace Tremain, daughter of the late liquor magnate, L.T. Tremain. . . ."

"I can see you standing there," I said. "What do you want?"

At last the figure straightened and moved away from the wall. I saw that it was a woman. She was wearing a very short skirt that barely covered the tops of her long, thin legs. I couldn't see her face but she had a big bush of short, curly hair. Relief made my knees go limp. I suppose it's foolish, but you don't think a woman is going to kill you. And then I thought, Oh. A woman. Of course.

"Are you looking for Eddy?" I said in a high, sharp voice. "He's not here right now."

She didn't answer, just stood there.

"He'll be back later," I said. "If you want to wait."

She made a slight movement with her shoulders, as if she was about to turn and walk out without speaking. Then she changed her mind. "No, thanks, honey," she said. "I got better things to do than wait for him." She had a rich, low Spanish voice with a sort of sexy huskiness in it.

"Well," I said into the gloom, "I can tell him you came by. Should I ask him to give you a call?"

I felt that she was smiling. "Don't bother," she said.

"Oh, it's no bother," I said quickly. "What's your name?"

She crossed her arms over her chest, shifting her weight from one foot to the other. "What's yours?" she asked after a moment.

"Mine? Why?"

"Why do you want to know mine?"

I laughed harshly. "Well, isn't this getting a bit ridiculous?" I said. "I thought I could tell him you'd stopped by, that's all. Believe me, I don't care who you are in the least. If it's such a big secret . . ."

"I'm a friend," she drawled. Her fuzzy black bush of hair was outlined by an aureole of white light. She cocked her head to one side. "Don't worry, honey," she said. "Not that kind of friend."

My breath felt hot in my lungs. "I'm not worried."

"Good," she said.

There was a brief silence, broken only by the sound of a step squeaking under her high-heeled shoe. "Because with Eduardo, let me tell you, there's no point in worrying," she added finally.

"Oh? Have you known him long?"

"Nobody knows Eduardo very long," she said.

"Oh?"

"That's right," she said. "'Oh' is right." She waited another moment, her shadowed face lifted toward me. "How do you like his . . . uh . . ." She waved her arm to indicate the rooms behind me. ". . . décor? Like he thinks he's gonna be leaving in a hurry, huh?"

She laughed. I couldn't help giving a dry smile in return.

"But he's a real attractive guy, huh? Man or woman, it don't matter to Eduardo, he knows how to get through. He just turns on the charm like a light switch. And off again, too. One time I come over and there's this little chickie sitting right here on the steps crying like she's gonna die. Tits big like watermelons. But Eduardo was tired of her already. Slammed the door in her face." She tilted her head back and smiled at me, waiting for me to react. I stared at her blankly.

"That wouldn't be you though, would it, honey?" she said. "You're never gonna be sitting on the stairs bawling over somebody."

"You don't think so? Why?"

"You're old enough to know better. Plus I can see you're

not the type." There was a brief silence. Then she said, "You're the rich one, aren't you?"

The words sank slowly into my mind. "Did he say I was rich?" I asked.

She shrugged. Suddenly she turned and clattered down the remaining stairs and yanked open the door. Sunlight and warmth poured across the threshold, and I saw that she was not as young as I had thought. She stood there squinting in the sudden brightness, pursing her lips thoughtfully. There were lines around her eyes and at the corners of her lips. "Celeste," she said. "You can tell him that Celeste said hello." The door banged shut behind her.

I went to the kitchen window, thinking I might get a better look at her, perhaps find out whether she had a car, or what direction she took. But she wasn't on the street. She had already gone. I sat down in one of his three chairs. Celeste, I thought. The things she had said kept chiming in my brain. Nobody knows Eduardo very long. Don't worry, I'm not that kind of friend. He just turns on the charm like a light switch. Man or woman, it don't matter to Eduardo, he knows how to get through. You're old enough to know better. You're the rich one, aren't you? You're the rich one.

He wasn't back in an hour. He wasn't back in two hours. It was early afternoon when he finally walked in, breathless and apologetic. I had been sitting at the kitchen table all that time. I hadn't listened to the radio. I hadn't written a note telling him good-bye. I hadn't moved.

"I'm really sorry," he said, putting some fragrant bags on the kitchen counter. "Are you ready to kill me? I got take-out because I knew you must be starving."

I stared at him. "Celeste said to tell you hello."

He was always good at keeping any sign of surprise or alarm from showing on his face. He simply looked at me, as if he was waiting with no great interest for me to elaborate.

"She said that you and she had a wild affair once," I told him. "She said neither one of you will ever forget it."

He smiled dryly. "Celeste said that?"

"Yeah. She told me all about you. Everything."

"Everything?"

"Every single thing."

"Such as?"

"Everything about you. All your women. All your secrets."

He leaned back against the kitchen cupboard. "Celeste doesn't know my secrets," he said. "So how could she tell them?"

I stared at him. In spite of everything I was still drawn to him, I felt his warmth, the magnetic pull of his body, all the way across the room.

"Does anybody know your secrets?" I said.

He shrugged, still smiling.

"She said, 'Nobody knows Eduardo very long.' What did she mean by that?" The bag on the counter was giving off a strong smell of eggs and fried potatoes. It made me sick to my stomach.

"Oh, well, who can guess?" he said. "Celeste likes to talk."

"Does she? I must say I didn't notice that. It was an effort to get two sentences out of her. Who is she?"

He shrugged. "She was my landlady." When he saw my expression he gave a sudden burst of laughter. "That's right. She lives over on Jones Avenue and when I first came to Toronto I had a room in her house. We've kept in touch, I see her once in a while. She's okay."

I decided to let it go. After all, Celeste's identity wasn't the important issue. I looked at his open, innocent face. "Did you tell her I was rich?"

His smile faded. He stared at me wordlessly.

"Because I'm not, you know," I said. "My father was rich but he made some bad business decisions before he died. All I have is a bit of property and a small trust fund. I'm not a big booze heiress. So if that's what you thought, you were mistaken."

He didn't speak. He was leaning on one elbow, looking at me with an unreadable expression.

"I hope you're not too disappointed," I said. In the silence I became aware of the soft hum of the refrigerator.

"Maybe you'd like to break it off now?" I said. "You can tell me. It's not going to break my heart."

He straightened and stared at me in disbelief. "Do you want to break it off?" he said.

"I don't know. It guess it would probably be the best thing, don't you think?" I stood up awkwardly, stumbling against the legs of the chair. "I wish you'd just tell me straight out, what is it you want from me, anyway?" I waited but he didn't speak. "No, you won't tell me, will you? I really have to wonder why I'm keeping on with this, it's insane. We have absolutely no common ground, it's like we're from different planets! And I don't know one bloody thing about you, I look around this place and you don't even have a photograph of anybody! Not one lousy photograph! I've never met anybody you know until today!"

He gave an abrupt laugh. "I've never met anybody you know either," he said. "Your sister was in town and you didn't even tell me until after she was gone."

"Well," I said, trying to think of a reply. After a moment I came up with one. "I just wanted to keep you to myself."

"Yeah, sure," he said.

A car went by on the road outside. I looked down at the smooth, empty tabletop.

"You told me you work in an office," he said. "But that's a lie. You're a professor at the university."

I cleared my throat. "How do you know? Did you read about that in the same place where you read that my father was rich?"

I was looking down at the table and I didn't hear him move but all at once he was standing in front of me. He took my hand and pressed it against his groin. I felt the hot, hard flesh through the smooth fabric of his pants. "This is our common ground," he said. I tried to take my hand away but he wouldn't let me. His eyes were so close that I saw myself dissolving in their black depths. His belt rubbed against my diaphragm and he pushed me backward with his body until the edge of the table cut into the backs of my thighs.

"So who cares about all that other shit?" he said. "We have this. Isn't it good enough?"

His shirt was hot under my arms. I felt the solidity of his shoulders, the nervous elasticity of his back, his tongue flickering against mine. It wasn't like the night before; perhaps it was only with the help of drugs that you were able to sweep aside all the barriers and feel such perfect completion. I was aware of everything that kept us apart: layers of clothing, belts and metal buckles, tense, resistant muscles, and suspicion, distrust, inability to believe, the tangle of his lies and mine. But he pressed against me, reached inside my clothes and touched me until I couldn't see, kissed me until I had no breath in my lungs, and I forgot everything else.

"Yes, yes, all right," I gasped. "Yes, it's good enough."

THAT NIGHT WE SAT on my upper balcony watching the glamorous shifting colours of the city in the dark water. It was another hot, still evening and many people were strolling on the shadowy boardwalk, trying to catch a breeze off the lake. We sat quietly, barely speaking. I had put on a loose, sleeveless dress and he was wearing a pair of white shorts that made a patch of luminous ivory against the darkness of his body, as though he were an image in a photographic negative. His bare feet lay in my lap and I rested one hand across his ankles. Even the pressure of his heels on my thighs, even the feel of his ankle bone under my fingers gave me pleasure. Down on the beach a man called out across the sand, "Dottie! Do you want a hot dog?" and the voice and words filled me with sensuous pleasure, as though they were music. I suddenly knew I wasn't going to France that summer. I gave up France in a moment, without regret. Instead I thought of Trewithen: its dreamy beauty and seclusion, the shadowy verandahs filled with fragrant breezes, the tall pines against a black sky dusted with stars, the night broken by a solitary loon cry, the long days of buttery light, the cool water against your sunburned skin, the hot taste of barbecued meat and the smooth taste of wine, the scent of trees across your face as you slept. I always wanted to keep it to myself; I never wanted to share it with anybody. But for some mad, inexplicable reason I wanted to show it to him.

"Are you going to take a summer holiday this year?" I asked casually.

He didn't move. When he spoke he sounded half-asleep. "I don't know," he said. "I haven't really thought about it." Sometimes when he was tired or excited, his Spanish accent became a bit more pronounced, and then his voice made me think of palm trees, dusty streets, hot pink neon, Latin rhythms.

"I have a cottage up north," I said.

"Yes?" He didn't change his position or his tone, but I had the impression that he had suddenly become alert.

"I've told you about it before."

"Yes, a little. Azure Bay, isn't it?"

"Azure Lake. The cottage has been in my family for years," I said. "My grandfather built it in 1929. He was the one who named it Trewithen. I told you that it means 'place of trees' in the old Cornish language, didn't I? My grandfather was born in Cornwall, England, and when he was a boy he always admired a country house in his neighbourhood called Trewithen. It was a big beautiful estate. My grandfather used to tell everybody that someday he was going to have his own Trewithen. Of course people laughed at him because he was the son of an unemployed tin miner, so no one thought he was going anywhere. But they should have known him better. My grandfather always did exactly what he said he was going to do."

"I think I saw some pictures in your photo albums," he said after a moment. "It has big porches, and trees all around it?"

"That's right. It's twenty miles from the nearest town."

There was a brief silence. I could hear his light, steady breathing. "It's a three-hour drive from here," I said.

"Yes?"

I looked across the hot, shimmering lake to the spire of the CN Tower. "I thought maybe you'd like to go there with me," I said.

"Yeah," he said immediately. I turned to look at him. He was smiling.

I stroked his foot. "Yeah, you would?"

"Yeah," he said. "I would." Suddenly he reached over and took my hand and began to swing it lightly back and forth between our two chairs. I don't know why but all at once there was a warm mist in my eyes, so that I could hardly see his face.

"Are you sure?" I said. "It doesn't sound too dull?"

"It sounds *magnífico*," he said.

Chapter Eleven

My MOTHER BOUGHT SEVEN NEW bathing suits every year. That way she could wear a different one for each day of the week. I can see her vividly, so sharply it's as though her image has been recorded on a film that I can replay in my mind. She wades into the bright, shallow water and methodically wets herself all over. Then she walks back across the sand, glittering with droplets that look like thousands of tiny diamonds, and settles into her reclining beach chair, prepared to lie in the sun for several hours. She is "working on her tan." There is an ice bucket beside her, filled with Coke bottles, so that she can replenish the drink in the tall slender glass that always sits within easy reach on a round white table. She has a stack of movie magazines and she reads her way through them as if she is studying for an exam, starting at the top one on the pile, frowning thoughtfully over stories like IS TIPPI HEDREN THE NEW GRACE KELLY? and PAUL NEWMAN: SEXIEST MALE

STAR? YOU DECIDE! Occasionally she is moved to read something aloud.

"Listen to this. 'Does love really conquer all? This is a question which Liz and Dick will have to ponder once the first flames of passion have died down and they have to contemplate the two shattered families they have left behind.'" She shakes her head disdainfully. "She hates to be called Liz, you know. Her friends all call her Elizabeth. I don't think she ever loved Eddie Fisher anyways. He was just there to pick up the pieces after Mike Todd died. I knew it wouldn't last. Richard Burton is a hundred times sexier. Don't you think? Which one would you pick? Huh?"

I'm lying on my stomach on a beach towel, reading one of my favourite books, *Tess of the d'Urbervilles* perhaps, and I can't bear to be interrupted by my mother's inane remarks. "Mom, please!" I cry in a tone of furious impatience. "I'm reading, do you mind?"

My mother rolls her eyes. "Just answer one question," she insists, holding up the magazine to show me a picture of Liz Taylor sitting on Eddie Fisher's lap and staring up coquettishly at an unsmiling, ironic-looking Richard Burton. "Which one is sexier? Be honest."

"I don't know and I don't care!"

Undeterred she turns and shows the magazine to Leslie, who is in the process of building an elaborate sandcastle with many towers, just so she can knock it down and stomp on it. "Les, what do you think?"

Leslie squints at the picture. "Wel-l-l-l," she says, considering the question intently, "Eddie Fisher is kind of handsome."

"Really? You think he's handsome?"

Hearing my mother's tone, Leslie is quick to qualify her opinion. "Kind of handsome, I said. But not very. He's not nearly as handsome as Rock Hudson."

My mother smirks scornfully, leaning back in her chair. "Rock Hudson. What a pretty boy. No, thanks. But Richard Burton, now. He's a *man*. Look at that face. And what about his voice? You could go for him for his voice alone."

The film winds down: we are three small figures on the beach in the fading light, the sun has fallen behind the western point, sending out a last few scarlet flashes before it disappears into the silky dusk. Faint lights appear on the other side of the water, and a magical stillness settles over us; we are timeless, we will never leave that beach. My father has just arrived from the city, he comes down the half-buried stone steps, the sleeves of a white sweater tied around his neck. He is in a good mood, so everything is all right. He walks to the end of the pier and stands with his hands on his hips, staring out across the glassy water. He turns, he says, "How about a row?"

Cut to the next scene. My mother sits in the prow, wrapped up in a jacket, her blonde hair turned white and her lips turned shiny black by the ghostly twilight. My father sits in the stern, manipulating the oars with no apparent effort. The quiet is broken only by the squeaking of wood in the oar-locks and the ripple of silvery water around the sides of the boat. He rows to the exact middle of the lake, and there we rest, the shore far away on all sides, dark and mysterious, twinkling with flecks of white light which seem to be mere reflections of the stars. In Port Azure, twenty miles away, they are setting off fireworks for Dominion Day. Because of the distance we cannot hear the gunpowder, we only see a soundless cascade of coloured sparks spraying across the sky and falling into the water. Leslie is so excited that she forgets where she is and tries to jump up in the boat, making it rock precariously, causing my mother to clutch the sides in terror, and I say, "Leslie, don't be so stupid, sit down!" but my father laughs and shifts his weight around so the boat rocks even harder. He always thinks Leslie is so funny. And then we row back to the pier, and we can see Trewithen on the cliff up above the beach, the long dark western lawn dotted with white clover, lamps in the windows, and on the verandah, behind the screens, china and a pale blue tablecloth are softly glowing in the light of two tall white candles, where the maids have set the table for dinner.

MOST OF THE TIME IT ISN'T LIKE THAT, of course. We are lying on the beach and my father appears at the top of the stone steps and calls down, "Vivian! Our guests are here." And my mother lowers her copy of *Silver Screen* with a heavy sigh and mutters, "Oh, boy."

The truth is we aren't often alone at Trewithen. Carloads of guests drive up from Toronto, and more appear from cottages down the road or on the other side of the lake. A portable bar is set up on the lawn and my father has the stereo moved out onto the verandah. He hates rock music and will never allow it to be played in his hearing. Soft, romantic songs like "Stardust Melody" by Nat King Cole and "All the Way" by Frank Sinatra drift down to the beach, putting people into a trance as they swim. The cottage echoes with the sounds of laughter and running feet and tinkling glasses.

I HAVE RETREATED TO MY ROOM, hoping my absence won't be noticed, but just as I am beginning to relax there is a sudden sharp knock on the door. I shrink down in silence, staring into the pages of my book, barely breathing.

"Grace." It's not a question; it's a word, my name, spoken flatly.

I wish I didn't have to answer, but I'm afraid to remain silent.

"I'm not feeling very well," I say in a soft voice, trying to sound weak and ill. "I'm just lying down for a little while."

He walks into the room and shuts the door behind him. He is wearing an elegantly loose blue shirt and white shorts, his legs are shapely and freckled, his hair gleams richly against the dark wood. I lie on the bed, holding my book like a shield, curled up and trembling like a scruffy little animal in the light of his bright, merciless eyes. "What are you doing?" he says. "We have company."

"I told you I don't feel well!" I cry. "My throat is sore and I think I have a temperature!"

"Grace, are you ever going to grow up?" His tone makes it clear how infinitely tiresome and dreary he finds me. "When you have guests you don't run to your room and hide like a scared mouse in a hole."

"I didn't invite them!" I hiss. "They're your guests, why can't you entertain them?"

Cold blue flames seem to flare up in his eyes, but he doesn't move and when he speaks he sounds very quiet and calm. "Since when do you talk to me like that?" he says. "Get on your feet."

I lie rigid, my head pressed into the pillow, staring at him.

"Didn't you hear me? I said stand up," he repeats in the same low, uninflected way.

My father is not a big man and I have never in my life seen him hit anyone or even touch anyone roughly. Nevertheless I am terrified of him; I feel that some kind of unspeakable violence might erupt from him at any moment. Without moving my eyes from his face I slowly straighten my legs and swing them over the side of the bed. He waits, motionless, his arms folded. Wretched tears fill my eyes and run down my cheeks.

"Oh, yes," he says with a sarcastic smile. "Cry. Just like a woman. What a good way to get out of a dilemma."

My knees are trembling and I have to summon all the strength I possess to keep back a sob. I feel how dull and clumsy my brain is, I loathe my ugliness and weakness. The goal is to be cold and elegant and ironic like him, exactly like him.

"I wonder sometimes, can you really be my daughter?" he says. "You're nothing like me." He waits a moment. Then he goes on in a soft, slow drawl. "Of course there's the red hair. I guess that's mine. That's the only thing you got from me."

Tears and mucus smear my face. I can't look at him. I look down through a hot blur at the dirty toes of my sneakers.

"All you ever want to do is sit alone with those books," he says. "There's nothing wrong with being well-read, but there are other things in life more important, aren't there? Well? Don't just stand there like a simpleton, answer me. Aren't there?"

I continue to stare hopelessly at my feet. Big wet drops fall on my blouse. "Yes," I say.

"Name some other things that are more important."

It's torture. I can't think, my mind is blank.

"Well?"

I rack my brains trying to figure out what I could say to satisfy him. It's impossible. Finally I have to shake my head. "I don't know," I blubber.

"You don't know," he says. "What a clever answer, Grace."

In the brief silence that follows, I can hear distant laughter and splashing from the beach. "But I don't think you're quite as stupid as you seem. What are you going to do with your future?" he says. "Do you think that just because I have money you never have to make the slightest effort?"

"No!" I cry.

"Well, what are you going to do? If you were a son you could go into the business, but as it is, that's never going to happen. Women stink in business and the few who don't stink stop being women and turn into aggressive witches. I hate that. I don't care what anybody says."

"I don't want to go into the business," I mumble.

"Of course you don't, because you don't have the right brain for it. You women, once your hormones take over, your intellects go right out the window. But what *can* you do? That's the big question."

I have to come up with an answer. I can't just stand here like a pathetic dummy. I blurt out a stray idea that suddenly drifts into my mind.

"I'll be an actress!" I say.

"An actress." His lips curl. "How original. When do you leave for Hollywood?"

I'm still staring down at my feet. My nose is leaking profusely but I don't want to draw attention to this by raising my hand to wipe it. After a moment I stammer, "A real actress, I mean . . . Shakespeare, and stuff like that."

"Stuff like that," he repeats mockingly. "Very impressive."

"Like at Stratford!" I protest. "I'll be like Perry Chandler, I'll move people and educate them to the—"

He gives an incredulous laugh. "Are you kidding? Do you think you could ever be like Perry? He's got presence and sophistication, he's informed on every subject you can name, he has a grasp of history that puts every event in perspective, he's entertaining, he's a terrific raconteur—he isn't some hare-brained female huddling in her room getting overheated and mooning over Victorian romances."

On the bed behind me my book is lying with its cover upward, *Tess of the d'Urbervilles* or *Wuthering Heights*, one of those, with a lurid illustration of a man and a woman clasped in a fierce embrace at the top of a windy cliff. I can feel my face burning with shame. How I wish I could shove that contemptible book out of sight, how I wish I could replace it with something serious and important, a biography of Napoleon perhaps, or a history of World War II by some famous general.

"One way a woman can really shine is in a social situation," he says. "She can be graceful and charming, she can put everyone at ease, she can provide an atmosphere for stimulating conversation, she can make a setting where everyone is at his best. That's not a small thing, that's a very big thing and very important. True, you don't seem to have any talent for it, but I expect you at least to try. You can improve. I'm not interested in people who won't even try to improve. When we have guests I expect you to smile and make conversation with them and do everything you can to see that their visit is pleasant. Do you understand that? I don't think it's too much to ask."

I don't seem to have any voice left. My groin itches with rebellion and misery. All I can do is give a jerky nod.

"What? I didn't hear you."

"Yes, I said! Yes, I understand."

"Who makes the rules around here?"

This is the litany. I know I have to go through it, there is no escape, so why drag it out? Just get it over with. But my throat clogs as I say the word. "You."

"And who follows them?"

165

I swallow hard. "Me."

"I," he corrects me. "I would have thought that someone who reads so much would know better grammar."

"I," I whisper.

"The Holland girls are in the white garden," he tells me. "You can start by offering them a drink and showing them where they can change their clothes for a swim."

I nod stupidly.

"You'd better wash first," he says. "You're a mess."

I'm in the bathroom, snuffling and blowing my nose, looking at my repulsive, swollen face in the dim, ferny light. I'm going to climb through the bathroom window and drop silently to the ground, I'll run, graceful as a panther, beautiful and strong, not ugly, not a mess, I'll run for miles in the woods, until it gets dark, I'll eat berries, I'll make friends with deer and rabbits, I'll cover myself all over with cool, dark leaves, I'll fall asleep for a hundred years. They will say I disappeared one day, no one knows what happened to me. My father will weep because it was his fault. Except I know he won't weep. He despises weeping, and nothing is his fault. He is right, that's all. He can't help it that he's always right.

THE HOLLAND TWINS are a couple of tall scornful blondes, and everything they see and hear causes them to glance at each other with smiles of incredulous amusement. They act as though they feel superior to everything in the world but each other. They follow me languidly from place to place, too bored and indifferent to come up with any ideas of their own. They make me so nervous that my shoulders and neck go stiff and the corners of my mouth ache, but I grin and laugh and pretend to have a good time, so my father will see that I can do it, that I'm not as hopeless as he thinks. But apparently he has forgotten all about me. He is busy holding court, sitting in a big white Muskoka chair while people gather around to ask him questions and laugh uproariously at his jokes. A woman's voice, shrill and half-drunk, echoes across the sunny lawn. "Oh, Laurie, you're such a scream!" And the Holland twins look at each other with their disbelieving, sardonic smiles.

I finally get them settled on the verandah, where they sprawl carelessly on a plush sofa, yawning and leafing through some of my mother's movie magazines. I pretend to look at a magazine too, but I feel too edgy to concentrate. I'm staring blindly at a large blow-up of Kim Novak, wondering how soon I can reasonably hope for the Hollands to go home, when one of them suddenly opens her eyes a bit wider and says, "God, what's that?"

An old, battered-looking Chevrolet has appeared on the curved driveway among the Rolls-Royces, Jaguars and Ferraris. An old man in a terrible straw hat is leaning out the car window, looking around quizzically. We all sit staring, wondering how on earth he got past the front gate and how long it will take him to realize he's made a mistake and drive away again. But he seems to have no idea of driving away. He turns off the ignition and sits there for a moment. Then he gets out of the car and begins to walk up the path. He is wearing a bright, checkered shirt with short sleeves, baggy grey trousers, and flat canvas shoes. He comes right up to the screen door and shades his eyes to peer through the wire mesh at us. The Holland twins look at him blankly, apparently believing that I'm the one who should deign to speak to him and tell him to get lost.

"Hi there," he says, nodding his head.

"Hi," I reply after a moment, distantly.

"Well," he says. "It was worth a long drive to see such pretty girls."

I don't need to look at the Holland twins to know what expressions are on their faces. I feel a frozen sensation in my own mouth. I don't want to encourage him by reacting to him in any way. I just gape at him, waiting for him to explain what he wants.

"I bet you're Grace," he says. A chill of horror makes my spine tingle. I have been proceeding on the assumption that he has taken a wrong turn somewhere and ended up at our place by accident. The fact that he knows my name makes it obvious that there is no mistake, that he has a purpose for being there, and God alone knows what that purpose is. The Holland twins are looking at me in cool amazement, waiting for me to respond.

"Grace," he says again, smiling ingratiatingly, "right?"

I seem to have no option. "Yes," I admit. I haven't moved from my chair.

"Is your momma around?" he says.

"Yes," I say, continuing to sit unmoving, staring at him through the screen.

He is wearing old-fashioned glasses with metal rims. One of his lower teeth is made of gold. "You go tell her Uncle Lubo is here," he says. "Okay, sweetheart?"

Somehow I manage to stand up. I can't look at the Holland twins, but I feel their incredulous, satirical gaze. My face is hot. I don't know which is worst: that this bizarre man has called me "sweetheart," that he claims to be related to my mother, or that he has a ludicrous, weird, foreign-sounding name like Lubo. I walk fast, almost running, down the verandah and out the double screen doors and around the side of the house. I don't look back to see what "Uncle Lubo" is doing, whether he is waiting or following me. I just want to get to my mother and dump the whole problem of "Uncle Lubo" in her lap.

She is standing on the western lawn with a group of people, holding a drink, her eyes blotted out by dark sunglasses. Her hair is a bouffant blonde globe around her face. It's Red Bathing Suit Day, and over that she's wearing a lacy beige beach jacket, with matching beige sandals. She looks absurdly glamorous and unreal. I go up to her, breathing hard, sweat prickling at my hairline.

"Mom," I gasp. "There's a weird man at the back door."

She turns and looks past me. I turn too. He has come around the side of the house and is standing there, unabashed, his straw hat pushed back on his head.

"Oh, my God," my mother says. Colour floods into her cheeks. The people who have been standing with her turn to look up the lawn. One of them gives a soft laugh and then stifles it.

"Oh, God," my mother says again. She hasn't moved. She doesn't seem happy, but I can't tell how she does feel. After a moment she raises her arm and gives a little wave. "God," she says in a low voice, stretching her ruby-red mouth in a smile.

Uncle Lubo responds to the wave by walking rapidly across the grass, grinning. I wish the ground could open up and swallow him, but it doesn't, of course. He keeps coming, big and flushed, his mouth open to reveal that flashing gold tooth.

"Polly!" he says. His eyes look moist behind the lenses of his glasses. "I can't believe it's you, I hardly recognized you, you look like a movie star!" And he envelops her in a huge hug, crushing her puffy hair, causing her to spill some of her drink on the front of his pants. "No, no, that's all right," he insists. "That's nothing. It'll dry in a minute. Gee, Polly, it's so good to see you."

My father has risen from the Muskoka chair. It strikes me that he is smiling in the same one-sided, ironical way that the Holland twins do. "Vivian?" he says.

My mother takes a deep breath and draws herself up defiantly. "This is my Uncle Lubomyr from Saskatchewan," she says. "Uncle Lubo, this is Laurie, my husband."

My father reacts calmly, coming forward with his hand outstretched. But Uncle Lubo ignores the hand, sweeps him into a voluminous hug, and follows that up with a big smacking kiss on the cheek. In spite of the tension and embarrassment, I almost want to laugh at the look on my father's face.

"So I finally meet the famous husband!" Uncle Lubo says. "You never come to visit us so I have to visit you!"

It takes my father a moment to recover his composure. He smooths his hair with both hands as he withdraws from Uncle Lubo's embrace. "I'm afraid I'm not quite as . . . demonstrative as you are, Lubomyr," he says, with a laugh.

Richelle Kosar

Uncle Lubo takes the remark as an apology. "Oh, that's okay, don't worry about it, Larry," he says, grasping my father's shoulder and giving him a friendly shake.

"Laurie," my mother corrects him.

"Right," says Uncle Lubo. "I can't get over it, Polly, you look like you just stepped out of a bandbox." He glances around at the other guests, all of whom seem to have been struck dumb.

"She was the best-looking girl in Saskatchewan," he tells them.

The Holland twins have wandered down from the verandah. I wish I could stop up their ears somehow, so that they won't hear one word of what is being said, but no, of course that's impossible. They have to stand there and hear it all.

"She won a beauty contest at her school," Uncle Lubo is saying happily. "She was the Snow Queen, remember that, Polly? All the boys were crazy about this girl."

My mother's eyes are hidden behind her sunglasses. She chews her lower lip and gives Uncle Lubo a nudge. "Oh, cut it out, will you?" she says.

"And nothing's changed," one of the men pipes up gallantly.

"You said it!" Uncle Lubo agrees. "She's still a knockout, isn't she?"

"Can I get you a drink, Lubomyr?" my father asks pleasantly.

"Well, that's the best offer I've had all day," Uncle Lubo says. "Give me a nice big glass of rye, Larry. With a little bit of water, and one little sliver of ice."

"It's *Laurie*," my mother repeats.

Uncle Lubo looks at her with his soft brown eyes. "What did I say?"

He sits in my father's Muskoka chair, with his straw hat on the grass beside him. Every once in a while he reaches down to touch it, as if to reassure himself that it is still there. He takes a dainty sandwich in his big hand, stares at its size for a moment, then swallows it in one gulp and takes another. He

170

has a second glass of rye, and then a third. He is delighted with Leslie and insists that she should sit on his lap. Leslie makes a face as his big bristly moustache rubs against her cheek. My mother sits beside him, one leg crossed over the other, smiling tightly. Her sunglasses remain firmly in place, so that no one can see her eyes.

He has plenty to say. He's just coming back from Niagara Falls. That was one sight he'd always wanted to see. Now that he's retired and the kids are grown up and the wife is dead, there wasn't a thing to hold him back and suddenly one morning he woke up and got into his car. It was a bloody long trip but worth every minute because man, those Falls are really something, aren't they, especially at night with all the coloured lights? Anyway, he decided he'd stop on his way back to visit his niece Polly, because he hasn't laid eyes on her for seventeen years, because she never comes home and all they ever hear from her is a Christmas card once a year. Wouldn't you know it, he gets to her house in Toronto and she's not there. By the way, some house! Let's face it, that's a mansion! The housekeeper said everybody was at their summer cottage at Azure Lake in Muskoka so he looked it up on the map and it looked like it was right on his way home. In Port Azure he stopped to ask for directions to Larry Tremain's summer cottage, stopped at the Lakeside Motel, and wouldn't you know it, the guy at the desk turned out to have a daughter living in Saskatchewan! No kidding! And Lord, when he first drove down the road and saw this place, he couldn't believe his eyes. Because he thought of a summer cottage as a little shack with a cookstove and some bunk beds. You remember that place we rented one summer at Waskesiu, Polly, sleeping bags all over the floor and it rained the whole week and we couldn't get the stove to work. . . .

He drains his glass and holds it out to my father for a refill without interrupting the flow of his conversation. My father turns without a word and hands the glass to the bartender, and a moment later the bartender discreetly appears at Uncle Lubo's elbow and puts a full glass into his hand. I don't think

Uncle Lubo has any idea who the bartender is, but each time he receives a new drink he turns and nods gratefully and says, "Thanks, buddy."

Senator Gilbert Holland and his wife Estelle are here. Carlo Falconi, the architect. Ted Farragut and Fred Hawthorne, two of my father's lawyers, and their wives. Charlie Walters, the CEO of Achison Incorporated, and his wife. Bill Twoomey of Twoomey and Ryan. Sterling Thomas, the president of Castlemaine Foods. Ted Richmond and Tyler Corkindale, board members at the Cheltenham Corporation. Steve Eldridge, the provincial Minister of Finance. A nice little collection of movers and shakers. They keep wandering into Uncle Lubo's orbit, listening bemusedly for a few moments, and then wandering away again. It's as though their limo driver or their plumber or their garbageman had suddenly walked in, sat down and tried to socialize with them.

Fred Hawthorne, who has been in the house taking a phone call, comes hurriedly across the lawn, his face taut with purpose. "Laurie," he says quietly, stopping beside my father's chair. "They're going private at fifty-five."

This cryptic statement seems to mean something important to the few people who are close enough to overhear it. Even Mrs. Twoomey, who is always expressing her absolute disregard for business matters, knows enough to stop talking and wait for my father's reaction. He smiles. "Interesting," he says. "That's a bit low, isn't it?" Fred Hawthorne grins.

"Did you talk to our friend?" my father asks through lips that barely open.

"He's in," Hawthorne says.

"Okay. Give Hazard a call," my father says. "Tell him to put together a team and go over the data this weekend. Say I want to be ready to move first thing Monday."

"Gee, Larry," Uncle Lubo remarks as everybody watches Hawthorne walking briskly back toward the house, "I guess you're a pretty big cheese, huh?" He is grinning and nodding, his gold tooth flashing. Perhaps he's sincerely impressed. But there is an edge, just the slightest edge, of combative mockery, as though he thinks my father is putting on an act of some kind, exaggerating his own importance. It's unbelievable. My father stares at him speechlessly.

Now Senator Holland speaks up. He was once a politician so he thinks he knows how to handle the common people. He gives a rich, deep politician's laugh. "Lubo, tell me—you say you're from Cardinal? I wonder if you know Richard Mercer, the M.P. from Cardinal riding. He's a very good friend of mine."

Uncle Lubo looks up, smiling. "Sorry, I didn't get your name."

"Gil Holland," Senator Holland says. "Just call me Gil."

"Well, Gil," says Uncle Lubo, "if Mercer's a friend of yours then I guess he must be okay, so I'm not gonna say anything against him. But he's a God damn Tory, excuse my French, and I have to tell you, I'm a socialist all the way."

Suddenly my father gives a loud shout of laughter, leaning his red head against the back of his chair. Uncle Lubo keeps smiling and reaches down to touch his straw hat where it lies on the grass.

WE STAND WITH HIM ON THE DRIVEWAY, surrounded by large, gleaming automobiles, my father, mother, Leslie and I. My parents must have had some kind of discussion about the situation, although I haven't heard it. My mother has changed into a pink shirt and a pair of white silk pants in the style that used to be called toreador pants. It is late in the afternoon, toward six, and the sun is honey coloured and the shadows are long and rippling over the grass. My mother talks, quickly, with too much expression, as though she is playing a part in a television program.

"See, we didn't know you were coming, Uncle Lubo. So we made all these other plans. We've got this dinner and dance we have to go to tonight. And we've got all these people staying here, you can see."

"That's okay, that's okay, Polly," Uncle Lubo says

cheerfully. "Don't you worry about me, I can sleep anywhere, the chesterfield is good enough for me. Or a sleeping bag on the floor, that's fine too."

"We wouldn't want you to sleep on the floor, Lubo," my father interposes smoothly. "We think you'd be more comfortable at one of the hotels in town. And of course I'm paying for it, I don't want any arguments about that."

Uncle Lubo just doesn't get it. Even Leslie gets it, but Uncle Lubo doesn't. He continues to protest, cheerfully and robustly. "Hell, you don't have to do that. I'm not gonna let you spend your money. I didn't come here to stay in some fancy hotel, I came here to visit Polly's family. I tell ya, I'll be happy on the floor. I mean it."

"But see, we made these other plans," my mother says desperately. "We've got this dance to go to tonight. A wedding dance, some friends of Laurie's. We have to go. So you'll be better off in town. You'll have a TV set—Laurie doesn't like TV in the country so we don't even have one here. And you can have a nice dinner, supper, I mean. . . ."

"And tomorrow morning of course you'll come back here for breakfast," my father adds in the same smooth, easy way. "And spend the whole day, if you like."

"Yes!" my mother agrees eagerly. "We'll take you for a ride in the boat and it'll be great."

Uncle Lubo continues to smile, although there seems to be a slight change in the shape of his mouth. He hasn't given up though; after a moment he says, "A wedding, hey? Well, why don't you just take me along? They won't mind one more, hey? You know me, Polly, I always like a wedding."

My mother's lips move helplessly. But my father isn't concerned; he is used to getting his own way. "I'm afraid we can't do that, Lubo," he says firmly. "It's one of those small, private affairs, by invitation only. You wouldn't know a soul there. You just wouldn't be comfortable. It's too bad, but we'll make it up to you tomorrow." And he smiles: a charming, easy, implacable smile. My mother is looking down at her scarlet toenails, chewing on her lower lip.

Uncle Lubo glances from one to the other. He is still smiling and his eyes are bright behind the shiny lenses of his glasses. I think for a moment that he's going to keep on arguing. I'm filled with impatience and a sort of intense, prickly discomfort. Why is he so stupid, why won't he just do what we tell him to do? Then he raises his straw hat and places it jauntily on his head. "Okay, sure," he says. "If that's the way it has to be."

My mother's voice is shrill with relief. "Honestly, we'll make it up to you tomorrow," she says, squeezing Uncle Lubo's arm. "You'll come for a great big breakfast and then we'll go on the boat and you can fish if you like and later we'll have a barbecue, we'll barbecue steaks and it'll be great."

"Steaks? Well, my mouth is watering already," Uncle Lubo says.

He has fallen into line and everything is all right, so I can't understand why the feeling of tension and unrest remains in the air. Everybody is smiling as though nothing is wrong. And after all, nothing terrible has happened. It's a purely social matter. You can't take someone to a place where they haven't been invited, can you? Even Uncle Lubo has to understand that.

"Polly's going to drive into town with you and see that you get settled," my father says. I've never heard him call my mother Polly before, but the name seems to glide off his tongue with perfect ease and simplicity.

"Oh, you don't have to do that," Uncle Lubo says. "How are you gonna get back if you come in my car?"

"Well, we've got that all figured out, Lubo," my father says.

"Oh yeah, do ya, Larry?" Uncle Lubo says.

"The Twoomeys want to go into town too, they want to do some shopping. So Polly can drive back with them. So it's all taken care of."

Uncle Lubo shrugs. Then all at once his face brightens as he thinks of something. "Oh, hey, I almost forgot," he says, walking around to the back of his battered car and opening the trunk. "I brought something to show you. I thought you'd get a kick out of seeing it."

He rummages around for a moment while we all wait rather stiffly, anticipating further embarrassment, unable to imagine what he can possibly produce from that cluttered trunk that will be of interest to us. At last he finds what he's looking for: an old, dirt-stained bottle with a ragged yellow label. He thrusts it into my father's hands triumphantly.

"A real antique, huh?" he says. "Isn't that something? I turned it up in my basement last month when I was putting in a new furnace. That's got to be forty years old."

My father stares at the bottle, nonplussed. Its yellow label has a crude blue logo on it, an outline of an angel with the words "Tremain's Elixir" arching clumsily around its head to form a big, ragged halo.

"What is this?" my father says with a thin smile.

"You don't recognize it? Oh, your old man would recognize it for sure. He was pretty big in our neck of the woods for a while. Old Louie Tremain, everybody had stories about him. For a while it was illegal to sell alcohol except for medicinal purposes, so Louie foxed 'em, he just changed the labels. Me and my brother used to go to the drugstore in Canora and pick up a couple bottles of Tremain's Elixir and we'd take it out on the prairie and sit in our old Model T and drink it down. Man, it was powerful stuff. Your fingers and toes'd still be numb two days later. Guys used to joke that Louie put a dash of sulphuric acid in his booze just to give it a bit of an extra kick."

I have seldom seen my father at a loss for words before. He just keeps standing there, staring at that old bottle with a slight smile on his lips.

"Course that drugstore stuff was just small-time," Uncle Lubo says after a moment. "He saved his best stuff for the rum-runners."

At that my father raises his eyes and looks at Uncle Lubo. Then he shakes his head, still smiling very slightly. "My father never sold to rum-runners."

Uncle Lubo laughs. "Now, come on, Larry. We're talking

about Louie Tremain, who used to work out of Saskatchewan in the 1920s? Geez, the rum-runners'd drive across the border and wait at the Royal Hotel in Sifton, sometimes it'd be after midnight when they'd get the word there was a shipment of Louie's booze waiting for 'em at the train station. You'd see their cars lined up for half a mile by the railroad tracks. I seen it myself."

My father calmly shakes his head, looking right into Uncle Lubo's eyes. "My father never sold to rum-runners," he repeats.

After a moment Uncle Lubo reaches up and tilts the brim of his straw hat over one eye. "Okay, Larry," he says. "If you say so. You keep that bottle anyway. A nice souvenir, huh?" He slams his trunk shut and walks around the car to open the door for my mother. Without a word she climbs into the front seat.

My father glances at Leslie and me with his remote, blue-grey eyes. "You kids go along too," he says. "Your mother's uncle wants to visit with you."

Neither Leslie nor I want to go, but we both know better than to argue with my father. Silently we get into the back seat of the battered old Chevrolet. There is a tear in the vinyl and some of the white stuffing is showing. Leslie looks at it with distaste and shifts over so that she doesn't have to sit on it. My father stands in the driveway as we pull out onto the road. He is still holding the old bottle in one hand. I catch a last glimpse of that blue angel with its big crude halo. My father raises his arm in a casual salute. Leslie and my mother wave back. Uncle Lubo and I don't.

My mother rolls down her window and the car is filled with a warm breeze. She ties a white scarf over her hair and stares through her dark glasses at the dusty windshield.

"Well, Polly, you sure got a rich one, huh?" Uncle Lubo says suddenly.

She gives a sharp laugh. "Yeah, I guess."

"I never even knew it was the same Tremain till about five years ago when your mother showed me a picture in a magazine. You were wearing a fancy blue dress. It said 'Laurence Tremain and his beautiful wife Vivian.' First of all, I couldn't figure out who they meant by this 'Vivian.' Then I go on reading and it says, 'son of Louie Tremain of Tremain Distilleries.' 'Well, God almighty,' I says. 'She married the son!' 'Jever meet the old man?"

"Yeah," my mother sighs.

"So what did you think of him?"

My mother shrugs. "He was okay." After a moment she takes out a cigarette and lights it. She blows a cloud of smoke out the open window, and white wisps drift back into her face. "If you beat him at checkers he'd get mad and throw the board across the room," she says.

Uncle Lubo laughs. "No kidding. Yeah, I always heard old Louie was a tough son of a bitch. Typical private enterpriser. No matter what Larry says, he did sell to rum-runners. That's how the money started rolling in. He was pal-sy wal-sy with all those big-time hoods like Lucky Luciano and Dutch Schultz. It was—"

"Oh, who cares?" my mother interrupts impatiently. "It's all ancient history anyway."

"Well, okay," Uncle Lubo says with an agreeable shrug. "Anyway, you're in good shape." He pauses briefly and I can hear the piercing song of crickets in the grassy ditch as we speed past. "You kind of had to call yourself a different name, huh?" he says.

My mother keeps staring out her window, smoking. "Yeah, I kind of did," she says.

Uncle Lubo nods. After a moment he says, "Lots of people can't figure out how to spell Popowich. They're always putting in two *P*s or an extra *T* or something. . . ."

My mother doesn't answer. I sit with my head against the warm vinyl of the shabby car seat, wrinkling my nose at the stale, dusty smell. I can't wait for the ride to be over. I can't wait to get rid of Uncle Lubo.

"Everything still the same?" my mother says after a brief silence.

"Still the same," Uncle Lubo confirms. "We thought you might come home for Nikola's funeral. Your momma felt kind of bad at the time."

"I couldn't!" my mother cries with sudden passion. "I told her! I just couldn't get away, and she knew that!"

Uncle Lubo nods his head thoughtfully. "She said Polly's never been back in all these years."

My mother presses her lips together. I am trying to think who Nikola might be. I have an obscure memory of someone I might have seen in an old photograph, although it's unlikely since my mother always claims she has no photographs of her family. Nevertheless the image persists in my mind: someone tall and skinny and sunburned, someone wearing glasses taped together at one corner, someone in a dark shirt and pants with baggy knees. Someone standing by a fence, looking into the camera without a smile, his arms hanging loosely at his sides, as if he didn't know what to do with them. Have I really seen a picture like that? And if I have, why do I associate it with the name Nikola? Another weird name, not English, not connected with anything familiar and civilized. I think how lucky it is that these alien relatives of my mother's live far away and we never have to see them.

"You know how it happened?" Uncle Lubo says.

"Yes," my mother answers quickly, as if she wants to stop him from talking about it.

But Uncle Lubo can't be stopped that easily. "They found him in the ditch by the road from Canora. He tried to walk home. Forty below, the coldest night of the year. Can ya believe it? He drank like a fish, Polly."

"You all did," my mother says flatly.

"Oh, well, we all liked a little drink once in a while," Uncle Lubo says.

My mother gives a sarcastic laugh.

"There's nothing wrong with that," Uncle Lubo says. "Once in a while you gotta set yourself free. But he really went nuts, Polly. It got so's that was all he was doing, your momma couldn't handle him and your brothers neither. He wasn't even working much anymore; he'd sit out in the barn and keep drinking till he passed out. That night he drove into town and when he come out of the beer parlour the truck wouldn't start.

The poor son of a bitch, I guess he went staggering out of town and down the road in the middle of the night, and then he must of got tired, or he just—"

"Oh, God!" my mother hisses. "Do you have to make me listen to this? I said she told me already! It was a hundred years ago!"

Leslie is holding her comic book in front of her eyes but I know she isn't reading it anymore. I stare out the window at the beautiful blue expanse of Azure Lake, envisioning a scene: a microscopic figure trudging along a dark road on the surface of a great white empty globe. Maybe as he lay down on the ground to sleep the clear, cold stars looked like Christmas lights revolving above his head.

"I forgot to take pictures," Uncle Lubo suddenly exclaims, slapping his forehead with one hand. "Damn, now you remind me to get out the camera tomorrow. I want to take lots of pictures to show them back home."

"I send her money," my mother says abruptly.

"I know you do. She brags about it, you should hear her. She keeps a picture of you on top of the TV set. The one where you're wearing the fancy long dress with the feathers. Do you remember that one?"

"Yeah," my mother says after a moment. She is looking straight ahead at the road.

"One day I dropped by to see how she was doing, you know I keep an eye on her the best I can, and she's got some poor school kid sitting in the living room with her, the kid's trying to sell magazines or something—boy, did he come to the wrong house! Mary's got him sitting there looking at all her scrapbooks and the poor little bugger can't escape. She always cut your pictures out when you used to be in the Eaton's catalogue, you know. Pasted them in scrapbooks. She still doesn't speak English too good but she's put it across to the kid just the same, this is her daughter, she's the one posing in all the nice clothes in the catalogues, she got married to a big shot, she lives in Toronto and sends lots of money."

My mother gives a short, sharp laugh and Uncle Lubo

smiles at her with a flash of his gold tooth. "She's got ten of those scrapbooks, I think. She's got you in bathing suits and party dresses and fur coats and nightgowns." My mother nods brusquely, rolling her eyes.

We take him to the Azure Inn. My mother walks briskly up to the desk, her sandals slapping against her heels. "We want a room overlooking the lake," she says.

The desk clerk shakes her head regretfully. "Oh, I'm sorry, but all those rooms are booked for tonight. We've got several nice ones on the other side though, looking over the garden."

"No," my mother says. "We really want one overlooking the lake. Mr. Popowich has come a long way."

"From Saskatchewan," Uncle Lubo adds helpfully. "Went all the way to Niagara Falls in my old Chevy. And now I'm on my way back but I stopped off for a visit."

"It would be for just the one night," my mother says. "I'm Mrs. Laurence Tremain. You know us, don't you? We want everything to be really nice for Mr. Popowich and please charge it all to my husband."

"Oh!" the clerk says. "Mrs. Tremain, I'm sorry, I'm new here, I didn't know it was you. Just a minute, I'll see what I can do." She goes into the back and shuts the door.

"Polly, you didn't have to do that," Uncle Lubo says in a low voice. "I'm happy with anything, you know me. You shouldn't waste your money."

"If you can't use it to get what you want, what good is it?" my mother says.

The desk clerk comes back. "We've had a cancellation, so I can give you the Pinewood Suite, Mrs Tremain. It's got a beautiful view and glass doors that open onto its own private terrace overlooking the lake. I'll have Terry bring up the bags."

Uncle Lubo's hat is tipped rakishly over his forehead. He leans across the desk and grins confidingly. "This is my rich niece," he says. "Nothing but the best for her old uncle."

The clerk gives him a bright, professional smile and hands over his key. My mother's face is flushed; she shakes her head and takes him by the arm. "She was the best-looking girl in Saskatchewan," Uncle Lubo says. "She was the Snow Queen at her school."

"Big deal," my mother mutters, laughing nervously in the clerk's direction and pulling Uncle Lubo away. He seems determined to blurt out this arcane detail of her past to any stranger he encounters. Who knows what he's going to come out with next?

By the time we reach the third floor he is puffing, out of breath. "Boy," he says, "for these prices, you'd think they could put in an elevator."

"It's an inn," my mother says. She is a bit breathless herself. "It's supposed to be quaint and old-fashioned."

"Oh," Uncle Lubo says. "Well, it's old-fashioned all right." And he laughs as though he has said something very witty.

His room is large and filled with a delicate, subtle fragrance of piny air and potpourri. Its wide windows display a vista of blue lake and green trees. The sun is low in the sky and soft amber light glimmers in the distant water. My mother flings open the glass doors proudly.

"Isn't it nice?" she says. "You have your own balcony. Look. A table and chairs. You can sit out here all evening and relax and look at the view. Isn't it beautiful?"

She keeps looking at him, wanting him to express some sort of excitement or pleasure. He doesn't seem to be as impressed as she wants him to be. He shrugs, glancing around. "The TV's pretty small," he says.

My mother's lips go tight. "So you don't like it," she says. "It's the best hotel in Port Azure. Famous people come here to stay and they think it's wonderful."

Uncle Lubo sits down on the edge of the bed. "Geez, it's hard as a rock," he says. "Oh, no, honey, of course I like it. It's great. I told you, I'm happy anywhere. Now, where's the liquor store? I'm gonna take a snooze and then I'm gonna get myself a mickey, and I'm gonna sit and watch the sunset. Have they got a Kentucky Fried place here? I'm gonna sit here with my whiskey and my Kentucky Fried, and it's gonna be nice."

"You can call room service," my mother tells him. "They'll bring you drinks and a wonderful dinner, anything you want."

"Well, honey, you know, I've kind of got my heart set on Kentucky Fried," Uncle Lubo says.

As we are going, he hugs each of us fervently and kisses us with his big, moist, whiskered lips. We leave him sitting on the bed, still holding his straw hat. It is hot on the street. I see a thin film of perspiration on my mother's forehead. We are supposed to meet the Twoomeys at a gift shop called Faye's Folly, and there is no particular hurry, but she is walking very quickly, her high-heeled sandals clicking like castanets.

"I don't like Uncle Lubo," Leslie says. "He's too kissy."

All along my mother has shown every sign of being just as embarrassed and annoyed by Uncle Lubo as we are. I expect her to groan and agree. Instead she frowns and speaks in a brusque, angry voice. "Well, he's just a dumb old hick from the sticks, so I guess you don't have to like him," she says.

Leslie, who always reacts strongly to anyone else's mood, immediately begins to whimper with remorse. "I didn't mean *that*," she says. "I didn't mean that, Mom."

My mother's full lower lip starts to quiver, as though she is about to cry too. "When he and my father came to this country they had five bucks between them and they thought that was a fortune. They didn't have anybody to buy them fancy clothes and tell them what books to read," she says, walking on fast in the hot, brilliant sun. We almost have to run to keep up with her.

"I didn't mean it, Mom," Leslie cries, rubbing her nose with the back of her hand.

"All they knew how to do was work like dogs," she says. "They picked the poorest farm in the whole province. It was half rock. That was just the kind of break they always got. When I was a kid we didn't even have an outhouse. I had to go out behind the barn and pee in a field."

She is talking too loudly; the word "pee" seems to hover in the air around us and I feel as if everyone else on the sidewalk has turned to look.

"I'm sorry, Mom," Leslie is sobbing. "I didn't mean it."

"Well, just forget it," my mother says harshly. "That's the best way."

THE AZURE LAKE COUNTRY CLUB is situated on a green hill overlooking the water. As you turn into its circular drive you can see the red shimmer of sunset in all its long windows. Our car is filled with soft, glamorous scents: my mother's perfume, my father's cologne, his freshly ironed shirt and polished shoes, her cosmetics and French cigarettes. She is wearing a narrow silver dress and her long legs glisten like satin. The smoke from her cigarette hangs around her in the twilit air like a veil. My father's shoes crackle on the gravel. He raises his arm in greeting to a man standing above us on the terrace. "Hi, Dave," he calls. Then he looks at me and immediately I feel my inadequacy, my lack of poise, my stupidity, my ugliness.

"Too much lipstick," he tells my mother. "She's not old enough yet to look like a tramp."

My mother takes a Kleenex from her purse. I feel the tremor in her fingers as she hurriedly blots my mouth.

"Sh-h-h-h," she whispers. "Don't cry."

"I have no intention of crying!" I hiss, quietly, so he won't hear me. But he has already turned away, is already walking up the driveway, his hands in his pockets, his hair gleaming in the light from the doorway, careless and youthful-looking as a college boy.

The ballroom of the Azure Lake Country Club has walls of glass, and doors opening onto the terrace on three sides. Sunset light tints the gleaming floor and stains the bride's gown with pink. She has caught up her long train and draped it over one arm rather dashingly, like a musketeer about to fight with a sword. The well-known debutante, Sally Sampson, daughter of Wilfrid Sampson, the steel baron. When she sees my father she laughs and takes his hand and says,

"Hi, Uncle Laurie!" He isn't really her uncle but she always calls him that. And he laughs too, a gay light-hearted laugh that we rarely hear when he is alone with just us. He brings that laugh out for company, for parties. He says, "We're here to dance all night!" And the music starts exactly then, as if the orchestra has been waiting for his command. A big orchestra on a dreamily lit bandstand. They are dressed in white suits and their horns shine like gold and they play "Stardust."

"Can I have champagne, Mom?"

"Well, I shouldn't let you but I guess you can have half a glass."

"Can I have champagne too?"

"No, Leslie, you're way too young."

"Gracie gets to have it!"

"Gracie is almost thirteen and you're only six, and you know it."

Leslie pouts and slumps into a chair with her arms folded across her chest. The champagne tastes even better because she can't have any. It is like ginger ale but more pungent and intoxicating. The golden bubbles tickle my nose and make me feel giddy. My father is dancing with Mrs. Twoomey, whirling her around the room; all she has to do is lean back in his arms and be carried by him, swiftly and beautifully, with perfect ease and rhythm. I think that someday when I'm older I'll dance with a man like that. I'll wear a long gown made of some sparkling fabric, I'll look stunning, and a man's hand will rest lightly and warmly on my waist, and he will move me through the patterns of light and shadow on a vast, dim floor while balloons and streamers drift silently down around us.

Shadowy figures are leaning over the walls of the terrace, smoking cigarettes and murmuring softly to each other, gazing at the scarlet sky behind the slim black pine trees. Suddenly I think of that old man, that old, funny, foreign man, sitting on his balcony with his "mickey" and his straw hat and his greasy fried chicken, watching the sunset. How awful it would have been if they'd let him come with us, how he would have ruined everything, barging in with his loud voice, telling people stupid things about my mother, kissing and hugging everybody, forcing children to sit in his lap. I don't want to see him ever again. I think how much better it would be if he just got into his horrible Chevrolet and drove away and left us alone, because we don't want him, we have no time for him, he bores and disgusts us.

At one in the morning, in the dark parking lot, still echoing with distant dance music, a group of us stand around an amazing car. It is a 1932 Alfa Romeo roadster, white as milk, long and sleek, with black tires and touches of gold. Even in the dark it glistens, as beautiful as a piece of sculpture. Its owner, a small, dark-faced man whose name I forget, leans against it proudly, demonstrating its special features.

"How much did you pay for it?" my father asks suddenly.

The dark-faced man trails his fingers caressingly across the long, low, gleaming hood. "I was at a classic cars show in Chicago," he says. "There was another guy bidding against me. I had to go up to thirty-five thousand."

An appreciative murmur runs through the group. It is 1964 and thirty-five thousand is still a considerable sum of money.

"I'll give you fifty thousand for her," my father says.

This is so unexpected and outrageous that there is a momentary silence. Then Wilfrid Sampson calls out, "Laurie needs another old car!" and everybody laughs. My father's penchant for vintage automobiles is well known.

"So?" he says to the dark-faced man. "How about it?"

The dark-faced man smiles, gives a nonchalant shrug, and drops his car keys into my father's hand. This produces a ripple of applause. People are always heartened by the exchange of expensive merchandise.

"Come by tomorrow and I'll have the cheque for you," my father says.

He leaps into the driver's seat and turns on the ignition. The engine gives a rich, deep purr and he closes his eyes and sighs with satisfaction. "Music," he says, and everybody laughs. Then suddenly his eyes move restlessly over us, eager and bright. "Who wants to come for a drive?" he says.

It is irresistible: the gleaming car and the scented summer night and his impulsive invitation. He leans forward, smiling, tapping his fingers on the steering wheel, offering excitement, speed, pleasure. Among us there is a general desire to respond, an intake of breath, a wish to cry out, "Yes!" But Leslie is the only one who is still enough of a child to give in to it. She was asleep earlier, lying on the sofa in the ladies' powder room, and the sofa cushions have left red sleep-marks on her face. "I do!" she screams, suddenly wide awake. "Let me go, Dad, let me!"

I know he'll take her. He always takes Leslie. Leslie is his favourite. I look down at the ground, distant and unsmiling. I hate him and I will never ask him for anything and he can drive Leslie and everyone else to the ends of the earth and I still won't give a damn.

Then he says, "Come on, Grace."

I raise my head. He is smiling at me as if he has never said cruel things to me, as if he has never called me a failure, a mess, a tramp. He is like this sometimes; after being hard on me all day he will suddenly relent, as though I have earned a reward by enduring his abuse.

I won't smile back, I won't make it easy for him, he is never going to know if he makes me happy. But inside, my whole being gives a wild throb of joy.

Leslie starts jumping up and down. "No, Dad! Please, Dad! Take me! Take me! Look at her, she doesn't even want to go!"

"Sure she does," he says. "Grace?" And he leans over to open the car door for me.

I sit beside him in the passenger seat, shining like a queen, willing myself not to grin, looking at them all, their shadowy faces, my mother's frown and Leslie's wide, teary eyes. The car leaps forward as though it is alive, spraying gravel behind us like confetti. You can smell the rich leather, the polished metal, all the expensive materials that have gone into its construction. The dashboard lights gleam like jewels.

Richelle Kosar

"Just one of those fabulous flings!" my father sings out into the vast, radiant night. My hair streams behind my head in the perfumed wind. The long gleaming nose of the car glides over the road like the prow of a ship. He is beside me, he likes me for a little while, for a little while I am the chosen one and he belongs to me alone. He is always beautifully dressed, always urbane, always in control, never embarrassing, never stupid, never crude and ordinary. There's nothing in the world he can't do. We drive along the lake road. We drive a hundred miles an hour. If he wanted to, he could drive right into the sky. The lake is blue, midnight blue, and the moon floats in it, the moon is like a silver wafer that you could catch in your hand and swallow whole.

"Isn't it great?" my father says. "Did you feel that? I think we just left the ground!"

Chapter Twelve

WE LEFT THE CITY ON A PERFECT SUMMER DAY, hot and sunny and clear, so clear that even objects at a great distance seemed unnaturally distinct, as though their outlines had been sharpened with a fine black pen. The air was delicate and flowed softly over my face and arms like a thin, subtle liquid with a light fragrance.

We had to take two cars. He said he might need his to drive back to the city for "business." He didn't offer any further explanation, and I didn't ask for one. Speeding along on the wide, glistening band of Highway 400 between the patchwork fields, I saw him behind me in the rearview mirror, his nondescript white car, his dark glasses, his tanned arm resting on the side of the window, his longish hair blowing in the breeze, edged with sunshine. I felt strangely free and youthful, the way I might have felt once at the beginning of summer vacation from school, when it seemed that there was a whole lifetime of long summer days ahead with nothing to do but read, run on the beach, lie in the sunlight and eat when I was hungry. The city had fallen away behind us, disintegrating on the horizon until it no longer existed. I had boxes of groceries in the back seat, provisions for a long journey. No one knew where we were going. The bright hot fields whipped past; the air hummed with crickets and windy grass. Occasionally I went over a rise or turned a bend and then thought I'd lost him, but after a few moments his white car would reappear, sailing easily into place behind me, and each time I felt a flash of pleasure, just like a teenage girl who spots her boyfriend's car on the street, I told myself sarcastically. Pathetic. But it didn't matter. I decided I was going to do whatever I pleased, and feel the way I felt, and to hell with it.

When I was a kid we always stopped at a town called Porterfield for lunch. A friend of my father's, George Stanbury, had a restaurant there, and we would eat a lunch of vichyssoise, cold chicken and fresh French bread, while George sat across from us discussing football and politics.

That day I drove right through Porterfield and Eddy followed me. Twenty miles further, I pulled into a shabby little gas station just off the highway. There was a diner attached to it, advertised by a hand-painted sign spelling out "Sherry's" in faded letters. I didn't remember ever seeing the place before, but it looked so old and dilapidated that it could have been there for fifty years. A tall, thin man with a red face came out of the dark garage and approached me smiling.

"Fill it up, will you?" I said. "How's the food here? Can we get a bit of lunch?"

"Sure," the man replied eagerly. "It's real nice. Home-cooked. Second cup of coffee for free."

He was about fifty and had very clear grey eyes that seemed unnaturally young set against his rough, weathered skin. Sometimes you're struck by the utter incomprehensibility of other people's lives. What was a fifty-year-old man doing in that shabby, forlorn place in the middle of nowhere, pumping gas? I heard tires crackling on gravel as Eddy's car pulled up behind me. It was a big day for the red-faced man, two customers at the same time.

"I'll be with you in a minute, sir!" he called out briskly.

Eddy got out of his car and walked toward me, looking back at the deserted road and the silent trees. He seemed fascinated and vaguely troubled. "God, it's quiet," he said. "Where are we?" I wondered if he had ever spent much time outside the city. But of course his family owned a large *estancia* in the Argentinian pampas. So he always said.

"We're going into the wilderness," I told him. "Be prepared."

The red-faced man felt bound to correct me. He probably thought we were Americans. "It's not that wild, actually," he said. "Another thirty miles and you're in Orillia. Quite a good-sized town."

The diner was empty. We sat at a table by the window, looking out on the gas pumps and the grassy ditch. Our waitress was a girl of about fifteen, wearing jeans and a pink blouse with "Gwen" embroidered on her breast pocket in bright curlicues.

"Hi, Gwen," Eddy said, glancing up at her with a lazy smile.

I'm sure she'd never seen anyone like Eddy before. He looked like a model in *Vanity Fair*, his sunglasses tucked into the collar of his loose linen shirt, his right ankle crossed carelessly over his left knee, his Rolex watch shining on his casual wrist, his white teeth gleaming in his smooth brown face. "Where's Sherry?" he said.

She stared at him in confusion, smiling weakly.

"Sherry's, right?" Eddy said, waving his hand to indicate the room and everything in it. "That's what it says on the sign."

"Oh. Oh, yeah. Sherry. She's . . . uh . . . she's not here." Gwen gave a nervous laugh, as if she'd made a joke, and shrugged her narrow shoulders jerkily.

Eddy smiled. He seemed to be completely aware of the effect he was having on that awkward adolescent girl, and he seemed to like it quite well. Nervously she pushed some hair behind one ear and shifted her weight. "So . . . uh . . ."

"So what should we eat, Gwen?" he said. "You tell us. What's the best thing on the menu?"

Gwen looked nonplussed, as if she had never been asked such a question before. She gave him a quick sideways glance, to see if he was kidding, and then rolled her eyes to the ceiling, giggling helplessly. "Oh, gee, I don't know.... The club sandwich is pretty good, I guess," she said. "You get french fries with that."

"That's what I'll have," I said. She glanced at me with a nod but I hardly existed for her. She was standing between us but all her senses had shifted to the side closest to Eddy. The tip of his canvas shoe was almost touching her leg. I thought in another moment he would brush his foot against her thigh. I waited for him to do it.

"Any other suggestions?" he asked. "What are you going to have for lunch?"

"Me?" Gwen laughed again and he laughed too, as though he found her absolutely delightful. "Oh, I'm skipping lunch today. I'm on a diet."

"A diet?" He raised his eyebrows in amazement. "What for?"

They went on that way for what seemed like a long time. I could have understood it if she'd been the least bit attractive, but she was scrawny and pale and vague, with pale, lashless eyes, a waif-like nonentity. That didn't seem to matter. He behaved as though he were entranced by her, as though every word she spoke was a pearl dropping from her mouth. He was finally persuaded to order a Denver sandwich, after she had explained to him, in great detail and with a lot of breathless giggling, what a Denver sandwich was. He watched her disappear into the kitchen. Then he turned his head and looked at me, smiling.

"What?" he said.

I was thinking that I must have been crazy to invite someone like him to Trewithen. I was wondering what had come over me to do such an absurd thing. I decided I would let him stay just a couple of nights, and then I would come up with some excuse to get rid of him, and he could go back to Toronto where he belonged. But I wasn't going to let him see how disgusted I was; I was going to pretend to be airily unconcerned. I started to smile. Then I changed my mind. Why the hell should I smile? "What was that all about?" I said.

"What?" His eyes opened innocently, but he was grinning.

"That," I said. I felt like leaning over and slapping his face, hard. See if he'd keep grinning then. " 'What are *you* going to have for lunch, Gwen?' " I mocked, bobbing my head from side to side.

"What's wrong with being friendly?" he said, still smiling.

"Is that what you call it?"

"Well, of course. What else?" He gave a light, maddening shrug.

I had a sudden impulse to stand up and push the table over on top of him. Then I felt shocked by the intensity of my anger. I decided I wouldn't say one word more. But my voice went on as if it had no connection to my brain. "I never knew you could be such an asshole," I said.

Colour came into his face. Good, I thought, good.

"You're jealous," he said.

"Jealous? Don't flatter yourself. Do you think I'm going to be jealous of some scrawny little teenage waitress at a gas station in the middle of nowhere? I just think it's boring . . . very boring and rude, to—"

"You're really jealous," he repeated in an incredulous tone. He leaned across the table, staring at me. I felt an angry warmth rising in my forehead and throat. He put his hand on my arm. I pulled roughly away.

"I told you, this has absolutely nothing to do with being jealous. It was rude, that's all. And really tiresome . . . and predictable, and it makes me—"

"I love it," he said. "Wow. It's exciting. Look at this, your eyes are almost black. I want to take you somewhere and have sex right now."

"Oh, shut up. You're unbelievable. You're such a—"

"I mean it. We could drive the cars a few miles further and then go into a field . . . lie down in that tall grass . . . no one on the road would even see us . . . let's. Why not?"

"Don't be ridiculous." I tried very hard to hold on to my anger, but it was no use, already it was evaporating in the heat of his teasing, seductive gaze. I could hardly keep from smiling a little. I let him put his hand back on my arm.

"Why not?"

"What about your Denver sandwich?" I said. "You don't want to miss that."

He laughed as if the words "Denver sandwich" were the funniest he had ever heard. He was still leaning across the table. His eyes were tangled up with mine. At that moment, Gwen returned carrying two large plates heaped with steaming food. Eddy bent over his and inhaled deeply.

"Oh, it smells wonderful, Gwen," he said. "I'm glad I listened to you." And then he glanced at me with a soft, meaningful smile. I realized that he had somehow managed to flirt with both of us in the same second.

When we left the diner the sun was high up in the sky and the heat seemed to be rising from the ground in waves. The brilliant afternoon light burned in the yellow grass, and the pine trees beyond looked invitingly cool and dark.

"In another hour and a half we'll be at Azure Lake," I told him. "We can go swimming right away. It'll be heavenly." Apparently I didn't care how manipulative he was, how flirtatious, how infuriating. He was standing beside me with his arm touching mine and that was all I cared about. At Azure Lake we would be all alone; I would have him entirely to myself for days on end, without any Gwens to distract him.

"Excuse me," a breathless, giggly voice called behind us. We both turned and saw her running across the gravel, waving some bills. "You didn't wait for your change." She was blushing and smiling, looking right through me to Eddy, as though he were standing there by himself.

He smiled at her in surprise. "No, it's for you," he said.

She chewed her lip bewilderedly, squinting her eyes at him as though he were too bright to be looked at directly. "But ...," she faltered. "It's so much."

Suddenly he reached out and touched her arm. He had put

on his sunglasses and all I could see was her distorted image reflected on the black shades. "No, it's not, Gwen," he said. "You keep it."

We walked toward our cars, leaving her standing there clutching the bills and staring after us with her mouth open.

"How much did you give her?" I asked him.

He shrugged. His smile had a twist in it. "The usual," he said. "I guess she's used to getting quarters."

"Yes," I said. "I guess she's never served a big tipper from the city before."

The sun had been beating ceaselessly through my windshield and the interior of my car was like an oven. Sweat broke out on my hairline as I fastened the seatbelt. I switched on the air conditioning and glanced in the rearview mirror. Gwen had walked toward Eddy's car and he was leaning out his window to talk to her. I couldn't hear what they were saying, but it didn't appear to be a short conversation. The food I had eaten, the greasy potatoes, the bacon and mayonnaise and bread, lay heavily in my stomach. A thin trickle of perspiration began to work its way down my spine. Gwen Nobody from Nowhere, I thought. My rival. Then for a moment a terrifying blankness came over me, as if I had forgotten where I was and what I was doing. I was a faceless, nameless thing looking into a smudged mirror at two strangers, a man in a white car and a mouselike girl in an airless, alien space. I stepped on the gas and shot out onto the highway. The speed seemed to restore me somewhat. My breath returned slowly to my lungs and the air conditioner began to dry the sweat on my forehead. Ahead of me an endless strip of gleaming concrete stretched out to the horizon. I was going over 150 kilometres an hour. He wouldn't be able to keep up with me. I was going to leave him behind. I would get to Trewithen, the solitude would be beautiful and enveloping, I would put on my bathing suit and walk into the warm blue water. The only sound would be the gentle splash of waves and the far-off muffled roar of someone's motorboat. After all, I didn't need him. I never needed anyone else at Trewithen.

But the white car sailed into place behind me, as though it had been fastened to me all along by a long, thin cord. His arm was resting on the edge of his window, his hair was blowing in the hot breeze, the same as before. It was clear that I would need a lot more speed to lose him.

In a little while I saw the blue sparkle of Lake Couchiching in the distance and then gradually the fields began to draw back from the road and the rock began to push its way forward. As always, the first glimpse of pink Muskoka stone gave me a childlike pang of happiness. Sometimes it jutted out of the water in a sheer promontory, other times it was long and flat as a table. So many summers I had lain on one of those flat pink rocks, feeling the smooth, sunwarm surface all along my back. So many times I had turned onto Highway 118 just south of Bracebridge and driven through the Huckleberry Rock Cut, craning my neck out the car window to see the tops of those dazzling pink cliffs towering above the highway. In some places the rock face was so smooth that it looked as though it had been carefully sculpted rather than blasted with dynamite. The Pre-Cambrian Shield, my father used to tell us proudly, as though he had created it himself. The oldest rock on earth.

So many times I had driven alone down that empty, sunny curve of road. But everything was different that afternoon, because the white car kept with me, glinting steadily in my rearview mirror like a flaw embedded in the glass. A sort of nervous anticipation began to take hold of me. I kept asking myself what had possessed me, why had I given in to a bizarre passing impulse and asked this man to come with me? My brain must have been clouded by sex, there was no other way to explain why he was the one I had chosen, out of all the people I had known in the past seven years since my father's death, to be my first guest at Trewithen—a sleazy guy named Eduardo Corona, it wasn't surprising that a person with a name like that would be a con artist, a drug dealer, a thug, a womanizer. But I couldn't stop and change my mind, it was far too late for that. He was right behind me, he couldn't be shaken, and he was about to enter the place that had been my private, closely guarded retreat for so long. When my car leaped over the top of the hill Trewithen spread out below me like a gift: the shimmer of bright water beneath the cloudless blue sky, the feathery trees waving in the soft air, the red and white flag snapping at the top of its bronzy flagpole, and the house itself, mossy green and lake-blue and cloudy white, as though pieces of the landscape had joined to form it and it had then settled between the pines, misty, unreal, almost like a mirage. "The domain of Trewithen," I murmured to myself. It was like a ritual that had to be repeated even though my father was no longer there.

I switched off the air conditioner, rolled down my window, and turned off the radio. The country stillness was beautiful and profound, only a faint rustle of blown leaves and the high thin hum of cicadas to break it. I turned off the highway onto our road, past the old black and white sign with its stern reprimand: PRIVATE PROPERTY! TRESPASSERS WILL BE PROSECUTED! A haze of golden dust swirled up behind me, and for a moment I lost sight of the white car. Then it reappeared, as solid and inescapable as ever. We drove into the shady drive, under the leafy canopy of poplar trees. At the far end you could see the gate, its old stone posts tilted slightly inward, the white paint on the crossbars weathered to a soft, woodsy grey. After the artificially chilly temperature created by the air conditioner the air under the trees felt soft and natural, full of green fragrance.

I got out of the car to open the gate. Eddy pulled up behind me and sat there behind his steering wheel. I didn't look at him as I jumped back into the driver's seat. He followed me between the two posts and in the rearview mirror I saw him stop and get out of his car to close the gate behind us. I watched him coldly, his fashionable sunglasses, his expensive clothes, his entire phoney, flashy façade. My God, I thought, I must have been out of my mind, this is a big, big mistake.

He jumped back into the white car and we went on. The

old wildflower garden was blooming like crazy. A rich tangle
of daisies and sunflowers and bluebells spilled down the slope
at the back of the house, buzzing with insects, alive with white
butterflies. I drove around it up to the top of the driveway and
parked. Eddy's car door slammed. I stood on the raked white
gravel, watching him as he walked toward me. I couldn't tell
from his expression what he was thinking.

"Well," I said, "we're here."

He lifted his eyes to look up at the wide, moss-green roof.
"It's big," he said in a tone of surprise.

"I told you it was big," I said.

"But I didn't think it was as big as this."

For some reason that irritated me. "You saw the pictures
in the albums. How big did you think it was?" I asked
sarcastically.

He didn't respond to either the words or the tone. He just
shrugged vaguely and looked past me at the large tubs of velvety red geraniums beside the back steps. "Is there a gardener
or something?" he said.

"Yes, there's a man in Port Azure. He and his wife come
out from town three times a week. He takes care of the gardens
and she takes care of the house. They've worked for us for
years."

"Us?"

"My family. I phoned to tell them we were coming so they
could get everything ready."

"This place is yours alone."

"Well, mine and my sister's, yes."

"But she's not here."

"She doesn't come here very often anymore. She never
loved it the way I did."

"Oh. She didn't like it."

"Well, she liked it, but not as much."

"Oh."

He was strangely subdued. Nothing he saw seemed to
awaken any reaction at all. Simple politeness demanded that
he utter a few complimentary phrases such as "Well, it's really

beautiful" or "What a perfect setting" or even "Very nice." But he didn't say a word. It was almost as if he was disappointed. After a moment he walked over to my car, opened the back door and lifted out a box of groceries. I unlocked the screen door.

"See?" I said. "The verandah is on three sides, south, east and north. There's an upper gallery too." I heard an artificial brightness in my voice. I sounded like a hostess worrying that her guests aren't pleased. He followed me across the long, cool, shadowy porch, nodding briefly, as if he wasn't particularly interested or impressed.

"Just put that box down on the table," I told him in the kitchen. "We'll unpack later." I thought surely he would say something about the kitchen because it was so large and airy, so cool because of the verandah's protection from direct sunlight, so animated with soft, swaying glimmers of green from the surrounding trees. Every year when we arrived at the cottage, my mother would take off her shoes and walk into the kitchen in her bare feet because she liked the feel of the wood floor. And Leslie would rush around and open all the windows and call out, "Look, the finches are back!" And you would see flashes of gold in the dark branches and for some reason I would always think of that fairy tale where the Emperor of China has a bird in a golden cage and he sets it free.

"Here?" Eddy said, and put the box of groceries on the polished wooden table.

"I'll pick flowers later," I told him. "My father always liked to have big bowls of flowers everywhere. I guess I got it from him."

"You'll pick flowers?" Eddy said. "I thought you'd have someone from town come and do it."

I looked at him sharply but his face was blank, without a trace of mockery.

"No, I like to do it myself," I said with an uncertain laugh.

Silently he followed me into the front room. Guests always used to exclaim in delight when they saw it. It was long and wide and the far wall was almost entirely glass, so perfectly transparent that you could forget it was there. You could stand just inside the door and look down the whole length of the room, past the verandah, all the way across the glistening blue of Azure Lake to the clear bright green of the distant shore. The western wall had a beautiful floor-to-ceiling alcove containing three tall arched windows of bevelled amber glass that made the vista of lawn and garden beyond look as though it were bathed in golden light, even on cloudy days. At the very top of the alcove, right under the roof, another small round window collected the sunshine in one broad shaft that poured downward and spread itself across the pine floor at our feet. The light and the polished cedar walls made you feel as though you were standing in a forest glade.

"On rainy days it's nice to have a fire in the fireplace," I said. "Of course it hardly ever rains in the domain of Trewithen." I could hear how idiotic I sounded, like some flaky real estate agent trying to sell property to a doubtful client. A few minutes before I had been full of hostility, wishing him far away. Now, just because he was so withdrawn and remote, I seemed desperately eager to please him somehow. "It's not too warm in here, is it?" I said. "There's no air conditioning. My father didn't like it, he liked the natural air. But there's usually such a nice breeze from the lake that you don't feel the heat. Does it feel comfortable to you?"

He shrugged carelessly. "Yeah," he said.

"There are two bedrooms on this floor, not counting the maids' room off the kitchen," I told him. "And six more bedrooms upstairs. The ones upstairs are the nicest ones. Come on, I'll show you."

He didn't move. "The maids' room off the kitchen?" he repeated.

"Oh, yes, well, it used to be the maids' room and I can't seem to get over calling it that. We used to bring a couple of maids with us in the summer. To cook and serve, and that kind of thing. My father had lots of parties."

He nodded thoughtfully. After a moment I turned away and started to climb to the second floor. He followed me. I heard his feet on the steps, the squeak of the wood. My chest felt a bit tight with inexplicable nervousness. I crossed the landing and opened the door of what I still thought of as my parents' room, even though it had been more than ten years since they'd occupied it. Mrs. Abbott had made the bed and opened the gallery doors and all the windows to let in the fresh air.

"This is where we'll sleep," I told him, glancing over my shoulder. He stood just inside the threshold, as though he needed permission to come further. His face hadn't changed; it was distant and unreadable. He wasn't his usual self at all, he wasn't even trying. For some reason I had imagined he would be excited and impressed by everything I showed him, or at least he would pretend to be. I had never thought he would follow me around in silence, barely rousing himself to nod or say "Oh."

"See the view?" I said. "Isn't it beautiful?" The northern windows and the gallery doors faced the lake; the two western windows had casements opening outward, so that you could lean across the windowsill and gaze down over the lawn and the white garden. "You can lie in bed and see the water," I said. "It looks wonderful in the moonlight. Once I saw a blue heron land right on the lawn. Do you know what a blue heron looks like?"

"No," he said. He was still standing just inside the door. His arms were folded across his chest.

"They have long, spindly legs and long graceful necks and their feathers are a sort of beautiful grey-blue colour. It was just before dawn and I don't know what made me wake up but all of a sudden my eyes were open and the lake looked all silvery in the first light, and then I saw him flying low over the water. He came in slowly and then he unfurled those long, long legs and landed in the grass. You should have seen the way he walked, he'd lift up one foot, and then the other, so daintily, just like a tall girl who didn't want to get her feet wet."

He smiled absently.

"You see all sorts of birds here," I said. "And squirrels and chipmunks and even a fox once in a while. Sometimes we used to come in the winter and you could even hear wolves howling. I've never actually seen a wolf though."

He uncrossed his arms and put his hands in his pockets.

"I don't know if you're interested in things like that," I said.

"Sure," he said.

"You seem so quiet," I said.

He twisted his shoulders and cleared his throat. "It was a long drive," he said. "I guess I'm sort of tired."

Maybe we should have brought Gwen along, I said to him silently. I'll bet you wouldn't be so tired then, would you? You'd be full of talk then, you'd have plenty to say, wouldn't you? Why don't you go back to the city where there are plenty of stupid little bimbos to impress? I'm sure you'd have lots of energy for that.

"There used to be a tennis court down there at the bottom of the lawn," I told him. "I don't play tennis so I haven't kept it up. But you can still see some of the court lines."

He walked over to look. I could feel him standing behind me, a foot or so away, as though it was too much effort to come any further. Don't strain yourself, I told him in my mind.

"Can you smell the flowers?" I said. "My grandfather wanted lots of gardens because the Trewithen in Cornwall had beautiful gardens. He had the white garden put in—all the blossoms are white—and also there's an herb garden and a rock garden and a winter garden. Once a friend of my father's was visiting with his mother from Atlanta. The mother was a real old Southern belle. They were down there on the lawn and all of a sudden she walked away and came back into the house. She said, 'Why, the smell of those white lilacs was so intoxicatin' that Ah thought Ah was gonna faint dead away!'"

I laughed. He nodded and gave a slight smile, as though he was humouring me. But you thought Gwen was terribly funny, didn't you? I said to him. Maybe you'd rather go back to that gas station and have some more witty conversation about french fries and Denver sandwiches.

"Let's go out," I said. "I'll show you the beach. You'll love the beach."

At the bottom of the front steps I paused and plucked a couple of fat red strawberries. They were warm from the sun and when you bit into them the juice sprayed across your tongue, hot and sweet. "Here, try one," I said, handing one to him. "When we were kids my sister and I used to get up early and come out here in our nightgowns to pick fresh strawberries. Then we'd have them for breakfast with cream and sugar. Mmmmmm, they're delicious. Go on, try it." He bit into his strawberry rather tentatively, as though it were a kind of fruit he had never seen before, strange and unappetizing. After chewing on it for a moment without expression, he nodded and said "Good" in a flat, toneless voice. I felt like taking him by the shoulders and shaking him.

We crossed the front lawn to the top of the cliff where the sunken stone steps went steeply down to the shore. The beach looked white in the sunlight, a little curve of shining sand with bright blue water lapping gently against it. I started down. After a moment I looked back and saw that he hadn't moved. He was still standing on the top step, staring out at the sparkling lake.

"Aren't you coming?" I said.

Without a word he started to follow me. He had rolled up the sleeves of his shirt to expose his well-shaped brown forearms, and his mouth was red from strawberry juice, but he didn't look happy or at ease. There was something stiff and unnatural about the way he walked, as though he was deliberately holding himself erect. I was usually in a festive mood the day I arrived at Trewithen. He was spoiling it for me; I couldn't relax. I felt as stiff and rigid as he looked.

On the beach I knelt down and let the water wash over my hand. His shadow fell across the sand beside me. "It's warm," I told him. "See how clear it is? Even when you swim out quite far, you can still see right down to the bottom." When I stood up I raised my wet hand impulsively toward his face. He jerked away as though my touch was repellent.

"What's wrong with you?" I said incredulously. "You've got strawberry juice on your mouth, I was just going to wipe it off!"

He turned aside and rubbed his lips roughly with the back of his hand.

"What's wrong?" I said again.

"Nothing," he said.

After a moment I went on talking. I didn't know what else to do. "This used to be a rocky beach," I said. "My father had tons of sand brought in. It was against some by-law, changing the shoreline isn't good for the environment, but he got around it somehow. I was just a tiny little girl, but I remember all the trucks. They had to come down over there where the slope is gentler. But even so, the brakes gave out on one of them and it ended up right in the lake."

"He got his sand though," Eddy said.

I was relieved to hear him speak in a normal tone. "Oh, yes," I said, laughing eagerly. "He didn't care how much trouble it was or how much it cost. He said he was sick and tired of having those sharp little rocks dig into his feet every time he went for a swim."

Eddy had raised his hand to shield his eyes from the radiant, sunlit water. He gave an odd, one-sided smile.

I was holding my sandals in one hand. I said, "Why don't you take your shoes off?"

For a moment I thought he was going to refuse. But then he bent over and unfastened his shoelaces.

"See, he was right, wasn't he?" I said. "Doesn't the sand feel good?"

He hesitated, still bending over, flexing his bare toes. Then his fingers moved slowly to roll up his pant-legs. Suddenly he looked about sixteen years old, a tall handsome boy whose youth and inexperience had made him stiff and inarticulate. I felt absurdly touched all at once; I almost forgave him for his strange behaviour. I felt like taking hold of his arm, but I didn't quite dare.

"That's the boathouse," I said. It seemed to float below the cliff at the eastern end of the beach, its pale green walls and dark green roof rising dreamily out of its own wavering reflection in the still water. "Do you want to see it?"

He gave a jerky shrug, as if to say that he was willing to go along with me, whatever I wanted to do, it was up to me.

"My father kept the big boat here sometimes," I told him as we walked toward it, our feet sinking down into the soft sand. "But it's gone now. We only have the launch and the rowboat. I don't know if you like rowboats. We could take it out later. It's nice after sunset."

He nodded, standing beside me in the shadow of the wall as I unlocked the door. Inside it was gloomy and damp, with a faint sound of dripping moisture. There were two large berths for boats. You could see the dim shape of the rowboat where it was suspended halfway to the ceiling on an automatic sling. Waves lapped softly against the pilings. The launch rested on planks above the murky, greenish water, the gold letters of its name gleaming dully against its dark mahogany bow.

"The *Gazelle*," I said, pointing it out to him. "She was one of the fastest boats on the lake in the 1930s but then she spent a long time in dry dock, until my father found her and had her restored. I'm not a great boat aficionado, but I do think she's kind of pretty."

Eddy nodded wordlessly.

"Do you think there'd be room for your boat here?" I asked. "Maybe sometime you could bring it." I have no idea why I said that. I still wasn't sure if it had been a good idea to invite him even once, and besides that I planned to tell him good-bye at the end of the summer, so what was the point in talking as though there would be many other visits, as though he and I would be going on together for a long time? But I kept it up. "You can bring a boat here by water all the way from Toronto if you want. My father did that a couple of times. He took the *Firebird* across Lake Ontario and down Lake Erie, then up through Lake Huron and Georgian Bay, right down Moon River into Lake Muskoka and through to Azure Lake. It took him about two weeks. We were standing up at the top of the cliff and we saw the *Firebird* coming around the inlet, very slow and easy, like a big white swan. That was such an exciting moment, to see it suddenly appear. Maybe you'd like to do that sometime with the *Caminito*."

He didn't reply. He seemed to be deep in thought.

There was a flight of narrow wooden stairs against the wall on the right. I led him up into the simple, sunny room on the second floor. Mrs. Abbott had cleaned all the windows and light was streaming in. The room contained a sofa with two wicker rockers and a wicker coffee table, two cots against the western and southern walls, two big white Muskoka chairs, a corner table with a lamp, a small fridge, and an antique radio, one of those big cabinet-sized radios from the 1940s.

"When my father was giving his big parties lots of people would stay overnight and some of them would sleep here," I said. "Sometimes I sleep here on the hottest nights because it's so cool right over the water like this."

I snapped on the radio. At first there was only static but after a bit of fiddling I found the CBC and a light, gay piano piece: Vladimir Ashkenazy playing Chopin's Fantaisie-impromptu in C-sharp minor.

"These Muskoka chairs don't belong in here," I said. "Let's take them outside."

He took one chair and I took the other. We carried them through the wooden doors and out onto the broad, bare deck at the front. The gleaming boards felt warm under the soles of my feet. We set the chairs down side by side facing the lake. Sunlight burned the top of my head and lay along my shoulders and arms like a cloth.

"It's too hot to sit out here now," I said. "But later on it'll be beautiful."

I leaned against the low white railing. Piano music drifted through the open door, quick and brilliant as sunlight rippling over the water.

"Do you see that red roof in the distance?" I said, pointing. "Way over on the opposite shore." He nodded. "That's La

Maison d'Azur, a restaurant. It's famous all over Canada. They make the most wonderful steak and seafood you've ever tasted. You sit on a terrace overlooking the lake and they hover over you and try to satisfy your every desire. The dessert chef trained at Le Cordon Bleu. We'll go there some night. You'll love it."

Suddenly a blue and silver motorboat streaked across the water, travelling at such a speed that its prow seemed to be pointing directly at the sky. It was far enough away that its roar was muted, but we could see the trail of white foam it left in its wake. A tall woman in a silver bathing suit was water-skiing, her long blonde hair blowing out behind her. She lifted one arm in a jaunty wave. I waved back. Eddy didn't. I turned to look at him and saw that he was trembling with an intense, unspoken emotion. His face was flushed, his eyes were bright with moisture, and his chest moved rapidly up and down, as though he had been running. I was astonished. I wanted to ask him what had happened but my lips moved without making a sound.

He felt me staring and gave a quick, hoarse laugh. He said, "I was just thinking of all the places I've been in my life."

I gaped at him, bewildered. After a moment he took a deep breath. "I've been so many places," he said. "I can't even remember them all. And now I'm here."

I didn't know what reply to make. "Yes," I said uncertainly.

He nodded and gave another quick laugh. The skin around his eyes had a damp sheen. "Sorry, I can't help laughing," he said. "It reminds me of home."

"What does?"

"All this."

I thought of that city I had looked at so often in my book: the parks, the drooping palm trees, the palaces and slums, the crowds of people, the labyrinth of streets. We were standing alone in a sunlit space, listening to Chopin, looking across the still, golden lake to the silent pines.

"Buenos Aires?" I said, confused. "It reminds you of Buenos Aires?"

All at once he straightened his body, shook his head and passed his hand briskly over his eyes, still laughing. After he had cleared his throat his voice came out firm and even. "Yeah," he said.

Behind us Ashkenazy produced his last dazzling crescendo and ended with a flourish.

Chapter Thirteen

Above the fireplace at Trewithen my mother and father stand in their wedding clothes, forever imprisoned in black and white, their hands clasped, looking outward and smiling with wide eyes, like two children all dressed up and eager for a journey. It always surprises me to remember what a small man he actually was; even in low heels she stands an inch or two taller than he. There is a rose in his lapel and she carries a bouquet of roses. I don't know whether those roses were red or white or pink or yellow. She is dressed in a light-coloured suit. That always struck me as so unlike her; she never wore suits. She liked bright colours, silks, shiny patent leather belts, spangles, glitter. Once I asked her why she had chosen to wear a suit on her wedding day, and it took her a moment to answer. Then she said, *Do you know how much that suit cost?* as if that explained everything.

So there she stands, in that tailored suit whose severe lines somehow make her look impossibly, almost laughably young—and actually she was young, barely twenty-one. He was young as well, only twenty-four. That picture didn't hang above the fireplace when they were alive. After his death I found it in an old cardboard box, and I had it framed and put there, where it seemed to belong.

"How old was he when he died?" Eddy asked, leaning against the mantelpiece, sipping vodka.

"Fifty-nine," I said.

"Oh. Not very old."

"No."

"Was he sick, or . . . ?"

"Heart attack," I said.

He nodded thoughtfully. "And she?"

"She was already dead, she'd been dead for a year and a half."

"So she was young too. What happened to her?"

"Car accident."

"Was she driving?"

"No," I said.

It was almost ten o'clock at night. The doors were open to the verandah and long shadows stretched across the floor, moving slightly in the warm breeze. He looked at me, his black eyes reflecting two flames of soft lamplight.

"Was anyone else hurt?"

"No. She wasn't wearing her seatbelt. She always hated them, they made her feel claustrophobic. She went through the windshield. She was thrown a hundred and fifty feet. They said every bone in her body was broken."

"Oh. *Dios mío*," he said.

I nodded, leaning back into the soft sofa cushions, looking up at her youthful, smiling face.

"And the driver?"

"Just a few scratches."

"It was . . ."

"A friend of hers," I said.

There was a brief silence, and country silence has a pervasiveness about it, a feeling that it goes on for miles, for eternity. Outside the wind whispered in the pine boughs, a sound so light, so faint and distant that you might think you had only imagined it.

"What about your parents?" I remarked. "I don't even know whether they're still alive."

He seemed to hesitate, as if he had to search for his reply. "No," he said after a moment, decisively. "Both dead."

"Both dead too. Well, we're in the same boat."

He nodded. He was standing there, his hair slicked back with water, holding icy white vodka in his long brown hand, tapping the side of the glass with a restless forefinger. No one like him had ever stood in front of that fireplace before. The dark air flowed through all the open doors and windows, smelling as fresh as if it emanated from the first night of the world. Every swallow of my drink tasted bracingly cold, powerfully refreshing and intoxicating. When he looked at me I felt it like a hand stroking my body.

"What were they like?" I asked. I didn't really care. I just wanted him to keep talking in that dark, quiet room while I sat watching him, he and I alone in a circle of soft light with the sweet-scented shadows all around. When he didn't answer me I said, "I don't think you've ever even mentioned your mother."

"Didn't I? Well, she died when I was quite young. I hardly remember her."

"That's too bad."

After a moment he had formulated his story and he began. "She was small and fair. She was convent-educated and married young. My father was a lot older than she was. He arranged the marriage with her father. He was madly in love with her but I don't know if she felt the same way about him. She got pneumonia and died when I was only four years old. The only thing I remember is sitting in her lap once and eating lemon candy out of a white paper bag. My father never got married again. There was a room at the *estancia* that had all her things in it, her Bible and rosary, her clothes and shoes, her jewellery and the veil she used to wear to Mass. He used to go in there sometimes and shut the door. Once he was in there for three hours and I started to get worried that something was wrong so I went to look. He was asleep sitting in a chair, and one of the windows had blown open and dead leaves had blown all over the carpet. He was holding one of her old shoes in his hand."

As always his way of telling things charmed me: I liked his ability to choose details for a special touch of poignancy. I smiled at him. My father would have found him contemptible. He would have hated it that someone like Eddy, a liar, a fake and a crook, could be standing on his carpet, drinking and talking expansively. I saw my father's sarcastic face, one eyebrow raised, I heard his superior, drawling voice. *There's nothing a woman likes better than a fast-talking piece of scum.*

I felt like laughing out loud.

Eddy took a long swallow of vodka and wiped his mouth with the back of his hand. "How much is a place like this worth?" he asked.

The abrupt change of subject startled me. "What? You mean, the cottage?"

"The cottage, the boathouse, the beach, all of it, the whole thing, how much would it be worth?"

"Well, I'm not sure. I've never thought about it."

"You've never thought about it?"

"No."

"You own this big piece of property and you have no idea what it's worth?"

"I know exactly what it's worth," I said dryly. "But if you're talking about dollars and cents, no. I suppose I could get the information from my lawyer. But why should I bother? It's not as if I'm ever going to sell it."

He stared at me. "How do you know?"

"Because I love it here. I'll never sell it."

"But what if you had to?"

"Why would I have to?"

He shook his head, smirking. "Say you needed the money."

I shrugged. "I won't."

212

"Are you that sure? You said you weren't rich."

"Well, not in a manner of speaking."

"Oh," he said. "Not in a manner of speaking."

"No. Not compared to some of the people around here. But I've got my trust fund, and a few safe investments, that kind of thing. I've got tenure. I'm in good shape."

"Say somebody offered you ten million dollars for it?"

I laughed, but he was standing upright, staring at me. "I'd say no," I told him.

"No. You'd say no to ten million dollars, just like that."

His scepticism irritated me. "That's right," I said. "I have no interest in money, and I've never understood why people are so obsessed with it. I told you I love it here. It would be like selling a part of myself. Why would I ever want to? Money is nothing compared to that."

"Not when you have a lot of it," he said, taking a swallow of his vodka.

"I told you I don't have a lot of it," I said quietly.

"Not in a manner of speaking," he said.

I stared at him. "What about your family?" I said. "Didn't they have a house in Buenos Aires and a ranch and a summer place in Mar del Plata? That's what you said, isn't it? So apparently they did all right."

His face didn't change. He kept leaning against the mantelpiece, holding his drink, and after a moment the clock beside his arm began to mark the hour with its even, elegant, bell-like chimes.

I set my glass aside. "Do you know what we should do?" I said. "Let's go for a swim." I stood up and began to unfasten the front of my loose cotton dress. He watched me, still a bit angry. His anger excited me. I had nothing on underneath my dress but a pair of underpants. In a moment I was naked. "We don't have to wear bathing suits," I said to him. "There's no one around for twenty miles. We can do anything we want." I bent down to unbuckle my sandals and then wriggled my bare toes against the soft rug. My pubic hair stood up like wire.

"Come on," I said to him breathlessly. "It feels great."

He continued to look at me for a moment. Then he drained his glass, set it down on the mantelpiece, and pulled his shirt over his head. Soon we were walking down across the damp grass, under a vast black sky crackling with stars. Our bodies looked white in the darkness. I heard him breathing. We were like wild creatures, like deer or foxes, moving along quickly on light feet, sniffing the air. The stone steps going down to the beach were smooth and warm. Below us the lake spread out like a dark, silken cloth, faintly shimmering.

"Ouch," he said behind me.

"Are you all right?"

"I tripped against something. It's so dark."

I reached up and took his hand. "I'll show you," I said. "I could go down these steps blindfolded." His fingers were hot around mine. We continued to go down. The air streamed over every part of my body, entered every pore, opened and cleansed me from head to foot. I felt as if I had never really been naked before. When I stepped onto the beach the grains of sand brushed the soles of my feet like a sexual touch. He let go of my hand and walked ahead of me. His vertebrae rippled in his long back. He stood at the shoreline and dipped his foot into the lake.

"You look like a Greek god," I said to him. Then I felt ridiculous for making such a stupid, extravagant remark. I dashed past him and plunged. He followed me. In a moment the water was swirling all around us, warm and slow as perfumed oil, and our limbs tangled together, my feet touching his knees, his thighs squeezing my waist, my toes on his hips, his shoulder against my breasts, his wet mouth over my wet ear. I had to gasp for breath, and when I lifted my face up into the air the earth seemed to tilt crazily, the horizon seemed to blur, the stars came pouring down around our heads with a sound like breaking glass and dissolved in the lake. After a while we ran up onto the beach and lay side by side to let the soft breeze dry our bodies. The air was as warm as mid-afternoon. I could smell a trace of his cologne on my own skin. "Let's just sleep here," I said.

"Here? On the beach?"

"Why not?"

"Do you do that?"

"I've never done it before," I said. "But I feel like it tonight."

"Okay," he said.

"Just a minute, I'll be right back." I went into the boathouse and climbed up to the second floor. In the pale light from the window I could see myself in the mirror, my white breasts and rounded belly, my wet tangled hair filled with sand. For a moment I stared in amazement because I looked so strange and unearthly, not quite human. A water sprite, I thought drunkenly, it's a midsummer night's dream.

Through bush, through brier,
Over park, over pale,
Through flood, through fire,
I do wander everywhere,
Swifter than the moon's sphere,
And I serve the Fairy Queen. . . .

I took a quilt from one of the cots, a bottle from the fridge, and a corkscrew from a drawer in the bedside cabinet. When I came back out into the shadow of the boathouse door, I saw him lying at a distance on the sand, white and naked and motionless, his arms above his head, as though he were a corpse that had been washed ashore after a violent storm. His absolute stillness stopped me for a moment; I stood there with the cold wine bottle dangling against my thigh, feeling the hair rise up on my scalp. It was as though we had entered a dimension where the usual laws were suspended; he could die, he could disappear as easily as that. But I had a fancy that perhaps in my new fairy-shape I could recover him, I could bring him back to life by pouring some wine into his mouth. He didn't open his eyes as I approached. Even when I crouched down beside him and bent over his face to tickle his cheek with my hair, his eyelids didn't flutter.

"Eddy," I whispered. He didn't respond. "Eddy, are you asleep?" I said softly. And then he blinked and opened his eyes, suddenly wide awake, sharply alert, with the face of someone fearful but ready to meet his fear, looking at me and then past my shoulder as though he expected to see someone else behind me. I dropped the things in my arms and climbed over him, clasping his wrists firmly and pressing him into the ground.

"You're my prisoner," I said.

"Good," he said.

"Aren't you afraid?"

"A little. But that's all right."

"Don't worry," I said. "I won't hurt you. Unless you ask me to."

He looked up at me, smiling, his eyes black and silky like water with no bottom.

"We have cold white wine," I said. "We'll have to drink it right out of the bottle."

"I'm already drunk," he said. "I don't know if it was the vodka or not. I'm flying."

"Me too," I said. All at once my elbows and knees began to tremble and I had to lie down against him. The pulse in his throat pounded loudly in my ear. It couldn't have been the same beach where I spent all those childhood summers, where Leslie built sandcastles and my mother read her movie magazines. It was a new place I had never been before, wild, rapturous and alien.

He said, "Just keep holding on to me, *querida*. I feel like I'm going to fall right off the world."

A meteorite dropped through the sky and broke apart in a shower of fiery sparks, sizzling and popping like distant gunfire.

Chapter Fourteen

THE NEXT MORNING I WALKED IN THE WHITE GARDEN, sipping a cup of coffee. The sunlight was bright, yellow as butter, warm on the top of my head, so warm it penetrated all the way down to the bottom of my feet and filled me with loose, lazy pleasure. Light was sparkling on the edge of my white cup. I put my face down to inhale the steamy aroma. I could smell the flowers too, tea roses, white narcissi, daisies, nicotiana, sweet alyssum, and the rich, loamy earth they sprang from. I could smell the grass, and the trees, and the fresh lake water. My clothes felt almost weightless on my body, as though only the thinnest of veils separated my skin from the soft air. We had lain on the beach in the breathless stillness just before dawn, and he told me the Spanish phrase for morning star, *lucero del alba*, words that seemed as beautiful as poetry. Tell me more Spanish words, I said, and he said *alegría* which means joy. *Feliz*, which means happiness. *Delicia*, which means delight. *Tierra*, which means earth. *Cielo*, which means heaven. All such beautiful words, I said, tell me more. He said, *Te llevo en el alma,* which means, I carry you in my soul. And then I had to turn my head away because I despise that kind of romantic fakery. I tried to change the subject by telling him some words in Italian, but he already knew them. His Italian accent was better than mine.

I had thought he was upstairs taking a shower, but suddenly I heard his voice speaking softly on the verandah. At first I thought he must be talking to me so I walked out onto the lawn, but he was standing inside the screen, half in shadow, and I saw that he had brought a cellular phone with him. I couldn't hear him very clearly, but he was speaking Spanish, and it sounded like a totally different language from the tender and melodious one he had revealed to me earlier. He took a couple of paces forward and then back, using one stiff hand for emphasis, and said curt, bitten-off things full of crisp consonants, things like *Está fregado!* and *No me jodas!* and *Ay, mierda! Mierda* sounded enough like the French *merde* that I thought I could guess what it meant, at least. I walked across the lawn and climbed the front stairs. If he saw me he gave no sign. Apparently he was so absorbed in his telephone conversation that he had forgotten about everything else. It was hard to believe he could be the same man who had lain naked on the beach only a few hours before. As I opened the screen door and stepped up onto the verandah, he turned and began to walk in the opposite direction, as if he didn't want me to hear what he was saying. That annoyed me and I walked right after him and sat down in the wicker rocker. He disconnected his call and punched out another number.

"Yeah, it's me," he said curtly. "I was talking to the guy in Montreal. He's going to be around for three days so you'd better leave this morning. He's at the Senator Hotel. Rodriguez. That's what I said. How the fuck should I know? Look it up in the phone book when you get there. No, you're not going to call me, I'm going to call you. Yeah, that's right. Good-bye."

Then he turned to look at me, pushing the aerial down and smiling cheerfully.

"What does *jodas* mean?" I asked.

He opened his eyes wide and gave a quick laugh. "It's a very rude word," he said. "Forget you heard me say it. You know what happens talking business with some guys."

"You're like those people you see on the street in Toronto who can't bear to be separated from their phones no matter what," I said. "Oh, hi, Joe, this is Moe. Just called to tell you I'm walking along Bloor Street now. Now I'm turning the corner onto Yonge. I'll call you again when I get to the next intersection."

He smiled and shrugged. "It was business," he said.

"I thought you were taking a holiday."

"I am, but this was important."

"As soon as my father died, I had all the phones taken out of here. I hate telephones on holidays."

He stared at me. After a moment he gave me a charming smile. "I'm sorry," he said. "Honestly, it was very important. But I told them I was turning the phone off so they couldn't call me. I told them I'd check in once a day and that was it. I'll do it when you're in the bathroom or something. You won't even know."

I couldn't overcome a certain stiffness in my mouth. "You can't even be away from it for one day, huh?" I said, not looking at him, squinting at the dazzle of sunlight on the lake. "You have to call in."

"You won't even know," he repeated. He was standing right beside my chair. After a moment he brushed my bare shoulder casually with the tips of his fingers. All at once I remembered some of the things he had whispered to me in the night. Sweet, obscene things. Heat rose delicately in my face.

"I'm thinking of getting out of it soon," he said suddenly.

"What? What do you mean, out of it?"

"Something big might be coming up," he said. "If it works out, I think I'll be able to retire."

I raised my head but he had averted his eyes. He was staring through the screen. I thought of asking what this "something big" might be, but I decided not to.

"You'll retire at the age of thirty-two?"

"Some people do," he said.

"And then what?"

He continued to stare out over the lake, narrowing his eyes against the brilliant sunlight. Finches were chirping gaily in the trees close to the house. There was a brief silence, as though he had never thought beyond that point before.

Finally I said, "Maybe I'll retire too and you and I can just live here together." I didn't mean it, of course, but for some reason it pleased me to say it.

"Yeah," he agreed. I don't think he meant it either, but he smiled and went on talking. "Every night we'll go for a swim after dark and then drink ice-cold wine and fall asleep on the beach."

"That's right. And in the morning I'll get up and make *café au lait*. I'll pick strawberries and we'll have them with sugar and cream."

"We'll barbecue steaks and eat them on the verandah by candlelight," he said. "Then we'll go somewhere and dance."

"Liar's Cove in Port Azure," I said. "There are dances there every Saturday night. It's a big pavilion with doors that open onto the lake. Duke Ellington and Louis Armstrong used to play there."

"We'll come home late," he said. "We'll light a fire in the fireplace and have sex on the rug in front of it. Now you're blushing."

"I am not."

"Yes, you are. And your hair will look like fire and I'll brush it for you. It'll crackle and give off sparks and my fingers will get burned." He laughed and his hand slipped across my cheek and into my hair, drawing it back from my temple. I felt his fingertips lightly caressing my scalp. I closed my eyes. He kept talking quietly. "Then we'll go upstairs and have sex on that big bed in the big front bedroom. Huh?"

"Yes," I said. It seemed a great effort to move my lips.

"We'll stop wearing clothes. We'll have sex on the lawn in the middle of the day. We'll have sex in that room in the boathouse."

"On a rainy afternoon," I murmured, leaning my head back against the palm of his hand. "With water thundering down on the roof."

"Oh, yes," he said. "I hope it rains soon."

"The summer will just go on. We'll never change, we'll never get tired of each other. We'll never get old," I said. "We'll never die."

"Right," he said.

Chapter Fifteen

HE KEPT HIS WORD AND I DIDN'T SEE HIM on the telephone for a long time after that. At night we went for drives along the lake, in my car with the top down, letting the wind stream through our loose summer clothes. We went to La Maison d'Azur and had dinner. They served us cocktails in the garden and then the maitre d' led us onto the large, cool terrace with its white tablecloths and tall candles and glittering silverware. We sat beside the lake and our reflections shimmered on its dark, shifting surface. The white-coated waiter brought us a bottle of champagne. "Mr. Franks sends his compliments, Miss Tremain," he said. "He hopes you have a very pleasant evening."

"Well, how nice," I said. "Tell him thank you so much."

Eddy was looking at me with a quizzical half-smile.

"The owner was a friend of my father's," I explained. "He always remembers me."

"Naturally," Eddy said with a laugh.

ONE DAY WE TOOK THE *GAZELLE* onto the lake. I let Eddy take the helm and he steered her sleekly and easily out of the slip and into the open water, as though he had been doing it all his life. I noticed that he was wearing the kid leather driving gloves he had bought at Hazelton Lanes.

"Isn't it a little warm for gloves?" I said.

"You get a better grip," he answered breezily.

The sun was pouring across the water, turning it into a sheet of white light so radiant that you could hardly see the small piny islands floating on its surface, wrapped in blue-green secrecy. I relaxed into the soft leather upholstery and stretched my feet out across the smooth mahogany floor. Right through the thick boards you could feel the thud of moving water against the underside of the boat. A fine crisp mist sprayed across my cheeks and sunglasses.

"She's so smooth," Eddy said. "She just glides."

"Oh, yes," I agreed. "She's a pretty good boat. Pick it up, Eddy. She can go a lot faster than this."

Eddy laughed and made the *Gazelle* leap out of the water. When she came down again she slid cleanly between the parting waves, without even a jolt.

"Oh, man," Eddy said. "I want one just like her. How much would she cost?"

"I have no idea," I said gaily.

The RMS *Segwun* came steaming around one of the dusky islands, clouds of pale smoke rising from her smokestack, her whistle tooting aggressively. You could see the lines of eager faces peering over the deck railings. There was a brief flutter of waving hands.

"What's this?" Eddy asked me.

"Oh, it's an old steamboat that takes gangs of tourists on a cruise of all the lakes," I said. "It goes all the way from Gravenhurst to the top of Lake Joseph, and the passengers get to gawk at Millionaires' Row and that sort of thing."

Eddy glanced at me. "Millionaires' Row?"

"That's a sort of nickname. Right down there, between those two islands, there's a channel with quite a few really palatial cottages on both sides, and I guess lots of people enjoy staring at them."

"Palatial . . ."

"Like palaces."

He nodded and repeated the word as though to fix it in his memory. "Palatial. Like palaces. They're more palatial than Trewithen?"

"Oh, God, yes, Trewithen is a model of simplicity compared to some of these places. Americans own quite a few of them."

Eddy grinned at me. "Oh, let's go and take a look."

"Are you serious? It's such a tacky thing to do. My father used to say it was typical of Americans that they'd build these enormous gaudy places and then complain when a bunch of yahoos came to gawk at them."

Eddy laughed. "Let's be *yahoos*," he said. "Let's gawk at these *palatial* houses."

"Oh, all right, if you insist." My reluctance was half pretence; it was a frivolous, sunlit afternoon and I was ready to do anything. "Just keep heading for that channel straight ahead."

The green headland of Deer Island rose up before us, with its tall flagpole and dazzling white curved pier stretching out across the watery reflections of dark trees.

"This half of the island belongs to the Gable family, the owners of Global Oil. They've spent summers here since 1910 or something like that. The cottage is up the hill, through the trees. You can't see all of it from here. It has twenty-five rooms. That middle boathouse is for their antique boat collection. They have everything from a Gentleman Racer to a 1924 Ditchburn cabin cruiser."

Eddy leaned down over the helm, trying to peer through the screen of dark branches. "What's that, I see something that looks like a fountain or . . ."

"Oh, that's a waterfall. They have a Japanese garden. Can you see the little curved footbridge? Lower down on the other side there's a big pond with water lilies."

"So you've been visiting at this place," Eddy said.

"Once or maybe twice, a long time ago. I was there with my parents. I'm not sure whether I ever met any of the Gables. There were always dozens of people around and I can't really remember who any of them were. Now, over there, on your left, is Echo Park, it belongs to Ezra Cannon, he's the head of Polaris Entertainment in New York City, if you've ever heard of it. Do you see that smaller cottage halfway down the hill, with the window-boxes? That's the children's cottage."

Eddy blinked at me. "The children have their own cottage?"

"Yes, they do. It's an exact replica of Snow White's cottage in the Walt Disney movie."

"You're kidding," Eddy said.

"No, I'm not. One summer Mrs. Cannon had a birthday party for the six-year-old, and she flew in a bunch of New York actors to play Snow White and the seven dwarfs."

Eddy laughed in amazement. "Actors? But . . . do you mean . . . ?"

"Yes, seven of them were dwarf actors. Or acting dwarfs. Actors who happened to be dwarfs. However you want to put it. It was a memorable occasion."

"Were you there?"

"Oh, heavens, no. I don't know the Cannons at all. But everybody in Muskoka knew all about that party. The ones whose children were invited went on and on about what an imaginative idea it was, and the ones whose children weren't invited said it was vulgar and pretentious. And of course there were a few nationalists who thought they should at least have hired Canadian dwarfs. . . . The Messers from Pittsburgh own the other half of Deer Island. See the waterslide? They can walk out on their deck in the morning, sit at the top and just slide all the way down to the water."

Eddy grinned, shaking his head. "Fantastic," he said.

"Why? There must be places like this in Mar del Plata, aren't there?"

"Yes, there are big, fancy places, of course. But this is one thing I have to say. No one ever flew in Snow White and the seven dwarfs."

"No, I should think not."

As we reached the southern tip of Spruce Island we suddenly seemed to be alone on the lake, as though all the other boats and people had vanished. The motor of the *Gazelle* made a soft, putting sound as it cut gently through the foamy wavelets. The water felt as warm as a bath. When you lifted your eyes, the white outlines of the Godfreys' gazebo became visible through the haze of sunlight, sitting right at the edge of a high ridge covered with a stretch of grass as green as a golf course. "We did know these people quite well," I told Eddy. "The Godfreys from Toronto. Every year at the beginning of July they have a huge party with an orchestra and dancing and a midnight supper. You can always hear the music and laughing all over Lake Belair, sometimes it goes on until dawn. They call it their 'Summer Rendezvous,' and there's always a different theme so you're supposed to dress appropriately. One year it was a Hawaiian luau, and another year it was Carnival in Venice, that kind of thing. One year you were supposed to come dressed as your favourite author."

Trying to take his cue from my attitude, Eddy toned down his enthusiasm. "Well, that sounds . . . okay. Wasn't it?"

"Not really. It was kind of unsettling, you'd be making conversation with someone who looked like Lord Byron, but all he could talk about was whether the Blue Jays were going to make it to the World Series."

The *Gazelle* burst out of Millionaires' Row, picking up speed as she streaked away from the two islands into the open expanse of Lake Belair. Eddy was staring straight ahead, his eyes narrowed against the glare of watery light.

"I had my fill of big parties long ago," I said casually. "Now I think the best parties are with just two people."

A smile formed on Eddy's mouth. Suddenly he reached across and gave my shoulder a brief, hard squeeze.

ONE NIGHT WE WENT TO A MOVIE in Gravenhurst and it was late when we started to drive back, eight-thirty or nine o'clock. The sun had dipped toward the horizon and the shadows had begun to stretch out, rippling like endless waves across the fields and the high pink rock. We took a slightly different route home so I could show him more of the countryside. He was interested in everything; he wanted to see it all. The road dropped away behind us; the tires seemed to skim over the concrete. I thought to myself that this was a part of my life separate from all the rest, a fragment of time unconnected to either past or future. I thought it was the same for him too. For a while we weren't caught in any pattern; we had broken free and we were driving down a highway going nowhere in particular, without history, without consequences.

We drove past the old Greenmantle airfield. He sat forward alertly, staring. "What's this?"

"British pilots trained here during World War II," I told him. "No one uses it now."

He wanted to stop and take a closer look. I didn't understand his curiosity, but I was willing to go along with it. The slamming of our car doors reverberated across the empty purple landscape. We climbed down a weedy ditch and crossed a field toward the cluster of dim, deserted buildings. Like all abandoned places, Greenmantle had a haunted feel about it, as though it echoed with voices and footsteps long gone. Crickets sang eerily from their hidden places in the tangled grass.

"So no one uses it now?" Eddy asked.

"Not for years. It was still operating in the sixties for a while. Sometimes during the summer it would get quite busy. A friend of my father's used to land his plane here once in a while."

"But not anymore?"

"Well, it was hardly ever used in the winter so it wasn't worth keeping up, really."

He stopped in front of the gaping entrance of a ruined hangar, staring outward at the faded but clearly visible outlines of a runway stretching away through the twilight. Although the ground was still warm, the air inside the hangar felt chilly and damp against our backs, as though it had not been disturbed in decades. You could hear the soft squabbling of swallows high up in the dusty rafters.

I stood close to him. I took his hand and pressed it against my breast. As always he responded at once, squeezing and caressing me with his long, skilful fingers. He never let me down, he was always ready to give me what I wanted. But when I glanced up at his shadowed face he was looking out into the dusk.

"Eddy?" I whispered. He didn't reply. After a moment I leaned against him, breathing in the smell of his shirt, his cologne, the faint sweaty dampness of his skin. Sometimes his smell alone could make me ache with desire. "Oh, Eddy," I said. I rubbed myself against him like a cat, I put my arms around him and squeezed his hard buttocks. Then he turned to me with a sigh. But even while he kissed me and unbuttoned my shirt, I felt that a part of his mind was fixed on something else.

We walked back to the car in silence.

That night we slept out on the boathouse deck, lying naked on an old quilt, gazing up at the starry black sky.

He told one of his stories. "This is something I heard once. There was a kid in Buenos Aires and he was walking along by the water one night. So he steps on something hard and looks down and it's a necklace of pearls. Real pearls, white like milk. They're just there, as if they've dropped from the sky. No one's around, there's no sign of anyone who might have lost this necklace or left it there. So the kid takes it home and sleeps with it under his pillow. During the night he has a dream. In the dream he's walking along the same beach in the dark and he sees the same pearls and picks them up. Then all of a sudden a man in a big panama hat comes marching down the sand out of the dark and grabs him by the collar and shakes him till his teeth rattle and the pearls fall out of his hand and the string breaks and all the pearls roll away in different directions

Richelle Kosar

across the beach. Then the kid wakes up crying because he thinks he's lost the necklace, and he's so happy when he realizes he was only dreaming. He looks under his pillow, still so happy, and there's no pearl necklace. It's gone. So he never knows whether he just dreamed that he found the necklace, or whether the man in the panama hat was real, and not a dream."

I smiled. "That sounds like something from Borges."

There was a slight pause while he assimilated that. Then he shrugged and said, "Maybe."

"Don't you think so?" I said.

His chest rose and fell with his even breathing. "Yeah, a bit," he said finally. I felt sure that he didn't have the least idea who Borges was.

"Do you know what I like best in all his writing?" I said. "I think it's called 'Inferno,' the piece about Dante and the leopard. I get tears in my eyes every time I read it. Do you know the one I mean?"

"Yes," he said firmly. After a moment he added, "I'm not a fan of his, though."

"Oh? Why not?"

He shrugged and said with sudden flat contempt, "He always bored me so much I couldn't keep my eyes open."

"How strange," I said. "I guess I thought any well-educated Argentinian would appreciate Jorge Luis Borges."

"It's pronounced Hor-hay," he said.

After that he seemed to go to sleep, and yet somehow I had the feeling he wasn't asleep, he was just lying there with his eyes shut. I lay beside him, motionless, the warmth of his arm against mine, looking at the metallic light on Azure Lake.

The next day I walked to the edge of the lawn and looked down at the beach and saw him squatting at the end of the pier like a boy, wearing baggy shorts and no shirt, his glistening arms resting loosely across his knees, his hair thick and black and shiny in the sunlight. The sight of him gave me a sudden rush of emotion, as though his presence had been completely unexpected and unhoped for. He was crouching there perfectly still, gazing at the water obliviously. So many things

230

about him gave me pleasure: the shape of his back, the texture of his skin, his clean brown limbs, his tea-coloured eyes, his mouth, his supple tongue, his clever hands. And his stories, his jokes, his easy charm, his secrecy, his dangerous edge, his exotic elegance with the touch of crudeness underneath. And the fact that I knew so little about him. And the fact that soon he would be gone. The time was short; one summer, already half over. The brevity of the affair was what gave it such intensity, what made it so sharp and strong. Already I could look forward to the time when I would come back again alone, and I would stand in the same place, gazing down at an empty pier. Already I could imagine the tender regret I might feel. I won't forget you, Eddy, I said to myself in voluptuous sadness, looking down at his unmoving figure, squatting there above the still, sunlit water. I'll never, never forget you.

AT THE END OF OUR THIRD WEEK at Azure Lake he came and told me that he had to go back to the city for a couple of days. He didn't say why, but I assumed he had just made one of his phone calls.

"I'll leave now and I'll be back tomorrow night," he said. "It's just a few things I have to take care of. Is that okay?"

I had been sitting in a lawn chair desultorily attempting a crossword puzzle. The sun was behind his head and I had to squint when I looked up at him.

"Sure," I said.

"You don't mind?"

"No," I said. "I'm used to being here by myself."

Suddenly he squatted down beside my chair so that his face was on a level with mine. "Don't get too used to it, though," he said. "Because I'll come back."

"Will you?" I said.

"Yeah," he said. "I kind of like it here. I can come back, can't I?"

"Oh, I guess so," I said.

He gave my hand a playful smack of a kiss and then walked away across the grass. After a few moments, I heard his car door slam and the far-off rumble of the ignition. The sunlight warmed my eyelids and my bare legs. I listened to his tires crackling on the gravel as he turned out of the driveway, and then the rumble of his engine died away on the air, leaving a sudden far-reaching cricket harmony and the distant ripple of water on the empty beach. I kept my eyes shut. From far away I could hear the tinkle of wind chimes on the front verandah. Suddenly a great wave of loneliness flooded over me. It was ridiculous. I was never lonely. I had to get up at once and walk. I went into the house and passed through to the kitchen. Our breakfast coffee cups were still sitting on the polished wooden table, the white porcelain tinted a soft green by the ivy over the window. It occurred to me that he would undoubtedly stop at that gas station again to see that little nonentity. Gwen. He would walk into that shabby café and she would come out of the back in her tight jeans and pink blouse, holding her pad and pencil, and her pale face would flush from throat to forehead with excitement and pleasure. He would say "Hi, Gwen," and give her that happy, flashing smile, as though she were the one above all others on earth whom he most wanted to see. She would have a cheap, cluttered bedroom up a narrow flight of stairs at the back of the café and she would take him there, nervous and apologetic, and he would sit beside her on the bed, gleaming like a prince in his expensive clothes, soothing her with his gentle hands, unbuttoning her pink blouse, staring into her face, murmuring soft, sincere compliments ... "Your hair is so beautiful, Gwen, I love your laugh. I've never felt such soft skin, my hands are shaking, you excite me, Gwen, lie back, lie back." . . . She would be stunned, tears would come into her pale lashless eyes because he was like someone she had only dreamed of, come to life. How he would love that.

I sat there at the kitchen table and thought it all through, detail by detail. In some strange way I savoured it; it filled me with a sort of hot, bitter pleasure.

Afterwards I got up and washed the cups and breakfast dishes. Then I changed my clothes and brushed my hair and put on some makeup. The front seat of my car was warm and stale-smelling. I hadn't been in it in days. The engine vibrated fitfully when I turned my key in the ignition but after a moment it sprang to life and I stepped on the gas pedal to make it roar. *Adieu, mes amis!* my father used to sing out when he was passing people on the highway in one of his extravagant automobiles.

The town of Port Azure is built on a hillside at the south end of the lake, and all its streets slant gently downward to the water. Once a rich American visitor forgot to put on his emergency brake and his Mercedes rolled right down Main Street and across the Azure Inn pier, finally burying its elegant nose in the mud right around the pilings at the bottom of the lake. That took place on Dominion Day in 1954 and the story still appears every July in the *Port Azure Tribune* in the "It Happened Here!" column.

The population of the town doubles in the summertime and even on a lazy Wednesday afternoon all the tourist shops were filled with people and there were small lineups at the checkout counter in the supermarket. I bought enough groceries to last another three weeks and had the box boy load them into my trunk. Then the heavenly scents from the Homewood Bakery drew me across the street. I bought two dozen peanut butter cookies and a dozen cinnamon rolls. The girl behind the counter smiled brightly at me and said "Thanks, Miss Tremain" as she took my money. I didn't have any idea who she was and I hated to be called "Miss Tremain" in that perky, bubbling way. It made me feel eighty years old. I gave her a blank look and the smile faded from her face. Probably after I left the store she turned to her co-workers and said, "Boy, is she ever snotty!"

Heading back to my car, I became so occupied with trying to remember exactly how long the Homewood Bakery had been operating that I wasn't alert enough to spot Kelly Wyatt in time to avoid her. Suddenly she blocked the sidewalk in front of me and said, "Well! Grace! Hi there!"

She was a few years younger than I, with white-blonde hair rolled into an elegant twist at the nape of her neck, and a face somewhat lined from years of relentless tanning. Her family owned a cottage at the southern tip of Azure Lake and she and my sister Leslie played together every summer of their childhood. I started to dislike Kelly the moment she became old enough to talk.

"Hi, Kelly," I said.

"So. You're back at the old estate, are you?"

I just nodded. Kelly didn't need anyone's help to carry on a conversation; she could go on for hours all by herself.

"Alone as usual? God, I envy you. I can hardly even imagine what bliss it would be to have a few uninterrupted moments to myself. Believe me, it's almost impossible once you have children. Of course the nanny came up with us, which is a help, but I've made a vow that I'm never going to be like my mother was, so uninvolved and uninterested. Because if you have no interest in kids as people, and no interest in your role as a parent—do you know what I mean?"

I opened my mouth, but Kelly didn't wait for me to respond.

"There's still time for you, Grace. Lots of women are starting late nowadays. Believe me, parenting is an experience like no other. It changes your priorities completely. You stop being all wrapped up in your own selfish concerns, you see what's really important and what just doesn't matter. For Easter I got Jessica a beautiful little outfit, an Elsa Rivers, do you know her? She designs exclusively for children, and it was such a ..."

My father used to say that Kelly Wyatt talked so much she foamed at the mouth. While she rattled on, I occupied my mind by imagining what it would be like to live with her, to have her around night and day, talking as you opened your eyes in the morning, following you from room to room with endless anecdotes, offering her opinions at lunch and recalling her dreams at dinner, whispering in your ear at night as you lay in bed trying to fall asleep.

"... so we decided to put in a solarium and a hot tub this year," she was informing me. "It adds so much to the value of the property. Although of course we'd never sell. Can you imagine anyone but the Wyatts summering at Lakeview?"

"No," I said.

"You'll have to come over once it's all finished. Of course I'm not sure when that will be, the workmen are so lazy, they show up late, work for fifteen minutes, and then it's time for a coffee break. The other day Jerry was so annoyed, he went down to the lakefront and they were all sitting around smoking and they said, 'We still have nine minutes left in our lunch hour.' Well, that's what unions have done to the working class in this country. You'd think they'd be grateful to have jobs, but not at all. They don't want to work anymore, they just want to sit around on their backsides and get paid for it. It's maddening how arrogant they are. I told Jerry about your father, you know, about that time he shut down the bottling plant in Quebec because the workers didn't want to take a wage cut? Well, boo hoo, things are tough all over. It was even on television, I remember that. All those union goons were bellowing insults and threatening to kill him, F this and F that, you know the kind of language people like that use, if they didn't have the F-word they'd be totally inarticulate. But your father was cool as a cucumber. He said he had no intention of letting 'disorganized labour' tell him how to run his business. 'Disorganized labour'! Jerry loved that when I told him. He laughed his head off. Well, let's face it, your father was a smart man."

I smiled and offered her a peanut butter cookie from my bag. She took one and bit into it and waved at somebody on the other side of the street, all without interrupting the flow of her chatter. Cookie crumbs quivered on her lower lip as she went on.

"The older you get the more you look like him, Grace. That hair! You and your father are the only people I've ever seen with hair exactly that shade of red. I remember once years ago, I must have been quite small, we were all sitting around some tables at Liar's Cove, and your father came in late, I think he'd been in the city and no one was expecting him that night, but suddenly he walked in the front door, and you could see that red hair all the way across the room even in the dark. The band was playing something by the Beatles or the Stones, lots of drums, and of course we all knew, even we little kids knew how he felt about rock and roll. So when he went over to the bandstand and called to the lead singer, everybody laughed. And then the band started to play 'Deep Purple' . . . It was probably the only slow one they knew. And your father strolled to the edge of the dance floor and held out his hand, oh Grace, he was supremely elegant, and your mother stood up and went over to him and they just glided away. She wasn't even dressed up, she had on shorts and flat shoes, but it didn't matter, I thought they looked absolutely glamorous. Do you remember that night at all?"

My legs were beginning to get stiff from standing so long. "No, I don't think so," I said. "Look, Kelly, I'm sorry but I really have to—"

"They were a great couple," she said. "I always thought they were perfect together. Even though she didn't have the background that some people thought was important. Do you remember Aline Schuyler, well, you know what a snob she was, she once said that marrying your mother was the only completely crazy thing your father ever did. She said if he'd been thinking sensibly he would have tried to ally himself with one of the established families, because with a father like old Louie Tremain he needed all the respectability he could get. Well. La-di-da. I tell you, I gave her such a look. As if you have to have ancestors who were United Empire Loyalists or something, I mean really. Who cares about that sort of thing anymore? Look at me. No one batted an eye when I married Jerry, and he's a Hungarian Jew, for God's sake."

"Kelly, I think I've really got to—"

"Yes, me too," she agreed. "Yes, I've got to be running. But do drop by soon and take a look at all our renovations. Jerry will be delighted to see you. You did say you were up here by yourself, right?"

I thought of Eddy driving along the highway, his window open, the wind blowing his hair. "Yes," I said. With a single word I wiped him out.

"Leslie never comes anymore, does she? You should make her come again. Wouldn't it be just like old times? I don't think she's been here since, I don't know, was it when she was still with Ivan?"

"Actually, I'm not sure. Quite a while, I guess. Well—"

"Ivan. What a character *he* was. Where does she find these guys? I don't mean Sid, he's fairly normal. But Ivan, what was he, thirty-five and still trying to make a living as a musician? I mean, come on. Grow up. And the way he always pretended to be such a radical, arguing about politics and writing all those putrid leftie songs. But he was perfectly happy to use Leslie's money whenever he wanted anything, wasn't he? And then of course Perry—well, I know he was a great actor and all that, but way too old for her, and so eccentric and moody. When she first told me about Sid, everything about him sounded right . . . just the right age, and a lawyer with Todd, Limbeck yet. I thought, Well, finally! It was such a relief!"

"Yes, I guess a lawyer is always a relief," I said.

"Well, of course I'm not talking about just any sleazy ambulance chaser," she responded seriously. "But a lawyer with Todd, Limbeck . . . you know that's got to be all right."

"Yes," I said. "Well, look, Kelly, I really have to—"

"Yes, me too," she said. "You be sure to drop by now."

"I will. Bye, nice running into you . . . ," and I finally got away. Walking back to my car, I heard her voice rise up in happy laughter as she cornered someone else and started all over again. It was wonderful to listen to the breezy rustle of poplar leaves and the far-off cries of children who had nothing to do with me. I even felt glad that Eddy was gone. Kelly Wyatt made you appreciate the benefits of solitude. As I drove down the Trewithen road with a festive scattering of pebbles, I started looking forward to the quiet evening ahead: a plate of pasta, wine so cold it misted the glass, the verandah at sunset, pages of a book illumined by one lamp, night turning the earth blue-black, stars sprinkled like motes of dust across the black, lustrous sky.

By nine o'clock I had eaten a nice meal, put the dishes away, and moved to the front porch with a third glass of wine and a book. The radio played softly, Debussy's "Claire du Lune." A poignantly fresh, subtle smell of shadowy flowers teased my nostrils. I opened *Middlemarch* to the first chapter and read the opening line: "Miss Brooke had that kind of beauty which seems to be thrown into relief by poor dress." After a while I became aware that I had read that sentence several times. For some reason it was hard to concentrate. Events in Victorian England seemed so far removed from my life that it felt as though they must have occurred in another universe. My mind remained stubbornly fixed on the present. Everything around me was peaceful but I didn't feel peaceful at all; in fact I felt so restless that it was actually a bit of a trial to sit still. Remarks of Kelly Wyatt's that I had hardly noticed in my eagerness to escape came back to irritate me. Even my flesh seemed to itch.

All at once I realized that I had not actually sat down to read a book in a long time. There I sat, holding *Middlemarch* on my lap, unable to summon the slightest interest in it. I had no interest in the Debussy either; it was too slow and pretty and dreamlike. I had to have something that moved. In a moment I was on my knees in front of the radio, fiddling impatiently with the dial. Suddenly the thin red station indicator quivered as a volley of drums and electric guitars exploded in the speakers. It was one of those rock numbers that make no attempt to be coherent, with nonsense lyrics sounding like *moola boola afro mocha cinderella coca-cola* interspersed with groans and falsetto wails above a steady, pounding, powerful drumbeat. *Primitive jungle yowling*, he always called it. *Ape music*. They used to drift across the grass in their silken clothes, dancing lightly and debonairly to "Moonglow." I twisted the volume button as far to the right as it would go and drums boomed out across the dark lawn, so thunderously loud that the screens stirred in their frames and the floorboards quivered beneath my bare feet. The world became all sound; it entered my body and made my flesh vibrate on my bones. I hoped it could be heard on the other side of the lake. I hoped it could be heard in the stratosphere.

I thought perhaps I should have a party of my own after all, just one, invite everybody in Port Azure, hire a heavy metal band or perhaps a punk rock group if any still existed, and ask them to bellow out a rendition of "Fuck the Queen." Out there in the panoramic darkness hundreds of bodies would be moving, shaking, jumping up and down, their feet trampling the perfect green turf, their legs kicking and their arms waving in the air, their hair tossing, their breasts bouncing crudely inside their loose clothes, and I would be right there among them, shrieking and laughing noisily, having the time of my life.

I flung open the screen door, went down the steps and began to dance all by myself, heaving my body forward and back, swinging my hair across my face, stamping my bare feet hard into the velvety grass. Sweat started to run down my back and chest and my hairline grew damp from my forehead to my neck, but I didn't stop until I was so exhausted that I could no longer stand. Then I collapsed and lay flat on the ground, panting, and still the drums went on hammering, inside me and out, as though my heart and the hearts of those hundreds of spectral guests had merged to make one immense, throbbing heartbeat. I could feel the earth rolling beneath me, I could feel the whole vast teeming planet turning in space.

He had said he would be back the next day. All afternoon I kept expecting his car to glide up the driveway but it didn't appear. Instead Mr. and Mrs. Abbott arrived from town. Lying on the beach below I could hear the hum of her vacuum cleaner and the whine of his lawn mower as he drove it back and forth, filling the air with the pungent scent of cut grass. They had always been a taciturn couple who did their work, took their money and left. It was hard to imagine them talking much even when they were alone together. I sometimes pictured them driving back to town, sitting side by side in their van, both staring straight ahead at the road, their mouths set in the same firm line.

Suppertime came, and although I didn't think I had any appetite, I ended up eating a rather large plate of leftover pasta. Then I took a bottle of cold wine and a glass onto the back verandah, where I could look out at the wildflower garden and the road. The thought crossed my mind that perhaps Eddy would never come back. Something had happened in the city, he had beaten someone up or been beaten himself, he had been arrested, he had found a new woman and was sitting across from her in a restaurant, enticing her with some erotic story.

The time passed very slowly. I began to feel only half-awake and the long pale road, stretching hazily away through the tall grass and between the trees, became like something I was seeing in a dream. A flock of birds sailed across the luminous sky and I watched them in a sort of sleepy ecstasy, as though they were only images, not real. It was a quarter after nine, just before the onset of real darkness, when at last a tiny white car appeared in the distance under the poplar trees, so far away, so ephemeral that it seemed to be part of a dream as well. It grew closer, its engine making a soft purr; it floated along as though it were barely touching the earth. I didn't move from my chair. The car rolled up the driveway and stopped. After a moment the door swung open and Eddy got out. His clothes looked pale in the ashy dusk. He paused for a moment, looking toward me through the screen, his arm resting on top of the car door, and I seemed to be caught in a breathless hush, as though for a second even the crickets stopped singing, even the breeze was stilled. I didn't move. I watched him cross the grass, quick and light-footed, his car keys jingling in his hand. He opened the screen door and stepped inside. A drop of perspiration trickled down between my breasts. The hair at the edge of my forehead was misty in the heat.

"I was waiting for you," I said.

Without a word he crossed the dim floor and knelt down in front of me. He clasped my upper body and pulled me forward. I felt his waist between my thighs and his breath burned the thin cotton fabric over my chest. My hands were full of his thick, silky hair.

Did you do this with Gwen too? I thought. Did you like it better with her?

Chapter Sixteen

A couple of nights later I was awakened by rain. I had been dreaming, a strange vivid dream in which my mother and I were driving down a sun-dappled country road in a place that seemed vaguely European. When I recall our real lives, I can't think of a single time that my mother and I went anywhere alone together, but in the dream it felt completely natural. She sat in the passenger seat, very young again and pretty, and suddenly she said, *Why don't we get out and walk for a while?* My mother never walked anywhere if she could help it; she was always wearing the wrong kind of shoes for walking. But in the dream her suggestion seemed normal and usual. We walked under the trees, and she lifted her beautiful young face in the sunlight. *Gee, isn't it nice?* she said. Then I opened my eyes into a thunderous darkness. Raindrops were hitting the roof like bullets and for a second I was terrified, unable to remember where I was. Suddenly Eddy sat up and I saw his wild, irrational eyes jerking about in their sockets as he tried to awaken and understand his position. Even though my hands were still trembling with my own alarm, I touched his back with my fingertips and said, "It's all right, it's only rain on the roof." Then he fell back against his pillow and closed his eyes, as though I had hit him hard on the top of his head.

In the morning the sun was shining and the lawns and gardens seemed to shine too, as though they had been washed clean during the night. The grass was emerald green and the wildflowers sparkled with gauzy moisture.

"Oh, smell that air," I said, opening the screen door. "It goes to your head just like wine."

Eddy was sitting in a wicker chair on the verandah. His face looked puffy from sleep and he hardly seemed to hear me. He held his coffee cup up in both hands as though the warmth gave him comfort.

"Are you all right?" I said.

He blinked and looked at me, startled. "Sure," he said.

"You look kind of pale."

"No. I'm fine."

"We really slept in. I don't know whether we should have breakfast or lunch."

"Brunch," he said. "Isn't that what it's called?"

After we had eaten we went down to the beach and had a swim. I left him lying in a deck chair on the sand and climbed up the stone steps. I was going to make a peach pie for supper. The peaches were sitting in a bowl on the kitchen table, round and rosy and golden, exquisite as a painting by Cezanne. I chose one and smelled it and held its soft fuzzy surface against my cheek for a moment. The bright breeze ruffled the curled edge of the calendar beside the window. It was the beginning of August. In six weeks I would be standing before a class of undergraduates with my lecture notes in front of me. Time was rushing away from me even as I stood there thinking about it. The hours were dwindling; I was already hurrying toward that moment in the future when we would have our cars all packed, ready to travel up that long drive and through the gate, back to real life. Maybe I'll keep him just a little longer, I thought suddenly. Just a little while longer. Just till Christmas. What harm could that do?

I put the peach back and bent down to get a bowl and a pie plate out of the cupboard. As I straightened up I thought I heard a car engine in the distance. I knew it couldn't be the Abbotts because they never came on the weekend, and other people rarely stopped by without invitation since we were so far from town and such a long drive from the main highway. But sure enough, when I glanced out the window there was a car at the far end of the poplar avenue, its chrome glinting in the sunlight. Damn it, I thought, who the hell is that? There were times when I wished I could encircle my property with a high stone wall and tall padlocked doors, so that no one could get to me unless I desired their company. I thought of pulling down the blinds and pretending not to be at home. But our two cars were sitting there in the driveway, so it was obvious we hadn't gone far. Someone like Kelly Wyatt wouldn't be discouraged by pulled-down blinds; she'd walk all over the grounds and down to the beach, calling my name. I tried to be optimistic. I told myself that it was probably just a trespasser, someone lost and wanting directions, and I would just tell them what they needed to know and send them on their way.

It was a blue car, a brand-new Lincoln. I didn't recognize it at all. It swirled across the driveway, rich and majestic as an ocean liner. I bent down, squinting, trying to see the lone occupant. A woman, I could tell that much, but the surface of the car window was made opaque by shifting reflections of light and shadow. Then the car door swung open and she stepped out onto the crunchy white gravel.

No! I hissed to myself, hunching my shoulders, bending my knees, as though I could drop to the floor and escape by crawling away on my belly. Shit, shit, shit, shit! I looked around wildly, longing for supernatural powers; I wanted to wrap up the cottage and the lawn and the beach and make the whole package disappear. But there was nowhere to hide, no way on earth to avoid what was about to happen. My sister Leslie, who had not been near Azure Lake in five long years, was apparently paying it a visit. It wasn't just a bad dream. She was there very definitely, walking up the stone path, wearing one of her outfits, a bright yellow shirt with black Charlie Chaplin faces all over it, and tight white pants, and high-heeled sandals, and large sunglasses with elaborately curved yellow frames. I felt as if I were frozen to the floor; I stood with the pie plate in my hand, trying desperately to think of a way out. She pulled open the screen door, walked through the verandah and tentatively stepped across the kitchen thresh-old. I saw her eyes behind the dark lenses of her glasses, flick-ering rapidly around the room. When her glance landed on me she gasped and pressed her hand to her heart.

"Oh, Gracie!" she said breathlessly. "God! I didn't see you standing there! You scared the bejesus out of me!" Without looking, she tossed her purse toward the table. It fell short and hit the floor with a dull thud.

"I'm sorry for just showing up like this," she said. "Don't be mad at me. I couldn't stop myself. I had to come. I should have let you know but how could I when there's no phone? Don't be mad." She took off her sunglasses and made an attempt to smile, but the corners of her lips quivered. Her eye makeup was smudged. "I woke up this morning and before I knew it I was in the car. I've been driving since seven a.m." All at once her mouth puckered in an infantile way and her eyes swam with tears. "Don't be mad, okay?" she squeaked. "I just wanted to come so badly."

It was obvious she was going through some kind of crisis, but I couldn't feel any sympathy for her. I didn't want her there, and there she was. It was just like Leslie to do whatever came into her head, without a thought about how it might affect anybody else. She was staring at me beseechingly, wait-ing for me to fuss over her and ask what on earth was wrong, but my lips wouldn't open. After a moment her tears over-flowed and spilled down her cheeks.

"Oh, God," she said. "You hate me. You wish I'd disappear." She sat down at the table, snuffling and wiping at her nose with the back of her hand. "I don't even have a Kleenex," she said. I took a box of Kleenex from the top of the fridge and set it in front of her. She yanked carelessly at the top one and a whole string of Kleenex came out of the box and trailed across her lap like toilet paper.

"I suppose I don't even have a right to be upset," she said after blowing her nose passionately. "Considering I'm the one who told him to get out. So I'm the villain, I guess. For the last two years he was so bloody cold and indifferent it hardly seemed as if we were living on the same continent. But I'm the one who threw him out, I'm the one to blame. I was supposed to let him use our house like a hotel, and have dinner every Sunday for his bloody parents, I was supposed to be happy to do everything while most of the time he could hardly rouse himself to remember I existed. So finally I couldn't take it anymore, right? I told him to get out. Two weeks later, he's with someone else. She's twenty-two years old. It's so typical, isn't it? So typical. You know, this is the first time I've cried about it. I haven't even felt like crying until today. As soon as I started driving up the hill, I got a lump in my throat because I couldn't help thinking of all those other times, driving along that road, you and I singing in the back seat, remember? At the beginning of summer, when we were so happy. And young and innocent. We'd come up over the crest of the hill and we'd see the lake down below and Dad would say, 'We're now entering Trewithen.'"

"The domain of Trewithen," I corrected her automatically.

"Yeah, the domain of Trewithen," she said, blowing her nose again. "I guess I wasn't sure it was going to be a permanent split. Dumb, huh? I guess I was actually stupid enough to think he might fall apart and beg me to take him back or something. How was I supposed to know he'd move in with a twenty-two-year-old girl about five seconds later, and make an idiot of himself? I think it's just so pathetic when a thirty-nine-year-old guy has to take up with a twenty-two-year-old girl. Can't handle a woman closer to his own age—wants to pretend he's a big man, and smarter and more mature and more experienced. With a little girl to look up to him, someone he can teach. Men really get off on that, they really do. I think it's sick. She's a law student. He used to talk about her all the time. How brilliant she was, how he was so impressed with her work. Hah. Yeah, I'll bet he was impressed with her work. Why was I such a dolt? Why did I make everything so easy for him?"

"So you think the marriage is really over?" I said.

She had almost stopped crying, but that question made fresh tears well up in her eyes. She looked at me speechlessly, pressing the Kleenex streamer against her trembling lower lip. After a moment I sat down across from her. There didn't seem to be much else I could do.

"I saw him yesterday," she gulped. "It was the first time I'd seen him since he moved out. He was with her. She was holding on to him and gushing all over him and he was lapping it up like honey. They can always find somebody, can't they? Why is that? Even when they're old and half-bald and boring and nasty and impotent, they can always find some woman who's happy to lick their shoes. Although I guess he isn't impotent with her. It was only me who left him limp!"

"Do you want a drink or something?" I said.

"Oh, no, don't worry about it, I'll get something myself if I feel like it. You know what, he wasn't wearing cowboy boots. It was a miracle! He always had to wear them, night and day. I told you that before, didn't I? . . . he's never been west of Sudbury but he wasn't happy if he didn't look like Clint Eastwood. I nagged him about those God damn stupid boots for five years but it was like talking to a brick wall. So what happens? Two weeks with her, and he's in Gucci loafers! When I saw that I could have strangled him! The rotten bastard!"

"What did he say?" I was having trouble concentrating on her rapid chatter; I kept thinking I heard a door opening, footsteps approaching. Any second Eddy might appear.

"Huh? Oh, I didn't talk to him. Are you kidding? The second I laid eyes on them I got out of sight fast. Well, I was wearing a pair of old jeans and my hair was a mess, was I going to let them see me looking like that? I stood inside Penne from Heaven and watched them. Although, you're right, I shouldn't have been lurking in the shadows like a bloody criminal or something. I should have just walked right up to them and said hi! You know what I'd love? A big glass of brandy. Have you got any brandy?"

I had a sudden foolish hope that she might just drink some brandy and then leave. "What do you think?" I said, standing up. "You only need one thing to be considered a good host, and that's a—"

"Well-stocked liquor cabinet!" she chimed in with a husky laugh, following me into the living room. The afternoon sun was pouring through the high windows and gilding the furniture and ornaments with a fine golden light. She sighed. "Oh, it's so good to be here," she said. "I can't tell you."

I poured some brandy into a glass and handed it to her. She took a deep swallow and then coughed. "Oh, God," she said. "Oh, it burns. It's great. You're not mad I came, are you?"

"After all, the place is half yours," I said. "I guess you can come whenever you feel like it."

"Oh, I know, but really, you're used to having it to yourself at this time of year. And really, it's more yours than mine. You're the one who takes care of the upkeep and pays the Abbotts and all that stuff. Everything looks just great. Dad would be very happy."

"Well, that's not why I do it," I said.

"Well, I know," she said. She clacked across the gleaming floor in her high-heeled shoes and opened the door to the verandah. "The lawn is so green," she said. "It's like a beautiful green salad, you could eat it. Why don't we sit out here?"

She chose the big wicker rocker and began to rock back and forth stiffly, holding her brandy glass in both hands. I sat on the red plush sofa. The lake was such a brilliant blue that it almost hurt your eyes. It was breezy and there were crisp white caps of foam on the bright waves. I stared at the empty cliff edge. Eddy had to be still lying down on the beach. Perhaps he had fallen asleep.

"I don't know why I thought of coming here," she said. "After I saw them together I felt so lonely and miserable I couldn't get to sleep all night, and then all of a sudden I thought of Azure Lake." She held her glass to her lips and took a sip. "I don't know whether it's the brandy or what," she said. "But already I feel a bit better."

"That's good," I said. Perhaps it would be all right. Perhaps he wouldn't even wake up till she was gone.

"Sid always wanted to go to his parents' place on Lake Erie and it wasn't nearly as nice as here," she said. "But of course I let him have his way. I wanted him to be happy. Why am I always such a fool? Perry liked Azure Lake, though. Didn't he?"

I must have looked blank. "Perry," she said. "You know, my first husband Perry. Oh, God. I've already had three husbands and I'm only thirty-four years old."

"Thirty-five years old," I said.

"I won't be thirty-five till September fifth," she said. "Come on, Gracie, give me a break, let me keep saying I'm thirty-four till the actual date of my birthday. Don't be too hard on me today."

"Oh, all right," I said.

A couple of red squirrels started chattering furiously in the branches of a maple tree. Other than that, it was deceptively quiet there on the verandah. My heart was beating dully and painfully. I was still buoyed up by my ridiculous hope that she wouldn't stay long. Drink fast, I told her silently, and then just go. Go. Go.

"I can't believe it's really over," I said. "Maybe you can patch it up."

"Why should I?" she snapped.

"Well—"

"He doesn't give a shit! He never made the slightest effort, it was like I was a piece of furniture. He was probably having an affair with her all along, he was probably ecstatic when I told him to get out! I'll bet it took him about five minutes to get over to her place and tell her the good news! Who's that?"

So it was already too late. Eddy was climbing the stone steps. He reached the top of the cliff and turned back to look across the lake, where a windsurfer was skimming over the water beneath a bright red and green and yellow sail. His towel was draped over his shoulder and his white bathing suit was so brief he seemed almost naked. I saw the way he would look to her: like a gigolo, too brown, too handsome, too foreign and sexy and flashy. She sat forward in amazement, squinting.

"Eddy," I said hopelessly.

She stared at me. "He's here with you?" she said.

"No," I said in a sharp voice, "obviously not. He must have come to rob the place but I guess he decided to take a swim first."

"You invited him here?" Leslie said incredulously. She could hardly have been more astonished if I had suddenly confessed to murdering somebody.

"Well, yes, Leslie, I guess I did," I said.

She set down her half-empty brandy glass. "Oh God," she said. "I thought you were alone."

"Didn't you notice there were two cars parked out front?"

"Oh God, I was so worked up I didn't notice anything." She gawked at me with wide, unbelieving eyes. "Is he . . . a friend, or. . . ?"

Her inability to understand the situation was really rather insulting. I gave her a flat, sardonic look. Her eyes opened even wider and she glanced back at Eddy, who was still standing down at the end of the lawn.

"Gee . . . I can't . . . he doesn't seem like your type, exactly."

"Oh, really? What's my type, in your opinion?"

"I don't know. Somebody professorial, I guess. An intellectual."

"What makes you think Eddy isn't an intellectual?" I asked ironically.

She blinked, and then gave a short nervous laugh. "Gee, I'm kind of stunned," she said after a moment. "I wasn't expecting this, it's kind of a shock. I just—I thought you'd be alone."

"Well, sorry," I said.

"So you're having a big romance and . . . and I'm barging in and ruining everything."

I looked at Eddy standing down in the hot white sunlight, his tiny bathing suit, his long naked torso, his longish, thick, black hair. "Oh, it's not a romance," I said.

"Not," Leslie repeated, as if she wanted to be sure she understood.

"It's a fling," I said.

"A fling," Leslie said.

"That's right. You know what that's like, don't you?"

"I guess so." She shook her head slowly from side to side.

"Or maybe you don't," I said. "You always have to marry everybody you sleep with."

"Oh, don't be mean," she said weakly.

"He's great in bed and he's charming and attractive and I wanted to have a good time. Can you understand that?"

"Yeah," Leslie said dubiously, "sure, of course." Eddy stretched his arms above his head in a lazy, voluptuous yawn; the muscles moved in his long back. His extravagant brown body seemed to float in leafy shadows. "But I'm just . . . amazed," Leslie said.

"Why?" I said sharply. "Did you think I'd sworn a vow of celibacy or something?"

"No, no, it's not that. . . ."

"We hardly ever see each other but you think you know all about me," I said. "Apparently I'm not quite so predictable after all."

"That's not what I meant," she protested.

"Maybe there are things in my life you don't have a clue about."

All at once her face contorted like a child's. "Please don't be mad at me," she said.

"Oh, for God's sake."

Tears brimmed in her eyes and rolled down her cheeks. "Please don't be mad at me now because I just can't stand it," she said. "I feel so awful, I feel so depressed, today I'm driving along in the car and I almost wished I were dead."

"Oh, come on."

"I did! It crossed my mind that I could just let go of the steering wheel. Who'd care, anyway? I mean it. Who would care? He forgot about me so easily, so easily! And now you're mad and you don't want me here—"

"Oh, I didn't say that. I wish you'd stop crying."

She fumbled in her pocket for her wad of Kleenex. "I know," she gasped. "I'm sorry I'm acting like such an idiot. I won't keep this up, I promise. It was kind of a shock, that's all, I was so sure you'd be alone. . . ." She gave me a quick, blurry glance and added hastily, "I didn't mean anything by that, okay? I shouldn't have just assumed no one else would be here. Even though you've never invited a single soul in years . . . but still, I shouldn't have assumed. I would have called but you're so strict, no phones allowed at Trewithen, how can any-body get through to you?"

"I know," I said. Eddy had started walking up toward the house. He had seen that someone was with me; he was smiling curiously. A sick, fluttering sensation went through my stomach.

"I'll only stay a couple of days, I promise," Leslie said, wiping her nose. "I'll go for walks and read my books and drive into town, you'll hardly know I'm here."

"Okay," I said. What else could I say?

The screen door opened and Eddy stepped through it. Leslie rubbed her face quickly and put her Kleenex away. Close up, leaning against the door frame, he seemed to flaunt his body proudly, as though he was pleased to show it to someone new. A wave of embarrassed warmth passed briefly over my face. He gave an engaging smile, flashing his white teeth.

"Hi," he said.

"Leslie, this is Eddy," I said. "Eddy, this is my sister Leslie." It seemed unbelievable that I could be speaking those words.

He took her hand and kissed it in a playful, courtly way. "Encantado," he said, like a phoney Latin lover in some old Hollywood movie. Leslie raised her tear-swollen face and stared at him wordlessly. Then I felt such a severe dislocation that the scene before me rippled like a kind of hallucination. I had thought I would always be able to keep things separate, but it had all gone wrong suddenly, and without giving me a chance to prepare, the two parts of my life had veered together and intersected. I had no idea who I was supposed to be.

IT RAINED AGAIN AFTER DARK and a damp, earthy chill rose through the wooden floorboards. We lit a fire and sat in front of it, Leslie in the armchair, Eddy and I on the sofa.

"Let's turn the lights out," Eddy said, reaching for the lamp behind him. "Let's have just the fire. Is that all right with you, Leslie?"

"I'd like it," she said.

Her face flickered redly in the sudden deep, echoing darkness. Eddy's hand lay on my thigh, so light it seemed almost insubstantial. We listened to the harsh crackle and snap of the flames.

"This is only the second time it's rained all summer," I said.

"Just my luck." Leslie gave a wry laugh. "I hope it stops by tomorrow."

"It will," Eddy said. "I'll see to it."

Leslie smiled at him. "Yes? What are you, a magician or something?"

"That's right. The Amazing Corona. I can always make rain disappear by morning."

"Well, you must be a good guy to have around," Leslie said.

"Just ask your sister."

"Oh, you're all right, I guess," I said.

"She always used to say that," Leslie said. "When we were kids I used to say, 'Gracie, do you love me?' and she'd say, 'You're all right.'"

Eddy's fingers squeezed my flesh softly. "Gracie," he said. "I like that. Can I call you Gracie too?"

"I wish you wouldn't," I said.

Leslie laughed, and her laughter seemed to rise and echo in the shadowy rafters high above our heads.

LATER HE AND I UNDRESSED IN THE DIM LIGHT of the bedside lamp. I opened one of the windows and leaned out. It was still raining and a shower of cold drops sprinkled my face and throat. Down in the wet darkness pale flowers were blowing against the frame of the trellis. The soft roar of falling water and the wind in the trees blotted out all other sound so that I could almost believe I was alone. But she was lying on the other side of the landing, staring up at the ceiling. And when I turned my head he was right there behind me, sitting in a chair, quietly unlacing his shoes.

"She's all broken up because her marriage is in trouble," I said. "She's only going to stay a couple of days."

"That's too bad," he said.

"Oh?" I said. "Do you think it's too bad?"

He stood up and unfastened his jeans. "That her marriage is in trouble, I mean. Why? Don't you want her here?"

"Oh, I don't care one way or the other," I said.

"Me either." He stepped out of his underpants and tossed them nonchalantly over his shoulder. They landed on the lampshade. My laugh caught in my throat as he walked toward me. With an easy motion he grabbed the bottom of my T-shirt, pulled it over my head and threw it straight up toward the ceiling. My hair crackled with electricity. He pressed against me and licked the rain from my neck. His tongue felt as rough as a cat's.

"Mmmmmmm," he said. "You taste like rainwater. So refreshing."

I put my arms around him. The wet wood on the window frame rubbed against my shoulder blades and raindrops trickled down into the small of my back. They were so icy cold they took my breath away.

Chapter Seventeen

It was thirty-one degrees celsius. Although my eyes were closed I could feel a brilliant watery light dancing on my eyelids. The waves hissed softly against the sand. I pretended to be asleep and listened to Leslie's voice, murmuring, rising and falling in the hot, breathless air.

"He said, 'Why didn't you tell me you were unhappy?' and I said, 'I did tell you! Over and over!' and he said, 'But I didn't think you were serious.' Can you imagine it? He was like that from day one, I shouldn't have been surprised. It was easier for him to pretend everything was a joke. I'm starting to think it was a miracle we lasted five years. Five lost years."

"So what did he do then?" Eddy asked. "He just packed his bags and—"

"Left. Walked down the street, carrying two suitcases, out of sight. I watched him and cried, isn't that pathetic? I couldn't see his face, but I'll bet he was laughing. I'll bet he was singing.

Going over to his girlfriend's house to crack open a bottle of champagne and celebrate. I did love him once."

"Well, he loved you too, didn't he?"

"I wonder if he did. Oh, I suppose so. For a little while. In the beginning. It never lasts longer than two years. I used to be a romantic and think that shit was eternal. God, talk about naïve. Everybody told me my second husband Ivan was more in love with my trust fund than with me, but of course I didn't believe it. Not even when I was paying to have his songs published and subsidizing tours for his band and buying sound equipment and renting studios. . . . I thought he was an artist and I was lucky to be able to help him. I'd be writing out the cheques and smiling, thinking how crazy he was about me. Stupid, or what? When I fall in love it's like I go deaf, dumb and blind. My first husband was already flirting with the bridesmaids, about five minutes after he'd put the ring on my finger. But I just thought it was charming!"

Eddy laughed. "Your first husband?"

"Yeah, I'm thirty-three and I've been married three times, isn't that awful? My first husband was Perry Chandler, maybe you've heard of him? No, well, I guess he's only world-famous in Canada. He's an actor, do you ever go to Stratford? Well, he's in a commercial too, a Chevrolet commercial? He looks asinine, he's sitting at the wheel and a crown appears on his head, and he says, 'I feel like a king!' Yeah, a king in a Chevrolet! That's about Perry's speed."

"How did you meet him?"

"He was a friend of my father's, actually. He was quite a bit older than me. Until I was twelve years old I never paid much attention to him, but then I saw him as Iago at Stratford. We were in the front row, and he walked downstage, looked into my eyes and said, 'I hate the Moor.' Oh, I felt the heat right through to the seat of my chair. I should have known I was in trouble right away!"

"So you had a romance with this Shakespearian actor when you were twelve years old, and he—"

"Oh, no, I didn't have a romance with him then. I guess I

had a crush on him, but then I didn't see him for a few years. He was off in New York and L.A. trying to become a big star. When he came back I was nineteen years old and I met him and my father in the old rooftop lounge of the Park Plaza. They were having drinks. He stood up and took my hand and said, 'Leslie, you have grown up beautifully.' He had this deep voice and these incredible, plummy British vowels . . . which was kind of bizarre since he was born in Manitoba. But oh, I fell for it like a ton of bricks, of course."

"Plummy?"

"Plummy. Yes. Like . . . round, and rich-sounding. You speak English so well, I forget there might be some weird expressions you haven't heard before. You hardly even have an accent."

"There are lots of English people in Buenos Aires," he said. "We used to visit back and forth. Some evenings my father would make a rule: English only until bedtime."

He didn't tell her that he'd gone to school in the United States. It was as though he'd come up with a story he liked better. I allowed myself a brief smile, as if I were dreaming of something pleasant.

THAT NIGHT WE SAT ON THE VERANDAH over the remains of dinner, holding our luminous wine glasses, breathing in the subtle scent of burning candles. Eddy's pale blue shirt had a sheen like silver.

"Look, there are some boaters down on the lake," Leslie said. "They're staring up at us. I'll bet they're thinking how lucky we are. They've stopped rowing. They're saying, 'Look at those three up there. What a beautiful table. Such tall white candles. Wow.' Eddy smiled; he seemed pleased with the fantasy that our table was a magical image suspended in the night for other people to gaze at longingly.

"They're thinking what a fabulous time we must be having," Leslie said. "Let's have a toast. Come on, Gracie."

"Cheers!" Eddy called out, clinking his glass against Leslie's with a ringing tone.

"Bottoms up!" Leslie said.

"Salud y guita!" Eddy said.

Leslie laughed breathlessly. "What's that?"

"Good health and lots of money."

"Salad ee geeta!" Leslie repeated loudly, with a comic accent. She was really enjoying herself. You would never have guessed that she was supposed to be grief-stricken over the breakup of her marriage. "Come on, Gracie, it's your turn," she said.

"Just calm down, will you?"

"Oh, we can be calm when we're dead! Right? Come on, don't disappoint the audience."

I wasn't even sure if that rowboat with its envious watchers was really out there on the water. However, people often find Leslie's gaiety delightful and I didn't want Eddy to think I was a sullen spoilsport. So I raised my glass and forced myself to smile. "Here's looking at you," I said.

WE LAY IN BED, SIDE BY SIDE. The silence was so deep that you could hear the squeak of boards settling or expanding. I thought of Leslie, lying in her bed across the hall. I wondered if she was awake and what might be going on in her mind. I wanted to take her thoughts out of her head and examine them closely.

"She's thirty-five," I said. "Not thirty-three."

"What?" Eddy said. But he knew exactly what I was talking about.

"Leslie," I said. "She always likes to pretend she's younger than she is."

"Thirty-five or thirty-three," Eddy said with a laugh. "What difference does it make?"

"None," I said. "It just annoys me, that's all."

WE WERE SITTING ON THE BOATHOUSE DECK, listening to the radio, drinking frozen daiquiris. When I look back on it now, I realize that we were drinking a lot on those long summer days. We started after lunch and continued till midnight, one, two a.m., falling into bed in a warm, sticky stupor.

Eddy took a long pull on his straw and then leaned back in his chair, flipping his sunglasses down over his eyes. "Ah," he said. "Perfecto."

"What would we be doing if we were in Buenos Aires now?" Leslie asked.

"We'd be shivering, and sitting inside by a stove, trying to keep warm," Eddy said.

"I always forget that the seasons are reversed. It must be so strange to have winter in July and August."

"It doesn't snow, like here. But it's very cold and raining all the time, day after day. When Perón came back to Argentina, they told him the Buenos Aires winter would kill him, and sure enough, it did."

"It did? For some reason I thought he was assassinated."

"No. He was a very old man, seventy-eight or so, and he'd been in exile for eighteen years. They wanted him back though. They couldn't wait to vote for him again. But after that, he hardly lasted a year. He got pneumonia. It was July 1974 he died, and I still remember the people lined up for blocks in the cold and rain, holding umbrellas, shivering and coughing, waiting to see him one last time."

Leslie was fascinated, apparently. She was leaning forward, hanging on his every word. "Did you see him?"

"Sure," Eddy said, with an offhand shrug.

"Really? You saw Perón's body?"

I took a noisy sip of my daiquiri.

"My father said we had to go, just to make sure he was really dead. His face was yellow and waxy-looking. He was smaller than I thought he'd be. I was thirteen or fourteen, with a big mouth. I turned to the person beside me and whispered, 'He wasn't so big up close, was he?' Then another man in front of us turned around and just glared at me. His eyes were full of big, bright tears, so they looked like stones under glass. I think if I'd said one more word he would have murdered me."

"No. Really?" Leslie said.

"People were always killing each other over Perón. Left-wing and right-wing, fighting all the time. This is how *porteños* show their feelings, they have a riot. On the day Perón came back from exile there was a riot at the airport and his plane had to be re-routed. A hundred people died that day. I saw a woman lying on her back on the cement with a long black trickle of something spreading out across the cement from under her head. One of her shoes was off and just lying beside her. She had a little round bullet hole right in the middle of her forehead. Her eyes were wide open."

"Oh, my God," Leslie said. "How horrible."

Eddy gave another casual shrug and sipped his drink.

"You know, if I think about it," Leslie said, "I don't think I've ever seen any actual violence. Not what you could call real violence. Except on television. Or in films. Isn't that unbelievable? I've never seen anyone killed or even hurt. Once at school in Switzerland, two girls got into a fight and one of them ended up with her nose bleeding all over her uniform. That's the worst thing I've ever seen. I mean, with my own eyes, not on television or in a film. What about you, Gracie?"

I stared down into the bottom of my glass, studying the melting shards of ice. I thought of that hot, moonlit night, the shocking crunch of metal, a man kneeling on the road with his hands to his face, the wet glitter of dark liquid on the pavement. "I'm the same," I said.

"We've had a pretty sheltered life, I guess," Leslie said.

Slowly I lifted my face to look at Eddy. His dark glasses concealed the expression in his eyes. After a moment he sucked up the rest of his daiquiri, then set his glass aside and folded his hands across his bare chest.

"The military took over soon after, didn't they?" Leslie asked. "What was that like? Did you know any families with disappeared ones?"

It was one of those questions to which Eddy had to devote some thought before replying. He gave himself a couple of moments by taking a handful of peanuts and popping them into his mouth. Finally he said, "*Desaparecidos?* No." After a moment he added, "I'm not political."

"You're not? Why?"

He shrugged. "Because it doesn't matter who's in the government, things are always just the same."

"I imagine there's a slight difference between a democracy and a military dictatorship," I said dryly.

"Maybe for you it would be different," Eddy said. "For me, there was no difference."

Suddenly Leslie laughed. "Remember what Dad always used to say? 'It doesn't matter who gets elected—as long as it's not a Red!'"

Eddy leaned back in his chair, smiling with one side of his mouth.

ONE MORNING WE DECIDED to have our breakfast coffee on the verandah. When I came out carrying a tray with the coffee pot and china cups, Leslie was sitting by herself.

"Eddy went to phone Toronto," she told me. "He said he had to do it while you weren't looking, or you'd kill him."

I smiled vaguely and started to pour the coffee.

"You sure are tough," she said. "Still have to prove something, even after all these years, huh?"

"Prove what?" I said. "I just think that if you're going to be on holiday, then you should be on holiday."

"Okay." She accepted a coffee cup and the sunlit steam rose around her mouth as she took a sip. After a moment she asked idly, "Have you seen any of the things from El Mundo de la Plata?"

"What?"

"Any of the silver work, I mean."

I must have looked completely mystified. Leslie laughed.

"You'd better drink your coffee," she said. "I don't think you're awake yet. The silver that Eddy's company imports. You must have seen some of the pieces, haven't you?"

"Oh," I said. "No, I haven't."

"Really? You should get him to show it to you. Some of it sounds really beautiful. He was describing an ornamental dagger with a silver handle in the shape of a bird. You should ask to see it."

"Yes," I said. "I should."

"Some of the pieces sound like collectors' items. You might want to consider buying something."

"Yes," I said.

"Did you know that Rio de la Plata means River of Silver? Literally."

"No, I didn't," I said.

For a moment we listened to the drowsy hum of insects in the rose garden. "You seem to be feeling a lot better," I commented idly. "You hardly seem upset at all. It's almost as if you've completely forgotten about Sid."

She sighed. "Yeah, it's easy to forget about things here. It all seems far away. I can hardly believe I was so hysterical over it. Why should I care what Sid does anymore? It's over. It's been over a year at least. I just didn't want to face facts." She picked up an orange and began to peel it thoughtfully. Its sweet citrus smell filled the warm air with juicy freshness. "You know what I was just thinking of?" she said dreamily. "I was remembering that Labour Day party, when Dad brought all the balloons. Do you remember that?"

"Of course."

"All those blue and white balloons, it seems to me there were hundreds of them."

"Yes, and he had the leaves spray-painted too. That was a bit much."

She stared at me, nonplussed. "The leaves? What?"

"Did you forget about that? It was so dry that year, no rain all summer, and the shrubbery looked a bit brown in places. Not the right effect at all, you know. So he had Mr. Abbott and a couple of other gardeners come out from town and spray-paint the brown leaves green."

Leslie put her hand over her open mouth and laughed. "Oh, my God. How decadent."

"Yes, well, all he ever wanted was absolute perfection."

"I didn't remember that about the leaves. All I remember is those blue and white balloons. They were like pieces of the sky just floating around in the twilight."

I saw him walking down the lawn, in sleek white pants and a shirt with the sleeves rolled up to reveal the golden-red fuzz on his forearms, his red hair dark with water and combed straight back from his forehead, his hands in his pockets, balloons rising soundlessly around him. I was skulking, as he would have called it, skulking in my bedroom upstairs, behind the curtains, sullen and ugly, with big glasses and pimples on my face, tense, stomach churning, already dreading the hours to come and the people I would have to meet, already feeling the stiffness of the forced smile on my lips, already knowing I would be a flop, tongue-tied, my mind as blank as a piece of paper, stuttering or my voice coming out too loud, who could blame them when they rolled their eyes at my inane remarks, snickered behind their hands, walked away bored? I would try too hard and still I would fail because I was stupid, stupid, stupid. So much better to stay alone in my room, hidden in the soft shadows, reading my book, pretending I was someone better. Hiding like a rat in a hole, he would say. Such a stupid, ugly little rat.

He caught one of the balloons and tapped it lightly, sending it up into the trees like a bit of white cloud. For a moment I thought he glanced up and saw me there on the second floor, just beyond the window. But perhaps not. He turned away immediately and then Leslie ran out across the lawn, all dressed up in pale pink silk, her hair curled and tied with white ribbon. *Hi, Dad! Look, I have a new outfit!* He nodded and smiled. *So I see! Very pretty.* She took his hand and they walked side by side on the grass. He tapped another balloon and it sailed upward to catch in the branches of the maple tree. Then Leslie laughed and hit one with her wrist, hit it so hard that it kept going up and up as though it were filled with helium, floating into the sky as lightly as a soap bubble.

"I wonder why Mom and Dad stayed together," Leslie said suddenly. "Do you ever wonder about that? They certainly weren't happy with each other."

"People didn't split up so easily then."

"But still. They drove each other crazy. I'm not even sure why they got together in the first place."

"Well, obviously she was exceptionally good-looking," I said.

"Yes, but do you think that's the only reason?"

"And he was rich," I said. "What other reasons do you need?"

"That's it, huh?" Leslie said. "She was good-looking and he was rich, so they got married and stayed together for thirty years."

"Sure," I said. "Why not? She was never going to find any-one with more money, and he was never going to collect a more beautiful trophy."

"God, Gracie," Leslie said with a laugh, shaking her head and looking away. "Sometimes you're so cold."

"No, I'm not," I said.

"But he was never even interested in anyone else. He was always faithful to her. How do you explain that?"

I stared at her in disbelief. "Oh, Leslie," I said. "For God's sake. Grow up."

"What? It's true. He never looked at another woman. Did he?"

"Well, let me see. There was Maureen Daley, that actress who worked with Perry at the St. Lawrence Centre one winter. There was Perry's sister Elaine. There was Cora Wilcox from the New World Foundation. There was a temporary secretary at Tremain Toronto one summer. Sylvia Platen, that junior partner at Dawson, Dawes. Aline Schuyler. Just to name a few."

Leslie was staring at me frozenly. "No!" she cried. "Not Aline Schuyler! He despised her!"

"Despising somebody doesn't preclude having sex with them, Leslie. In fact, sometimes it adds extra spice. Didn't you know that?" My mood was improving. It was just like the old days when it had been one of my great pleasures to strip away some of my little sister's childish illusions.

After a moment she placed her coffee cup carefully in its saucer. "So according to you Dad had affairs with all these women. How can you possibly know for sure? I suppose you listened to people gossiping and you just—"

"The Christmas party at Neville Park Boulevard in 19 . . . I think it was 1972? I walked into the library and Maureen Daley was sitting on the desk and he was all over her. Her blouse was wide open, her bra was down around her waist . . . They were so tangled up they didn't even notice me, so I just turned around and walked out again."

Leslie struggled to find an explanation. "Oh, well, Christmas parties, people have a lot to drink and get carried away, it doesn't mean they're having an affair, necessarily."

"One afternoon I saw him coming out of Sutton Place with Aline Schuyler, arm in arm."

"Well, Gracie," Leslie said. "People meet at hotels all the time, they have lunch, they have cocktails, they go to business meetings. . . ."

"There's only one kind of business he could have had with Aline Schuyler."

"How do you know?"

"He patted her bum while she was getting into the taxi, Leslie."

"So? What does that prove?"

I sighed. She was starting to give me a headache. "Look," I said. "Men are never faithful. I would have thought you'd realize that by now."

"Never?"

"They can't help it," I said. "It's a biological imperative. In the natural world the male is programmed to impregnate as many females as possible, to ensure the survival of the species."

"Oh," said Leslie. "Is that what it's all about?"

"Yes," I said.

He was standing on the balloon-filled lawn, beside the painted shrubbery, holding Leslie's hand. He called out, *Vivian! Make sure the bartender's got enough booze.* My mother's voice responded from somewhere inside the house, and he laughed impatiently. *Well, yes, it is important, Vivian. If you want to be a good host, the main thing you've got to have is a well-stocked liquor cabinet!*

"THE TRUTH IS IT'S BEEN OVER FOR AT LEAST A YEAR," Leslie said. We were in her car, her big blue Lincoln, gliding down the highway like a ship on the sea, gliding through a soft, dusky, clover-scented wind. "I just didn't want to admit it to myself. I even thought of getting pregnant. What a disaster that would have been!" Thin gold bracelets tinkled on her tanned wrists. "Luckily Sid had absolutely no interest in—you know, doing it. With me, that is! I'm sure he was bonking the law student every five minutes."

"Every five minutes?" said Eddy in mock awe. "What a macho."

Leslie laughed gaily. "Well, you know what I mean. It wasn't often that he had anything left for me. I started to feel like such a dog. You can't help it. You keep hearing excuses all the time, he's tired, or he thinks he's getting the flu, or he has to get up early in the morning, or his stomach's been queasy ever since he ate the pot roast, or he's got an earache, or he has a brief to prepare, or he strained his back playing tennis, or there's too much pollen in the air and his hay fever is acting up, or he's depressed because the Maple Leafs didn't get into the playoffs. . . ."

Eddy laughed heartily in the back seat. People often found Leslie very funny.

"Then you look at yourself in the bathroom mirror," she said. "And all of a sudden you see how old and fat and drab you are. You know you've lost it, nobody's ever going to give you a second look, ever again."

"That's ridiculous," Eddy said. "You look great."

Leslie gave a quick, happy laugh, glancing over her shoulder. "Oh, thanks," she said. "You don't have to say that."

"It's true," Eddy said.

I was staring ahead through the windshield, watching the white line disappear beneath the gleaming body of the car.

"You look almost as good as your sister," Eddy said.

I felt my lips stretch into a reluctant smile. There was no doubt about it; he was good. He never forgot me; he found a way to flatter us both.

We drove into the parking lot of the Azure Inn. On the patio shadowy figures sat around at tables illuminated by yellow lamps. The lake was beautiful that night, clear and black with brief flashes of fiery sapphire blue. We walked across the grass. Leslie was wearing a tight red T-shirt and a full black skirt covered with tiny red flowers. She had gold hoops in her ears. I thought she looked like a Hollywood gypsy but apparently Eddy liked the effect. They walked ahead through patches of soft amber light, talking and laughing, and I felt as though the gloom of the tall pines had fallen over me, separating me from them.

"Is this okay?" Leslie said, pulling back a chair and sitting down. "Remember that time Uncle Lubo stayed here?"

"Oh, God," I said. "Please don't remind me."

Eddy had started to light a cigarette. He looked at us over the clear bluish flame of his lighter. "Who?"

"Uncle Lubo," I said. "It's a long, boring story. Let's not get into it."

"You know, sometimes I think we should go to Saskatchewan and see if we can find any more of Mom's relatives."

"What on earth for?"

"Well, they're our relatives too, after all. Uncle Lubo is the only one we've ever seen. Don't you think it would be interesting to find out what they're like?"

I sighed and leaned back in my chair. "I imagine they're all like Uncle Lubo."

"We don't know that."

"I doubt whether I'd have much to say to a bunch of prairie farmers. Five minutes on crops and the weather, and then silence. I don't think it's worth travelling two thousand miles. On top of that I'm sure they'd want something from us."

"We don't know they're a bunch of prairie farmers," Leslie said. "They could be anything. And what makes you think they'd want something? Except for Uncle Lubo they've never even come near us."

She didn't really give a damn about those distant, unknown relatives. She was just showing off for Eddy's benefit. "Well, then, you go and find them, Leslie," I said. "Tell them I said hello."

"I think I will sometime." Suddenly she turned to Eddy, who had been listening attentively. "Our mother was a Ukrainian farm girl from Saskatchewan," she told him. "She decided to come here to the big city and seek her fortune."

There was no reason on earth to tell him things like that. He already knew as much about our parents as he needed to know. But she was impossible to control. She would tell anybody anything, without a moment's thought.

"She didn't know what would happen. She just packed up a suitcase and walked down a dirt road all the way to the highway and waited for the next bus. I always thought that was so great. After she got here she became a model. She modelled clothes for the Eaton's and Simpson's catalogues and she was a model at an auto show at the Exhibition Grounds. And my father always had a big interest in cars, so . . ."

"Oh, so that's where he met her?"

"She was wearing a silver-blue bathing suit and silver high-heeled shoes, and she was posing beside a yellow Rolls-Royce. He was with a whole group of rowdy guys. They were all standing together staring at her, or maybe at the car, she wasn't sure which. But she picked my father out. She hoped he was the one who'd come over. And sure enough, he did."

I was annoyed that the whole subject had been introduced, but on the other hand I wasn't going to let her dominate the conversation completely. "Yes, he said 'Hi, beautiful,'" I remarked dryly. "Isn't that a clever beginning?"

"Yeah," Leslie laughed. "And then he said, 'If I buy this car, will you go out with me tonight?'"

"So right away she knew she'd hit the jackpot," I said.

"Oh, come on, Gracie, don't be so cynical all the time! She said, 'I'll go out with you whether you buy it or not.' She was only twenty-one. She said she'd never seen a man so well dressed before. She always remembered the jacket he had on, it was soft grey suede, and it had a belt."

"Did he end up buying the car?" Eddy asked.

"No. Well, he didn't have to then. That's what he said to her. He said, 'Well, I'm glad I don't have to buy it because actually I've already got a Rolls.'"

"That was out of character," I said. "He always said it was so vulgar to boast about things you had."

"He wanted to impress her," Leslie said. "She must have shaken him up."

"Nothing shook him up," I said.

Suddenly drinks arrived at our table, delivered by a teenage boy in black pants and a black bow tie. Mystified, we stared at the three tall, frosted glasses filled to the brim with creamy, tropical tints: green and pink and gold.

"What are these?" I said. "Did we order them?"

"I didn't," Eddy said.

"Waiter?" I said. "Just a minute—" But he was already gone.

"Oh, let's just drink them," Leslie suggested. "They're so pretty."

Laughing and toasting each other a bit raucously, we raised the glasses to our lips. I could almost have believed I was having a good time. But below the surface something hot and painful was boiling around.

"They were married for over thirty years," Leslie said. "But Gracie doesn't think they ever loved each other."

"I never said that," I said.

"Gracie doesn't believe that people love each other," Leslie laughed. "She thinks it's all a matter of economics."

"I never said that," I repeated tonelessly. "Economics and biology is what I said."

Eddy was tasting his drink. "Mmmmmm," he said. "This is very unusual. I think there might be rum in it, but I'm not sure."

"Oh, she's a tough cookie, Eddy," Leslie said. "Did you know that?"

Eddy lifted his eyes and looked at me. "Is she?" he said.

"You should have seen her when we were teenagers. We were in Palm Beach one winter, right? We were sitting in a courtyard off Worth Avenue, waiting while our mother did some shopping, and these two sexy-looking guys walked over."

I snorted. "Sexy-looking!"

"They were, Gracie! Especially the taller one, I still remember him, dark hair and such a lovely, slow, sexy smile. They were musicians. I think. Although they never actually said. . . . Why do I have the idea they were musicians?"

"Because they were wearing cheap suits."

Leslie laughed. "Anyway, the taller one said, 'Hello, Red.' But Gracie pretended not to hear him."

"I don't answer to 'Red.'"

"So he tried again. 'Mind if we join you and your friend?' Well, I was only about thirteen and I just about died of excitement. That he called me Gracie's 'friend,' like he thought I was grown up, you know? Right away I started sliding over to make room for them to sit down. But Gracie gave the poor guy a look that would have frozen water and said, 'You must be joking. We're waiting for someone, so please leave us alone.' You should have seen his face! He just wilted like a tulip, and he and the other guy sort of crawled away."

Eddy was watching me over the rim of his tall glass, smiling enigmatically, a smile that didn't seem to affect the thoughtful expression in his eyes.

"I didn't like his attitude," I said after a moment. "He acted as though we should fall down in awe just because he deigned to speak to us. So I thought, Well, I'll show him."

"Our father used to be like that too," Leslie said. "He'd give somebody a look and they'd shrivel. He didn't have to say a word."

"I was never in his league when it came to withering looks," I said. "I think you're right, Eddy, it's rum and something else. A liqueur of some kind. I can't place it."

"But poor Dad, he had some insecurities too."

"Oh, sure he did. It's probably one of those drinks that lull you into thinking they're not very strong, and then suddenly you're under the table."

"He was never the same after Cheltenham."

"Oh, come on, Leslie. He made some stupid mistakes and he had to pay for it. Don't turn it into a big drama."

"But he was different afterwards. It was obvious. He lost his confidence."

"I didn't notice any big difference. He had less money, that's all. You know, our grandfather could always name every ingredient in a drink. One sip was all he needed, and then he'd list them off. One ounce of bourbon, half an ounce of dry vermouth, half an ounce of sweet vermouth, a dash of Angostura Bitters and a half teaspoon of lemon juice."

"I stopped by Dad's office one morning about a month before he died," Leslie said. "I wanted to drop off some theatre tickets. It was the weirdest thing. He was just sitting at his desk. I mean, he wasn't talking on the phone, or dictating letters, or going through papers, he was just sitting at an empty desk, drinking a glass of Scotch. It wasn't like him at all. It kind of scared me. I said something like 'Gee, Dad, isn't it kind of early for Scotch?' And he said, 'No, it's always the right time for Tremain Gold Label.' Just like in the ads, a little joke. So we were sitting there chatting, nothing serious, just idle conversation, then all of a sudden you know what he said? He said, 'I fucked it all up, didn't I?' "

"You must have been dreaming. He would never have said a thing like that."

"Yeah, I know, I couldn't believe it either, I was stunned! I said, 'Dad, what are you talking about?' But he just poured himself another drink. He said, 'The bastards were out to get me. I forgot to watch my back. That's always the first thing you've got to remember, and I forgot.' Well, of course I knew he was talking about Cheltenham."

"Oh, for God's sake."

"He was obsessed with it, he really was."

"What's Cheltenham?" Eddy asked.

"The Cheltenham Corporation," Leslie explained. "It was on the way to becoming one of the biggest conglomerates in North America. That was what our father was going for, anyway. Didn't you ever take Eddy to Tremain Towers?"

"No, of course not," I said coldly. "Why on earth would I? God, I can't believe how fast I've drunk this. What do you think, should we order some more?"

"Dad was having a huge office complex built on Lakeshore Boulevard West," Leslie explained to Eddy. "It was going to be the new headquarters for Cheltenham. It was never quite completed but you can still see it from the Gardiner Expressway. There are two sixty-storey glass towers with an atrium between, and landscaped grounds with two marble fountains. Everything had to be absolutely the best quality. Brass fixtures, mahogany panelling, marble floors. Dad didn't care about the cost, it was his baby. He was always driving people out there to look at it."

"Those big blue towers? On Lakeshore Boulevard?" Eddy nodded. "Sure, sure, I've seen that. It belongs to you?"

"Not anymore," Leslie laughed. "I don't know who owns it now. The last I heard, it was sitting half-empty. No one wants to rent office space way out there. But our father had big ideas and he didn't care what anybody said. He was sure Tremain Towers was going to be an absolute mecca for business."

"Who cares now?" I said. "Where's our waiter? Eddy, do you see him?"

"No," Eddy said. "He's disappeared. So what happened to spoil things?"

"Dad kept expanding Cheltenham. His vice-president, a man named Frankenheimer, would negotiate new acquisitions and Dad never wanted to sell any assets so instead he kept taking out more loans at higher and higher rates. But that was okay for a while. In 1981 Cheltenham had assets worth about ten billion dollars, isn't that right, Gracie?"

Eddy listened to this extravagant figure without even blinking.

"How should I know?" I said. "It's such a beautiful summer night, I can't believe we're sitting here nattering about acquisitions and assets and debts. I'm bored to tears."

"Dad got an offer from a Montreal consortium to buy a parcel of Cheltenham companies, and if he'd sold then, he'd have made a killing. Frankenheimer thought they should take the offer so what did Dad do? Bought out Frankenheimer instead. He couldn't bring himself to sell a thing. He wanted to keep it all and add more."

"Add value, add value," I said. "That was one of his favourite maxims."

"Yeah. Cheltenham was his big dream."

"Sure," I said sarcastically. "His big dream was to avoid paying taxes. Don't give up equity, borrow against it. Another famous maxim. He didn't think it mattered how much debt he accumulated, because he was the great Laurie Tremain. He could walk into any bank in the world and they'd lend him a hundred million on his word alone. 'Books? You want to see my books? What kind of a rube are you? Do you know who I am?' Then they'd hand it over in a hurry and apologize for being so gauche as to ask questions. I'll bet he saw himself just sitting up there in his big blue skyscraper, looking down on everybody from on high. Tremain Towers. His monument to himself."

"His brain never stopped," Leslie said. "He was sort of like a chess master, he had all the moves in his head. And he kept inventing new moves and starting new games because otherwise it wasn't enough of a challenge."

I snorted scornfully. "What she means is that he tried to grab as much as he could in the shortest possible time."

"Well, that's Gracie's way of looking at it."

"Every time he bought a new company he'd lay off half the employees and cut everything else to the bone, just so he could finance his next big transaction. I wonder how thrilled those companies were to be pawns on the master's chessboard."

Leslie stared at me. "How do you know so much about it? You always said you had no interest in Cheltenham."

"I don't," I said.

"I'm not even sure when he started to get into trouble. I guess maybe I noticed that he was on the phone a lot—I mean, even for him. And he was kind of intense. Usually you'd never hear him raise his voice, but one night I remember he took a call after dinner and all of a sudden he started yelling and then slammed down the receiver, and I was sort of shocked. But still, I just thought it was ordinary deal-making. Didn't you?"

"That's what it was," I said.

"Anyway, on the night of Dad's fifty-seventh birthday there was a big party at Winston's in Toronto and when we came out of the restaurant a reporter from the *Globe and Mail* rushed up and said, 'Mr. Tremain, a group of bondholders have just announced they're seizing Tremain Towers. They claim Cheltenham Corporation has defaulted on its last two payments. Any comment?' Oh, the look on Dad's face. As though somebody had punched him in the stomach. That was the first inkling I had that anything was seriously wrong."

"Oh, come on, he didn't bat an eye," I said. "It was the same deadpan mask he always put on when he was talking to reporters."

"Well, of course he controlled himself. But just for one second he looked completely stunned. Then he said—"

"He had that dry smile, as if it didn't matter in the least. He said—"

"'No comment.' And then he hustled us into the limo and we drove off. Remember how he just sat there without a word? I knew it had to be something really deadly because usually he'd have been grabbing the car phone and calling dozens of people and wanting answers and giving orders . . . but that night he just sat there as if he was in a daze. Of course Mom didn't have a clue, she kept chattering about the food at Winston's, remember? She didn't think it was as great as everybody always said, for example the chocolate soufflé was too runny. 'Didn't you think it was runny, Laurie? Come on, that soufflé was runny, just admit it.' And Dad said, 'Yes, Vivian, you're absolutely right.' Those were the only words he spoke all the way back to the house."

Our teenage waiter bustled up to the table with a tray of new drinks. I stared at him in amazement. "What is this?" I said. "We didn't order these."

"Don't you want another round?" he asked.

"Well, yes, but we ..." I looked at Eddy. "Am I going crazy?"

"That day in his office Cheltenham was all he could talk about," Leslie said. "He kept drinking Tremain Gold Label and staring at Grandpa's portrait, the one with the nick in it, where Grandpa threw the telephone that time. Peter Hazard was still the biggest villain. He said Peter Hazard was the one who screwed him completely."

"Who was Peter Hazard?" Eddy said.

"Really, Eddy, what possible difference can it make to you?" I asked. But Leslie didn't seem to find it at all questionable that a stranger like Eddy should show such a fascination with our father's ancient business dealings. "Peter Hazard was the president of the First Metropolitan," she explained. "He and Dad were friends. Dad was even on the First Metropolitan board of directors for a while. He'd brought them a lot of business. So he thought they'd bail him out. Most of the other big banks started getting tough all of a sudden and wouldn't extend him any more credit."

"Better late than never," I said.

"He had lots of proposals about restructuring Cheltenham's debt, but they all involved him staying in control of the corporation, and nobody wanted to hear. That must have been so strange for him. They were always so eager to listen before."

"Yes, it must have been the biggest shock of his life when they stopped kissing his ass."

"But he thought he could depend on Peter Hazard. When Peter played hardball he took it as a huge betrayal."

"I don't know why," I remarked. "He always said business had nothing to do with friendship. Another maxim to live by."

"What happened?" Eddy wanted to know.

"Dad had to agree to step down as both president and CEO of Cheltenham and he had to give up controlling shares to First Metropolitan at rock-bottom prices. He ended up with less than three per cent of the corporation. And he had to sell the corporate jet and all his other unencumbered assets. Luckily Tremain Distilleries was in Aunt Lucy's name, so they couldn't touch it. But it was as though Peter Hazard wanted to just take Dad to the cleaners, humiliate him completely."

"If he'd been in Hazard's position he would have done exactly the same thing. Business is business. Personal relationships don't enter into it. Isn't that what he always said?"

"I guess he didn't see it that way when it happened to him."

"I guess not."

"That day in his office he said, 'You can't trust anybody. How could I have been such an asshole that I forgot that?' And he kept going on, all the other things he should have remembered and should have done. Finally I said, 'Oh, Dad, what does it matter now? We've still got more than most people.' Well, you can imagine what he thought of that."

I smirked and stared down into my lush pink-green drink.

"What did he think of it?" Eddy asked.

"Oh, he had no patience with that kind of talk. Having more than most people doesn't mean a thing. If you're a real player your money doesn't just sit in a vault, it builds. You put it out there, you manipulate it, you work it, you use it, and it expands, you take it to the skies. That's what counts. You should never have to look back, if you're any good. I think Cheltenham was the first time he ever lost, and it was such a big loss. He always loved winning so much. He never knew what it was like on the other side. He couldn't forgive himself, he had to keep trying to figure out what went wrong."

Pink droplets had splashed onto the tablecloth and I briskly wiped them away with my napkin. "Our waiter is totally confused," I said. "Pretty soon the people who are actually ordering these drinks are going to start getting impatient."

Leslie was sipping her new drink and going on obliviously with her story. "He seemed so tired and edgy, I never saw him like that before. He kept looking up at Grandpa's picture. He said the whole Cheltenham thing would have handed Grandpa a big laugh. He said, 'The old man always told me I wasn't going to cut it, I wasn't tough enough.' God, Grandpa sure was a mean old bird, wasn't he? He never gave an inch. I don't remember him very well, only that he always seemed to be mad about something. Even when he was telling a joke he seemed to be mad underneath. I remember once he slapped his driver in the face because the guy was a minute late bringing the car around. Smack, right in the face, the guy actually staggered. Unbelievable. No one could get away with that sort of thing now. No, Grandpa was definitely not a nice person."

"He came to this country with ten dollars in his pocket and he made a fortune," I said. "I guess he didn't have time to be nice."

"No, you're right," Leslie agreed. "But he wasn't easy to live with, to put it mildly. That's why Aunt Lucy got married so young and moved to California, just to get away from him. No, it's true, she told me herself. She said when he came into the room it was as if he sucked up all the air and there was none left for anybody else. Actually I sort of remember feeling that way too. Didn't you?"

I shrugged. "Not really."

"Dad thought everybody was laughing at him after Cheltenham. 'All those sons of bitches,' he said, 'I know they all got a good laugh watching me crash and burn.' It made me so sad, Gracie. I felt so sorry for him. So I started crying, you know me, tears were pouring down, I said, 'Dad, that's not true, nobody could ever laugh at you,' I said, 'Of course you're tough, you're the toughest and smartest of them all!' But no, he wouldn't listen. 'Rags to riches to rags,' he said. Apparently that's what Grandpa predicted would happen. He was sure Dad would screw it all up after he was gone. 'You're just like some damn woman, just like your mother, just too soft.' That's how Grandpa used to talk. Poor Dad. He smiled as if it were funny, but I could see that he really didn't think it was too funny. You know, I think his hand was actually shaking when he picked up his glass."

"You always overdramatize," I said. "Two weeks after he lost control of Cheltenham he was in the winner's circle at the Queen's Plate, making champagne toasts and having the time of his life. I don't think Cheltenham broke his heart."

Eddy was sitting quietly, glass in hand, one arm resting on the back of his chair, watching us with a bemused expression.

"I guess it was a different story for some of the share-holders, though," I said. "When the shares dropped into the cellar some of them lost their entire life savings. I wonder if that even crossed the great man's mind while he was drinking Gold Label and wallowing in self-pity."

Leslie shook her head. "See, Eddy? I told you she was tough."

Eddy looked at me with a smile. "Yes," he said.

At that moment a pair of long, thin, tanned arms slipped around Leslie's neck from behind. Leslie gave a start and tilted her head back. "Oh, my God!" she squealed.

"Hello, stranger!" Betsy and Rob DeJong were standing on either side of Leslie's chair, laughing. I hadn't seen them approach. They seemed to have materialized out of the atmosphere. Apparently they had colour-coordinated their outfits; she was wearing a long silk dress in a rich green and brown pattern, and he was wearing brown pants and a dark green shirt. I knew they had to be in their sixties but their matching golden tans made them appear several years younger. They were enveloped in an aura of Chanel No. 5; it was difficult to tell whether the scent originated with him or with her. Leslie jumped up to hug them, first Betsy and then Rob and then Betsy again.

"You're such a bad girl!" Betsy said. "You haven't been to

Azure Lake for an eternity! I couldn't believe my eyes when I saw you!" She glanced in my direction. "Hello, Grace."

"Hello, Betsy," I said. "Hi, Rob."

"I see you're enjoying the Knickerbockers," Rob said.

"What? You mean, the drinks? You're kidding, were you the ones ordering them? We couldn't understand . . ."

Betsy gave a tasteful, tinkly laugh. "We were sitting way over there when you walked in. 'Let's send them some drinks,' Rob said, 'let's see how long it takes them to figure it out.'"

"Those are genuine Knickerbockers just like they make at the Knickerbocker Club in New York," Rob said. "Every time they hire a new bartender here, I have to go in and show him exactly how to make them. The secret is one tiny splash of mint. That's what makes a perfect Knickerbocker."

Eddy had stood up when Leslie did. He leaned forward across the table and gave a winning smile. "Why don't you join us?" he said.

"Oh, I'm being so rude," Leslie cried. "Rob and Betsy, this is Eddy Corona, a friend of ours from Toronto. Eddy, Rob and Betsy DeJong. They have the place with the green gazebo, right across the lake from Trewithen."

A friend of "ours," she called him. He was not her friend; he was mine. I stared at her coldly, but she didn't seem to notice. She was too busy signalling the teenage waiter to bring extra chairs.

As Rob sat down he called over his shoulder, "Another round of those fine Knickerbockers, too, if you please!" And he winked at me. I smiled vaguely in response. Already I was longing for them to leave. "Corona," Rob said to Eddy. "Are you in tobacco, by any chance? Corona makes me think of the cigars. Great cigars."

"No," Eddy said smoothly. "My family's in the import-export business. Leather, vicuna, lapis lazuli . . . but silver is our specialty."

"Eddy's from Argentina," Leslie told them.

"Honestly?" said Betsy, resting her head against the back of her chair and looking at Eddy through her eyelashes. "I have to admit I'm really quite ignorant about Argentina. I only know about Evita, llamas, and gauchos. End of list."

"Before I came here I didn't know about Canada either," Eddy said. "I thought it was full of snow and Eskimos."

"But you thought the Eskimos would buy silver, I guess," I said in a soft voice.

Eddy's eyes flickered at me for a second before returning to rest on Betsy's colourless face. "It was a gamble," he said with a grin. Betsy laughed her tinkly laugh.

"Where's Sid?" Rob wanted to know. "Did he come up with you?"

Leslie looked down at the table and then raised her eyes with a smile. "I might as well tell you," she said. "Sid and I have split up. It just happened a couple of weeks ago. No, it's all right, I'm fine. I really am."

We had several more rounds of Knickerbockers; I lost count. Leslie regaled us with the details of her breakup. Rob and Betsy claimed that they were totally unable to comprehend Sid's stupidity in preferring any other woman to her. They also expressed their conviction that Sid had to take the blame for everything that had gone wrong. We all clinked our glasses and Rob made a convoluted toast which had something to do with new beginnings. Eddy told a story about an Argentinian wife who had taken revenge on her unfaithful husband by drugging him and then clipping off his penis and sewing it to his forehead. Betsy was so scandalized and so overcome by the humour of it all that she had to lean forward hysterically and rest her hand on Eddy's knee. All the time I listened and nodded, smiling when they did and laughing when they did. Something odd was happening though; with each successive Knickerbocker they seemed to recede to a greater distance, until I felt as though I were looking at them through the wrong end of a telescope. They were reduced to dinky figures in a circle of glass, moving and gesturing incomprehensibly.

Later we stood on the Azure Inn pier and saw Rob and Betsy off. Apparently they had invited us all to a barbecue the following week; apparently we had accepted. "The Wyatts and the Godfreys will be there too!" Betsy called to us. "It'll be like old times!" Chanel No. 5 drifted back across the silvery water as their launch put-putted away. "Come over to Trewithen anytime!" Leslie cried. "Just jump in the boat and come!"

I stared at her in disbelief. After a moment she turned and saw the look on my face. Then she shrugged sheepishly and rolled her eyes. "Well, what else could I do?" she said. "They invited *us*."

"You always said you detested the DeJongs," I said. "Didn't you say they were the most pretentious people in the world?"

"Well, they are, Gracie! But a person has to be polite!"

"So now you've told them to drop by anytime. And we have to go to their place for a barbecue and Kelly Wyatt will be there. Kelly Wyatt, the one you said you wanted to avoid at all costs."

"Oh, shit, yes! Isn't it awful? A whole evening with her, and she'll tell me over and over again how terribly sorry she is about Sid, but she always knew what a disaster it would be if I married him! I'm going to need serious drugs! No, how about this? We'll call them and say we can't come because I've broken my leg. No, wait—I've gone blind! My mother always warned me it would happen if I didn't learn to control myself —but no, we can't call them because there are no phones at Trewithen— maybe we could get some carrier pigeons—or what about smoke signals. . . ." She ran back to the top of the pier, laughing tipsily. Eddy stood there watching her, laughing too.

THERE WERE CLOUDS OVER THE MOON that night and our room was so dark you could barely see your hand in front of your face. I felt Eddy's arm against mine. I listened to his soft breath.

"She's been here a week already," I said. "I don't think it'll be much longer."

"I don't care," Eddy said. "It's kind of fun having her around."

Every day when I woke up I longed for those mornings before Leslie came, the sun-filled silence, the soft sound of the boathouse radio as we took off our clothes on the beach and made love, the delicate touch of his limbs in the sultry water at midnight, the long, winy evenings, sitting on the verandah with his feet in my lap, one of the straps of my sundress slipping down from my shoulder, and then suddenly he would push the dress further down and stroke my breast with the sole of his foot. The days were passing, September was coming. Every day that Leslie stayed she robbed me of something. But apparently the things I longed for meant nothing to him. He liked to have her around; he thought it was fun. No doubt he had been getting bored with just me alone.

"So you don't want her to leave," I said quietly. There was a tremor far down in my throat, but I was glad to hear that my voice sounded strong and cool.

"Well, she's good company," he said. "Sometimes you two finish each other's sentences, do you realize that?"

I breathed gently, in and out, in and out. "You think she's good company?" I said.

"Sure," he said. "And I know a lot more about you than I did before."

My head went light with sudden rage. "Oh, is that so?" I said. "What do you think you know?"

He didn't answer. The silence was heavy, almost tangible. After a while the hot pulse in my temple began to slow down.

"Maybe you'd like to make it a threesome," I said brightly. "You, me and her. Do you think that would be a good time?"

I waited, staring at the ceiling. I felt him turn slightly to look at me. "You've done that before, haven't you?" I said. "More than two?"

After a moment he spoke casually. "Yeah . . . you?"

"Of course. Never with my sister though, I must say that would be an interesting new twist."

"Are you serious?"

"Absolutely."

He seemed surprised, but not too surprised. He must have heard plenty of far more perverse suggestions in his lifetime. "What about her, would she go for something like that?"

"Well, I don't know, we'd have to ask her. She's not quite as . . . adventurous as I am, but she might like the idea. There's nothing wrong with it, is there? It's just bodies, after all. Bodies, skin, pleasure. No harm in that. What do you think, should we ask her?"

Again I waited, listening to the throbbing darkness. My tortuous rage seemed to expand with each moment of silence. At first I thought he was pondering the question deeply, but then suddenly it occurred to me with crystal clarity that he wasn't doing that at all. He was simply trying to figure out what answer I wanted to hear the most. Finally he came up with it. "We can if you want to," he said. "But I'm happy just with you."

Damn him, damn his shrewdness, damn his rotten subtlety! I gave a harsh snort of laughter. "Well, isn't that sweet!" I said.

He was looking at me in the darkness. He reached out and rubbed my cheek lightly with the back of his hand. "I mean it," he said.

All at once my throat was gripped by a harsh pain and I had to press my lips together and swallow hard. Apparently my brief, violent anger had released other emotions too. It took a moment before I could trust myself to speak. "I just . . . I can't help thinking how nice it was when we were alone here," I heard myself say at last. "Didn't you think it was nice?" The tremor had risen into my voice; I heard it clearly; I heard how weak and beseeching and lovesick I sounded, just like any stupid woman.

"Of course," he whispered. What else was he going to say?

"I sort of wish she'd go so it could be like that again," I said. God, what had come over me, why did I have to say that? My face burned with shame.

He rolled over and pressed his body against me. "Me too," he said. Of course that's what he said.

Chapter Eighteen

THE DAYS WERE GROWING SHORTER. I think I was the only one who noticed this. In mid-July the sky had stayed light till nine p.m. and then twilight came slowly, spreading like a velvety shadow from the lake, turning to darkness in such subtle shadings that we hardly noticed the change until nine-thirty or a quarter to ten, when suddenly one of us said, almost in surprise, "Look, it's dark." Then we walked through the domain of Trewithen, he and I, climbing up the lawn, hand in hand, toward the tall walls that were going to enclose us in hot, vibrant secrecy.

That was all over. It was mid-August and the sky began to darken by eight and we had social obligations. The night of the DeJongs' barbecue, the descending sun was still bright on the water as we nudged the *Gazelle* in among all the other boats at their dock. Smells of cologne and cooking meat mingled in the warm air. Up on the flagstone terrace in front of the house, groups of people in pale clothes stood holding cocktails, the liquid in their glasses glimmering in the soft, fading light. Rob was wearing a tall chef's hat and an apron with the words "World's Biggest Sizzler" in fat red letters across the front. "Hi, Tremains!" he called, waving a barbecue implement at us through the smoke from the grill. "Hi, Ed! Steak or chicken? It'll be ready in ten!" Then a thin blonde figure detached itself from a group at the corner of the lawn and stamped its foot emphatically on the ground. "Leslie, is that you? I can't believe it! You get up here right away! We have to talk!" "There she is," I said. "Have fun." Leslie groaned under her breath but a second later she was grinning broadly and raising her arm in a happy wave. "Kelly! Hi! Is it really you?" At the same moment Betsy floated across the grass and slipped her arm around my waist. I noticed that her other hand settled lightly on Eddy's shoulder and stayed there. "Grace," she said, "so glad you could come. Guess who's here. Kent! We weren't expecting him until next weekend. Anjelica had to stay in town but he was able to get away early. Isn't that lucky? He said he hasn't seen you since university. You'll have a lot of catching up to do!" I smiled bravely. "Oh, yes," I said, "great." "Now, Eddy, the other night you mentioned you're a yachtsman," Betsy purred, looking up into Eddy's eyes. "Well, almost the entire Belair Boat Club is here tonight so there are lots of people you'll want to meet."

The sky arched above us like a great inverted bowl. It was beginning to change to cobalt blue, although a pearly glow of white and pale lilac still lingered around the horizon. Then there was an eerie, breathless moment when the last rays of light gilded all of us, lit our bodies with a supernatural white-yellow radiance below the vast rolling darkness. I sat on the boathouse dock with a plate on my lap, and I could look far across the water to the opposite shore, to the faint outline of my own boathouse almost hidden in twilight shadow, to the pale ivory railings of Trewithen's upper gallery, obscured by the tall pines. I tried picturing the empty beach and the waves washing against the sand, but it was hard to concentrate because Kent DeJong was sitting beside me, talking and eating heaping forkfuls of potato salad. He looked like a big-scale version of his father Rob: the same wide, freckled face, the same spiky sandy hair, the same thick shoulders and broad knees, but in Kent everything seemed a bit enlarged, a bit cruder and less clearly defined. He told me that he and his wife Anjelica had just returned from a Mediterranean holiday. Apparently Anjelica was the sales manager for a chain of beauty products called Naturally Natural. "Nothing tested on animals, no harm to the rainforest, all very P.C.," Kent said, waving his fork in the air. "They've made a great advertising shtick out of P.C., in fact. That's what I tell her. Of course she doesn't want to look at it that way; she says it's 'ethical marketing.' So I tell her, 'Hey, fine, honey, you call it anything you want.' They made a five-mill profit last year, just in the Greater Toronto area. If 'ethical marketing' sells like that, then give them 'ethical marketing.' I'm all for it."

I watched the sky as it continued slowly to change its colour; the lilac at the skyline began to deepen and spread upward until it merged with the inky blue to create a wholly new shade, a great wash of purple flecked with the white of occasional stars. After a while only a thin black line of land marked the difference between sky and water. In the grass up beside the house the turquoise kidney-shape of the DeJongs' heated pool glistened like a jewel, and Leslie was standing next to it, watery reflections rippling across her body as she entertained a group of eager listeners with her tales of marital discord. "So I said, 'Perry, what is the meaning of this?' and he said, 'Baby, I swear to God, we were just rehearsing, it's the nude love scene in Act II'—" Wild laughter rang out across the dark lawn, but the people down in the jacuzzi didn't even turn their heads; they were too absorbed in Eddy's equally fascinating account of his struggle against the hurricane. He was sitting up to his chest in steamy liquid, smoking an aromatic cigar, his arms resting along the polished sides of the tub, and various faces were tilted toward him like flowers toward the sun. Betsy DeJong sat right at his side, her damp hair hanging in tendrils around her powdery jowls, her wet brown hand clasping his wrist. I thought how repellent it was to see a sixty-year-old woman who couldn't accept the fact that her time was over. By then Kent DeJong and I had moved to the upper deck of the boathouse and every time Kent stopped for breath I could hear Eddy's distant voice pronouncing phrases like "the waves were fifty feet high...," "my boat jumped right up into the air...," and then his listeners would murmur in amazement, and Betsy DeJong would say, "That's incredible, Eduardo!" Eduardo? I thought. Where the hell did that come from? He was loving it, of course. He was in his element.

"It's too bad Anjelica isn't here because you two should meet," Kent told me. "You and she would hit it off, I'm sure. She loves to read when she has the time. Right now she's into Martin Amis and Julian Barnes and that whole Brit crowd. Maybe in the fall, we can arrange a dinner. I'll give you my card."

We were among the last to leave the party. Rob and Kent stood on the dock to see us off; Betsy was suffering from a migraine, probably brought on by sexual tension, and she had gone inside to lie down. The two men waved to us as we pulled away. When I looked back over my shoulder, they seemed to be standing right on the water, the shimmering yellow reflections of the boathouse lights spraying out from the soles of their feet.

"Be sure to call in September!" Kent reminded me.

"A new conquest?" Leslie asked me. She had flung herself down across the two back seats and rested her head against the side of the *Gazelle* so that her long hair almost trailed into the water.

"Sort of," I said. "He wants to set me up with his wife. He thinks we'll adore each other."

Leslie laughed gaily above the roar of the motor as we streaked out onto the lake. The wind was tropically warm; you could almost imagine that the dark shapes on the horizon were palm trees, not pines. The *Gazelle* spun out a vast lacy arc of foam across the silky black water.

"Well, it wasn't quite as ghastly as I thought!" Leslie shouted over the noise of the boat.

"It wasn't?" I said.

"No—not quite. How about you, Eddy? Did you think it was awful?"

Eddy was wearing his kid-leather gloves and holding the wheel with one hand, as though he were operating a toy boat. He smiled, looking straight ahead toward Trewithen. "No," he said. "I didn't have a bad time actually."

"Well, you made a big hit with the women, that was obvious!" Leslie cried with a laugh. "Kelly Wyatt could hardly take her eyes off you. She said she couldn't blame me for ditching Sid, if I had someone like you around. I said, 'Oh, no, Kelly, Eddy and I are just friends.' But you know how that sounds. Right away people think you're just trying to be coy."

Eddy snickered. I felt the corners of my lips getting stiff. "I suppose it didn't occur to her that he might be with me," I said carelessly after a moment.

"Well, I said to her, 'Actually Eddy is with Grace, not me.' And she was amazed, and said you told her you'd come up here alone."

Eddy's grin faded somewhat. He glanced at me, a brief expressionless look. I didn't allow myself to get confused or defensive, even for a second. "Well, of course that's what I told her," I said at once. "I'm not like you, I'm not eager to discuss my private life with everybody I meet on the street."

Leslie propped herself up on her elbows and stared. I folded my arms over my chest. I wouldn't look around. "What's the matter?" she said incredulously. "Are you mad at me?"

"No," I said. "Why should I be?"

The days went by and she never mentioned leaving.

"Good morning, Leslie," Eddy would say as she walked sleepily into the kitchen, rubbing her eyes, her hair in attractive disarray. She would smile at him with frank pleasure, catching her hair in one hand and rolling it up on top of her head, staring at him through her eyelashes. "Good morning, Eddy," she would say.

"Coffee?"

"Oh, yes, please. Mmmmmmmm. Eddy. Did you make it? I don't know why, but it tastes especially good today."

WE WENT FOR A WALK after supper one night. Eddy walked between us like a prince with two consorts, graciously bending his head first to one and then to the other. The tips of his fingers touched the inside of my arm. I wondered what he was doing with his other hand. The cool-smelling pines rose up so far that their feathery tips seemed to spear the clouds. One night my mother walked down the same path. The pale globe of her hair floated away and disappeared into the murky dusk. My father was standing on the steps of the verandah, smoking a cigarette. He hardly seemed to notice her departure but after a few moments he strolled casually in the same direction. I saw his red head moving slowly through the dark trees. They were gone a long time and when they reappeared they were walking along together, not touching but side by side. She was holding a white iris in one hand, swinging its long stem idly. He took a small step sideways and his arm brushed against hers. She smiled and lifted the iris to smell its perfume.

Leslie laughed at something Eddy had said. She always behaved that way with men: leaning toward them eagerly, devouring them with her eyes, basking in their attention, praising them, flattering them, raising a funhouse mirror so they could see themselves fabulously enlarged. And oh, how quick they were to respond, every last one of them. *Oh, Daddy, you're the toughest and smartest of them all!*

My feet felt stiff in my thin canvas shoes. I kept gazing distractedly into the dark underbrush, because I didn't want to look at the two of them. I could see the lake, a distant silvery glitter through the thick black branches.

"This is still your property?" Eddy asked, and Leslie answered him on his other side. "Yes, right up to the bridge."

We crossed the worn boards; you could look down

through the cracks and see the glint of metallic water below. It was a brook with no name; sometimes it would dry up completely and then reappear after a couple of rainfalls. That night in the strange clarity of the twilight its tinkly gurgle sounded faraway, unreal, rather melancholy.

We came out onto a deserted stretch of road called the McKinley Trail and walked along the deep ruts to Stoney Joe's Dairy. Mrs. Stoney Joe was behind the counter, just as she had always been during the long days of our childhood, and she still looked like the perfect woman to run an ice cream shoppe, smiling and hearty, with rosy cheeks and snow-white hair, her large body wrapped in a white apron stained with strawberry syrup. She exclaimed in delight at the sight of us. "I haven't seen you two girls together for so long! I remember when you'd both come in here on your summer vacation from school. Don't tell me—a sugar cone with two scoops of Heavenly Hash, and a waffle cone with the Chocolate/Pralines Combo. Right? You see? I always remember." She glanced at Eddy, a flicker of a look that managed to convey curiosity, appreciation and wonder, all in one or two seconds. "Now you, let me guess. You want something big and rich."

She kept chattering cheerily as she leaned into the big deep-freeze with her ice cream scoop.

"They used to come in here all the time," she told Eddy. "Such cute little girls, so well-behaved." She handed Leslie and me our cones, displaying her deep, rosy dimples. "That's a credit to your parents," she said. Leslie gave a puckered grin and ducked her head sheepishly.

"Your mother dressed you so well too," Mrs. Stoney Joe said. Her plump fingers were moving swiftly and expertly to construct Eddy's banana split. "Lovely sundresses, always so crisply laundered. You two always looked like you'd just stepped out of a bandbox. And you used to wear pigtails, both of you. The cutest pigtails! I always meant to ask your mother how she did that kind of a braid, with the ribbon twined right through, but then it would slip my mind whenever I saw her. How did she do it anyway?"

We waited until we were almost back to the bridge before bursting out laughing.

"She makes me feel about ten years old! What was she talking about? Did we ever wear pigtails?"

"It was French braid," I said. "And Mom didn't have a clue how to do it. That was Edith Fish. She always said that French braid was both elegant and practical."

"That's right, that's right! For your thirteenth birthday, she braided in a strand of seed pearls, remember? She was the reason we were so sweet and polite, she had us scared into submission for sure! Remember what Dad always said? The only real nanny is a British nanny. 'Now, girls, stand up straight. Leslie, please hold your stomach in, it's not ladylike to have a prominent tummy.'"

"Yes. Of course she loosened up once in a while after she'd smoked some dope."

"What! She never!"

"Of course she did! Don't you remember those funny-smelling cigarettes? Mom and Dad would be away, and we'd be sitting with Edith and Marge and Frederick in the kitchen, and she'd bring one out and light up. How could you forget this? One night you said, 'Edith, can I have a puff?' and Edith said, 'Certainly not, these are just for grown-up people.'" I imitated Edith sucking in some smoke and closing her eyes in rapture.

"She never! I don't believe it!"

"It wasn't till years later, when I was at university, someone brought out a joint and there was something so familiar about the way it looked, and then when I got a whiff, I thought, Oh my God, Edith Fish was way ahead of her time!"

My voice seemed to carry up to the highest branches of the trees. I wondered why I was talking so loudly.

"Where could she have gotten it?" I said. "I can't imagine marijuana was that common in Toronto the Good in 1960. Maybe she had a contact. Maybe an ancestor of the one who supplies you, Eddy."

If Eddy was startled he didn't show it. He was busy spooning ice cream and banana chunks into his mouth and didn't even pause. But Leslie turned her head and looked at us both with a surprised smile. "What?"

"Eddy has a great contact in Toronto. He got us some really great dope and some coke too."

Leslie's eyes fluttered. "Coke? You're kidding. I'd be sort of scared to try that. Isn't it terribly addictive?"

"Not at all," I said with a breezy laugh. "Well, maybe crack is. But we had that beautiful, fine white powder. The champagne of drugs. You sniff it into your nostrils and then you think you're in paradise. I was delirious. It's true though, I wouldn't want to do it too often. Just like Edith Fish would say . . . 'Girls, it's not ladylike to feel delirious.'"

"Oh, God, yes. It reminds me of the time when—"

We went on in the same gay, girlish, fraudulent way for most of the walk back. I strained to keep it up; it was far better than listening to Eddy's insinuating conversation and Leslie's over-eager response to it. I wanted to bore and irritate him; I wanted him to find us shallow and phoney. But the trouble was he never seemed bored and irritated when we launched into our tedious reminiscences. He didn't seem to think it was shallow and phoney at all. He always listened and laughed and asked questions as though he wanted to absorb every last detail we could dredge up. I always had to ask myself why a man like Eddy Corona would find our long-ago, uptight, vapid girlhood so endlessly fascinating.

By the time we got back to Trewithen I was tired, physically tired as though I had just done some kind of intense, punishing exercise. I switched on the kitchen light and we all blinked in the sudden yellow glare. Eddy reached out and rubbed the corner of Leslie's mouth with one finger. "Chocolate," he said. Then he put his finger in his own mouth and sucked on it.

For a moment it seemed to me that the light bulb had shattered and filled the room with shards of glass and electricity: a calamity so sudden that one is dazed and can't react. Water burned beneath my eyelids. I could hardly see, and yet I saw vividly, I saw a swift, evanescent blush on Leslie's face as she turned away, I saw the faint smile passing momentarily across Eddy's mouth. I thought I could grab something and break it, and then I would have something sharp to hurt one of them. I didn't know which one it would be.

But that would have been an insane over-reaction—losing my temper and behaving like a virago, simply because a man with whom I was having a trivial fling casually wiped an ice cream stain from my sister's cheek. I turned away from them and walked across the room. I opened a cupboard. I heard myself say, in a voice so hollow that I seemed to be speaking from inside a tunnel, "Why don't we have some gin and tonic?"

We sat in front of the empty fireplace. It was too warm to have a fire. Lamplight enclosed the three of us in a small circle; beyond it shadows stretched out across the polished floor and the tall amber windows stared opaquely down the lawn to the misty white garden. I held my cocktail glass in both hands and looked at the ashes in the fireplace grate. I was sitting on the floor and Eddy sat behind me in the old moss-green armchair. I could feel his presence there. I held my back rigidly straight. I thought I couldn't stand it if any part of him touched me.

"When you come back you should bring some silver work from El Mundo de la Plata," Leslie said. He was driving to Toronto the next day to take care of some "business."

I continued to stare at the ashes. "Yes, Eddy, why don't you?" I said.

"Should I?"

"Oh, do," Leslie said. She was speaking in her best bright, flirty, gushy tone. "We'd love to see some of it. It sounded so beautiful when you described it. Maybe I'll even buy a piece. It'll be a souvenir of the summer Sid left me. Or I left him, or whatever it was. The happiest summer of my life. I'm only kidding. But I'm starting to think it was the best thing that could have happened."

"Are you," I said.

"Yes, because why hang on to something that's stone-cold

dead? Isn't that right? Walk away from it, go on living. It's not as if we have so much time. We can't afford to waste any of it. It's better to be free."

I noticed how fine the ash was, fine as powder. They might have exchanged a glance behind me, but I didn't see it.

"Do you ever miss Argentina?" Leslie asked suddenly. "I'd like to go there someday."

"Grace and I are going," Eddy said. "You can come with us. We'll go on my boat. We'll sail into the Rio de la Plata bay like royalty. I'll show you everything. When I'm walking down the street with two such gorgeous *gringa* ladies on my arms, everybody is going to be so envious, they'll be saying, 'That Eduardo, how did that son of a bitch get so lucky?'"

"Oh, yes!" Leslie cried enthusiastically. "When will we do it?"

"Soon, maybe."

"Really? Soon?"

"Yes," Eddy said.

My fists were balled up in my lap. Sometimes I woke up like that, my fingers stiff from clenching them all night in my sleep.

"I've never been to South America," Leslie said. "Oh, wait, that's not true. Sid and I were in Cartagena once, he had some business meetings there for one of his clients. You could see all the drug lords' palaces on the hillsides. With electric fences and security guards. It drove Sid crazy. He had a real bee in his bonnet about drugs. He always used to say drug dealers were the worst lowlife scum in the world and they should all be executed."

Leslie laughed, as though this were funny. I felt a thin, electric shiver in the base of my neck. There you go, Eddy. Take her to Buenos Aires on your boat. Kiss her ass. I waited to hear what he would say. He didn't say a word. After a moment she went blithely on.

"What bothered me most was the terrible poverty. I never dreamed it could be like that. I thought I'd seen poverty before but I didn't have a clue. You'd be driving by on the highway and you could see right into the shantytowns, hundreds of little hovels made out of cardboard and tarpaper and I don't know what, with smoke coming out the doors, and sewage running down the middle of the street, and kids playing in it, kids hardly more than babies, wearing filthy T-shirts and no pants, squatting in the dirt and splashing around in the shitty water. You could actually smell the shit, and see it, the grass in the ditch all stained with brown, it almost made you gag. I saw this woman behind an awful shack covered with dirty paper. She was standing on a pile of garbage and hanging up pieces of rags on a clothesline. How would you be able to do it? How could you wash clothes and hang them up on a line, in the middle of a hellhole like that? I think I'd kill myself. I wouldn't be strong enough, I'd have to kill myself."

A pulse in my head was throbbing so loudly that it was difficult to hear what she said. I kept expecting Eddy to answer her, but he didn't.

"There were a couple of street kids, we saw them every day outside our hotel. Fernando and Manolo. They were so cute, especially Fernando. He was nine and Manolo was eight. They both spoke English quite well. Lots of the street kids spoke some English, I guess so they could talk to tourists and ask for money. One day we wanted to take them to eat in a restaurant. It wasn't a fancy place, just an ordinary tacky restaurant, but still, the waiter didn't want to let them in. He said, 'Señora, don't pity them, they're vermin, that's all they are.' He said it right in front of them. I got out my wallet. I was so worked up my hands were shaking. I'd just had money changed so I had quite a lot of cash, and I took it all and pushed it into his hand and I said, 'We want a table by the window right now.' You should have seen their eyes!"

She made me sick. I kept wanting Eddy to respond, but he remained stubbornly silent. Finally I said, "You always like to make big melodramatic gestures, but actually it would have been a lot smarter to give the money to some local charity. They probably could have used it to feed ten kids for a month."

"That's what Sid said too. But I don't know, I wanted those

two particular kids to sit down in that restaurant and be waited on!"

I nodded, still gazing at the fireplace grate. "What happened to them after you left?" I said.

She was silent for a moment. "I don't know," she said finally. After another pause she added, "You're right. I should have done more."

"If you're so concerned maybe you should sign over part of your trust fund. Think how many street kids you could help."

Leslie nodded slowly. "You're right," she said. "I should look into that."

"Why don't you go right now and write a letter to Ted Farragut?" I said.

"I'm going to," she said. "I've had too much gin to write a coherent sentence right now, but I'll do it tomorrow." I knew that by tomorrow she would have forgotten all about it.

Into the stillness the clock on the mantelpiece began to drop its silvery chimes. I felt Eddy's solid, motionless presence behind me.

"I guess Argentina isn't as poor as Colombia, is it?" Leslie remarked at last.

I heard Eddy clear his throat and shift his weight in the chair. "No," he said. "It's not as poor."

"But there's poverty there too," I said.

"That's what Dad always used to say, remember? 'There's poverty everywhere, always was, always will be, even though the bleeding hearts don't like it. Some are strong and some are weak, and the weak ones go under. We can only take care of ourselves, we can't take care of the whole world. Survival of the fittest. Too bad, but it's the law of nature. We're animals just like the others, no better, no worse. Grow up and accept it.' Poor Dad was a bit of a reactionary. I don't think he meant half of what he said."

"Don't you," I said.

"My uncle had a *finca* in Paraguay," Eddy said suddenly. "A ranch. My uncle wasn't a very nice man. My father who was a very religious Catholic used to say that Uncle Carlos would spend eternity in the first circle of hell. It would have to be the first circle because Uncle Carlos would never accept anything less than first. He used to send his agent to hire poor guys from the streets of Buenos Aires and Montevideo and Sao Paulo. The agent would promise them a fine salary and great working conditions. They'd come driving onto the *finca* on the back of a truck, standing up and singing, as if they already had the money in their pockets. Uncle Carlos had a barracks behind barbed wire and worked them like slaves. If they couldn't keep up the foreman would beat them and if they talked too much he'd beat them and if they asked when they'd be paid he'd beat them. Once or twice someone would die from a beating and they'd be buried in a field. I remember seeing the mounds of earth with bits of grass blowing over them."

"But how could he get away with it?" Leslie said.

"They were *desechable*, that's the word my uncle used. Uh . . . disposable in English," Eddy said with a shrug. "These guys had nothing and they were worth nothing except for the bit of work you could get out of them. And there were always lots more to take their place. My uncle said he was doing the government a favour to take care of them."

Leslie shook her head. "How disgusting," she said.

"He really believed it," Eddy said.

They were both so phoney it turned my stomach. I saw Eddy suddenly in my mind, walking along the boardwalk and stepping off it into the white sand in front of my house, glittering in the darkness as he came up through my garden, gold at his wrist and around his neck, hair curling on the collar of his pink silk shirt, the scent of Calvin Klein's Obsession in the folds of his clothes, his stomach full of wine and pasta. I hate you, I thought, you revolt me. Then I was filled with such a piercing desire that for a moment I couldn't see the ashes in the grate anymore, only the vision of him walking through my garden in his gaudy pink shirt.

"Once when I was visiting Uncle Carlos I got to know one

of them," Eddy said. "He was a young guy, eighteen or so, about my age at the time. I talked to him often. He'd never been in the country before. He said he'd never seen so much grass, not even in Palermo Park which is a big park in Buenos Aires. At night he didn't like how quiet it got, he'd have to make some kind of a noise to be sure he hadn't gone deaf. The night sky made him nervous too. He wasn't used to it being so big and black. He said in Buenos Aires at night the sky was always red and there were lots of big bright electric lights, not all those little stars so faint and far away. In the end he escaped."

"Escaped!" Leslie exclaimed. "How?"

"One night I was driving back from town and I heard gunshots so I got out of the car. The back field was full of men running and the foreman was firing his rifle into the air and shouting. For some reason I knew without any doubt who they were chasing. And then all of a sudden I saw him, he ran across the riverbank fast as lightning and dived in. When he came to the surface a whole fountain of silvery water sprayed up all around his head. Bullets were singing through the air and for a couple of minutes he disappeared and I thought, Oh Christos, they've shot him dead. But then all of a sudden there he was on the other side, climbing up out of the water. What a crazy bastard, he actually had the nerve to turn around and wave. And he yelled out, 'Adiós, maricones!' It means, well, very rude, it's a word that means faggots, fairies. These guys are still shooting at him but there he stands, waving! Calling them *maricones*. Then he's gone into the trees. We never saw him again after that."

Leslie let out a long breath. "Well, good for him," she said. "Good for him." She had been absolutely riveted, her eyes moving back and forth to follow each sweeping gesture Eddy used to embellish his story. Sid had never told stories like that. Ivan had saved most of his creative energy for the members of his band. Perry had never talked that way except when he was onstage. She was like a small child, enthralled by an unusual new toy. I had seen her like that before, of course. Many times.

A sort of exhaustion made all my nerves quiver and my neck was beginning to ache from holding my head so erect. I sat there with my hands in my lap.

"Did you ever find out what happened to him?" Leslie asked.

"No," Eddy said.

"He jumped on a magic white horse and galloped down the highway and became the king of Argentina," I said.

"No," Eddy said after a moment. "There's no king in Argentina."

"No?" I said. "I thought there was."

"No," Eddy said.

"I thought fairy tales always had a king," I said.

There was a brief silence.

"Let's have some more gin," Leslie said.

"That's an excellent idea," Eddy said.

I don't know what time it was when we finally climbed the stairs. It felt to me like the exact middle of the night, when many long hours have already passed but many long hours are left to be endured. Leslie paused on the landing, looking at us, a delicate shiver making her shoulders twitch.

"It actually feels a bit chilly," she said in a soft voice. "Well, good night." Then she laughed. "I don't know why I'm whispering. I should be holding a candle or something. I feel like Jane Eyre."

"I guess that makes me the mad wife," I said.

"Oh, Gracie." She laughed again and trailed off into the shadows, her hair floating around her like a veil. I walked past Eddy into the bedroom and stood at the open door to the gallery, staring out at the dark lake. I decided I wouldn't have sex with him that night. He could go to hell. I waited for him to come up behind me and put his hands on my shoulders so that I could stiffen and walk away. I was going to speak politely, distantly, I was going to say that I wasn't in the mood. See how he liked that. I stood without moving, my fingertips tapping the door frame. But he didn't come. Then I heard the bedsprings creak. When I turned my head I saw that he had simply taken off his clothes and got into bed. He was lying on his side with the top sheet flung carelessly over his body.

"What are you doing?" I said. I didn't sound cool and distant the way I had planned; my voice had an ugly high edge in it.

His eyes were open but he didn't look at me. He spoke into the edge of his pillow. "I told you. I have to get up early in the morning. I'm going to the city."

"Oh. Yes, that's right," I said. Something was hurting the inside of my chest, pressing against my sternum like a thin, cold blade. "I guess you should have gone to bed hours ago, in that case. But it's funny, you didn't seem tired at all. You couldn't stop talking, you went on and on."

"Did I?" he said. "Sorry."

"What are you sorry about?"

"Okay." He was still lying on his side with his mouth against his pillow. "I'm not sorry then."

Furious tears prickled at the edges of my eyes; a ball of tears welled up in my throat. By lying there on his side he seemed to be offering me an insult so profound it couldn't be ignored. I stared out blindly into the windy darkness.

"What's the problem?" he said. "You don't want me to go to sleep without fucking you, is that it? You have to get fucked at least once a day or your *crica* will dry up."

The words expanded in my brain like a small explosion. I thought of several things I could do. I could say how dare you speak to me that way, and walk out of the room. I could say get out of my sight, you son of a bitch. I could break the window with my fist. I could slap and punch him, I could go to the bathroom and get a razor blade and cut his face.

I turned around to stare at him. He had rolled over on his back and his eyes were black as oil. "Yes," I said. "It's true, I like sex. Can you handle that, or is it just too much for you?"

"Shit, no, I'm always ready. Isn't that why you like me?"

"Yes," I said. "That's why."

He grabbed the sheet and flung it off the bed. "Well, get over here then. Come on, let's go. I wouldn't want you to be disappointed."

"That's right," I said. "Don't disappoint me." I walked over to the bed. I could hardly see him through the blur of moisture in my eyes. He grabbed my forearm and pulled me down so roughly that my neck snapped. The room was blazing with bright, white electric light, as though surgery were about to be performed. He grabbed the waistband of my shorts and yanked them down over my ankles.

I stared up at the shadowy ceiling.

"Take these off," he said. "Can't you help at all? Or do you want me to do everything?"

"Yes," I said. "I want you to do everything."

I felt his fingers tearing at the thin crotch of my underpants. The threads pulled apart without making a sound. "There goes fifty bucks," he said. He shoved me backward. I bumped my face against the footboard of the bed and a thin, sweetish taste of blood filled my mouth. He put his hands on my knees, pushed my legs open, and with one sudden brutal motion forced himself up inside me. I wasn't ready for it and my tissues seemed to stretch out like elastic before it breaks. Pain flowed up into the roots of my hair and down to the tips of my fingers. The mattress vibrated beneath me. "Does it feel good?" he hissed in my ear. "Is this what you want? Tell me. Talk. Say if you like it."

I had to clench my jaw to keep from screaming. "Fine," I said. The mattress went thump, thump, thump against the bedsprings. My teeth clattered against each other like little pebbles.

After he was finished he heaved himself away from me and lay on the other side of the bed. I was shaking; the centre of my body felt pulpy and tender and bruised, as though I had been beaten from the inside. I was afraid to move too quickly; after a moment I turned over very cautiously and let my damp cheek rest against the rumpled sheet. The sharp white light revealed the nails in the wooden floor, the strands of wool in the woven rug, and dozens of fine lines in the palm of my hand. My tongue seemed to quiver as it touched the edges of my dry lips. I could still taste blood.

"How was that?" he said.

"It was all right," I said.

WHEN I CAME DOWNSTAIRS the next morning, Eddy's car was gone and a light sunny silence lay over the back yard. The dust in the road had already settled; he had been gone for quite a while. Leslie was sitting outside in a lawn chair between two wooden tubs full of blood-red geraniums. Her fair skin gleamed with suntan oil. She had been up for hours, making blueberry tea biscuits, brewing coffee, then opening her eyes wide in innocent surprise when Eddy walked into the kitchen.

- Oh, hi, Eddy! I had no idea you were leaving this early.

- Hi, Leslie. What's that wonderful smell?

- Oh, that? I just felt like making some biscuits this morning. Why don't you have a bit of breakfast before you go?

- Who could say no to an offer like that?

- You'll be back soon, won't you, Eddy? It'll be awfully quiet around here without you. I really love listening to you talk. You've had such an interesting life!

(He shrugged modestly and she looked up at him with those big, bright, eager eyes, bursting with innocent fascination and desire. And he gave her a lazy, seductive smile.)

"Hi," Leslie said, as I crossed the grass. "I made some blueberry biscuits."

"I saw them on the kitchen table. You must have been feeling ambitious today."

"I woke up at six a.m. and couldn't get back to sleep. I had the strangest dream last night. I dreamt I was in a liquor store and I wanted to buy some Courvoisier and there was a bottle on the top shelf, so high up I could hardly reach it, so I was groping for it and all of a sudden it fell and broke and splashed all over my legs. A clerk came up to me and told me I'd have to pay for it. But when I opened my wallet, all my money was gone. What do you suppose a dream like that means?"

"How would I know?" I said, lowering myself into a chair. There was still a secret harsh soreness deep inside me. Leslie didn't know about it. It gave me a strange sort of dirty pleasure that she didn't know.

"My shrink would say it's an anxiety dream. Well, according to him, practically everything is an anxiety dream. But remember Mom's dream book? In the dream book it said that anything to do with wallets or purses meant sex. If you lost your wallet, it meant losing your virginity. But what does it mean if you still have your wallet, and it's empty? I'm afraid to even think about that one."

"Were you up when Eddy left?" I said casually.

"Yeah. He left about eight-thirty. He was crazy about the biscuits. He ate three. He said when he got back he'd cook us a real Argentinian feast."

"Did he really." I closed my eyes. The sun was hot on my eyelids; for a moment I swam in a dim red light.

"I like him," Leslie said with sudden guileless enthusiasm. "He's such a nice guy."

"You think he's nice."

"Yes."

I opened my eyes. "Leslie, sometimes you're so unbelievably naïve," I said.

"What do you mean?"

"He isn't nice," I said. "Nice is the last word to describe him."

She stared at me, amazed. "What are you talking about?"

"You always like to believe everything men say," I said. "No matter what they tell you, no matter how far-fetched it is. It makes me laugh to see you sitting there drinking it in and begging them to go on. He could say he'd just arrived from Mars in a spaceship, and you'd stare at him and say, 'Really?'"

Leslie turned red. "Oh, that's not fair," she said.

"He's a con artist," I said. "Isn't that obvious? He makes up stories just for the pleasure of it. I'm not even sure he's really from Argentina."

She seemed even more electrified than I could have hoped. She sat up straight in her chair and gaped at me. "What?" she said in disbelief.

"I don't think he has a silver business," I said. "I think he's involved in drugs."

"Drugs!" Leslie echoed weakly.

The shock on her face made me smile. In spite of her three marriages, her money, her shrinks, her thirty-five years of restless motion, she retained a sort of childlike innocence about some things, like a fifties housewife.

"Why do you say that?" she asked.

"I just think so. He never goes to an office and I've never seen an office or any sign of one. He takes care of business at all sorts of odd hours. He always uses a pay phone or a cellular phone. Once I found thousands of dollars in cash in his duffel bag. Once I saw him smash a guy's face against the hood of a car. This was on a street in Toronto in the middle of the night."

Her whole body was turned toward me. Her eyes searched my face helplessly. "I can't believe it," she said at last.

"You can't believe it, but you had no trouble at all believing he was at Perón's funeral."

"Did you ask him about any of this stuff? What did he say?"

I shrugged. "We've never discussed it."

"You haven't even asked him about it? Why not?"

"I suppose I didn't really want to know."

After a moment she leaned back in her chair and stared out at the empty road. "So you're telling me that Eddy is a fraud and a violent criminal."

"Well . . . that's sort of a negative way of putting it."

"Someone who sells drugs and beats guys up on the street, but you brought him here to Azure Lake and introduced him to all those people—"

"You're the one who was so eager to go to that bloody barbecue. Up until then I hadn't introduced him to a living soul."

"I wasn't eager. And you're the one who's having a love affair with him."

"No, not a love affair, I told you it was a fling."

"A fling."

"That's right."

"You're having a fling then. A fling with someone who you say is dangerous and violent—"

"But he's always been real sweet to me," I said sarcastically.

"You don't believe a word he says, you don't trust him—"

"Well, Christ, Leslie, what is so wonderful about trust? I think it's completely overrated. It's never been something I prayed for," I said. "Where's the drama in it? I like his imagination. I like the way he's always re-inventing himself. And I must admit that I haven't always told him the truth either. That's not what I'm looking for."

She gazed at me. "What are you looking for, Grace?" she asked finally.

I thought for a moment. "Excitement," I said. "Thrills."

"Thrills," she repeated blankly.

"That's right," I said. "I want to know I'm alive. I don't want to marry some dreary corporate lawyer and spend five years decorating a bloody house and waiting around like a faithful dog until he condescends to have sex with me."

I didn't pause to see her startled, pained expression. "I'm starving," I said over my shoulder, walking toward the house. It was true, I suddenly felt very hungry. I went into the kitchen, smeared butter on a biscuit, and wolfed it down. It tasted so good that I ate another one, chewing ravenously and licking the buttery crumbs from my fingers, as though I hadn't swallowed food in days.

Chapter Nineteen

"She was so beautiful and she hardly said a word," my father remarked one day. "I thought she was mysterious." Then he laughed.

My mother didn't look up from her magazine.

"She could sit for an hour and not open her mouth once. I used to study her, trying to figure out what she was thinking. Isn't that a good one?" He laughed again.

A damp grey breeze made the screen doors rattle.

"She told me she was from California." He stared at her as he spoke. "I actually believed it for a while."

My mother turned a page. The ends of her long blonde hair fluttered. We were sitting on the verandah. It was a rainy afternoon. Leslie and I had been playing Scrabble.

"I got a bit carried away," he said. "I pictured her walking along the beach at Malibu, at dawn, carrying a parasol. Well, in my defence, I was young. She told me she had to be careful to protect her skin from the sun, she burned so easily. Such a

fragile little flower. How could I have guessed that she was a
hardy Ukrainian peasant who used to drive a tractor through
the fields from dawn to dusk?"

A casual listener might have thought this was good-
natured banter, but we all knew it wasn't. He had been in one
of his moods all day. Maybe they had had a fight the night
before, or maybe it had nothing to do with her. Whatever the
reason, he wasn't behaving like his usual self, talking con-
stantly on the telephone, walking restlessly back and forth,
laughing, snapping his fingers, full of energy and organization
and authority. Instead he had been sitting for hours in the
same wicker chair, hardly moving, staring through the wet
screens toward the dull grey lake, ice tinkling in his glass of
Scotch. His unnatural stillness seemed to charge the atmosphere with electricity; we had to pretend everything was
normal even though it felt as if we were waiting for a bomb to
go off.

"I never drove a tractor," my mother said, still without
raising her eyes from her magazine.

"Oh," he said. "I'm sorry, I thought you did."

"That isn't a word!" Leslie cried. I had created "cryptic"
which gave me a triple word score. "Dad! That isn't a word, is
it?"

He leaned forward slightly to look at the board. "Yes, it's a
word," he said. "Only Grace would think of it." He wasn't
being complimentary. He thought my facility with language
was a very second-rate, feminine sort of talent. Stoically I
wrote down my score while Leslie slumped in her chair with
a disgusted grunt.

Then there was a brief silence. Rainwater splashed down
from the eavestrough into a barrel at the side of the house. My
mother turned another page. He stared at her, rattling the ice
in his glass.

"I would have thought that by now you'd know everything there was to know about every two-bit actor in
Hollywood," he said. "But apparently not. However, I guess I
should be grateful that you're so easily entertained. The five

hundredth story about Rock Hudson and Doris Day? Oh, goody, I can hardly wait!"

Her lips tightened. She closed her magazine and set it aside.

"Oh, no, please don't stop on my account," he said.

"Double word score," Leslie said in a very low voice.

"It was raining just as hard as this the first time I ever saw Toronto," my mother commented suddenly. "It was night-time. It was the biggest city I was ever in. I got off the bus with fifty whole bucks and ten minutes later somebody stole it."

We all looked at her in surprise, waiting for her to go on. But she sat in silence, tapping her fingers on the cover of *Movie World*.

"So then what did you do?" Leslie asked finally.

She chewed her full lower lip, remembering. "Nathan Phillips Square wasn't there then. There were a bunch of cafés and strip clubs around Old City Hall. So I go into the Blue Ribbon Grill, I still remember the name, and ask if I can use the phone. The guy behind the counter sets the phone down in front of me and I start to dial and then all of a sudden I'm crying and I have to hang up 'cause I don't even know who to call, I mean the police or what. The guy was real nice, I don't know what I would have done without him. Mel Kaminsky was his name. He said there was a room in the back where I could stay overnight and then in the morning I could—"

My father gave a sudden harsh bark of laughter. She turned red. "It wasn't like that," she said.

"Oh, no, of course not," he said.

"It wasn't. He didn't expect anything for it, he—"

My father took a sip of his drink. "Well, but some women are whores just because they like it."

The word "whores" detonated in the rainy stillness like the bomb we had been anticipating. Leslie and I sat rigidly, staring down at our Scrabble tiles. After a moment my father's chair squeaked as he leaned over to replenish the Scotch in his glass.

"Some men like to think so, anyways," my mother snapped

back. There was a brief silence. I listened to the rain falling with a gentle rustling sound onto the grass. "You can't even believe in a thing like ordinary kindness," my mother said. Her voice wavered suddenly and tears formed in her eyes. "Can you? Boy, I feel real sorry for you."

"Oh, that's right," he said with a long, weary sigh. "Cry. Just like a woman. That's always good."

"He was sweet to me. He made me up a bed. A perfect stranger. With clean sheets and an extra blanket. I was only nineteen years old. He patted my head and said not to worry, everything would be okay."

"So that made it easy to spread your legs," my father said lightly.

Her chair screeched as she pushed it back and stood up. He raised his eyes and stared at her coolly. "I don't believe in ordinary kindness because there's no such thing," he said. "That's not cynical, that's a fact. Everybody who's kind wants something for it, even if it's only gratitude. Do you think even Mother Teresa is totally without self-interest? She's after God's approval. See what I'm doing for you, God? Don't you love me now? Everybody's thinking of himself first. And that includes you too, Polly."

At the name "Polly" she blinked as though he had slapped her face. She opened her mouth to answer him but he went on smoothly before she could say a word.

"I'm sure you didn't mind giving some free nookie to some poor old greaseball in the back of his greasy spoon, just to say thanks. I don't blame you, it was all you had. But you were after a lot bigger fish than Mel Kaminsky, weren't you? Back on the farm I'll bet you looked at yourself in the mirror, after dark when your mother was in bed and your old man was out in the barn getting plastered. Didn't you? I can see you, you took off your clothes and looked at yourself in the lamplight, you thought, Wow, I'm hot stuff. Somebody's going to pay big bucks for this. Don't tell me it didn't cross your mind more than once, Polly. Don't be embarrassed to admit it. As it turned out, you were right."

"Maybe you're afraid Mel Kaminsky got a better deal than you," my mother blurted out accusingly.

He took a small sip of Scotch and smiled with one side of his mouth. "No, not at all. I'm not complaining about my deal. It seemed to be worth it, at the time. But as I said, I was young."

"Yeah," she said. "So was I." Then she flung open the screen door and walked out into the rain and across the streaming grass, taking long rapid strides as though she were crossing an empty field. She was wearing high-heeled sandals and one ankle buckled, but she righted herself and went on. For a moment I imagined that I was inside her body, I could taste the great gulps of fresh, wet air. She dropped out of sight going down the stone steps to the beach, but a moment later her blonde head reappeared, and I saw the tail of her pink blouse floating above the grey, misty water. She had walked right into the lake without even taking off her clothes. It flashed across my mind that she might keep going and drown herself, but I was paralysed and couldn't do a thing to save her.

My father was looking at Leslie's alphabet tiles. "Monotony," he suggested. "M-o-n-o-t-o-n-y."

SHE HAD JUST HAD HER HAIR DONE, its colour freshened, its curls renewed. She was leafing through an old photo album, her legs crossed, one foot swinging restlessly.

She tapped a manicured nail against a picture of herself in a dazzling ice-blue evening gown, hosting some long-ago party. "See me here?" she said in an oddly objective way, as though she were speaking of a complete stranger. "When you look like that they'll give you just about anything," she said. She thought about it a moment. "For a little while, anyways," she said.

I SAW HER TALKING TO HIM once or twice. He was a small, wiry, very young guy who had come with a work crew to rebuild a stone wall at the back of our property in Toronto. I saw her standing in the sunlight, her hair in a white blaze, smoking a cigarette, wearing tight pants and high-heeled shoes, looking like an aging Hollywood starlet, like the California girl she once claimed to be. He had taken off his shirt; he was moving rocks and his back gleamed with sweat. He said something and she laughed. I had never heard her give such a loud unrestrained laugh before. He nodded and grinned up at her, blinking. She was still attractive; she looked good for her age. And he knew she was rich; money surrounded her with glamour and made her radiant. And maybe he liked the way she laughed at his jokes. What she saw in him I don't know.

The night of the accident we waited while my father went in to identify her body. When he came out he immediately lit a cigarette. He was very pale but his hands were steady. We went and sat in the car. Leslie sobbed quietly and blew her nose. He looked straight through the windshield at the dark, empty street. Trees rustled softly in the night breeze. I could smell lilacs.

"I know who the guy was," I said. It was difficult to talk through the constriction in my throat, but I went on anyway. "He was one of the labourers, he helped build the stone wall."

My father took a deep drag on his cigarette and blew a cloud of smoke into the darkness.

"He was only about twenty," I said.

"Oh, Gracie, stop it," Leslie whispered tearfully into her Kleenex.

"He was black, too," I said.

"Gracie, come on," Leslie begged.

My father flicked his cigarette out onto the road and gripped the steering wheel with both hands. The flesh of his face seemed to quiver—with grief, with rage? "God damn bitch," he said thickly. It wasn't clear whether he was referring to my mother or me.

"They were in a Toyota," I said. Wild laughter rose up into my mouth and made me choke.

After a moment he said, "She never gave a damn." Two tears slid down his cheeks like small shiny stones.

"That's right, Dad," I said. "Cry, just like a woman."

"ONCE HE COLOURED WITH ME," Leslie said.

"Oh, come on."

"He did! When I was sick with chicken pox. Edith Fish hadn't ever had them so she couldn't come near me, and Mom wasn't around for some reason. I had a Flintstones colouring book and he coloured one side and I coloured the other. He had Pebbles and Bamm-Bamm riding Dino in the Bedrock Dinosaur Derby. He started to colour Dino yellow and I said, 'No, Dad, Dino is purple!' He said, 'Oh, I forgot,' and put down the yellow crayon and picked up the purple one. Then we heard Grandpa coming down the hall, you know the way Grandpa's cane always made that thump, thump, and Dad threw down his crayon and walked away fast. God forbid that Grandpa should catch him colouring Dino the Dinosaur!"

AUGUST 25, 1985 was a hot, sultry day, but the Toronto General Hospital was air-conditioned and rather chilly. Leslie and Ivan went down to the cafeteria to get some coffee. I sat beside my father's bed, listening to the steady beep beep of the cardiac monitor. His red hair looked unfaded and crisp and healthy, but he had an intravenous needle in his arm, a nasal tube supplying oxygen, a number of cathodes taped to his chest and a catheter draining his urine into a plastic bag. I expected that at any moment he would demand to have all these things taken away. He would never put up with anything that caused him discomfort—he was used to silk sheets, gourmet food, satin smooth liquor. He was always in charge. I couldn't believe that he would allow his body to betray him, just like some poor man's.

I thought he was asleep, tired out. Against his doctor's orders he had been talking on the phone for hours, asking questions, making agreements, issuing directives. "What do you mean, they want to negotiate their fees now? We haven't even closed the deal yet. What have they actually done for us?" "Five million for their God damn advice? That works out to about fifty grand a word. Tell them I never saw any diamonds dropping from their lips." "Buy up at least sixty thousand shares of Excelsior, it's going at twenty-one bucks so now's the time to grab it." "Okay, my price is $2.5 million. Want to split the difference?" "Not interested. No way. Because it's overvalued. One point five is the best we could do. Okay, then. We're in." "No, I'm not going to get my shorts in a knot over a lousy million. It was only a paper loss." (With a triumphant, joyous shout of laughter): "That old bastard! You remind him I've got sixty per cent now and I'm king of the castle! See what he says to that!"

But finally he had set the phone aside and was lying back on his pillows, apparently sleeping. His face looked very pale, almost grey. I saw a pulse fluttering in his throat. Then suddenly he opened his eyes and looked right at me. I was startled and sat forward in my chair.

"Get Hawthorne on the phone for me," he said. "I know a way to take Cheltenham back."

He seemed so lucid, he spoke in such a commanding tone, that I half-rose from my seat, ready to obey. But then his eyes fluttered shut, and his head turned to one side. Later he murmured something in his sleep. "Rags to riches to rags," he said. About two hours after that he died.

The next day he was paid the tribute he would have appreciated the most. Tremain Distilleries shares dropped two full points.

Chapter Twenty

I WAS WALKING IN THE WHITE GARDEN. I had had three glasses of wine already and it was only two p.m. I heard Leslie's voice from the verandah, bright and happy and vivacious: "Hi! You're back!"

Instantly my heart contracted with a painful, spasmodic twist. Leslie was laughing; apparently the things I had told her about Eddy had had no effect. He answered her in a low, humorous murmur.

Perhaps you two would like it if I just left you alone, I thought. You're so terribly happy to see each other and have so much to say, my presence is going to be a bit of an intrusion, isn't it? God knows I wouldn't want to intrude. If there had been any way of reaching the beach without being seen, I would have gone down to the boathouse, turned on the radio, and sat on the deck until they came to find me, if they ever did. I wouldn't care, they couldn't touch me, I would just float on a current of Mozart, free of all the dirty, messy feelings that threatened to boil out and scald everything around me.

But there was no way I could reach the stone steps without being spotted from the verandah. I smoothed my hair with my hands and licked my lips. My wine-drinking had produced a slight headache and a dry mouth. The light seemed too blindingly bright when I walked into it; I had to squint. Leslie was sitting in the wicker rocking chair and he was standing beside her. He turned his head and looked at me through the sun-splashed screen. For a second I had a sort of eerie sensation that he wasn't really there; he had receded into my mind like a dim, sweet memory, and that was where he would be safest, that was where I wanted him to be.

He smiled. "Hi," he said.

I didn't smile in return. I felt stiff and awkward. I wasn't sure what attitude I wanted to take, whether I should be cold, or angry, or casual, or forgiving. When I opened the screen door he stepped forward and put one arm around my shoulders and gave me a brief, fervent hug. "You just washed your hair, didn't you?" he said. "Ah. I love the smell of that lemon shampoo."

Apparently he had decided to be charming and ignore any past unpleasantness. Of course. His warm fingers squeezed my shoulder. I felt such a longing to relax against him, just for a moment. But that would have been too easy. Leslie was looking up at us with wide, bright eyes. Don't worry, I told her silently, this is just his act, it doesn't mean a thing. He likes you better now. My eyes felt like they were full of bits of glass. I sat down on the porch swing. Its springs squeaked faintly.

"I feel slightly tipsy," I said. "Soon it's going to be September and I'll have to get out of this habit of drinking wine so early in the afternoon."

"Oh, don't think about September," Leslie pleaded. "It's going to be summer forever."

"That's right," Eddy agreed. "We won't let it end."

"So did you have a successful trip?" I asked casually, picking up a cushion and fingering its silky tassel.

"I had a very successful trip," Eddy said. All at once he laughed out loud. "Yes, very successful. I think soon we'll be sailing to Buenos Aires. When summer is ending here, it's beginning there. You'll see the jacaranda trees, all in bloom. We'll sit in a café on El Paseo de la Recoleta and drink tall glasses of vodka and lemon."

"What are you talking about?"

"I'm working on a deal," he said. "I don't want to jinx it by saying too much. But it's big. It's very big." He looked at us both, laughing breathlessly, his face alight. "I'm afraid you might hear my phone ring a few times in the next couple of days," he told me. "Don't be mad, it's only for this one occasion. I'm setting something up. I might have to leave suddenly and be gone for two or three days. I'm not trying to be mysterious, but I don't want to jinx it. It might mean a lot of money. I mean—maybe seven figures." His voice lingered over the words, as though he were savouring the taste of them. He said it again. "Seriously. I'm not exaggerating. Seven figures."

Leslie and I were both staring at him, rather nonplussed. I had never before heard him speak with such naked eagerness about anything. It was exciting, and also rather tawdry.

"We're going to have an Argentinian evening," he said. "I've brought Argentinian wine, made in Mendoza. The best wine in South America is made in Mendoza, at the foot of the Andes Mountains. Grace already knows that. We're going to have steaks and they're going to taste better than at La Cabaña, which is the finest steakhouse in Buenos Aires. I've brought tango music. I went to Sam the Record Man and bought all the CDs they had."

Leslie was always ready to be caught up in a man's enthusiasm. She leaned forward eagerly. "Let's get dressed up too!" she suggested.

"Yes!" Eddy agreed. "We'll wear our best clothes. Everything tonight will be the best." He turned his head and his glance brushed against mine like a physical touch. A sort of shakiness passed through my elbows and knees. I was glad

I was sitting down. He'll look at her that way too, I reminded myself. He's good at it.

His duffel bag was sitting by the screen door. Suddenly he bent down and opened it. "Oh, and I have a surprise," he said. He produced two packets wrapped in tissue paper and set them before us on the wooden coffee table. His long slender brown fingers worked nimbly on the wrapping and like a magician he revealed what it contained. Suddenly our eyes were dazzled by silver, blazing hotly in the sunlight.

"From El Mundo de la Plata!" he declared with a flourish.

They were exquisite pieces, finely wrought: a tall bird with spectacularly long, graceful legs, and a crouching panther with tiny topaz eyes.

"They're wonderful!" Leslie exclaimed, throwing me a quick, meaningful look. "What beautiful workmanship!" I ignored her.

Eddy nodded gravely. "Yes, one of our artisans did a silver chalice for King Juan Carlos of Spain," he said. His audacity so astounded me that I had trouble repressing an appreciative laugh. He said it so easily, so glibly, "one of our artisans . . . King Juan Carlos of Spain."

"But these are special gifts for the two Tremain sisters," he said. He picked up the silver bird and placed it in Leslie's hands.

She gasped in disbelief. "Oh, no, Eddy! They're way too expensive. You've got to let me pay for mine!"

Eddy held up his hand, carelessly magnanimous. "Please, just forget it. I want you to have it."

She shook her head and looked at me with a shrug and a helpless smile. He bent over beside my chair and indicated the crouching silver cat in its bed of crumpled tissue paper, its yellow eyes glinting in the sunlight. "See?" he said to me. "The leopard in Jorge Luis Borges. You said it was your favourite."

So he had remembered that. He had remembered the name Jorge Luis Borges and could toss it off fluently, as though he had known it all his life. He really was a clever man. As he straightened up his thigh brushed against my shoulder. A slight tremor went through my fingers as I took the leopard in my hand.

But he had to give her something too. That spoiled it all.

THE SILVER BIRD SAT ON HER BUREAU as Leslie dressed for dinner.

"Where did he get them then?" she asked, leaning forward to the mirror to put on lipstick. She was wearing a black dress with a wide black shiny belt, and gold earrings gleamed against her ear lobes. Apparently on that hysterical morning when she was sobbing and throwing things into a suitcase, getting ready for her desperate drive to Azure Lake, she had somehow thought to pack an evening dress and jewellery.

"Keep your voice down," I said quietly. "I imagine he bought them somewhere."

She took a Kleenex and blotted her lips. "He combed the city to buy some silver for us just so that he could claim it was imported by his non-existent company. Why would he go to all that trouble?"

"Because that's the sort of thing he does."

"He goes through all sorts of complicated manoeuvres just to trick people."

I looked down at the thin fabric of my green gown. I suddenly felt it was dowdy and uninteresting. Or perhaps too gaudy, too obvious. I looked old beside her, the lines around my eyes showed up clearly. She was thinner, her neck was longer, her skin was smoother. I got restlessly to my feet, thinking I would go back to my room and change into something else. Mentally I checked off the items in my closet, but each one seemed wanting in comparison to her simple black dress.

"I doubt whether it was that complicated," I said dryly. "There's lots of silver on sale in Toronto."

She shook her head and straightened, fluffing up her hair. "I don't know, Gracie, instead of coming up with all these elaborate explanations for everything he does, it seems to me it would be so much easier just to believe him."

"It wouldn't be easier for me," I said. "But you can believe him if you want to so badly."

She opened her eyes wide in innocent surprise. "I don't care!" she said with a laugh. She twisted her hair in a knot and held it in place on top of her head for a moment, then let it fall with a heavy sigh. "It's hopeless," she said. "Look at yours. You should always wear it down like that. I mean it, Gracie. It's stunning. Especially with that shade of green."

I felt an unexpected hot flush of pleasure so intense that it made my throat go tight, as though I wanted to weep in gratitude. This was followed immediately by violent anger. Flatterer! I wanted to say. Liar! Don't you dare try to fool me, I can't be fooled by anybody's phoney compliments!

I walked toward the door, trying to concentrate on something real and solid, the feel of the doorknob under my hand, the floor under the soles of my shoes. I needed more wine, a lot more wine. I longed to be sleepy and calm; I wanted to feel as though I were floating on warm water, peaceful and half-conscious.

Eddy was climbing the stairs. "The steaks are grilling," he said. "And the table is set. Dinner will be served in ten minutes, ladies."

I walked out onto the landing. He was wearing sleek black pants and his shoes shone like mirrors. I could smell the oil in his hair. The sun was setting over the lake, casting soft pink light through the tall windows and onto the polished floor below, filling the air with ashy reflections of his silky pink shirt.

He paused, gazing upward. "You look fabulous," he said. "You both do."

She had come out to stand behind me, my sister, my shadow, my inescapable twin, bright where I was dark, gay where I was gloomy, better than I, luckier, kinder, prettier, ready to take everything I had.

WE STOOD IN THE HALF-DARK, waiting for the music to start. His hand firmly clasped my waist and I could feel the tension in the muscles of his legs. His shirt felt smooth and slightly damp. I saw our dim images in the gleaming floor. Leslie was sitting in the old red plush armchair, holding a glass of cognac.

"This was never polite music," he said. "It got started in bordellos and bars and shantytowns, with the gangsters and prostitutes."

"What instrument is that?" Leslie asked as he began to move me slowly backward.

"A *bandoneón*. Like an accordion. This one is called 'Carolina.'" His breath tickled my ear. I felt the pressure of his body against mine; he moved me without difficulty, backward and forward, to the side, in a circle. It was as though he were carrying me and my feet barely touched the ground.

"It says . . . uh . . . once you belonged to me, Carolina," he translated in time to the passionate tenor voice pouring from the stereo. "This dark street echoes with the words you spoke, when you said you loved me, when you said you were mine. Life is . . . just a breath of air. Years pass . . . like the brief flight of a bird across the summer sky. It's so long since you went away but it seems like only yesterday. My soul still cries out for you . . . my heart cries your name. You betrayed me and left me alone . . . but I can't stop wanting you. I weep when I think that someone else is holding you in his arms. Tonight I'm drinking strong wine to ease . . . the torment of my desire. I hold up my glass, I drink a toast to you, my beautiful Carolina."

The music ended but he kept moving, drawing me along with him. I had had more wine at dinner, a lot more, but I couldn't feel its effect. If we had been alone I might have let my face rest against his shoulder. I might have let go, I might have said something to him when he spoke those feverish tango lyrics. But I had to keep erect. My neck ached from holding my head up so straight. She was always there, she was there in a corner of my vision, she swirled past when he turned me, I saw her even when she was at my back, sitting there in the depth of the armchair, her earrings shimmering, watching us and sipping her brandy.

"God," she said. "It's really passionate, isn't it?"

"The emotions are so exaggerated," I said. "If you listen closely it starts to sound a bit ridiculous."

"Oh, no," Eddy disagreed. "In the tango all feelings are big. Once I heard it sung by a street singer in Buenos Aires, standing on a corner in the late afternoon, an old man with shabby clothes, and blind, his eyes were the colour of milk because of—what is it in English?"

"Cataracts?"

"Yeah. His hat was in front of him for people to put coins in. He looked about seventy and so frail he could hardly stand, but when he sang his voice was like a young man wild with love. He was the best tango singer I ever heard."

Suddenly he released me. I had to shift my feet quickly to keep my balance. It had become quite dark, and I had a feeling that we were glittering inside that deep, soft darkness like hard little jewels in a black velvet box. "But now, *señoras y señores*," he said, "we'll have something completely different, because this is Buenos Aires and we get bored very quickly! We're tired of the tango, we want something more modern." The CD player slid open and he inserted a new disc. After a moment, a cool, jazzy Latin rhythm filled the room. He turned to Leslie and held out his hand. "Please, señora, you've simply got to join us."

She laughed and jumped up. "I thought you'd never ask!" She lifted the hem of her skirt and held out her foot. "You see I've worn my dancing shoes!" She was so awfully cute. He liked it, of course. He grabbed her wrist and twirled her around. She gasped and leaned against him very briefly as though she were dizzy and had to catch her breath. If I had turned away for two seconds I would have missed it. However, I didn't turn away and I didn't miss a thing. I saw her fingertips touch his shirt-front, I saw her fleeting upward glance and the subtle smile in his brown eyes.

We danced together, all three of us. His hand rested on my

waist, her hand rested on my shoulder. His thigh rubbed against me, her hip bumped lightly against mine. If I opened my eyes, her eyes were staring directly into mine from his other shoulder and she blinked and gave me an artless, happy smile, as though she were still my little sister, as though we were driving somewhere on a picnic. A poisonous vision floated into my mind, it was the *ménage à trois* I had facetiously suggested to Eddy, I saw us all together, our limbs dimly entwined, our hair drifting across our shadowy faces, our drunken lips touching . . . but I knew how fantastical it was, how impossible, because I kept dissolving from the image, leaving only the two of them. They turned to each other gladly. They didn't even remember me.

"On the Avenida del Libertador in Buenos Aires there were dozens of nightclubs," Eddy said. "And the best one of all was the Café del Jazz. It was on the second floor of a building, it was half a block long. You could see the windows at night, all lit up. Cars would park outside, Mercedes, Rolls-Royces, Alfa Romeos, all the best cars. You could watch for hours, all the people who came and went, it never got dull. Oh, the women, they had long hair and long legs, and they wore spike heels, it was hard to believe they could walk on heels like that, but they did, sometimes they even ran from their cars to the doorway. You could smell their perfume and their French cigarettes all the way across the street. The lights changed colour all the time, pink, green, gold, blue, and sometimes they were very bright and sometimes kind of dim and dreamy. You could see people up there in the windows, having drinks and being served big steaming plates of food and getting up to do the mambo or the twist." Suddenly he laughed and squeezed my waist. He probably squeezed her waist too.

"You know, I think if there was such a thing as heaven it would be just like the Café del Jazz!" he said extravagantly. "Yeah, and God is going to be standing up there in an Armani suit and he's going to say to me, 'Hey, Eddy! Come on up and have a dance.'"

Leslie gave a breathless squeak of a laugh. At the same

moment I felt a sudden wave of nausea so strong that it made a fine film of sweat spring out across my hairline. Too much beef, too much wine, too much bread, too much bile, all of it swirled around in my stomach and threatened to explode. His soft breath stirred my hair. Leslie's hand was heavy on my shoulder. I didn't want to leave the two of them alone, but I also didn't want to be sick all over his beautiful pink shirt.

"I'll be right back," I said brightly, pushing myself away and going waveringly toward the stairs. The floor seemed uneven and slippery; I felt that I had to walk very carefully to avoid falling.

"Are you all right?" Eddy laughed. He thought I was drunk. He thought it was funny that I was drunk. "Perfectly," I said in a light, precise voice. "Why?"

Upstairs in the bathroom I leaned dizzily over the toilet and waited to vomit, but nothing happened. The Latin music drifted up the stairs, sensual and rhythmic, full of brass and drums. They were down there dancing together in the dim light. Now that I was out of the way, was he taking the opportunity to whisper something in her ear, was she sighing and pressing her face into his neck? Of course she would give lip service to me and my feelings. This isn't right, I feel so guilty because Gracie is my sister and I don't want to hurt her. And he too would pretend to be thinking about me. She's great, I have feelings for her, I really do. But this is different. I can't help myself. I want you so much. Oh God, I want you too.

I couldn't throw up. All the white porcelain was glistening and it hurt my eyes. A woman's voice sang in Spanish, teasing and sexy. The only words I could make out were "ooo-la-la, ooo-la-la-la." I heaved myself to my feet and looked in the mirror. My hair was hanging around my face like a slightly parted curtain. I was pale and ghostlike. I looked sick and old. Nausea lay in the pit of my stomach like a heavy mass. I stared into my damp, feeble eyes. "Oh God please help me," I whispered out loud. I don't know why I said that.

After a while I went into the bedroom. A span of soft light fell across the floor from the hallway. I sat on the edge of the bed and held on to the footboard. The music went on, slower now, very slow, with a syncopating bongo that seemed to bop around inside my skull. Through the dark windows I could see the long moonlit slope of the lawn, the pale gleam of the white rose arbour, a thin veil of mist over the old tennis court. I thought I would have to go to the bathroom again soon.

His duffel bag was sitting beside the closet door. Suddenly I realized it was a different bag from the one that had contained the silver. Two duffel bags? And the one beside the closet seemed to be packed absolutely full, so that its sides bulged. The mass in my stomach rolled over and I put my hand across my mouth, but nothing happened. The husky woman's voice sang on, repeating a word that sounded like "perfidia." Was it someone's name or did it have a meaning similar to the English word—perfidy, perfidious?

I dropped down to my hands and knees. It seemed quite natural to do that. The floorboards vibrated faintly beneath my palms. I crawled over to the duffel bag and unzipped it. It was crammed to the top with money, fifties and hundreds, so many bills it would have taken hours to count them all. I crouched there with my hands in my lap, looking at it. Something hard and round was pressing against my knee. I didn't investigate immediately because for a moment I seemed to fall into a dream, listening to that voice sing "perfidia." Perhaps it was a name, like Perdita or Pamela. My hands felt limp, as though they were barely attached to the rest of my body. The hard, round object, whatever it was, had been placed in a side pocket of the duffel bag. Finally I unfastened the straps and opened the pocket wide. Inside was a gun. I touched it with my fingertips. It was very cold. A sense of absolute unreality came over me. I was sitting there on the floor with a bag of money and a gun. I knew it wasn't the sort of thing that happened in real life. I thought of the Godfather movies. The camera pans over the wall, down across the half-lit arm of a woman, across the shadowy green of her dress, and reveals the gun gleaming in her hand. But she doesn't fire it. Because women never fire guns in the Godfather movies; they stay at home with the children while the men go out and kill each other.

I had never held a handgun before. It was deceptively small and quite heavy. When I lifted it and tried to point it at the wall its weight made my wrist tremble. The trigger curved against my finger, so ordinary, so inoffensive, a small and simple metallic object like the hook of a bottle opener. It was hard to believe that a little thing like that could actually cause pain and death. I thought I could go downstairs with it, point it at them and say, I'm tired of this and I'm going to put a stop to it. Only as a joke of course. Just to see the fear and disbelief in their eyes. I leaned forward and rested my face against the gun barrel. Its coldness seemed to relieve my nausea for a moment. Then I replaced it in its pocket and zippered up the top of the bag. My knees quivered as I got to my feet. I walked out to the landing. They were still dancing. He was a good dancer. He was good at everything. I saw the rhythmic motion of his hips. His cheek rested against the side of her head. They were oblivious to everything but the music and each other.

"I think I'm going to bed," I said finally. I put a friendly, easy tone in my voice. They stopped dancing and turned their faces up to me. "I'm not feeling too well," I said, with a faint laugh. "Too much wine."

"Will you be okay?" Eddy asked, full of concern.

Don't pretend you care, I thought. You phoney, lying bastard.

"Oh, sure," I answered cheerfully. "I just need to sleep it off."

There was a brief pause while we stood at our separate levels, I in the shadow of the landing, they down below, side by side in the shifting lamplight.

"Can I bring you something?" Leslie wanted to know. "How about some clear tea, that might help."

"No, no." It was very difficult to speak normally. "Don't worry, I'll be fine." I waited a second. I don't know what I was waiting for. Finally I said, "Good night, then."

"Good night, sis."

"I'll be up in a few minutes," Eddy said.

Don't do me any favours, I thought. Don't think I believe in your phoney sympathy. Don't think I need your God damn kindness. I hope you rot in hell. I smiled. "Okay," I said.

I shut the bedroom door behind me. Acting cheerful and normal had taken such an effort that I felt exhausted. I turned out the light. I took off my dress and shoes and lay down on the bed in my underclothes. Below me the merciless Latin beat went on, light and happy and fast, full of bongos and maracas and castanets and horns, it would never end, it made you think of coloured lights, of swirling skirts and shapely legs, of laughter and sex and champagne corks popping. I was always going to be alone in the darkness, listening to dance music from far away. I had to press the backs of my hands against my eyes to quell a rush of stupid, self-pitying tears.

He didn't come up. It was too dark to see my watch, but I knew more than a few minutes had passed. Tick, tick, tick. He couldn't tear himself away. They were down there alone. It was amazing that they would be so obvious about it. Apparently it didn't matter to them what I thought. Tick, tick, tick. Nausea rose in my throat but I still couldn't vomit. They were still talking, they were still dancing. She had to have a man, couldn't live without one for even a day. Lose one, get another fast. Their voices were whispering beneath the music. I tried to hear what they were saying, but I couldn't hear it. They took the glasses out to the kitchen. Who would make the first move? She would turn around and look up at him, that eager, wide-eyed, half-shy look that was like a written invitation, and of course he wouldn't resist it, he wouldn't even try. I could hardly breathe. It was so hot in that bedroom, stifling hot. An hour had gone by, at least an hour, maybe more. Suddenly the bedroom door clicked open. He came in and shut it behind him. The music had stopped. It was like a cessation of pain to hear the silence.

He leaned over me. I tried to keep my eyes shut, but my eyelids quivered uncontrollably. "You're not asleep, are you?" he whispered.

"What time is it?" I said.

"I don't know."

He was checking on me and if I was asleep maybe he would go back to her, that was it. She was waiting, she was lying on her back exactly the way I was, in her dark room on the other side of the landing, breathing quietly, listening for him to come.

"Still sick?" he asked softly.

His hair smelled of sweet-scented oil. I kept my eyes closed. I couldn't bear to look at his face. "I feel really nauseated," I said. "But I can't throw up."

He touched my forehead with the palm of his hand. "It's so hot and stuffy in here," he said. "Wait a minute. I know what to do."

I heard him open the windows and the gallery door. The mild, poignant fragrance of roses drifted across my hot face. He went into the bathroom and turned on a faucet. In a moment he was back. The bed sagged as he sat down on it. He touched the strap of my bra.

"Why don't you take these things off?" he said.

"Why?"

"Because they're so constricting. You can't relax. Take them off."

I waited a moment. Then I sat up abruptly and looked straight ahead into the darkness as I took off the bra and underpants. I dropped them on the floor and lay down again and shut my eyes. Water dripped into a basin and he touched my face with a cool, wet cloth. He wiped my forehead and smoothed my hair back with his other hand.

"How does that feel?" he said.

"Good," I said through dry lips. It was more than good; it was soothing and refreshing, it was as miraculous as a fountain in the desert. He squeezed water onto my chest and it ran down my ribs.

"The sheet's going to get wet," I said.

"It'll get dry again. This is what we used to do in Buenos Aires to cool off on a hot summer night."

"My eyes are so tired," I said.

"Rest them, then," he said. "Just close your eyes and rest."

The water flowed over my belly, rich and slow as a cool lotion, wetting my pubic hair and trickling down between my legs. I heard myself sigh. Tension seemed to be evaporating from my muscles with each touch of that cool cloth against my skin. He had lain down beside me on the bed and moved some pillows aside to make room for the basin of water. He was as relaxed as a sultan in a harem. Apparently I had no pride or strength of mind; apparently I couldn't help myself and had to behave like a spineless puppet, so easily soothed, so easily pacified by his slow, delicate, clever hands. He was smiling to himself, thinking how simple it all was, how you could move from one to another and keep everybody happy. I tried to summon some resistance. Liar, I called him silently, bastard. It's quite possible he's actually killed people, he carries a loaded gun in a duffel bag, and that duffel bag is sitting five feet away, black and bulging, while he leans over me, tenderly sponging my body. He seduces my sister; then he comes to seduce me. It's humiliating, it's vile, surely I'm not going to let him get away with it, surely I can't put up with it, can I, I can't want it, I can't get any pleasure from it, can I, can I?

"Lift your arms," he said, and I did. He held the cloth at one wrist, then the other, and the cool water ran down over my elbows and into my armpits, easing my restlessness, consoling my sorrow, stilling all the pulses of pain and disbelief. He wet the cloth again and held it against my temple and the water slipped down through my hair like cool, delicate fingers. Water splashed softly into the basin like drops falling into a pool in the middle of the night.

"Be careful with that basin," I said suddenly. "It's very old, my father's sister found it in an antique store in Germany and had it shipped here. It could never be replaced."

"Okay," he said. He touched my breast with his smooth, damp palm and it took my breath away. I kept my eyes closed. The gun was there, iron-cold in the pocket of the bag. He had put bullets in it and strapped it briskly into its envelope. His hands were as soft as silken cloth on my skin.

"I'll buy you another one," he said after a moment.

"I just said, it can't be—"

"Of course it can be replaced," he said. "Anything can be replaced if you have enough money. You know that. I'll buy you another one, and we'll use it just for this."

I didn't answer him. I kept my eyes closed. Everything had faded away. I was aware of the warm breeze, the soft darkness, the sound of water, and the touch of his hands on my body. That was all.

"What else shall I buy you?" he said. "A new car. A convertible, so you can drive around with your red hair blowing in the wind and everybody will stare at you. How about a ring? What's your favourite stone? How about an emerald? An emerald set in gold. I saw a ring like that once. Do you like jewellery?"

"Sure," I said.

"How about a Hermes purse? Would you like something like that?"

"What do you know about Hermes purses?"

"I know lots of women like them. I'll get you one. What else? A new house in Toronto? Wouldn't you like a new house in another part of town? I'll buy you a new house and you can keep the one in the Beach too. And I'll buy more boats, a launch like the *Gazelle* and a Gentleman Racer like Rob DeJong has, that small one that can go like lightning. Oh man, a small boat's great when you're going top speed and it jumps right out of the water and flies! I'll buy you your own fast boat too. Do you want one?"

"All right," I said.

"And clothes," he said. "You look terrific in green, like tonight. I'll buy you something in every shade of green."

"Not lime green," I said. "I hate lime green."

"Every shade except lime green. After we leave Buenos Aires we'll go to Mar del Plata and I'll buy a summer house facing the ocean. We'll dance on the beach at night. You'll be naked and I'll cover you head to foot with diamonds."

And what will you cover Leslie with? I asked silently.

"Are you feeling better now?"

"Yes," I said.

He set the basin aside and leaned over me. His bare shoulders gleamed in the light from the gallery, but I could hardly see his face, only its dark outline. "All the way back in the car, I thought how I'd make love to you tonight," he whispered.

He was treacherous beyond belief, he knew just the thing to say to pierce my heart.

"Oh," I said. My jaw trembled with the effort it took to keep my voice from quivering. "I wasn't sure you still wanted to."

"Always," he said, bending closer, looking into my face.

I gave up trying to hold back my tears; they flooded warmly into my eyes and it was almost a relief to let them come. He saw them; he saw everything. There was no defence against him. It was unbearable to be so helpless, so exposed, so stupid and ugly.

Chapter Twenty-One

I HAD BEEN AWAKE FOR AN HOUR, staring at an unmoving patch of white light on the ceiling. Birds were twittering noisily in the trees outside the open window. I wished they would shut up. There was an evil taste in my mouth. Eddy was lying on his back, his legs sprawled apart, his mouth half-open, a trail of saliva on his chin. I wondered what I was doing lying in bed beside such a strange, crude, ugly man. The antique basin was sitting in the middle of the rug, a cloth floating in its cloudy water. I closed my eyes. I wanted to go back to sleep and dream I was somewhere else, far away. When the cellular phone rang right next to my head, the sound seemed to be muffled in a blanket and I hardly reacted to it. But Eddy was awake in an instant; he sat up and then fell across me in his haste to grab it. For a moment his flat belly pressed against my face and I could hardly breathe. Then he twisted away and got off the bed.

"Yeah?" he said crisply, walking to the window. The sun

shone so brilliantly around him that I could see nothing but his dark silhouette. He was holding the phone to his ear, bending slightly at the waist, listening intently. His shape and outline reminded me sharply of my father; it seemed to me that I had seen my father in exactly the same position, standing at a window, leaning over, talking briskly into a telephone, tapping his fingers restlessly against the window ledge.

"Yeah. Right. Four o'clock. That's good. Yeah, I've got it. No, I think tomorrow's perfect for a vacation. Yeah, okay. And then drive to Miami. I've got a couple of guys there really interested in the merchandise. So it won't be a problem. Okay."

He pushed the antenna down and set the phone aside, frowning thoughtfully, absorbed in his plans. Without looking right at it, I took note of the duffel bag, still sitting beside the open closet door. Suddenly he remembered me and turned around.

"I'm sorry," he said quickly. "I had to take that call. That was it. It's all set."

"Is it?" I said.

His face was alight with excitement. "I'm leaving tomorrow after lunch," he said. "I should only be gone a couple of days."

I nodded, lying unmoving, looking up at him. I felt slightly removed from myself, as though my mind and my body had drawn apart and were connected only by tenuous threads.

"After this I'm going to retire," he said. "Seriously."

"Are you?" I said.

"From my business, I mean," he said. "I'll do something else."

"Like what?"

He looked at me blankly, as though he hadn't expected such a question. "Well," he said after a moment, "I'm not sure yet."

He picked up a hairbrush from the bureau and absently ran his thumb over the bristles. "One thing is, I'd like to read some books. You could help me with that. You could make up a list for me. I've never had much time for reading."

"No? Not even when you were going to school in the United States?"

He didn't hesitate. "Oh, well, you know, I was young and I was too busy having fun." He lifted his eyes and gave me a sudden, charming smile. My lips curved automatically in response, but my mind was floating at a distance, cold and detached.

"I heard you say you were driving to Miami," I said. "That'll take longer than a couple of days."

He laughed. "Oh, no, that's just an expression. Driving means flying."

"It does? I never heard that expression before."

He shrugged and smiled. "A contact of mine is flying down from Montreal. He's going to stop and pick me up at that airfield, the one you showed me. And then we're going to fly on to Miami."

"The one I showed you?"

"Yeah. The one near Good Hope."

I felt a strange chill in my upper spine. He was talking about Greenmantle. I remembered that warm evening, the deserted hangar, the pungent smell of weeds, his hand dreamily stroking my body. Obviously he had been planning something the whole time, storing everything in his mind. "The one near Good Hope," he said casually, as though it had been familiar to him from childhood. Its inclusion in his sleazy schemes brought them uncomfortably close, almost as if I were involved somehow, as if I could be considered an accomplice.

"But you saw how dilapidated it is. I told you, no one ever uses it anymore," I said.

"That's okay. He'll land and then we'll take off again. The plane'll be on the ground for about five minutes. It's not a big deal. This guy, my contact, he has his own private plane. He flies to Miami all the time." He walked over and sat beside me on the edge of the bed. "How do you feel this morning?" he asked solicitously.

I moved my legs so they wouldn't be touching him. I didn't want to be asked about how I felt. I didn't want to be reminded of the previous night. I didn't believe in it, I didn't believe any of it had really happened, the heat and the cool water on my skin and his hands touching me and my dumb acquiescence. Take off your clothes and that person took her clothes off, lift your arms, and immediately she did it, no more will power than a mannequin. Say a kind word and she bawled like a baby. Stupid cow. That wouldn't be the way I would act. I was a lot tougher than that. I had been so drunk and sick that it hadn't even been me.

"Yes, I feel fine," I said.

He bent over and kissed me. Remotely I felt his lips brush against mine. He straightened and looked at me. I smiled vaguely.

"Let's go and have a swim," he said.

"You go ahead. I just feel like lying here a bit longer. I feel lazy today."

"Hangover?" he said teasingly.

"No," I said, looking at him with a blank expression, as if I had no idea to what he was referring. "I'm fine."

He put on his tiny, tight white bathing suit, flung a towel over his shoulder, and paused in the doorway. Behind his shoulder the hallway looked gloomy, as though the bright morning sunlight had been unable to penetrate there. "Are you going to come down a little later?" he asked.

"Sure," I said.

I waited a moment or two after he had shut the door. Then I got out of bed and went to check the duffel bag. For some reason I thought something might have changed while I slept: he might have moved the money, or the gun, or both. Or perhaps in my stuporous state of mind I had dreamed the whole thing, and when I unzipped the bag I was going to find rumpled clothes and sneakers and a bottle of men's cologne. But no, it was still there, all those bills, thousands, hundreds of thousands of dollars, and I could feel the hard barrel of the gun through the cloth pocket of the bag; I didn't need to see it to know it was still there too.

I went to the window. He was crossing the sunny lawn and

Leslie was beside him. It was as though they had arranged to meet. They walked side by side, her shoulder bumping companionably against his upper arm, his head bent slightly to speak to her and listen to her replies. They were not laughing; they were talking seriously and thoughtfully, as though they had many serious and important things to say to each other.

I DON'T REMEMBER THE DETAILS of that afternoon very clearly. I only remember that it seemed very long, that I thought the interminable hours would never pass. The sky was a perfect, tranquil blue and the sun seemed to be fixed in it immovably. It was always going to be three-thirty and I was going to have to spend an eternity on that beach in my bathing suit, with Eddy on one side and Leslie on the other. I held a book open in my lap and stared at the sharp black printing on the bright white page. It could have been Egyptian hieroglyphics for all the meaning I derived from it. My mind drifted backwards; fragments of old memories flashed and shifted like the bits of coloured glass in a kaleidoscope, changing the pattern over and over again, never producing the same one twice. Leslie came bursting through a door, wearing jeans and a bright red sweater, and she said, *I'm going to get married! Perry loves me and I love him!* Then she came through a different door, wearing a grey skirt and an orange silk blouse. *I'm going to get married! Ivan loves me and I love him!* She always loved somebody; somebody always loved her. I remembered old hurts, things that had happened so long ago I had thought they didn't matter anymore. They came back with a terrible immediacy, old trivial hurts which seemed to carry such a sharp, exaggerated pain that they seared my eyes behind my sunglasses. Someone who said he'd phone me and never did, someone who pretended to love me and then disappeared without a word, all a long time ago when I used to care about such things.

"Is there any of that beer left?" Leslie said. "Usually I hate beer but on a hot day it's just the thing. How about you two?"

"Sure," Eddy said. "I'll get it."

"No, that's okay, I'll get it."

"We'll both get it." They laughed together, lively, full of high spirits, like teenagers.

"How about you, Gracie?"

"Wine," I said. "Just bring the whole bottle."

Eddy leaned over and playfully twisted a lock of my hair around his finger. "Are you sure you want to do that?" he said teasingly. "Remember how you felt last night?"

I stared at him through the dark lenses of my glasses. He was smiling. I couldn't force myself to smile in return. "I'm fine," I said.

"Anyway, hair of the dog," Leslie said, standing up and stretching her arms above her head.

"The . . . hair? The dog?"

She laughed merrily and caught hold of his elbow as he came around behind my chair. "I always forget English isn't your first language!" I heard her say. "The hair of the dog that bit you. It's supposed to be the cure for a hangover. You have some of the same stuff that made you sick in the first place."

"But what does that have to do with dog hair?"

Their happy, laughing voices faded away as they went up the steps to the lawn. They were having such a good time. I wondered if they enjoyed torturing me, or if they simply thought I didn't notice what was going on. I couldn't decide which possibility was worse. The time, which had been standing still, suddenly began to move again. I saw that it was late afternoon and the shadows had become long and wavy on the pale sand. I sat alone on the beach. There were no boats to disturb the placid surface of the lake. The tall dark pines stood silently against the sky. The summer was over.

They didn't return. I saw myself from a distance, a pathetic, solitary figure on a lawn chair, forgotten by everyone, a dupe, a loner, a loser. It was a role they were forcing me into, it wasn't my fault, there was nothing I could do. Four-thirty, four thirty-five. Still they didn't come back. I sat rigidly, sweating in the sun-steeped silence, gripping the hard wooden arms of my chair, watching the water draw back from the shore to leave a gleaming strip of wet sand. Four-forty. My mind was filled with dim imaginings; I saw her standing with her bathing suit down around her ankles, the hypocritical slut, he pressed his hot face into her belly, oh God she whispered, oh Eddy. Four forty-five. I sat forward, straining my ears, but I couldn't hear a sound. Neither his voice nor hers. No laughter from the lawn, no feet on the stone steps, no tinkling glass as they came back carrying beer bottles and a wine bottle. Only the rustling pine needles, only the gentle lap of the waves. I would never have believed they could be so cruel. Four-fifty. I decided to wait until five. Then I would go up there. I relived that day in Kew Gardens, the bare, glossy trees, the puddles of water in the grass, there was a man at the corner of my vision but I ignored him, I got up and walked away. I went home and spent a quiet evening reading Jane Austen. In July I went to the south of France. I sat in a garden in Provence, sipping a glass of red wine. The sun was setting, turning the vine leaves on the wall a fiery orange. I was happy. Four fifty-five. A step squeaked. Here they come. Oh, thank God, they're coming. No, the steps are empty. They aren't coming. They didn't give a damn what I thought; they weren't afraid of what I might do. Five o'clock. The sunlight was the colour of honey. My legs felt very stiff when I stood up, as though the muscles had been clenched tight for hours. She knew he was with me. She knew I didn't want her to stay. But she stayed anyway. And she was just going to take him, the way she always took everything she wanted, without the slightest hesitation. She couldn't endure unhappiness; she had to be happy all the time, she had to be loved. She didn't know what life was all about; she only knew the good part, the easy part. She should have to learn, I thought, she should be taught, someone should teach her. I remembered all the things he said to me, the things he whispered, the look on his face, the way he pretended to care about me. Then she came, laughing and flattering and flirting, making it easy. They all want it to be easy, don't they, they can't resist anything so pleasant and easy. They say they despise women's tears, women's softness, women's emotions, women's love, but secretly they long for it, they're miserable without it, when it's offered they run to it, they shelter in it. I hate them for pretending not to want it, and wanting it all along. And they are never, ever going to get it from me.

My bare feet made no sound as I walked across the hardwood floor in the front room. I couldn't hear their voices. All the doors on the upper landing were closed. I seemed to be panting, as though I had been running hard, or sobbing. There was a line of light under the kitchen doors. I smacked them open with the palms of both hands. Eddy was holding a mop and leaning against the fridge door. Leslie was sitting on a chair, her legs curled up beneath her, reading from a magazine. They had heard me coming. I imagined it as a stage comedy scene: two illicit lovers realize someone is approaching and leap apart, snatch props, strike chaste poses. They turned their heads and looked at me with wide, fake-innocent eyes.

"Oh, Gracie, you wouldn't believe it!" Leslie cried. "What a time we've been having! First of all, we broke a wine bottle. Can't you smell it? All over the floor! What a mess! We used towels and newspaper and you-name-it, and still couldn't soak it all up."

"But don't worry," Eddy said, "it wasn't the last bottle." He indicated a tray on which they had placed a freshly opened bottle of wine, two bottles of beer, and several glasses. I walked across the damp tiles, poured myself a drink and took a deep gulp. I managed to avoid looking directly at either one of them.

"I got so thirsty sitting down there all by myself," I said.

"Then Eddy looked in the broom closet and found that old mop," Leslie went on. "And this old magazine was all crumpled up under the shelf at the back." She displayed the cover, a bright blue background with white lettering, a twenty-year-old model with a board-flat stomach, large breasts, full lips and lots of tousled hair. "It must have been Mom's, right, because you and I were always way too intellectual for *Cosmopolitan*, weren't we? Listen to this." She laughed gaily. " 'Test Your Romance Quotient.' Isn't it too much? You should hear some of the questions! So far Eddy's got a perfect score."

"I'll bet," I said, holding the wine glass to my lips and staring out across the verandah at a cloud of golden bumblebees hovering over the wildflower garden. I seemed to have a bee-buzz inside my head.

"Just listen," Leslie said. "Number five. 'My idea of an exciting evening is: A) driving my Ferrari down a mountain road at twenty miles per hour over the speed limit, B) watching an NBA final, C) playing poker with the boys, or D) taking my lover to a secluded country inn and hanging a DO NOT DISTURB sign on the door.' "

"D," Eddy replied.

"Oh—!" Leslie appealed to me. "What do you say, Gracie, is that really what he'd choose?"

"I have no idea," I said, taking another swallow of my wine, watching the bees. "Why are you asking me?"

After a moment Leslie gave a rather nervous laugh and returned her attention to the magazine. "Well. Okay, number six. 'Planning a romantic dinner for two, I would be sure to include: A) hamburgers, beer, and Monday night football, B) Scotch, steak, and Tony Bennett, C) rum and coke, fish and chips, and the Beatles, or D) candlelight, champagne cocktails, and Chopin.' "

"D," Eddy said.

I laughed. "Such esoteric tastes for a dope peddler," I said.

There was a momentary silence. Finally it was possible for me to turn away from the sleepy, sun-filled garden and look at them. Leslie sat dumbly holding the magazine in both hands as though she had forgotten what she was doing with it, the traces of a slight, foolish smile lingering on her mouth. I looked straight at Eddy. His face had gone red. I smiled at him so broadly that the corners of my lips hurt.

"What?" he said slowly, with a laugh.

"Oh, come on," I said. "Please. I've known it all along. How stupid do you think I am?"

"Look," Leslie said.

"He's got a bag upstairs jam-full of money." I addressed this to Leslie although my eyes didn't move from Eddy's face. "I'm talking about cash money, Leslie. Hundreds of thousands of dollars in cash. He's got a gun too. A loaded gun. What do you think about that?"

Eddy struggled to recover. "I suppose I'm a bit eccentric sometimes in the way I handle my finances."

I heard myself give a bark of laughter. A sort of white-hot triumph was shooting through me like a rocket; I was in control again, I was powerful, they couldn't hurt me anymore. I pulled the cork out of the wine bottle and poured myself another full glass.

He continued doggedly. "No, I mean, I guess it's ridiculous, but I don't always trust banks, sometimes I feel better working with cash. And when you're carrying a lot of cash it only makes sense to have something to protect yourself. I know it's kind of unusual. Actually I hate guns. It's only a precaution."

"Please," I said. "I beg you. We weren't born yesterday, we know all about dope peddlers. Everybody knows. We've all read the newspapers. Even sweet, trusting Leslie knows all about it, don't you, Leslie? What parasites you are, what . . . vultures. The lowest of the low. So low, so selfish and depraved you can't work for a living, all you can do is prey on other people's weaknesses. Get people hooked and then suck them dry. Destroying neighbourhoods . . . just destroying entire . . . neighbourhoods and cities! Wrecking people's lives! Pushing dope to innocent little school kids! We know the sorts of things you do. We know all about it. We know. We know." Words were bursting out of me so wildly that a foam of spittle collected at the sides of my mouth.

"Gracie, calm down," Leslie said fearfully. But I hardly heard her through the roar of blood in my ears. Eddy was still looking at me. The colour had died out of his face. I saw his chest rise as he took a deep breath.

"I don't sell to school kids," he said.

"Oh, no? You don't?"

"No," he said. His voice was suddenly calm and straightforward. "School kids don't have money. I sell to people with money. What they do with it afterwards is their own business."

I threw Leslie a defiant, joyous look. There, you see, what did I tell you? She had laid the magazine down on the table and her hands rested shakily on top of the buxom model's toothy grin. She seemed to be more concerned with me than with Eddy. She shook her head and repeated, "Gracie, you've got to just calm down."

"Don't tell me to calm down," I said. "I'm calm."

"I've never twisted anybody's arm," Eddy said in a low, quiet way. "Do you think I make people want this stuff? They want it for reasons that have nothing to do with me. They come to me for a product, and I sell it to them and make a profit. Supply and demand. That's the free enterprise system, isn't it?"

"Well, you can rationalize it all you want," I said. "But the fact is, you ruin people's lives. Because of you people suffer and die! And you make money from it! There's no way around that, is there? You're a bloodsucker! Can't you just admit it?"

He stood there, looking at me levelly. There was no emotion in his face. Perhaps he was starting to hate me. I didn't care if he hated me, as long as he knew I had never, ever been fooled.

He said, "People suffer and die because of booze too. Lots of them. A lot more than from cocaine. Was your old man responsible? He sold it to them. Was he a bloodsucker?"

I couldn't believe that he was attempting to argue with me, bringing my father into it. "Don't be so simplistic," I said. "It's not the same thing."

"It isn't?" he said. "Why not?"

"Our father was an industrialist," I said. I was surprised to hear a slight quavering in my voice. "He had lots of business interests. Alcohol was just one of them. And of course, there's the small detail that selling alcohol is legal."

"It wasn't legal in the twenties though," he said. "But that didn't stop your grandfather from selling it by the truckload. He even had a little airline going between southern Ontario and northern Michigan. The rum-runners used to circle the field and flash their headlights to show the planes where to land. He made quite a small fortune out of it. And then your father took it over and made it bigger."

"Apparently he's been reading up on our family history, Leslie!" I cried. "I don't know if we should be flattered or revolted!"

"There was a big movement against booze in your grand-father's day," Eddy said. "People called it evil. Some minister made a speech and said the whole country was going to fall apart if somebody didn't stop all the get-rich-quick liquor guys from destroying the souls of the younger generation. But that never worried your grandfather for a minute, did it?"

"This is ridiculous," I said. I could hardly get my breath. I actually had tears in my eyes. "Our grandfather started with almost nothing, and after he made it big he gave a fortune to charity. Senators and members of parliament came to his funeral!"

"I can give money to charity too," Eddy said. "Then they can come to my funeral."

"They wouldn't take your lousy money!"

"No? Pretty soon they forget where it came from, don't they? All they care about is that you've got it."

"Don't hold your breath! They won't forget where yours came from!"

"Maybe in fifty years cocaine will be legal too," Eddy said. "And they'll just admire me for being a good businessman. Just like your grandfather."

"Look, alcohol is entirely different from cocaine! People have been using alcohol for centuries, it's part of human culture!"

"People have been chewing coca leaves for centuries too."

"Oh, well, Indians and peasants!" I said.

"That's right," Eddy said. "Don't they count?"

In the momentary silence I heard my own ragged breathing. My forehead felt damp.

"Such a fast talker," I said. "I suppose you've come up with a lot of good answers over the years. I suppose they make quite an impression in a courtroom."

"I've never been in court," he said. "I've never even been arrested."

"Well, good for you. I guess you're pretty smart."

His eyes looked very black, with a shiny, impenetrable surface, like onyx. "Yes," he said. "I am smart."

"However, the fact remains that you're committing a crime and if you were caught you'd go to jail for a long time!"

"I said I was going to retire. I'm just going to do this one last deal, and then I'm quitting." Suddenly I thought how absurd he looked, standing there in his dinky bathing suit, holding that old mop, trying to justify himself.

"But why quit if it's such a great career and you're so proud of it?" I said. "Lots of money and excitement, meeting new people all the time, carrying a big fat gun, terrorizing anybody who steps out of line, that's all part of it, right? How can you give that up? Do you really think you can?"

He didn't answer me, just stood there holding the mop.

"Don't give it up," I said. "Because what would you be then? A sleazy nonentity."

"Oh, Gracie," Leslie begged.

"I must admit, there was sort of a nice little dirty thrill having sex with a criminal. I must admit I did enjoy it for a while. Eduardo Corona. Isn't that a fantastic name? Right off a cigar box. The perfect name for a thug."

"She doesn't mean it," Leslie told Eddy.

That enraged me. I wanted to grab the bottle of wine and swing it at her head. "How would you know what I mean?" I said. "Seriously, Leslie, he was a pretty good lover. Yes, admittedly a bit primitive, but what he lacked in finesse he made up for in energy. Go ahead and try him out. If you haven't already."

"Oh, no!" she gasped, leaning forward across the table.

"Gracie, no, you've got the wrong idea!" She was overacting; the exaggerated display of shock and amazement didn't convince me for a second. I poured more wine. Some of it slopped onto my fingers. I couldn't remember whether I had drunk two glasses and this was the third, or three glasses and this was the fourth.

"But be sure to have an AIDS test afterwards," I said. "That's what I'm going to do."

"Oh, God," she stammered in a husky voice. "I see what you're thinking, but it's—"

"Oh, come on," I said. "Why do you always have to be so God damn coy? Don't worry about me for a second. Don't even think about me. Go ahead and do it right here on the floor if you feel like it. Always do everything you feel like doing, Leslie, don't let anything stop you, don't let anybody get in your way. Maybe you'd like some privacy. That's fine because I'm happy to leave. Happy. Believe me."

Eddy made a move as if to come toward me. I thought that if he touched me I would do something crazy and desperate. I lurched away from his outstretched hand toward the screen door.

"In fact, all I want right now is to get out of here," I said. "It'll be like heaven to have you two out of my sight!" I meant to speak emphatically and firmly, but the tone escaped me and came out in a sort of hysterical sob.

"Wait a minute," Eddy said.

I couldn't bear to listen to his voice and continued to talk right through it. "So long!" I said. "Don't worry about me, just have a wonderful God damn time! So long!" I was still carrying my wine glass, spilling a bit of it on the front of my bathing suit as the screen door swayed backward and bumped my elbow. I saw my car keys in the basket on the window ledge and snatched them up with my free hand.

By that time Leslie was crying. Of course. It was just like her, the two-faced tramp.

"Oh, Gracie, you're not going to try to drive?" she gasped. "Wait a minute, just sit down for a minute and—"

"You make me puke," I said. It felt wonderful to say that to her.

I let the door bang shut and walked across the grass and the crunchy gravel. I was wearing a bathing suit and sandals, carrying car keys and a glass of wine. It seemed to make perfect sense to get into my car and switch on the ignition. The car seat was pleasantly warm under my bare thighs. I squeezed the wine glass up against my groin and held it there while I stepped on the gas and backed down the driveway. Their figures were a distant blur in the doorway as I whipped past and turned onto the road. My brain seemed to be intensely focussed. The cottage faded into the dust behind me, and the two of them dropped down into my mind like pebbles to the bottom of a pond. I've got to drive to town, I thought, I've got to get there fast, so I can buy more wine at the liquor store. The road stretched ahead of the car like a gleaming silver band, running right up into the sun. I didn't feel drunk. I felt the need to concentrate very hard on the task I had set myself, driving, keeping the car in the right lane and heading in the right direction. The steering wheel was like a live thing under my hands; it wanted to pull away from my control and I had to use a great deal of strength to hold it in place.

The streets of Port Azure were busy that night. It was ten to six and cottagers were still wandering in and out of the tourist shops, or loading their cars with groceries, or strolling along the sidewalk eating ice cream cones. I hoped against hope that I wouldn't see anyone who recognized me. Incognito, I thought, adjusting my sunglasses and tilting my head back to lick the last drops out of my wine glass.

There were several cars in the parking lot behind the liquor store. As I turned off the ignition, I remembered vaguely that Port Azure was hardly Rio; I couldn't recall ever having seen a grown woman on the street wearing nothing but an unadorned bathing suit. Once you had passed puberty a beach jacket was the very least you could get away with.

Who gives a shit? I said to myself. It's a resort town, after all. If they can't take it, to hell with them. Then I realized that

I hadn't brought any money with me. Even that didn't cause me any great consternation. Put it on my bill, I said to myself with a haughty flourish of one hand.

The surface of the parking lot was uneven and I had to walk carefully to keep from tripping. No one looked up as I entered the store. Several people were browsing in the aisles. One man with wrinkled canvas shorts and sunburned knees glanced around as I walked past and stared rather openly at my bathing suit, but I ignored him. The wine bottles glistened brilliantly in the sunlight; all the labels were unnaturally bright and vivid. Then suddenly I decided wine wasn't enough. I wanted something stronger, something so pungent and powerful that it would numb my brain. Scotch. Forty proof.

The boy behind the counter was young and fair-haired, with a flush of acne along his jawline. I knew I'd seen him before. I looked at him through the lenses of my dark glasses and gave a friendly smile.

"I'm Grace Tremain," I said, enunciating the words very carefully so he wouldn't get the impression that I'd had too much to drink already. "I come in here all the time. Would you do me an enormous favour?"

He too couldn't keep his eyes from flickering nervously down over my bathing suit. Men are all such imbeciles, I thought contemptuously, widening my smile. "I'm having a beach party with several guests," I said. "And wouldn't you know it, we ran out of liquor. So I said I'd go to get some more, and I've driven all the way into town, and now I realize that I forgot to bring my purse. Oh, I could just kick myself!"

He smiled and shrugged, apparently sympathetic.

"Listen, do you think you could just trust me for the money until Monday? You know my family, don't you? My father was Laurence Tremain. We have the big cottage at the north end of the lake. Trewithen. We've been in this area for forty-five years. I swear I'll come in first thing on Monday to pay you."

The red spots darkened on his sallow cheeks. He ducked

his head slightly and gave another shrug, a nervous twitch of both shoulders. "Sure," he said.

"Oh, you're wonderful! I'll be eternally grateful! Thank you so much!" I watched him putting the bottles into a brown LCBO bag. I read the warning caption: Please Don't Drink and Drive. "It's ironic," I was moved to comment.

His eyes flashed at me and he smiled, eager to please but not sure just what I meant. "This is Tremain Gold Label," I explained. He shook his head bewilderedly. "Tremain," I said. "Do you get it?" I said. "What I'm actually doing is buying liquor from myself. In a manner of speaking. Isn't that rather funny? My father would be proud of me. Keep it in the family was his motto." I wasn't aware that my voice had been especially loud but suddenly I realized everyone in the store was looking at me. Go ahead and look, I thought. Grace Tremain, I heard them whisper. That's Grace Tremain. I took my bag under my arm and straightened my sunglasses. At the doorway I paused and ostentatiously adjusted the bottom of my bathing suit. The spandex snapped like a pistol shot. Behind me they all jumped.

Then I was back in the car with two bottles on the seat beside me. I was driving down through Azure Park toward the patches of blue water that I could see through the trees. After a while the road became bumpy and rutted. I was looking for a secluded crescent of sandy shore, so small it could hardly be termed a beach. I had discovered it once years before and always meant to go back. Again my mind seemed to be intensely fixed on a single idea: to find that bit of empty sand and sit there in silence until the darkness spread soothingly across the water and enveloped me. I imagined the last red rays of sunlight flashing through the shadowy pines and setting alight the white wine in my glass. But no, wait, I wasn't drinking wine anymore. It was Tremain Gold Label. It's always the right time for Tremain Gold Label.

My memory becomes confused at this point. I think I found the place I was seeking, although it might have been a different place that only resembled the one I remembered.

There was a warm, flat pink rock which I sat on. I opened one of the bottles and the whiskey fumes went up into my sinuses and made me dizzy. My hair felt heavy on my shoulders, slightly damp with perspiration. There was an ache in my body which seemed to begin in my throat and spread down through my chest and upper arms. Far away in the bright distance, coloured sails floated and shimmered in the light. But it was quiet where I sat in the shade of the tall pines. So quiet I could even hear the trickle of whiskey across my tongue and the sound of my throat muscles contracting to swallow it down. I dreamed of falling asleep there, dying there, vines growing around my limbs, shrubs springing out between my toes, saplings sprouting through my empty eye sockets, how peaceful it would be when the cool wilderness completely overwhelmed my quiet, emotionless skeleton. The light changed imperceptibly, from deep gauzy yellow to scarlet to ashy pink to a rich, measureless dark blue. Water dampened my face; it seemed to me that I was crying for my lost childhood, my innocence, my longing, my belief that someday that longing would be satisfied. Thoughts went through my mind with the potency of hallucinations: I saw myself or someone like me dancing, floating across the lake, dropping fiery sparks from her dark garments as she rose into the endless blue ether, carried aloft on a vast, reverberating loon call.

After a while I seemed to be in my car again, although I didn't recall walking to it or getting in or starting to drive. It was travelling fast, making a low roar, causing the wind to whip my hair into a mass of tangles. I felt as though I were not controlling it in any way; it was speeding along by its own volition, carrying me somewhere, and all I could do was let it carry me. I was sitting in the driver's seat and yet I was hardly there; I felt only a slight attachment to that gross, fleshy body slumped over the steering wheel. All around me the fields were dark and enormous, each blade of grass was edged with silver and the smell of the night air was sharp and spicy and sweet, intoxicating as any drug ever created. I was like one of those western riders in a rodeo show, standing easily upright on the back of a galloping horse, holding the reins with one casual hand, raising the other arm in a salute. I remembered my father singing that night when he drove the 1932 Alfa Romeo roadster down the lake road after Sally Sampson's wedding.

Then I was down on my knees in an overgrown ditch, throwing up. Crickets hummed around me in a loud chorus; the strong, bitter smell of weeds stung my nostrils. I don't know how long I crouched there in that ditch on my knees. After a while I felt much better and clearer in my mind. I got back into the car and continued to drive.

There were no lights in any of Trewithen's windows. I parked a hundred feet back from the front gate because I didn't want them to know I had returned. Their cars were sitting silently at the end of the driveway. Obviously they weren't out driving frantically around the countryside, looking for me. They were nearby, obscured by the soft darkness, together. My feet crunched loudly on the gravel. I stepped into the soft grass and stood looking up at all the dark, empty windows. Nothing stirred, nothing revealed itself. I was holding a bottle of Scotch in one hand; the glass rested against my thigh. I raised the bottle top to my mouth and took a deep swallow. My lower lip felt pulpy as though I had bruised it somehow, but I couldn't remember doing anything to bruise it. Eventually I walked around the eastern wall of the house. The shadows were even deeper there because of all the trees clustering close. The flagstone path showed dimly against the black lawn. I thought if I stood absolutely motionless I would hear them whispering to each other. There was a scurrying sound under the maples, a swift indistinct shape like a large squirrel or a small cat. I stood listening, holding my bottle. After a moment I did hear something, a distant murmur, almost indistinguishable from the breeze gently rustling the leaves. They were on the front verandah. They hadn't lit a candle or turned on a lamp. They were just sitting there in the dark. I couldn't see them from where I stood, but I knew they were there. I walked quietly, close to the wall, and as I walked their voices became clearer. My heart began to beat in harsh, painful anticipation.

"That's what was always so hard to understand," Eddy said.

What was hard to understand? What?

Leslie didn't answer.

"But you wouldn't know about that," he said after a moment.

"I guess not," Leslie agreed very quietly.

Know about what?

I sat down on the ground with my back against the wall of the house. Very slowly I raised the bottle and took another drink. My bruised lip seemed to be bleeding a little and a taste of blood mixed with the taste of Scotch. The screen of the verandah was right above my head. They were sitting side by side on the old red plush sofa, looking out at the lake. They both sounded tired. What did they have to be tired about? They were acting relaxed and companionable, like an old married couple. They weren't thinking about me at all; they had other things on their minds. I could have been lying dead on the road for all they knew or cared.

"Remember those kids you were talking about the other night?" he said. "The ones you met in Colombia?"

"Yes."

"I was like that once. I was on the street."

"You were?"

"Yeah. My sister and me. We were both on the street for awhile."

Chapter Twenty-Two

WHEN I WAS VERY LITTLE WE LIVED in a small village in the pampas in the west of Argentina and my father was a farm worker I think, Eddy said. I hardly remember about that. I remember going to school sometimes and I learned to read very fast so a nun there liked me and gave me a storybook. This book had coloured pictures and my sister and I were always looking at them and pretending to be in them. What? Oh, I don't know, they were *cuentos de hadas*, what's the English? Fairy stories, I guess. I liked those fairy stories. There were pictures of *castillos* and dark forests and sleeping princesses and *caballeros* riding beautiful horses. That kind of thing. I don't know what ever happened to that book.

Then we had to leave our village. Well, I hardly remember it. But I think the government came, and there was some big company that was also involved, and they were going to build a dam so there would be electricity for everybody in the west, something like that. But after the dam was built our village would be underwater, so we had to leave. Where they moved us it was much smaller than the place we had before and there wasn't any land to grow vegetables or keep animals, so we didn't last there very long. So that's how we came to Buenos Aires. Everybody said there was lots of work in Buenos Aires. Then my father wasn't around anymore. I don't remember. I just know after a while he wasn't around. When? Well, I was very small, so it must have been the sixties, late sixties?

In Buenos Aires after my father was gone my mother became a *puta*. I mean a prostitute. It was her only way of making money, but she wasn't very good at it. She was too old and not pretty enough and not very skilled in sex so nobody would pay much for her. She died. I don't know what it was, maybe . . . *fiebre tifoidea*? Yes, that's right, typhoid fever. My sister was ten and I was nine. Then we were on our own. We were living in a *villa miseria* near La Boca, but we had to leave because we couldn't pay any rent. *Villa miseria*? Oh, like a . . . like you said the other day . . . shantytown, yeah, that's it. Shantytown. Oh, yes, you've got to pay rent in a shantytown too. Of course. You can't live anywhere for nothing. Even on the pavement, someone will make you pay. We begged for money and we'd go through the garbage in the alleys behind some of the restaurants, looking for food. One night we found half a chocolate cake, and that was a celebration. It had a few bugs on it and it was a little wet from old coffee grounds, but we cleaned it up and ate it and we had chocolate all over our faces and man, it was great.

Oh, yes, there was a place called the Fuentes Instituto, but no one wanted to go there. It was crowded and dirty, one bathroom for a hundred kids, and the older ones would get together and beat you up and fuck you, and like that. Some kid who ran away from there told us about it. He said it was just as bad as the Reformatory and that was all I needed to know because I'd been in the Reformatory twice, once for ninety days and once for thirty and believe me, one day was already too long. They caned you and shaved your head and took away your clothes. Oh, well, sometimes I was a *carterista*, that is, stealing things from people's pockets, or a *caimanero*, stealing ladies' purses, and I got caught. One night the second time I was at the Reformatory a boy got knifed and then he just lay there on the cement floor and no one would go near him. He was a big dumb guy, always bragging about how big his muscles were, it was the only thing he had to brag about. He kept calling out, yelling and laughing, saying, "I can't die. I'm too big and strong, I can't die." It started to drive us crazy to hear him saying that over and over again, so finally somebody told him to shut up and I remember he opened his mouth as if to answer but instead of words this big gush of blood came out and he put his hand in it, and looked at the blood on his fingers so surprised, like he didn't even know what it was. When they were taking the body away the superintendent said, "Well, one less cockroach to worry about." So I didn't want to go to any place that was like the Reformatory. My sister and me, we figured we were better off on our own.

One afternoon in La Recoleta there was a rich *porteño* family having tea and sweets at an outdoor café and the children were eating ice cream cones and oh, those ice cream cones looked so good it was making our mouths water. The mother wanted to teach her kids about charity, I guess, so she gave each kid a peso and said, "Give it to these poor children who are less fortunate than you." Well, the second we had those coins in our hands, my sister and I ran to the ice cream shop and bought two cones for ourselves. When the mother saw us walking past with those cones she was very indignant and said to her husband, "Look at that, they didn't really need the money at all." I guess she thought we should have bought something else besides ice cream cones. But there wasn't much you could buy for a peso. It was a hot summer afternoon and my sister and I sat under a big ombú tree in the shade and ate our ice cream and watched all the people in the cafés, sipping tea in their beautiful clothes. We pretended to be like them and said things to each other like "Would you pass the sugar, darling?" and "What do you think, should I be wicked and order another pastry?" I think that was the happiest afternoon my sister and I ever had.

The winter wasn't so good. In Buenos Aires it doesn't get

as cold as in Canada, but it's very damp and rainy. Then of course people don't sit outdoors and they're in a hurry and don't want to stop to give you money. One time my sister and I hadn't eaten anything for two and a half days. Your head would start to feel light. When you smelled food cooking from the back doors of restaurants, it would make your eyes water. It was all you thought of, food, food, every minute it was on your mind. We found some pieces of bread in a garbage can but it was so old and hard it hurt your teeth to try and bite it. There was a pizza cook in La Boca who sometimes gave us leftovers so we went there to see if he had anything for us. We stood at the back door in the rain. He was a big, fat guy with a big fat belly, always sweaty and smelling of garlic. He stood in the doorway and he said to my sister, "I'll give you a whole fresh-baked pizza for a fuck." Yes, my sister was ten years old. But she wasn't a virgin. Sometimes when my mother was alive the men who had her would want my sister too and who was going to stop them? I mean there we all were together in our little shack made out of newspaper, all they had to do was roll off my mother and roll onto my sister. And anyway they would pay extra sometimes because my sister was young. That started when she was about eight years old so she was used to it. But she didn't like the pizza cook; she didn't want him to touch her. She ran away. Then the cook was angry and slammed the door in my face. So I ran after my sister and when I caught up with her I slapped her hard. I was really furious. I said, "What's the matter with you? A whole fresh-baked pizza!" She was crying. She said, "But I hate him. He's fat and he stinks!" I kept thinking about that pizza, how it would have tasted, hot out of the oven, with melted cheese and tomatoes and sausage. Jesus, I could have just about cried myself. I wanted one bite of that pizza, just one bite. It wasn't as though she hadn't fucked any fat, smelly men before, worse than him. Sometimes I even found men for her to fuck, and she always did it. So I don't know what got into her that day. Maybe it was because the pizza cook asked. Usually nobody asked, they just threw her down and did it. But the pizza cook asked, so maybe she thought that meant she could say no. I said, "It would have been over in two minutes, you stupid bitch!" I slapped her again and she cried harder. She said, "It's fine for you, but you don't know what it's like."

I didn't say anything but the truth was I'd done it too. She didn't know that, I never told her. In Argentina you're supposed to be a macho, you're supposed to die before you let somebody stick it up your ass. A macho doesn't let himself get fucked like a woman. But at the Reformatory it happened more than once, they'd hold you down and do whatever they wanted and you couldn't stop them. And you never got anything for it either. But once behind the Casa d'Oro in San Telmo, that's a part of Buenos Aires with a lot of night-life, this great big guy shoved me up against a wall and gave it to me hard and it hurt so bad I thought I was going to die, but afterwards he bought me steak. I was still hurting and I even had some tears in my eyes, but each mouthful of that steak took away the pain and filled my whole body with pleasure and happiness. So it was worth it. And I thought, If you get steak for it, then I'm ready, I'm bending over, come on, give it to me again.

So I was mad at my sister for being such a fool. I kept slapping her in the face. Yeah, I was younger but I was the man, I was the boss, so I had to show her I wasn't going to put up with crying or any other women's shit. Then I walked away and left her standing there in the alley in the rain. I went to Palermo Park and hung around. I thought I might see some people eating and maybe they'd leave some food behind. Or I thought maybe I might try to grab somebody's purse, even though I was nervous about it because I didn't want to get caught and sent back to the Reformatory. But there were hardly any people in the park because of the rain. I took some handfuls of grass and ate that, just so I could feel it in my mouth, so I could feel myself chewing something and swallowing. But after the grass got into my stomach it made me sick and I had to throw up. I kept heaving and heaving but nothing came up except a dribble of green spit.

We had a big cardboard box we slept in sometimes. It was in a vacant lot a block from El Caminito in La Boca. I went there and lay inside it and my teeth started to chatter. I dreamed about that pizza we could have had, and then I dreamed about steak and fried potatoes and paella and bread and churros dipped in chocolate and all the other things I wanted to eat. It got dark and then my sister came. "Look, Eduardo," she said. "Look what I've got." She'd sneaked onto the metro and gone over to Barrio Norte where a lot of people live, and she found some crackers and some wrapped-up meat in a garbage can. I said, "This is dog food, you dumb *puta*!" She said, "Oh, no, it's sandwich meat!" I said, "It doesn't look okay." She said, "Oh, no, I'm sure it's all right, I picked out the best parts." I was still mad at her. I said, "We could have had a whole fresh-baked pizza, you stupid whore." I ate some of the crackers. They were stale but after I'd eaten three I felt as if my muscles came back to life and I could sit up straight and I could smell the rain in the air and I could hear the music from the cantinas in Calle Necochea. Funny how even a little bit of food could do that. My sister made a fire to cook the meat she'd found but she was so hungry she couldn't wait and just heated it up a bit and then ate it. She said, "It's all right, go ahead and have some." She was pushing the meat into her mouth with both hands and bloody juice was dribbling down her chin. It made me sick to see her. "*Dios*, you're ugly," I said to her. I wouldn't eat any meat, I just ate the crackers. She had one or two, and I ate all the other crackers in the package. After that we lay side by side in the cardboard box and listened to the cantina music. She tried to take hold of my hand but I wouldn't let her, I yanked my hand away, I was still mad at her and besides a macho doesn't do any *marica* stuff like holding his sister's hand. They were playing a tango called "Buenos Aires de mi corazón" ("Buenos Aires of My Heart"), and people were singing along with the *bandoneón*. "Buenos Aires de mi corazón, I left you long ago but every night you fill my dreams. Your music makes me forget my sadness, your perfume lifts my soul. On your streets I walk with the one I love. On your streets we're always young. I hear you calling to me, I long to see you once more. Buenos Aires de mi corazón, when I come back to you, all my troubles and hardships will end."

When I woke up the next morning, my sister wasn't lying beside me anymore. I saw her later that day. She was lying on her back in some yellow grass in an empty yard. I think she must have felt sick that night after eating the meat and climbed out of the box so she wouldn't wake me up, and wandered away. Her eyes were wide open and she was dead. I think it was the meat that killed her, although who knows? It could have been anything. After a while they came and took her away. I was hiding in an alley across the street and watching. I didn't want them to see me because I was afraid they'd take me to the Fuentes Instituto. They didn't ask anybody what her name was. They didn't care about things like that. Just one less cockroach to worry about. I couldn't stop remembering that the last thing I said to her was when I called her a stupid whore, and ugly. I wished I'd said something else. I wished I'd let her hold my hand. It wouldn't have hurt anything, no one was there to see and think I was an *hermanita*, oh I mean a sissy, a sissy-boy. She had a pretty name. Her name was Carolina. Yes, just like in the tango song I played for you the other night.

It wasn't very long after that I stole a drum. There were a bunch of guys from a military band sitting at a café on Avenida de Mayo. The military weren't in power then, but they were always around. These guys had been marching in a parade for the Nueve de Julio celebrations, and they were sitting all together having a beer. I thought they were all generals. I was only a kid and didn't know that generals never march in parades, they just sit up on a balcony and watch the parades go by. But these guys were dressed so beautifully, I thought they had to be generals. They were wearing dark blue jackets and bright red sashes, and they were having a good time, talking and making toasts and laughing. They had all sorts of shiny brass instruments, cornets and trombones and tambourines and cymbals, and one old guy had a great big bass drum which was sitting on the sidewalk behind him. It wasn't a brand-new drum but it was pretty and shiny and it had red ribbons tied on it, and I don't know why but I thought I should take it. When you're on the street you're always looking for things to take.

Anything that looks as if it might be worth a few pesos. Your eyes go right to it, like a reflex. And sometimes you just have to try, even if you might get caught and sent to the Reformatory. That drum was sitting there on the sidewalk and everybody was turned away, nobody was paying any attention to it, so I walked over and picked it up and walked away with it. That was how easy it was. After I'd walked half a block, I ducked into an alley and then I ran like hell. I thought if any of those damn generals saw me they'd send the whole army after me and they'd take me to a dungeon somewhere and shoot me with electricity till I had no manhood left. So I ran as though I was being chased by wild dogs, and it wasn't easy because the drum was almost as big as I was. It wasn't till I was miles away that I dared to stop and look it over. It was the kind of drum you wear on your back, with straps over your shoulders and around your waist to hold it in place. The drumsticks were fastened to it, one on each side, and there were little cymbals attached to the top of it, and there was a cord that you pulled which made the cymbals bang and the drumsticks hit the drum right in the centre. I loved that drum. I liked all the red ribbons and it was so big and bright and when you pulled the cord it made such a boom and a crash! It was the prettiest thing I ever held in my hands. I was thinking I was going to sell it for a lot of money, but then I got another idea. I was always noticing beggars who sang or danced or played the harmonica, and the people with money were always more generous about opening their wallets because they felt they were getting something in return, something interesting or some little bit of pleasure. They didn't hate the ones who did something nearly as much as they hated the ones who just asked for a handout. I couldn't sing or dance or play the harmonica but I thought maybe I could beat the drum and people might give some money for that. I had to rub some dirt on it and try to make it not so gorgeous, so people wouldn't wonder how a street boy came to own such a thing.

Still, I had to fight for it more than once. Somebody was always trying to take it from me. A lot of times I had to sleep with my head on it and it wasn't a very soft pillow! Once I was sitting with a whore I knew, Crazy Carmen. She was a bit old but she kept her body in great condition and she used to boast that she could do twenty-five men in a day. Her boyfriend Marco was a fence so I was always taking stuff to her place to sell to him. She had a back porch and sometimes for a peso she'd let you sleep there overnight if she was in the mood. Anyway she got the idea that I should sell Marco the drum. I said no, it wasn't for sale, but she grabbed it and started to walk out with it, so I ran after her and shoved her and hit her with my fist. I'd seen Marco hit her so hard she fell against the wall, so I figured a little punch from me wasn't going to bother her too much, but I guess she'd take things from her boyfriend that she wouldn't take from a *pibe* off the streets, because she spun around and all of a sudden she had a knife in her hand, I don't know where that knife came from, and she cut me, right in my side, right through to the bone. I remember running down the street dragging the drum, and blood pouring all down my side like a river and filling up my shoe. They were shoes I found in the garbage dump, and they were too big for me, and my foot kept slipping around in this puddle of blood inside the left shoe so I stumbled every time I took a step. People just kind of backed away from me, they didn't like the look of me and I didn't blame them, I would have backed away too. I kept thinking of that big dumb guy at the Reformatory, I was scared that blood would start coming out of my mouth and that would mean I was going to die. But I made it to the emergency hospital and they sewed me up. I kept one hand on the drum the whole time they were doing it.

Another time I fought an older boy, he was about sixteen and almost a foot taller and he was determined to have that drum. He caught me in an alley near where my mother used to live. Sometimes a woman who was my mother's old friend would let me sleep in her shack if I satisfied her. It wasn't too difficult. All you had to do was rub against her, say "I love you," stick it in, pull it out, and she was asleep. On really cold nights or on nights when it was raining hard, I would usually go to her place.

So one morning I was walking in the alley behind her shack, carrying the drum, when the tall boy came around the corner. I knew who he was. I'd seen him before. He had one green eye and one brown eye, and the iris of the green eye turned to one side, so he always looked wild and *loco*. People used the gutters of that alley as a toilet, and he held me down and pushed my face into the shitty water and said, "Drink it." I tried to hold my breath and press my lips together, but I could smell it and taste it and it made me gag. We wrestled for a long time. He was strong but not as mad as I was. I clasped him around the neck like a lover and bit a chunk right out of his cheek. I still remember what it was like in my mouth: wet and salty and filled with gristle. So that day I tasted shit and I tasted the flesh of a human being. He ran away, with both his hands over his face and blood pouring out between his fingers. I was amazed and proud, I felt myself growing tall with pride that I could be so savage like that. I knew then I wasn't like a cockroach, they better not dare try to touch me or take things from me or fuck with me anymore because I had power, I was a killer. I wished there was someone who had seen this happen to me. But there was no one to see it. So I picked up my drum, and I knew it was really mine then because I fought for it and won. I remember that the street was all full of cold pink light, it was very early, just dawn. I could still taste that crazy guy's blood in my mouth. It tasted good.

I can't say I had much talent as a drummer. And of course I never had anyone to teach me what to do. I just beat on it with all my strength. And I taught myself a trick, which was that I would stand on one foot and whirl around in a circle as fast as possible, still beating on the drum all the time. I would go to Palermo Park or Parque Lezama or to any area of the city where there were street cafés. I would walk up and beat my drum and say, "Señoras y señores, me llamo Eduardo, el Rey del Tambor!" (Ladies and gentlemen, my name is Eduardo, the Drum King!) "And tonight you're lucky because the Drum King is going to perform for you!" Then I'd pound my drum like mad and crash the cymbals and spin around so fast they could hardly see me or who I was, boy or girl, man or woman. They'd stare with their mouths open. Sometimes the police would come or the waiters would run out of the cafés and chase me away. But not often. Mostly they left me alone. Sometimes the police would even stand and watch me like everybody else. I had an old felt hat that my mother's friend gave me, and I would go from person to person or table to table, and I would bow and smile and hold out the hat for money. There were slow nights when my whole body would be trembling with exhaustion and all I'd have in the hat were three or four coins. But other nights that hat would be heavy with money and I'd walk down the Avenida Corrientes with my drum on my back and buy hot empanadas from a street vendor, they're like little meat pies, and nothing was ever so delicious as those empanadas, they were stuffed full of juicy beef and spices, and I could have as many as I wanted, I could keep eating until my belly was bursting. And on those nights the Avenida Corrientes looked like a river of coloured light, neon red, electric blue, all the colours so bright and shiny you almost thought you could bite into them like candy.

Once I went to Belgrano, a pretty neighbourhood with shops and cafés and churches. It was after sunset and the streets were getting dark and most of the shops were closed, but I came across a restaurant where lots of people were sitting at tables outside and a couple of waiters in black pants and white jackets were standing in the doorway. There were lamps on all the tables, lamps with little yellow lampshades. I saw two women eating omelettes and drinking wine from tall glasses. Two rich women. One was wearing a white linen dress and gold earrings. Their perfume was in the air and I thought it smelled the way gold would smell if gold had a scent. So I stood on the sidewalk and beat on my drum and said, "Señoras y señores, me llamo Eduardo, El Rey del Tambor!" I heard the woman in the white linen dress say to her friend, "What is it? Is it a dwarf?" I stepped forward and took off my hat and bowed. I said, "No, señora, I'm not a dwarf, I haven't yet reached my full height but in other respects I'm man-sized!" and I took my balls in my hand and gave them a little shake. Her friend was shocked but the woman in the white linen dress laughed out loud, and so did everybody else. Even the waiters laughed and poked each other. It was always good if you could tell a joke and make them laugh because then they liked you more and would give you more. So I made them happy that night and they were all smiling at me, all liking me. And then I adjusted my drum and stood on one foot and whirled around. The red ribbons flew around me and the whole street spun around, the yellow lamps, the gold earrings, the white linen dress, the perfume and the waiters' white jackets and the laughing faces, round and round in a beautiful blur, and I made my drum boom so loud God in heaven must have heard it. Afterward they gave me quite a lot of money. One of the waiters went inside and came back with some paper packets of sugar. Sugar was good, it gave you a burst of energy so you could go on for hours. And the woman in the white linen dress called me over and handed me four thousand pesos, which at that time was worth almost ten dollars. It was the most money I'd ever been given by one person. She had black hair and her lipstick was red and shiny and I felt as if I wanted to run my tongue over her mouth to taste that lipstick. And I wanted to eat the food off their plates and drink the wine from their glasses and smoke their cigarettes, I wanted to feel their soft clothes on my skin, and I wanted to ride in a car, and sleep in a fluffy bed with two pillows, and wear a gold ring, and smell perfume all night, and not live and die in the God damn shit. I thought, Why can I not have these things? Holy Mary, Mother of God, show me the way to get them. It was like, some nights even after I'd swallowed a dozen empanadas and my stomach was so full it couldn't take one more mouthful, underneath that, even then, there was a big empty space where I was still hungry, and that space was always there no matter how much I ate. That night in Belgrano, all of a sudden I felt as if I'd had that hungry place my whole life and even before, forever and ever, and it had got so big that nothing could ever fill it up, except if I swallowed the whole world.

Chapter Twenty-Three

IT WAS A GOOD STORY. HE SAVED HIS BEST STORY FOR LESLIE.

I think it ended there, but I can't be sure. I closed my eyes for a moment and when I opened them again, his voice had stopped. The branches of the trees were black and spiky against the soft, star-filled sky. All I heard was a whisper of air through the black leaves. I waited but there was no sound from the verandah. I had no idea how much time had passed, whether I had closed my eyes a moment or an hour ago. I squinted at the dim face of my watch. It seemed to say three o'clock, but that was no help at all because I couldn't remember what time it had been when I first crossed the lawn. The night had turned cool and I felt cold in my bathing suit. My hair was a tangled mass with leaves in it and bits of grass. My knees looked dirty, as though I had been crawling on the ground. I couldn't remember crawling.

Were they sitting up there on the verandah in silence, waiting for me to reveal myself? I willed myself to remain absolutely motionless, to breathe without making a sound. One of the wicker chairs would creak, one of them would cough. But nothing happened. I realized my fingers were sore from the pressure of squeezing my hands into tight fists.

He was smart; he always knew what to do. He had found the perfect role to play for Leslie. She loved to feel pity; she wanted to be a rescuer. She would envelop him in her embrace, rock him like a child, shower him with attention and gifts, raise him to the sky. He would make his last deal and then retire. He would move into Leslie's house. He would be Leslie's fourth husband. She never recognized when something was completely rash and inappropriate, she never had qualms or doubts, if she wanted to do something she always went ahead. She didn't understand that he was an outlaw and had to remain so; that was his definition. If she brought him inside and made him one of us, it would ruin everything about him that I loved. "I'm so happy," she would tell me over the phone. "I love him and he loves me." "Eddy and I are going to Europe," she would say. "He's never been there before. I can't wait to show him the Mediterranean!" "Eddy and I are having a Welcome to Summer party, and we want you to come." They would put me in the spare room. Leslie would have picked flowers in her garden and arranged a big bouquet in a vase beside my bed. "Eddy and I are so glad you could come, Gracie. We're always glad to see you."

I can't endure this, I thought. I cannot accept it. No. I can't go on living if this happens.

I got to my feet. My joints were stiff from sitting so long on the damp ground. I moved slowly down the side of the house, trailing my fingers along the stone. The verandah was empty. They had gone. I hadn't heard them go; I didn't know whether they had left minutes or hours before. They were inside the house, though. I stood on the grass looking through the tall windows at the darkness and the empty, moonlit floor. They had gone upstairs.

The screen door squeaked as I pulled it open. I stopped and waited, but there was no answering sound from the interior. I moved cautiously, like a housebreaker. I had been cold but now I felt hot. The ends of my hair tickled my damp, sweaty forehead. The living room stretched away from my feet like some vast, deserted ballroom; my black, distorted shadow trembled across the silvery floorboards.

Please God, I thought, pausing on each stair, let him be in our room alone. Let him be there lying on the bed. If he's there I'll forgive him, I'll believe him. Please God, I'll do anything you say if only you let him be there.

Like most prayers, that one wasn't answered. Light from the windows poured across the tight, smooth bedspread and the round rug. Everything was exactly the way it had been when I left the room that morning, so long past.

I stood in the open doorway, holding my breath, listening with my whole body. They were naked together, somewhere close by, he was pressing his hot face into her throat, just the way he did with me, she was gasping with pleasure the way I did, he was whispering the same sweet obscenities into her ear. They didn't care if they destroyed me, they didn't care if they broke my heart. My heart is broken, I said to myself. My heart is broken.

My hands were steady as I unzipped the side pocket of the duffel bag and took out the gun. How quickly their pleasure would evaporate when they saw it. How terrified they would be. I wanted to see their terror, I wanted to hear them pleading with me. It was the only thing that would relieve the awful pain in my chest. They thought they could make a fool out of me. I had to show them. No one ever made a fool out of me. Not me.

The gun was heavy. It pulled at my arm as I walked across the landing. I thought they might be in Leslie's room, but on the other hand, they might have chosen one of the other bedrooms, just to be on the safe side. I didn't want to open the wrong door, because wherever they were they might hear it and be warned. I knelt down on the floor outside Leslie's room and pressed my ear against the door panel, listening for a sigh, a murmur, the creak of bedsprings. Nothing. They thought they were being clever, they were hiding in one of the unused rooms, but I knew I was going to find them, all I had to do was be very quiet and listen very hard. I crawled along the hall close to the wall, so close my shoulder rubbed against the varnished wood, holding up the gun so that it didn't scrape on the floorboards. When I reached the next closed door, I placed my ear against the thin wooden panel and listened. It was hard to hear anything above the mad hammering of my heart. But after a couple of moments I decided, No, not here either. And I hurried on, a frantic, clumsy crawl to the next door.

Then it was as if a part of myself that had been asleep suddenly woke up. It was as if I suddenly rose to the ceiling and looked down at myself. What I saw was an ugly, demented animal in a dirty bathing suit, crawling along the hallway on its hands and knees, its hair full of dust and leaves, scuttling close to the floor, hunched over, snarling and muttering to itself and sniffing the air to find its prey. Horror overcame me, pinned me to the floor like nails. For a moment I could no longer tell which was up, which was down. The hallway filled with a lunatic wind that screamed around my ears, lifted me up, whirled me around. For the first time all day I asked myself, What am I doing? But even the "I" was nebulous; the boundaries of my identity had lost their precision and it felt as though my consciousness were melting away into a huge, dark space. I clutched the gun in both hands. It was the only solid thing I had to hold. I felt its smooth barrel, the point of the trigger, the hard curve of the butt. I don't know how long I crouched there. I wasn't sure if I would ever be able to stand, but finally I did. My knees, my elbows, my ankles, every part of my body was shaking convulsively as I walked back across the landing, crossed the threshold of my room, and shut the door behind me with a click. My image floated dimly into the mirror: I saw my wild hair, the deathlike pallor of my skin. The gun was so heavy I felt I couldn't hold it anymore; I would have to let it drop. Instead I raised it and touched the barrel to my lips. Then I opened my mouth and clenched my teeth around the hard metal. My reflection watched me with hollow, shadowy eyes. I wondered what it would be like. Would you hear the click of the trigger, would there be a slight pause between that click and the moment the bullet tore into your head, would there be terrible pain, would you be aware that your brain was exploding—or would there be instant, simple, blessed oblivion? In another second I would do it, just because it was so easy, so much easier than going on, one movement of one finger and relief would come at last, endless relief.

After a while—a minute, half an hour?—I set the gun down on the bureau. Then I lay across my empty bed with my face against the counterpane. I had lain in exactly the same position once before, exhausted after one of the big Tremain summer parties, running into my parents' room because someone else was using mine. I had lain there smelling the same smell, a faint, ancient whiff of eau de Cologne that reminded me of my mother.

THE SUN ROSE OVER AZURE LAKE, merging sky and water in one vast expanse of soft pink light. There was no breeze; all was still and at peace. Daylight spread silently over the pale green walls of the boathouse, across the wet, gleaming sand, up the stone steps. It raised the mist from the lawn in a delicate, golden steam, it crept along the curved arms of the wicker chairs on the verandah, it warmed the flower petals and dispersed their sweet fragrance in the air, it illuminated the faded lines of the old tennis court.

I was lying flat on my stomach with my face pressed into the bedspread. The fabric was damp from my saliva. No one had awakened me, no one had come to inquire. My head didn't hurt, my stomach wasn't upset. In fact, I hardly felt present in my own body. It was as though I had died during the night and my revival was still uncertain. I had a sensation of vague, distant pain, like the beginning of a toothache. There was no sound anywhere in the house. I thought perhaps they had got up early and driven away, unable to face me. They were driving fast down the road, feeling guilty but crazily happy nonetheless. I know a great place to have breakfast, Leslie was saying. We can eat and relax and think about what we should do.

It seemed to take an enormous effort but I pushed myself up to a sitting position. I sat on the edge of the bed with my hands in my lap. There was grit all over my skin. My finger-nails had dirt under them and one knee was stained with dried blood. I was a mess. I will go and have a shower, I thought, but I didn't move.

Suddenly the cellular phone emitted a loud, demanding buzz. The sound was so unexpected and so near that I almost jumped out of my skin, and my sluggish blood awakened and began to flow rapidly through my veins. I'm not answering it, I thought, it's nothing to do with me. But after the third ring I leaned toward the bedside table and looked at it. It seemed to vibrate impatiently, insisting on my attention. Finally I pulled out its antenna and raised it to my ear.

"Hello?" I said. My voice sounded amazingly crisp and clear, as though I were wide awake after a peaceful night's sleep.

There was a startled intake of breath on the other end, and then an intense, listening silence.

"Hello?" I said again. "Hello?"

At last a sharp, nervous man's voice spoke warily. "Who's this?"

"Who's this?" I countered.

There was another pause. I waited and then I said, "Look, this is idiotic. What do you want?"

He seemed to hesitate. Then he said firmly, "I want to talk to Eddy. Can you put him on?"

"He's not here right now," I said.

"Shit! He didn't leave already, did he?"

"Leave? I don't know."

The man gave a groan. There was a sense of urgency in his tone and in his breathing, as though he longed to drop the phone and run. "He was planning to make a trip today," he said sharply. "Right? You knew that."

Miami. His last big deal. "Oh, yes," I said. "Well, his bag is still here, so he couldn't have left yet."

He let out a quick gust of breath. "All right. Good. You're his chick, aren't you? I don't know your name. The redhead?"

His chick. The redhead. It almost made me laugh to hear myself described that way. "Yes, I guess that would be me," I said.

"Okay, so I want you to give him a message, right? Can you do that? It's very important."

"All right," I said.

"Tell him Terry called and I said it isn't a good day to start a vacation. Okay? A very bad day for a vacation. He definitely should not go today. Will you tell him that? Find him and tell him right away. Okay? Got it? Just answer me, honey, I'm in sort of a rush here. Have you got it, or not?"

"Yes, I've got it," I said. "It's not especially complicated."

"Okay, good. And tell him not to try calling me back because I'm not gonna be around for a couple days. Tell him I'll try to call him later in the week."

"All right," I said.

There was an abrupt click, and then dead air.

"Hello?" I said. "Are you still there?" But he was gone. Slowly I pushed the telephone antenna back into its socket. Then I stared at the duffel bag, at its unzipped pocket hanging open. I remembered taking the gun out. What had I done with it, where was it? But I didn't want to think about that. All at once my lethargy seemed to evaporate. I walked quickly over to the bureau and yes, the gun was there just where I had left it. I returned it to the duffel bag and zipped it into place with quick, efficient fingers. Then I went into the bathroom, stripped off my filthy bathing suit and stuffed it deep down in the laundry hamper. The hot water poured down over me, blinding and deafening me, washing away all the stains, all the dirt. After I stepped out of the shower I put on my terrycloth robe and it smelled fresh and clean. I could look at myself in the mirror, at my plain, clean, soap-scrubbed face and my long, clean, wet hair. It was as though the night before had been washed away, had swirled down the bathroom drain and disappeared. Sunlight streamed through the high arched window and made the water droplets gleam on the red tiles. Everything was all right. I went back into the bedroom. I got my hairbrush and sat on the window ledge, feeling the warm sun across my lap. The lake was a brilliant, foamy blue. It was a beautiful August day, and later than I had thought. The clock on the bedside table said that it was almost one-thirty in the afternoon.

After a while, I don't know how long, I heard footsteps on the stairs. No voices, just footsteps, mounting steadily. I was aware of my heartbeat, but otherwise I felt quite calm. I didn't turn my head when the bedroom door opened. I continued to brush my hair, looking out at the distant blue water.

"Hi," he said.

"Hi," I answered, still without turning around.

"I slept on the front verandah last night," he said after a moment.

"Oh?" I kept brushing my hair, long even strokes. "Why?"

"I thought I'd see you when you came home but I must have fallen asleep," he said. "When I looked a few minutes ago I saw your car parked way down the road. Why did you park way back there?"

I shrugged. "It was the middle of the night and I didn't want to disturb anybody," I said.

He was standing just inside the doorway. "I had some breakfast, or lunch or whatever you want to call it. There's coffee if you want any."

"How about Leslie?" I said. "Is she up too?"

His voice was calm and uninflected. "I haven't seen her since last night."

The toothache pain was beginning to intensify. It spread through my face, it made my throat ache. "No?" I said.

"She must be still sleeping. We sat up late talking."

"Really. You must have had a lot to talk about."

"We drove around for a while looking for you. Then we didn't know what else to do so we just sat here waiting for you to come back," he said.

Liar. What a filthy bastard of a liar he was. "Finally about three a.m. we gave up," he said. "Where were you?"

None of your damn business. He was never going to know anything real about me. Never, never, never.

"I drove to the other side of the lake," I said gaily. "I went to visit the DeJongs. I forgot about the time."

After a moment he said, "We were worried."

I squinted at the light on the water. "Why?" I said, with a laugh.

"Why? Because you drove out of here at about ninety miles an hour with a glass of wine in your hand, and—"

I laughed again. "Oh well," I said. "I'd had too much to drink, that's for sure. I used to be able to handle it, but I must be getting too old. Betsy gave me a lot of coffee and sobered me up."

There was a brief silence while he digested that. The sun was so bright it hurt my eyes. I wanted him to go. Go, I told him silently.

"Anyway, you weren't so worried that it stopped you from going to bed and sleeping like a stone," I said lightly.

"How do you know how I slept?" he said.

Maybe I should ask Leslie, I answered silently. But I shrugged my shoulders and kept brushing my hair, watching a boat with a gleaming silver arrow on its hull, streaking above the water like a rocket.

"Besides, Leslie said you'd done this before," he told me.

I lowered the brush to my lap and stared down incredulously at the black bristles. "What?" I said.

"She said you always used to get mad about something and storm out. Then you'd come back later and pretend nothing had happened."

I had to take a deep breath to still the sudden trembling in my hands. "That is absolutely fantastic," I said. "I might have done it once before, about a hundred years ago. So she says I 'always' storm out. 'Always.' That's so typical."

He kept standing in the doorway, looking at me. After a moment I raised my arm and resumed brushing my hair.

"I have to get ready to leave," he said finally. "It's about two hours to that airfield, isn't it?"

This isn't a good day for a vacation. Find him and tell him. This isn't a good day for a vacation. The words chimed dully in my mind.

"Isn't it?" he repeated.

"Yes," I said. "An hour and a half if you drive fast."

I heard him checking the duffel bag, rapidly unzippering it and zippering it up again. He threw the closet door open with a bang and pulled out a jacket.

"Good-bye then," he said curtly.

I didn't turn around. I kept staring at the lake. *Find him and tell him right away. It's a very bad day for a vacation.* The toothache was in every part of my body, it was in my ear lobes and my eyelashes and the roots of my hair. The hard bristles of the hairbrush scraped against my scalp.

"Good-bye," I said.

He started to go out. I stared outward, but my vision had blunted and all I could see was blinding sunlight. He hesitated in the doorway.

"Look," he said. "After this I'm giving it up. I really am. This is the last one."

"All right," I said.

"I mean it," he said.

"I know," I said.

"Do you believe me?"

"Yes," I said.

He took a couple of tentative steps toward me. My insides tightened. I looked down at the brush and began to pick out long strands of hair.

"And we'll go to Buenos Aires, like we said. Right?"

"Sure," I said.

He was standing right behind me. Do not touch me, I thought.

"We won't have to stay there forever," he said. "I just want them to see me with my boat and my beautiful redheaded *condesa*."

"Your what?"

He laughed. "That day in Kew Gardens," he said. "The sun was shining on top of your head and your hair looked like it was on fire. I'd never seen hair that colour before. You were wearing that gorgeous pale green Armani suit. I thought you looked so fine and proud, like a *condesa*, that's what I called you in my mind. When you spoke to me I couldn't believe it. Usually I'm the one who has to make the first move. I said to myself, Eddy, this is going to be your lucky day."

He put his supple, treacherous hands on my shoulders. I could feel his breath on the top of my head. I had to swallow hard to keep a sort of nausea from rising in my throat.

"Oh," I said. "Is that how it was?"

"Look, your sister's very nice," he said. "But I've never gone near her. You're the one I want. You know that."

I almost laughed out loud. I almost shook him off. I almost said, Do you really think what you want matters in the least?

I stood up. The hairbrush fell against my bare foot and left a stinging pain. I grabbed the cellular phone and held it out to him.

"Don't forget this," I said. I looked at his cheekbones. In that way I managed to avoid looking at his eyes.

"I could leave it here," he said. "Then I could phone you from Miami."

"Oh, no," I said. "You'd better take it. Maybe you'll need it."

"Okay," he said, putting it into his jacket pocket. He was standing two inches from me. I had no room to turn around. I stared at the collar of his shirt.

"Everything's all right, then, isn't it?" he said.

"Yes, everything's all right," I said.

"I'll be back in a couple of days," he said. I nodded. My back was pressed against the window frame. He bent his head. I had to let him kiss me. His mouth was dry and hot.

"Are you sure you don't want me to leave the phone?" He was standing against me; his hands cupped my neck, holding my face against his throat. I could feel the texture of his skin under my cheek. The smell of his cologne penetrated my brain and made me light-headed. I saw him walking down a street, walking in his easy, graceful way, hands in the pockets of his green jacket, becoming smaller and darker in the distance. I saw him turn the corner out of sight.

"No," I said. "I'll talk to you when I see you."

He stepped back. With an effort I raised my eyes and looked into his face. He was smiling. He seemed to believe that he had won, that he had fixed everything. He was pleased with himself. I saw that he wasn't so smart after all. I was the better liar, I was far more devious and cynical than he.

He picked up the duffel bag and paused in the doorway. Teasingly he placed his hand over his heart. "Te llevo en el alma," he said, with his old charming smile.

I smiled back. "So long, Eddy," I said.

I listened to his feet running down the stairs and crossing the wide floor. I heard the kitchen doors swing open and shut. There was still time to go after him. It wasn't too late. I sat completely motionless, feeling the light breeze lift the long ends of my hair. Far away, far away, a car door slammed, an engine rumbled. There was still time, if I ran and shouted. But I didn't move. It was only a phone call, I told myself. How can a trivial thing like a phone call make a difference in anyone's life? If it was really important Terry would call back. Or he would call Terry. He was probably dialling Terry's number that very moment. He was roaring down the road, the dust was swirling around him, he was gone. I sat on the window ledge in the peaceful, sun-filled silence. The light was warm on my face.

Chapter Twenty-Four

LESLIE WAS IN THE KITCHEN. SHE WAS WEARING JEANS and a striped T-shirt and her hair was brushed and tied back in a neat ponytail. Two suitcases were packed and sitting beside the door. She was standing next to the polished pine table, holding a coffee cup in both hands and staring through the screen.

"Good morning," I said in a harsh, bright voice. "Or, no, sorry, I guess it's afternoon, isn't it?"

Her shoulders gave a twitch and she turned around. She looked flushed and teary. Of course she had to say good-bye to Eddy too, I thought. She had been in the kitchen all along. She had waited while he went upstairs to get his bags, and as soon as he walked back into the kitchen she threw her arms around his neck and pushed her moist lips against his and stuck her tongue down his throat. Oh Eddy, she said, I love you, oh Eddy, I'll miss you, oh Eddy, I wish you didn't have to go.

"Did Eddy get off all right?" I said.

She blinked. She said, "I guess so. He was already gone when I came down."

Sure.

I poured myself some coffee. The hot steam rose into my face and made my eyes water.

"I'm leaving today," Leslie said.

"So I gather," I said.

"That's what you want, isn't it?" she said.

I had to laugh. "Leslie, I wanted you to leave three weeks ago," I said. "Now it doesn't make any difference."

It never took much to make her cry. One angry word, one frown would do it. Immediately her eyes filled up and her lower lip vibrated. "Why didn't you just tell me?" she said squeakily.

"I did. But you had other things on your mind."

"You never told me. You said it was okay if I stayed."

"Well, there's no use arguing about it now." I sat down at the table and stared out the window. The place where his car had been parked was empty.

"I didn't mean to spoil anything for you," she said weepily.

I didn't answer.

"You said you didn't love him. You told me that a dozen times."

"So you thought it was all right to move in."

"I didn't! I'd never do that!"

I didn't have the energy to argue. I wrapped my fingers around the warm china. The coffee had a spicy scent. *I made the coffee this morning. Oh Eddy, did you? It's absolutely delicious!*

"All right, yes, I guess I flirted a little bit," she admitted after a moment. "I mean, I know that. But it wasn't serious. It's just that he was so interesting and attractive, and I . . . felt so lonesome and sad. . . ."

"You haven't been to Azure Lake in five years, but this year you had to come. And then, oh, you just couldn't tear yourself away. You had to hang around day after day. Week after bloody week. And I certainly didn't get the impression that I was the irresistible attraction. 'Oh, Eddy, how fascinating!' 'Oh, Eddy, that's incredible!' So cutesy and goo-goo-eyed and breathless. Why can't you ever just sit back and shut up? But no, you always have to gush and slobber over people until they're so puffed up they can hardly see straight. You've been like that your whole life. You could never stand it unless everybody in the room thought you were adorable. I'd bring friends home and there you'd be like a shot, rolling your eyes at them and giggling and tap-dancing and doing cartwheels and telling them how wonderful they were. . . . I thought surely you'd have grown up by now, I mean, God, you're thirty-five years old. But no. You haven't changed one iota! You're always so eager to give everybody exactly what they want. It's really kind of sickening. He always fell for it too, even though he liked to think he was so tough and cynical. But even he just couldn't resist it. 'Oh Dad, you're the most wonderful father in the world!' That's all it took. And he turned into a pile of mush just like everybody else. It used to make me laugh, it really did."

My tirade seemed to be too much for her and she made no attempt to respond to it. She just stood there staring at me helplessly, tears running down her cheeks.

" 'I forgot how peaceful it is here at Azure Lake,' " I said, imitating her breathy little-girl voice. " 'It's the first time in months that I've felt happy.' 'Oh, Eddy, tell us more about Buenos Aires.' "

"He was so nice to me," she stammered, rubbing at her nose with a crumpled Kleenex. "He was sweet to me and with Sid I felt like such a dog for such a long time. I just flirted a little bit, it wasn't serious. And you kept saying you didn't love him. You said it was only a fling."

"Yes, but it was a good fling. And now it's all over."

"It's over?"

"Yes. So take heart, Leslie. It all worked out fine for you, as usual. Didn't it?"

"What do you mean, over?"

"Over. You understand what over means, don't you?"

"You didn't break up with him or something?"

"He's not coming back." I spoke the words quickly and dryly, but a moment after they were out, their meaning suddenly throbbed in my chest. He's not coming back. He's not coming back.

"Did he say that?" Leslie looked stricken. I wasn't sure what that look signified.

"I don't think he'll be coming back here," I said. "I guess there's always a chance he could find his way to Clarendon, though."

She stared at me with an expression of stunned disbelief.

"Pretty soon he'll make you forget all about Sid," I said. "Right?"

She came and sat down on the other side of the table. I sipped my coffee and looked out the window. It seemed to be a great effort to maintain my relaxed posture. I felt that if I let myself go my hands and arms would begin to tremble uncontrollably.

"Look," she said. "It was just a little flirting. That's all it was. It wasn't serious."

"You keep saying that."

"It's true. And I think Eddy really cares about you."

The banality of that remark repelled me. She actually thought I could be taken in and comforted by such a feeble cliché. It was an insult; it made my stomach turn over. "Oh, please!" I said. I put my cup down so hard that coffee splashed over the rim onto the tabletop.

"Really," she repeated, leaning toward me. "Gracie, I honestly think he—"

"Please!" I said again. "Please, please just shut up!" I had to stand; I couldn't bear to sit there across from her and accept her sincere, beseeching look. "I can't listen to this crap! Do you honestly think I'm that dense? He 'really cares about me.' You've been watching too much daytime television. I'm stupid and ugly, I'm boring, God, I'm not even young. He only liked me because of the money. It's always, always the money, one way or another!"

She gaped at me in horror, as though I had suddenly fallen

to the floor and had a convulsion. And perhaps in a way I had. A hot mist of embarrassment rose in my eyes.

"Oh, Gracie, what are you saying?" she breathed. "Stupid? And ugly? Why would—"

I forced myself to swallow, to shrug, to give a dismissive laugh. "Oh, forget it. Sometimes I get carried away with my own rhetoric. Anyway, it's all academic. Do you think I want him now? You can have him, he's all yours. What do I want with cheap scum like him?"

"Oh, Gracie," she said. "He's better than that. You know he's better than that."

"What makes you think so? Oh, yes, of course. I forgot. He's a good-looking man so naturally he has to be full of admirable qualities."

"But he's had such an incredible life. You'll never guess what he told me last night. When he was just—"

"Oh, yes, the street-boy story. The boy with a drum."

She was surprised. "He told you about it too?"

"No, I heard it last night, when he was telling you. I was sitting outside."

"You were—"

"Sitting outside. Yes. And I heard it all. I had to smile to myself. He was really in top form, and he certainly knows how to pick his audience. He'd never have dared to tell me that story. He'd have known I wouldn't buy it in a million years."

"You wouldn't buy it? What does that mean?" Her eyes searched my face in disbelief. "Oh my God. You're not going to tell me it was just another thing he invented."

"I think he listened to you babbling about street children a few days ago, and he used it. He thought, Now here's a real bleeding heart, this'll have her going through a box of Kleenex in two minutes flat. He always knows how to get to people."

"All those details. His sister. The red ribbons. The woman in the white linen dress. He made it all up."

"I said he was good. He probably saw a woman in a white linen dress once. He remembered the song about a girl called Carolina. Once he watched a parade and a boy marched by beating a drum with red ribbons on it. He takes a little bit from one place, and a little bit from someplace else, and weaves it all together in a convincing pattern."

"It couldn't possibly be true."

I laughed. "Don't you know that people like him always have an agenda? They always have a sad story about their hard lives, so that well-meaning, gullible types like you will feel sorry for them and think all their sleazy behaviour is justified."

Leslie stared at me with wide, burning eyes. "People do suffer, Grace," she said suddenly. "It's not just a sad story."

"I know that."

"People suffer, they have nothing, they're in despair. They starve and die. It happens. It happens to children."

"I know that, Leslie," I said impatiently. "I don't need you to lecture me."

"Everybody isn't like us. We're just a small minority. There are millions on the street. In every part of the world. With such—"

"Yes, yes, I know. But he wasn't one of them."

"Why not?"

"Because he wasn't."

She waited, gazing at me. "I believe him."

I smiled. "Of course you do."

"Who would you believe, Grace?" she asked abruptly. "Name somebody."

It was ridiculous, but for a moment I couldn't think of an answer. I was aware of the hum of the refrigerator and a fly buzzing against the window. Somehow she had managed to turn the conversation against me; all at once I was disconcerted, slightly on the defensive. She looked ugly; her eyes were tear-swollen and some hair had escaped from her barrette and stood up around her temples in messy strands.

"You can't think of one single person whose word you trust," she said. "Can you?"

"Shakespeare," I said. "Jane Austen, George Eliot, Thomas Hardy. Henry James. Tolstoy."

She blew her nose. "Oh," she said. "Dead writers. That's easy."

"Great writers, yes, of course, what's wrong with that? When you're face to face with people they're full of lies and evasions. They've always got an underlying motive, they exaggerate, they try to vindicate themselves, or impress you, or get something from you—nothing is ever straightforward. But a great writer tells the truth and that's what I want, the truth, pure and simple."

Her tired, swollen eyes rested on my face. She said, "'The truth is rarely pure, and never simple.' *The Importance of Being Earnest*."

I stared at her. She shrugged and blew her nose. I felt my lips turn downward in a small, reluctant smile.

"Perry played Lady Bracknell one year," she said. "Remember? He loved that part. Lots of Rs to roll. 'P-r-rism! Wher-r-re is that baby?'"

I wouldn't have thought it possible that I could laugh with her that morning about anything on earth. But I actually heard myself give a snicker.

"Oscar Wilde was always a bit too fey for my taste," I said after a moment.

"All right, I have another one," she said. "'The world is not thy friend, nor the world's law. / The world affords no law to make thee rich, / Then be not poor, but break it.'"

I gave her a blank look.

"That's what Romeo says to persuade the apothecary to sell him poison," she told me.

I smiled and shook my head. "Wasn't Perry a little long in the tooth to play Romeo?"

"County Paris," she said. "After the apothecary scene he always swept onstage in a beautiful purple cloak." She paused, chewing her lip. "You know what else I was trying to remember? Wasn't Cheltenham involved in some big hydro-electric project in South America in the sixties?"

"Cheltenham? What's that got to do with anything?"

"Well, last night Eddy said that his family had to move to

Buenos Aires because some companies came in to build a big dam and their town was going to be—"

"Oh my God! You're really stretching it now! It's not enough that you have to swallow everything he told you, but now it all turns out to be our fault, is that it? How neat. Yes, the big bad capitalists are to blame for everything. Isn't that just—"

"Oh, that's not what I meant! But think, wasn't Cheltenham involved in some big South American project?"

"I have no idea what Cheltenham did. I never had the slightest interest in Cheltenham, and neither did you. Where are you getting this from?"

"Oh, I don't know, I seem to have a vague memory of Ivan ranting at me about Cheltenham and the World Bank and some South American consortium—I don't know, maybe I haven't got it straight."

"Ivan! He was a complete lunatic, and most of the time he was half-stoned! You're going to start dredging up things that Ivan said in a hashish stupor ten years ago?"

"No . . . but I'm sure there was something about Cheltenham going into South America in the late sixties when Dad first started to expand, and a bunch of farmland was flooded, thousands of people were moved from their villages, and the reservoir got stagnant and polluted a whole large area so there were clouds of mosquitoes even in towns thirty miles away, blah blah blah, things like that, he went on and on. . . . Maybe it was Brazil though, not Argentina. I wish I could remember it better."

"Didn't Eddy say it was a project that was supposed to bring hydro-electric power to the entire west? That doesn't sound so terrible to me. It sounds like progress."

"But if whole areas of land were destroyed and everybody lost their homes . . ."

"God, Leslie, progress doesn't come easily! Sacrifices have to be made, sometimes a few people get hurt. It's a trade-off. If we always held back for fear of hurting somebody, we'd still be living in caves! We have to take risks, we have to move forward."

"Oh, yes, but I'm sure Ivan said that most of the power ended up being used by a couple of big smelters, the ordinary population didn't see much of it. That consortium was probably thinking more about making a profit than they were about progress."

"Well, I'm sure that's true! People don't just do things out of pure altruism, whether you like it or not. They have to get something for themselves. It's human nature. Take off your blinders and see the world the way it really is."

Leslie was looking at me with an odd expression. After a moment she said, "It would be kind of ironic, though, wouldn't it? If it turned out that Cheltenham was involved in the same South American project that meant Eddy's family had to move to Buenos Aires?"

"Don't be so simple-minded."

She sighed and tapped her fingers on the tabletop. "Okay, I guess that's something else you don't want to believe."

"It's not a question of wanting to believe it," I said. "It's just too far-fetched."

"All right," she said.

"Anyway, the less you believe, the less likely you are to be screwed," I said with a sarcastic laugh.

Slowly Leslie raised her eyes. "You know who you sound like, don't you?"

For a moment I didn't grasp exactly what she meant.

"It's like he's been sitting right here in the room," she said.

Then I understood. I felt as though she had punched me in the stomach. My own words repeated in my mind with a ponderous reverberation. For a moment the room seemed to vibrate from it. But I forced myself to swallow, to take a deep breath. I couldn't let her see that she had gotten to me. "That's a pretty stupid remark," I said evenly. "Just because I can see things objectively . . . just because my mind isn't filled up with a bunch of sentimental clutter and I know how the world really works . . ."

She shrugged, got to her feet, and went to the sink to rinse out her cup. I watched her. I had to hit her with something too, to pay her back.

"This is what I predict," I said. "You'll get married again within a year. Because you just can't relax unless you're married to somebody. And you'll be so in love, and you'll tell everybody you meet, whether they're interested or not. And there'll be such good times. And you'll be so happy, the way you always are."

"I'm not always happy, Grace," she said tiredly.

She left a short time later. She said she would phone me in Toronto in a couple of weeks. I said fine. I watched her swirl around the driveway in the shiny blue Lincoln. In the distance, with her untidy ponytail and her striped T-shirt, she looked like a child, like my maddening little sister of long ago, bouncing up and down behind the steering wheel, saying Dad, Dad, can I drive, let me drive! And he melted as always, he said, You can sit in my lap.

I never sat in his lap. He never put his hands over mine. He never rested his chin on the top of my head and said, What a smart little girl.

I looked at my watch. Eddy must have reached the Greenmantle airfield by that time. *It's a very bad day for a vacation.* Words from a pulp novel. Ridiculous to think that anything irrevocable could happen because in a fit of pique I had failed to relay a message like that. No, I was sure he would be all right. But I was through with him, just the same. When he came back I was going to tell him so.

I WALKED DOWN THE STONE STEPS to the beach. Three beach chairs were still gathered together in a semi-circle. I sat down in the middle one. Soon I would have to put all the chairs away and lock the boathouse doors. Already the air seemed cooler. One of the trees on the opposite shore had a few red leaves.

One autumn day, on an afternoon that was still as warm as August, we lingered on the beach. Everything had been packed away in readiness for our return to the city. My mother wanted to have one last dip in the lake. We sat on the stone steps and watched her run out of the dazzling water, pulling off her bathing cap to loosen a glorious cloud of shining blonde hair. She stood there laughing, her white bathing suit and her tanned skin sparkling as though diamond dust had been sprinkled down upon her from above. It was one of those times when her extraordinary beauty hit you like a physical impact, like a blow to the chest, knocking the breath out of you, filling your throat with a sort of ache, because suddenly you were reminded of everything in life that was brief and lovely and could not be held. Slowly my father raised his hand as though to shield his eyes. *Jesus*, he said huskily, *is she real or am I only dreaming?* Always eager to relay compliments or good news, Leslie jumped to her feet and shouted, *Mom! Guess what?* But my father took her arm and pulled her down. *Shut up*, he said. *You don't have to tell her that.*

I saw Eddy crouching at the end of the pier in the sunlight. But no, that was just a memory too, and already it seemed far away in the past. Everything had turned out just as I always knew it would. The season had changed and I was alone again and the place where he had been was empty forever. And I was going to stop thinking about Eddy. It was time to get back to my real life.

I opened my book and began to read. "Emma Woodhouse, handsome, clever, and rich, with a comfortable home and a happy disposition, seemed to unite some of the best blessings of existence, and had lived nearly twenty-one years in the world with very little to distress or vex her."

Chapter Twenty-Five

Iᴛ ᴡᴀs ʟᴀᴛᴇ ɴᴏᴠᴇᴍʙᴇʀ, ᴀɴᴅ ʙᴀʀᴇ ʙʀᴀɴᴄʜᴇs waved like sticks across the damp grey sky. I sat on the streetcar with my briefcase in my lap, watching the streets glide by: the shabby teenage strippers wobbling on their impossibly high heels as they stood outside Hot Mamas having a smoke, the pimple-faced boys asking passers-by for spare change, the drunks rolled up asleep on a patch of wet grass across from the Salvation Army Men's Hostel. The city was getting worse, people kept saying, soon it would be unlivable, like an American city.

The night before I had dreamed that I was walking across the Greenmantle airfield, stepping over the tangled grass and the faint outlines of old runways, passing the boarded-up buildings. The wind was cold, and made a dreary, moaning sound. I walked and walked into a yawning emptiness. Then, in the way of dreams, I was in a forest, with brambles stinging my legs and roots tearing at my feet. I saw a white car, falling apart, overgrown with weeds and vines, sinking into the earth, its windshield smeared with bird shit and dirt and dried rain. I had to look inside. One of the car doors was ajar and I pried it back. In the middle of the sagging front seat I saw a pile of leaves and hair and lint, and suddenly a huge black rat squirmed up out of this nest it had made, baring its long yellow teeth. I screamed and woke up thinking that the air must be ringing with my frantic voice, but there was no sound in my dark, stuffy bedroom except my heart pounding so wildly it seemed ready to burst out of my chest.

He had never come back. His car was rotting somewhere in the woods around Greenmantle.

I had planned to leave Azure Lake the day after both he and Leslie drove away, but I ended up lingering. There was so much to do, I told myself. I had to pack up my clothes, and all the food in the kitchen; I had to let the Abbotts know I was leaving so they could close everything for the winter. So it happened that I was still there on the day he had said he was going to return. From the moment I woke up on that morning I was in a state of vague agitation; every sound made me jump, made my stomach turn over. I didn't expect to see him ever again, and I refused to give him more than a passing thought, but I kept glancing out at the long, sunny road, waiting to catch a glimpse of white in the distance, a glitter of chrome. The afternoon seemed to contain hundreds of hours. He hadn't said what time he thought he'd be back. The twilight spread darkly through the trees and across the lawn, leaving only the lake alight. I didn't want to go down to the beach for fear I wouldn't hear his car if it came. Instead I sat in the back yard, at the picnic table. I couldn't eat anything. I wanted to smoke, but I had no cigarettes, and I wanted a glass of wine, but I had promised myself I wasn't going to drink any alcohol for a while. I didn't want it to become a problem.

I sat at the picnic table until long after it was dark. I listened to the crickets, to the soft breeze in the trees. My mind was empty. I just watched the road.

I don't remember what time it was when I finally climbed

the stairs and undressed and lay in bed. He could still come, I said to myself. He could slip into bed beside me the way he had in the past, smelling of the wild night, his breath tickling my ear as he whispered Hi, sorry I'm so late. I took one of my pillows and pressed it against the vacant feeling in my body.

He was ruthless, he was intelligent, he knew what he was doing, nothing could happen to him. I just couldn't believe that one missed phone call, one unrelayed message had done him any serious harm.

I don't remember sleeping that night. I remember lying on my bed, watching the sunrise fill the sky and the lake with soft, pearly colours. I lay without moving, listening to the pervasive stillness. The air was warm but my arms and legs felt stiff, as though with cold. I knew at last, beyond doubt, that what I had told Leslie was true. He wasn't coming back.

He had left a few things behind. Nothing very important: some shirts, a pair of jeans, a pair of dark slacks, and the green jacket he had bought at Hazelton Lanes, with the kid leather driving gloves tucked neatly into one pocket. I slipped my hand into one of the gloves. It was almost as though his fingers had left an impression behind, a light pressure, a fleeting warmth. I packed everything in a box and put it up in the attic.

On the way back to the city I took a long detour so that I could drive past the Greenmantle airfield. I don't know what I thought I might see there: something dramatic and frightening perhaps, police cars, the rotating light of an ambulance, yellow tape blocking off a scene of devastation—or just some sign of him, some small sign that he had been there. But there was nothing at all. I parked the car by the side of the road and stood at the top of the ditch. The wind blew the sunny grass back and forth around my feet. In the distance the ruined buildings stood silent and empty. For one heart-stopping moment I thought I glimpsed a bright flash of metal through the trees beside the old airplane hangar, but when I stepped across the ditch and squinted I saw that it was only a pool of rainwater mirroring the sunlight.

After I had been back in Toronto for a week or so, I drove past his house. I waited until nightfall so my car would be less conspicuous on the street. The second-floor windows of his apartment were all in darkness. His car wasn't in the driveway. I parked and sat for a while. A light rain began to fall. Once I thought I saw a deep black shadow hovering just inside the window frame of what had been his kitchen, as though someone were standing there looking out. But it was only my imagination. There was nothing but blank glass reflecting the floating lights of the street.

Leslie phoned me one night in mid-September. "Hi," she said. "It's me."

"Hi," I said.

"How are you?"

"Fine," I said. "How are you?" I pressed the phone against my ear, listening avidly for background noises, the scrape of a chair, someone clearing his throat, any sound at all. I could picture her holding one finger to her lips to warn him to be silent, and him sitting there across from her in the lamplight smiling, giving her a wink.

"Oh, I'm okay, I guess," she sighed.

"Have you heard from Sid?"

"No, not a word. All his stuff is still here. All his clothes. Maybe I'll just pile it all up in the back yard and set it on fire. There's so much of it, what a fabulous blaze it would make. Are you back at school? How's it going?"

"Oh, the usual. I've got too many classes, and there's a troublemaker in my Lit. 102. Every time I open my mouth she wants to argue. If I said the sun rose in the east, she'd disagree with me."

Leslie laughed. "Squash her!" She hesitated momentarily. Then she hurried out the words. "Have you seen Eddy?"

"No," I said.

"You haven't?"

"No," I said. "Have you?"

There was a pause. I thought I might have heard a door open or close. Perhaps the click of a cigarette lighter. Or the rustle of a magazine page being turned.

"No, I haven't, Grace," she said. "Of course not."

"All right," I said.

"He's back in town though?" she asked after a moment.

"I have no idea," I said. It was impossible to be sure what was going on. Perhaps she knew no more about it than I. Or perhaps he was listening on the extension, hand over his mouth to suppress his laughter.

"Wouldn't he call you if he was back?"

"Why?" I said. "I told you we were through."

"Well . . . but you think he's all right, don't you?" Or perhaps he had promised to get in touch with her when he returned, and she hadn't heard from him, and she was worried. They'd had a rendezvous; he hadn't shown up. Perhaps he had been sick of both of us, her as well as me.

"I'll tell you what I think," I said. "I think he's in Miami right now. I think he's walking down the street with a wad of bills in his pocket. I think he's wearing a Rolex and smoking a Cuban cigar. I think he's got a blonde on one arm and a brunette on the other, and they're both twenty years old and they've both got big breasts. I think he's having a great old time. I think he's tired of cold winters and he's never coming back."

"Oh," Leslie said.

I waited, listening intently. But I couldn't hear anything except her breathing. Finally she said, "I'm going away for a while."

"Oh, really?"

"Yeah. To L.A. Maybe stay with Aunt Lucy. I just want to get away from here. I need a change of scene. I keep imagining myself walking beside the ocean. Remember what Dad always called California? Land of Cheap Fantasies."

"Yeah. He was always so superior about things that everybody could afford. The Pacific Ocean was sort of tacky because even the riffraff could look at it."

"Oh, Gracie." She laughed, then coughed. "Come on. He loved the ocean." There was a pause. "Well. I'll let you go." I heard her swallow. After a moment she gave a nervous sniff. "Hey, look, you're not still mad at me, are you?"

My fingers hurt from gripping the receiver so hard. Did I hear someone else's breathing besides hers? Was someone standing next to her, leaning forward to listen?

"No," I said brightly. "Why would I be?"

"Because you know I never meant to hurt you," she blurted out. "If I did, I'm really sorry."

It was just like her. She wanted to have her own way, and she wanted everybody to love her too. He could have been standing behind her squeezing her breasts while she spoke to me and asked for forgiveness. That was exactly the sort of thing she would do.

"I don't want you to hate me," she said with her eager, hopeful laugh. "After all, you're my only sister." No matter how hard I strained I couldn't hear any sounds except the ones she made herself. It was possible that she was really alone, that she had always been telling me the truth.

"I don't hate you," I said. "Say hi to everybody in California. Send me a postcard."

"I will." She hesitated. "Well, bye, sis."

"Bye, sis," I said.

After I had hung up I felt strangely upset and agitated, as though I hadn't said what I wanted to say. A clump of words was caught in my throat, struggling to untangle and burst out. I'm so lonely, Leslie. I'm afraid I've done something terrible. How ridiculous. Someone was always making a confession to Leslie. It was because she was far too easy and forgiving with people, especially the ones she loved. She would never blame you, no matter what you did. She would understand; she would make excuses for you till the bitter end. She would say, You couldn't help it, Gracie, it's not your fault. I stood by the telephone and suddenly my heart swelled until I thought it would break open with my longing to hear those soft words. But I knew that wasn't what I really needed, or deserved. I needed someone to be hard on me, hard as stone, hard as flint, hard as iron. I needed rock so impenetrable that I could beat myself against it and leave no trace.

The next day after school I drove down Lakeshore

Boulevard East. It was a beautiful Indian summer afternoon, with yellow leaves drifting down onto the water through the warm, smoky air. I parked in the parking lot, walked casually into the office of the Royal Marina and leaned on the counter. "Excuse me," I said. "Does Eddy Corona still have a boat moored here?"

A rosy-faced, blond teenager opened the register and turned several pages. "How was it spelled?" After I had told him, he shook his head. "Nobody by that name."

"No? Are you sure? Eduardo Corona. His boat was called the *Caminito*. A fifty-two-foot yacht."

He shrugged. "Sorry. Nope."

"He's a tall guy with dark curly hair. He has a very slight Spanish accent. I thought everybody around here knew him."

The boy shrugged again. By that time he was staring at me curiously. "Sorry, I haven't been working here very long. Jim will be back in fifteen minutes, maybe he can help you."

"Oh, no, forget it," I said. "It's not that important."

I walked slowly from pier to pier. The warm breeze seemed to have perfume in it; it filled me with aimless longing. I couldn't find the *Caminito*. I didn't want to ask anyone else about it for fear of arousing further interest. What I was looking for was nobody's business but mine.

A few days after that I went to the Metro Reference Library and found some books about hydro-electric power in South America. Since the early sixties there had been several large-scale dam-building projects, including a number in Argentina. Most of them had had the participation of the World Bank and various foreign-owned corporations; most of them had involved what was called "the destruction of ecosystems and the displacement of human populations." I didn't recognize the names of any of the companies, but some of them might have been Cheltenham subsidiaries. To find out for sure I would have had to look closely into Cheltenham's early history and the idea of that made me ill. I could imagine how Eddy would smile if he knew I was giving so much credence to one of his stories, and how pleased Leslie would be to see me treating her speculations so seriously. I thrust the books aside and went home.

A couple of weeks later I had a visit from the police. The weather was still warm and I was sitting in my garden reading a new Alice Munro story in the *New Yorker*, when suddenly two men in badly fitting suits walked around the corner of the house and came down the path.

"Hi. Miss Tremain?" the taller one said as they approached. "Your maid told us you were out here."

It was Elvira's afternoon to clean. But fine, let them think she was my maid if it suited them. "Yes?" I said.

"We're from the Metro Police. I'm Detective Sparks and this is Detective Leidecker. Can we ask you a couple questions?"

I looked up at them with an incredulous smile. "About what?" I said.

"Do you know a man called Eduardo Rivera?"

I was calm, quite calm. I closed my magazine and stared at them. They seemed rather ill at ease. The shorter one kept shifting his weight from one foot to the other. "No," I said.

"No? But you were seen with him several times in the past few months. During July and August he made some phone calls from the Muskoka area, where you have a summer cottage."

I smiled. "Thousands of other people do too," I said.

"Maybe you know him by a different name. Eddy Primo? Eddy Corona?"

I could feel the pulse in my throat beating steadily. "Oh, yes," I said. "I know someone named Eddy Corona."

The taller man had drab fair hair and very pale grey eyes. He made me think of a painting whose colours have faded. "And when was the last time you saw him?" he asked.

"Why?" I felt my stomach drop slightly, a soft sickening sensation. "Has something happened to him?"

There was a momentary silence. I waited, listening to the soft breeze in the shrubbery. "He's gone missing, Miss Tremain," the taller one said finally. "We were hoping you might be able to give us some idea of his whereabouts."

I allowed myself a soft, astonished laugh. "Me? Why on earth would you think that?"

The shorter one spoke up for the first time. He wanted to sound tough and aggressive, but couldn't carry it off; he stammered over a couple of words. "Didn't you have a p-pretty close r-relationship with him, Miss Tremain?"

"Close?" I said. "Hardly. It was more like a casual friendship. What makes you think he's missing? I had the impression he travelled quite a bit. How do you know he's not just away on a business trip?"

"A business trip?" the shorter man said with a sharp, nervous laugh. "Is that what you c-call it?"

I shrugged and smiled quizzically, as though I didn't understand. The taller man finally spoke in a rather weary voice. "Miss Tremain, surely you were aware that Corona was a known drug dealer and was under police surveillance."

That was my cue. I stared at them for a couple of beats. Then I tucked my magazine under my arm and stood up. "Gentlemen, I don't think I have anything more to tell you."

"Please, Miss Tremain," the taller one began, and the shorter one was talking too, leaning toward me belligerently, saying, "Now just a minute—"

I was taller than he was; I paused and looked down into his sharp, nervous little eyes. "If you want to ask any other questions, I think you should contact my lawyer," I said. "Ted Farragut at Farragut, Blaney, Marr."

"Miss Tremain," the taller one said placatingly. "There's no need to get excited. This is just an informal inquiry and we hoped you might be willing to cooperate."

"I assure you I'm not the least bit excited," I said. Then I turned away from them and started to walk toward the house. "I can't cooperate because I don't know anything," I said over my shoulder. "I knew Mr. Corona very casually and he never discussed his business with me. In fact I don't recall his ever mentioning it, even once."

"Okay, but just a minute," the shorter man was saying to my back. I crossed the terrace and pushed open the sliding door.

"If you have anything else you want to discuss, please call my lawyer," I said, pulling the door closed and snapping on the lock. They stood on the garden path for a moment, squinting in the brilliant sunlight. Then they left.

I could hear Elvira's vacuum cleaner whirring upstairs. I sat down on the sofa, still holding my magazine. My hands had been perspiring and the picture on the cover was a bit smudged.

He had "gone missing." They wanted to know his "whereabouts." For some reason I thought of the description I had given to Leslie on the phone: Eddy walking down a street in Miami smoking a fat cigar, a voluptuous woman on either arm. Suddenly I thought it might be true. It actually made me feel better to think it was true. Somewhere he was laughing, drinking, eating, having sex, spending lots of money. Perhaps someday I would even see him again, after years had passed, after all the pain and anger had faded. I would run into him on some street somewhere in the world, and he would look just the same, and he would come toward me with his big white grin.

The silver leopard he had given me was sitting on the bookcase. I kept meaning to put it away in a box in the closet, but for some reason I couldn't bring myself to do that. Its topaz eyes winked at me lonesomely in the late afternoon sunlight.

THE POLICE VISIT WAS IN LATE SEPTEMBER. Two months had passed without any further news. As I walked along the boardwalk, bits of snow were beginning to fall into the grey, churning water of the lake. I had two collections of essays to mark. I was looking forward in a dull way to working at my desk with a cup of hot tea at my elbow.

A newspaper had been stuffed part-way into my mail slot. I didn't have any papers delivered, so I thought it must have been meant for one of the neighbouring houses. I tucked it under my arm, unlocked my door and walked into the kitchen. The room was chilly and grey in the fading, wintry afternoon light. I laid the paper down on the table. It was a trashy tabloid which I normally wouldn't have soiled my fingers by touching.

On the front page was a big, gaudily coloured picture of the Prime Minister wearing an Indian headdress and looking like a buffoon. I put the kettle on to boil and turned up the thermostat. Snow was beginning to fall more heavily and flakes hit the windowpane with a soft, hissing sound. Idly I opened the newspaper and spread it out on the tabletop. The headlines were just what you'd expect from that kind of a rag: HOCKEY COACH ACCUSED OF SODOMY . . . HOOKER MURDERS LONG-TIME JOHN. . . . I yawned and turned the page. There was a blunt pain behind my eyes. I thought of getting up and finding some aspirin. Then I saw it on page three, a feature story surrounding a dark, grainy picture of a man's smiling face. For a moment it felt as though my body had been gripped and squeezed by a giant, cold hand. The roots of my hair crackled and turned to ice; my heart began to pound so hard it made my throat hurt.

DRUG DEALER MEETS BLOODY END

Eduardo Rivera (a.k.a. Eddy Primo, Eddy Corona, Eddy Torres) wanted a life of luxury, and he thought pushing dope would be the quickest way to get it.

It didn't work out that way.

Metro police now believe that Rivera died in late August at an isolated airfield in New York state, his body riddled with bullets. Three months later the case has not been solved.

"It's pretty obvious someone tried to turn the guy into a piece of Swiss cheese," said Detective Harry Wallberg of the New York state police.

Rivera was probably Argentinian, although at various times he also claimed to be from Santiago,

Chile; Sao Paulo, Brazil; Lima, Peru; and Mexico City,
Mexico. According to some acquaintances he came
from a privileged background, while others insist that
he started out with nothing. In the mid-'80s he settled
in Toronto, where he quickly built up a dependable
network of drug smugglers and couriers.

Although known to police, Rivera was never
arrested. He kept a low profile, renting a modest
apartment, driving an old car, never drawing
attention to himself. In time he managed to amass a
small fortune, including a 60-foot yacht.

The last summer of his life Rivera intended to pull
off the biggest deal of his career, then quit.

He had created a couple of sham corporations in
Toronto to launder money, but he rarely used them.
Instead he deposited large sums with friends. In July
of this year, he started gathering it back.

He had a simple scheme: to buy a large shipment
of cocaine for $1 million, sell it to drug connections
in Miami for $5 million, then sail away to freedom
on his yacht.

One of his connections, a small-time Montreal
dealer, arranged for Rivera to fly from an airstrip
somewhere in northern Ontario to a secluded airfield
at Ludlow, New York. He was to be met at Ludlow by
a second plane carrying the cocaine. It is believed the
second plane was to take him to Miami where he
would sell the dope for a quick profit.

"He shouldn't have gone," said a friend who did
not wish to be named. "No one he trusted was with
him, and he was carrying all that money. But he liked
to take risks. Once he sailed straight into a hurricane
just to see how it felt."

In response to an anonymous phone call reporting
an "accident," state troopers arrived at the Ludlow
airfield that warm August evening just in time to
spot a plane taxiing down the runway without lights,

then taking off. After searching the area they discovered Rivera in a ditch a few feet from the tarmac.

"He was lying on his back and his eyes were open," said Detective Wallberg. "You would have thought he was just resting if you only looked at his face. He wasn't dead yet. He said something that sounded like 'Señor Tom Boar' or 'Ray and Tom Boar.' It was hard to make out. After that, he just stopped breathing."

Police speculate that Rivera might have been trying to identify his killers. However, there is no one with the name Boar among Rivera's known contacts.

Rivera had no money or identification and he was dressed like a hobo, according to one of the porters who helped to drag his body into the hangar.

"We didn't feel sorry for him," said another airport employee. "All of us knew what he was."

A former landlady of Rivera's, with whom he invested more than $150,000, recently liquidated all her assets and left the country. So far police have found no evidence to connect her with his death.

It appears that other contacts in Toronto simply pocketed the tens of thousands of dollars Rivera left with them. His yacht and other effects have been either sold or stolen.

Although many people profited from his death, Rivera's body remained unclaimed. It is buried in an unmarked grave.

The teakettle was screaming on top of the stove, gushing out clouds of steam. It took me a moment to understand what that loud, shrieking sound was. When I stood up my knees trembled so badly that I had to lean against the cupboard. I turned off the stove and shifted the kettle to another burner. My chest was moving rapidly up and down, as though I couldn't breathe properly. The grainy black-and-white picture blurred before my eyes. It didn't even look much like Eddy. I thought perhaps it was all a mistake, the story was about some stranger, someone named Eduardo Rivera whom I had never met. Or it was a trick, his last big trick, making me think he was dead when actually he was in California, he and Leslie were sitting on the terrace of my Aunt Lucy's house, hands clasped, gazing out at the misty, romantic beach.

Words tolled in the back of my mind, a memory was trying to come forward and I didn't want it to come forward. But it was going to come. I could feel it coming. I started to walk toward the living room but suddenly I couldn't go any farther and had to sit down in the middle of the cold, gritty kitchen floor. This is absurd, I told myself, I'm reaching for this, it must be my pathetic desire to give everything a sort of literary significance that causes me to find meanings and connections where none exist. But of course that was something Eddy and I always shared: our appreciation of a good story. If he had been telling it himself, he would have wanted to give it a powerful and dramatic finale.

Yes, it made sense. Perfect sense. And perhaps I really did want to believe it, after all. His low voice returned to me and chimed in my head, I heard him talking feverishly in the hot, dreamlike darkness.

Señor Tom Boar. Ray and Tom Boar.

Señoras y señores . . . El Rey del Tambor.

Ladies and gentlemen . . . The Drum King.

Epilogue

SOMETIMES AFTER I GO TO BED I IMAGINE how Trewithen must look now: the silent pier glittering with ice, the boathouse with the canoe and the launch suspended from ghostly rafters, the stone steps climbing to the frozen lawn, the blank windows staring emptily outward, the furniture swathed in white cloth, the snow falling endlessly into the dark lake. I think of Eddy's clothes, his jacket and gloves, all folded up in their chilly box in the attic.

Even if I had told him about the phone call, he might not have listened, I say to myself. He might have gone anyway. I'll never know for sure.

Then after a while I close my eyes and dream of Buenos Aires. Not the real Buenos Aires, but the one he created in my mind. It shimmers against a dark sky: gorgeous and mythical, brutal and romantic, an unearthly city where anything can happen, anything is possible. On a shabby street a man leans from the window of a ramshackle bus and picks a succulent, golden orange. A seventy-year-old tango singer fills the shadowy boulevards with the voice of a strong young man wild with love. A gypsy woman whispers someone's fortune behind scarlet blinds in a cluttered room smelling of sandalwood and cats. A spidery widow seduces a fourteen-year-old boy in a transitory hotel beside an enclave of vast stone mansions for the dead. A rich traveller loses all her clothes and jewels in a game of gin rummy. A boy finds a necklace of pearls on the beach, and it disappears from beneath his pillow. A poor neighbourhood gleams like a stage set against a sky resembling a backdrop of dark blue cloth. A heavenly nightclub rises over the pavement, full of food and wine and hot colours and music. A starving girl refuses to sell herself for a fresh-baked pizza. And a boy whirls around in a cloud of red ribbons, beating his drum till it booms like thunder, and his rewards are money and some packets of sugar and a woman's smile. He bows low and winks, he cocks his shabby hat over one eye and walks away jauntily in the twilight, his drum on his back.

And one day a man leaves home to make his fortune. Years pass and then one fine summer afternoon a white boat enters the harbour. Flags blow from its upper deck and a stranger stands there, dressed in fine clothes, manipulating the wheel with ease and grace. People begin to gather on the dock. Who is it, they wonder, who could it be? The words of the tango singer drift through the clamorous air. How passionately he sings his gutter songs about loss and pain and undying love, as if gangsters and whores could really know about such things. But surely they know just as much as anyone else.

In the tango all feelings are big. You trusted me and I lied to you, you carried me in your soul and I let you go; I loved you more than the world and yet I betrayed you; in the long winter nights I weep for that brief summer when you were near me; I can't forget you; my heart aches from wanting you; my body hungers for your touch, I look for you everywhere and never find you, I'm sorry, forgive me. . . .

The man on the boat doesn't hear, he is too far away, off in the shining distance, sailing over the perfumed water, his face uplifted, his curly hair rippling in the breeze, like someone in a glossy magazine. His belly is full of good food, and his brain is teeming with triumphant, fantastic dreams. He rides his fast white boat, high above all the God damn shit and misery, so high and fast he almost seems ready to leave the earth. And a murmur goes through the crowd, now they recognize him, now they remember him.

"It's Eduardo," they say to each other. "Imagine that! It's Eduardo coming home, and he looks like a million bucks."